Danielle Steel has been hailed as one of the world's most popular authors, with over 570 million copies of her novels sold. Her many international bestsellers include *A Good Woman, Rogue, Honour Thyself, Amazing Grace, Bungalow 2, Sisters, H.R.H., Coming Out, The House,* and other highly acclaimed novels. She is also the author of *His Bright Light,* the story of her son Nick Traina's life and death.

D0493237

Also by Danielle Steel

A GOOD WOMAN	MALICE
ROGUE	FIVE DAYS IN PARIS
HONOUR THYSELF	LIGHTNING
AMAZING GRACE	WINGS
BUNGALOW 2	THE GIFT
SISTERS	ACCIDENT
H.R.H.	VANISHED
COMING OUT	MIXED BLESSINGS
THE HOUSE	JEWELS
TOXIC BACHELORS	NO GREATER LOVE
MIRACLE	HEARTBEAT
IMPOSSIBLE	MESSAGE FROM NAM
ECHOES	DADDY
SECOND CHANCE	STAR
RANSOM	ZOYA
SAFE HARBOUR	KALEIDOSCOPE
JOHNNY ANGEL	FINE THINGS
DATING GAME	WANDERLUST
ANSWERED PRAYERS	SECRETS
SUNSET IN ST. TROPEZ	FAMILY ALBUM
THE COTTAGE	FULL CIRCLE
THE KISS	CHANGES
LEAP OF FAITH	THURSTON HOUSE
LONE EAGLE	CROSSINGS
JOURNEY	ONCE IN A LIFETIME
THE HOUSE ON HOPE STREET	A PERFECT STRANGER
THE WEDDING	REMEMBRANCE
IRRESISTIBLE FORCES	PALOMINO
GRANNY DAN	LOVE: POEMS
BITTERSWEET	THE RING
MIRROR IMAGE	LOVING
HIS BRIGHT LIGHT:	TO LOVE AGAIN
The Story of Nick Traina	SUMMER'S END
THE KLONE AND I	SEASON OF PASSION
THE LONG ROAD HOME	THE PROMISE
THE GHOST	NOW AND FOREVER
SPECIAL DELIVERY	GOLDEN MOMENTS*
THE RANCH	GOING HOME
SILENT HONOUR	

* Published outside the UK under the title PASSION'S PROMISE

For more information on Danielle Steel and her books, see her website at
www.daniellesteel.com

To my beloved children,
Beatrix, Trevor, Todd, Nick, Sam,
Victoria, Vanessa, Maxx, and Zara,
who are the Hope and Love and Joy
in my life!

With all my heart and love,
Mom/d.s.

Whatever happens, has happened, or will happen,
I still believe in Love, whatever orthodox,
unorthodox, ordinary, or extraordinary form it takes.
Never give up Hope.

d.s.

One Day
at a Time

Chapter 1

It was an absolutely perfect June day as the sun came up over the city, and Coco Barrington watched it from her Bolinas deck. She sat looking at pink and orange streak across the sky as she drank a cup of steaming Chinese tea, stretched out on an ancient, faded broken deck chair she had bought at a yard sale. A weather-worn wooden statue of Quan Yin observed the scene peacefully. Quan Yin was the goddess of compassion, and the statue had been a treasured gift. Under the benevolent gaze of Quan Yin, the pretty auburn-haired young woman sat in the golden light of the sunrise, as the early summer sun shot copper lights through her long wavy hair, which hung nearly to her waist. She was wearing an old flannel nightgown with barely discernible hearts on it, and her feet were bare. The house she lived in sat on a plateau in Bolinas, overlooking the ocean and narrow beach below. This was exactly where Coco wanted to be. She had lived here for four years. This tiny forgotten farm and beach community, less than an hour north of San Francisco, suited her perfectly at twenty-eight.

Calling her home a house was generous. It was barely more

than a cottage, and her mother and sister referred to it as a hovel or, on better days, a shack. It was incomprehensible to either of them why Coco would want to live there—or how she would even tolerate it. It was their worst nightmare come true, even for her. Her mother had tried wheedling, insulting, criticizing, and even bribing her to come back to what they referred to as "civilization" in L.A. Nothing about her mother's life, or the way she had grown up, seemed "civilized" to Coco. In her opinion, everything about it was a fraud. The people, the way they lived, the goals they aspired to, the houses they lived in, and the face-lifts on every woman she knew in L.A. It all seemed artificial to her. Her life in Bolinas was simple and real. It was uncomplicated and sincere, just like Coco herself. She hated anything fake. Not that her mother was "fake." She was polished and had an image she was careful to maintain. Her mother had been a best-selling romance novelist for the past thirty years. What she wrote wasn't fraudulent, it simply wasn't deep, but there was a vast following for her work. She wrote under the name Florence Flowers, a nom de plume from her own mother's maiden name, and she had enjoyed immense success. She was sixty-two years old and had lived a storybook life, married to Coco's father, Bernard "Buzz" Barrington, the most important literary and dramatic agent in L.A. until his death four years before. He had been sixteen years older than her mother and was still going strong when he died of a sudden stroke. He had been one of the most powerful men in the business, and had babied and protected his wife through all thirty-six years of their marriage. He had encouraged and shepherded her career. Coco always wondered if her mother would have made it as a writer in the early days without her father's help. Her mother never asked herself the same question and didn't for an instant doubt the merit of her work, or her myriad opinions about everything in life. She made no bones about the fact that Coco was a disappointment to her, and didn't hesitate to call her a dropout, a hippie, and a flake.

Coco's equally successful sister Jane's assessment of her was loftier, though not kinder: Jane referred to Coco as a "chronic underachiever." She pointed out to her younger sister that she had had every possible opportunity growing up, every chance to make a success of her life, and thus far had thrown it all away. She reminded her regularly that it wasn't too late to turn the boat around, but as long as she continued to live in a shack in Bolinas like a beach bum, her life would be a mess.

Her life didn't feel like a mess to Coco. She supported herself, was respectable, she didn't do drugs and never had, other than the occasional joint with friends in college, and even that had been rare, which was remarkable at that age. She wasn't a burden on her family, had never been evicted, promiscuous, pregnant, or in jail. She didn't criticize her sister's lifestyle, and had no desire to; nor did she tell her mother that the clothes she wore were ridiculously young, or that her last face-lift still looked too tight. All Coco wanted was to be her own person and lead her own life, in the way she chose. She had always been uncomfortable with their luxurious Bel-Air lifestyle, hated being singled out as the child of two famous people, and more recently the much younger sister of one. She didn't want to lead their life, only her own. Her battles with them had begun in earnest after she had graduated with honors from Princeton, went to Stanford Law School a year later, and subsequently dropped out in her second year. It had been three years since then.

She had promised her father she would try law, and he assured her there was a place for her in his agency. He said it helped to have a law degree if you were going to be a successful agent. The trouble was she didn't want to be one, especially working for her father. She had absolutely no desire whatsoever to represent best-selling authors, scriptwriters, or badly behaved movie stars, which were her father's passion, bread and butter, and only interest in life. Every famous name in Hollywood had come through their house when she was a child. She couldn't imagine spending the rest of her life with them, as her father had. She secretly believed all the stress of representing and indulging spoiled, unreasonable, insanely demanding people for nearly fifty years had killed him. It sounded like a death sentence to her.

He had died during her first year in law school, and she stuck it out for another year and then dropped out. Her mother had cried over it for months, still berated her for it, and told her she lived like a homeless person in the shack in Bolinas. She had only seen it once, and had ranted about it ever since. Coco had decided to stay in the San Francisco area after dropping out of Stanford. Northern California suited her better. Her sister Jane had moved there years before, but commuted to L.A. frequently to work. Their mother was still upset that both her children had moved north and fled L.A., although Jane was there a lot. Coco rarely went home.

Coco's sister Jane was thirty-nine years old. By the time she was thirty, she had become one of the most important film producers in

Hollywood. She'd had a dazzling career so far, and eleven record-breaking box-office hits. She was a huge success, which only made Coco look worse. Her mother never stopped telling Coco how proud their father had been of Jane, and then she'd burst into tears again, thinking about her younger daughter's wasted life. Tears had always worked well for her, and got her everything she wanted from Coco's father. Buzz had thoroughly indulged his wife and adored his daughters. Coco liked to believe at times that she could have explained her choices, and the reasons for them to him, but in truth she knew she couldn't have. He wouldn't have understood them any better than her mother or sister did, and he would have been both baffled and disappointed by her current life. He'd been thrilled when she got into law school at Stanford, and hoped it would put an end to her previously extremely liberal ideas. In his opinion it was all right to be kind-hearted and concerned about the planet and your fellow man, as long as you didn't carry it too far. In her college days and before, Buzz thought she had, but he had assured her mother that law school would get her head on straight. Apparently it hadn't, since she dropped out.

Her father had left her more than enough money to live on, but Coco never touched it, she preferred to spend only what she earned, and often gave money away to causes that were important to her, most of them involved in ecology, the preservation of animal life on the planet, or to assist indigent children in Third World countries. Her sister Jane called her a bleeding heart. They had a thousand unflattering adjectives for her, all of which hurt. Coco readily admitted that she was a "bleeding heart," however, which was why she loved the statue of Quan Yin so much. The goddess of compassion touched her very soul. Coco's integrity was impeccable, and her heart was huge and constantly focused on kindness to others, which didn't seem like a bad thing to her, nor a crime.

Jane had caused her own ripples in the family in her late teens. At seventeen, she had told her parents that she was gay. Coco had been six at the time, and unaware of the stir it made. Jane announced that she was gay in her senior year in high school and became a militant activist for lesbian rights at UCLA, where she studied film. Her mother was heartbroken when she asked her to be a debutante, and Jane refused. She said she'd rather die. But in spite of her different sexual preferences, and early militancy, essentially she had the same material goals as her parents. Her father forgave her once he watched her set her sights on fame. And as soon as she achieved it, all was well again. For the past ten years Jane had lived with a well-known screenwriter who was a gentle person and famous in her own right. They had moved to San Francisco because of the large gay community there. Everyone in the universe had seen their films and loved them. Jane had been nominated for four Oscars but hadn't won one yet. Her mother had no problem now with Jane and Elizabeth living as partners for the past decade. It was Coco who upset them all deeply, who worried the hell out of them, annoyed them with her ridiculous choices, her hippie life, her indifference to what they thought was important, and it made her mother cry.

Eventually, they blamed Coco's attitudes on the man she was living with when she dropped out of law school, rather than their effect on her for years before. He had lived with her during her second and final year of law school, and had left law school himself without graduating several years before. Ian White was everything her parents didn't want for her. Although smart, capable, and well educated, as Jane put it, he was an "underachiever" just like her. After leaving school in Australia, Ian had come to San Francisco, and opened a diving and surfing school. He had been bright, loving, funny, easy-going, and wonderful to her. He was a rough diamond and an independent sort who did whatever he wanted, and Coco knew she had found her soul mate the day they met. They moved in together two months later, when she was twenty-four. He died two years later. They were the best years of her life, and she had no regrets, except that he was gone, and had been for two years. He died in a hang-gliding accident, when a gust of wind crashed him into the rocks, and he fell to his death below. It was over in an instant, and their dreams went with him. They had bought the shack in Bolinas together, and he left it to her. His wet suits and diving gear were still at the cottage. She'd had a hard time for the first year after he died, and her mother and sister had been sympathetic in the beginning, but since then their sympathy had run out. As far as they were concerned, he was gone, and she should get over it, get a life, grow up. She had, but not the way they chose. That was a capital offense to them.

Coco herself knew that she had to let go of Ian's memory and move on. She had been out on a few dates in the last year, but no one came close to Ian. She had never met a man with as much life, energy, warmth, and charm. He was a tough act to follow, but she hoped that someday someone would come along. They just hadn't yet. Even Ian wouldn't have wanted her to be alone. But she was in no hurry. Coco was happy living in Bolinas, waking up every day, facing each day as it came. She was on no career path. She didn't want or need fame to validate herself, as the rest of her family did.

She didn't want to live in a big house in Bel-Air. She didn't want anything more than she'd had with Ian, beautiful days and happy times, and loving nights, all of which she knew she would carry with her forever. She didn't need to know where her next steps would lead, or with whom. Each day was a blessing unto itself. Her life with Ian had been absolutely perfect and exactly what they wanted, but in the last two years since his death, she had made her peace with being on her own. She missed him, but had finally accepted that he'd gone on. She wasn't frantic to get married, have children, or meet another man. At twenty-eight, none of that seemed pressing, and just rolling along in Bolinas was more than enough for her.

At first, living there had seemed odd to her and Ian as well. It was a funny little community. The local residents had chosen years before not only to be inconspicuous but to virtually disappear, like Brigadoon. There were no road signs to indicate how to get to Bolinas, or even to admit that it was there. You had to find it on your own. It was a time warp that they had both laughed at and loved. In the sixties it had been full of hippies and flower children, many of whom were still there. Only now they were weather-beaten and wrinkled and had gray hair. Men in their fifties or even sixties, headed for the beach with their surfboards under their arms. The only shops in town were a clothing store, which still sold flowered muumuus and everything tie-dyed, a restaurant full of grizzled old surfers, a grocery store with mostly organic food, and a head shop that sold every possible kind of paraphernalia and bongs in all colors, shapes, and sizes. The town itself sat on a plateau that hung over a narrow beach, and an inlet separated it from the long expanse of Stinson Beach and the expensive houses there. There were a few beautiful homes tucked away in Bolinas, but mostly there were families, dropouts, older surfers, and people who, for whatever reason, had chosen to get away and disappear. It was an elitist community in its own way, and the antithesis of everything she had grown up with, and the high-powered family Ian had fled in Sydney, Australia. They had been perfectly matched that way. He was gone now, but she was still there, and she had no intention of leaving anytime soon, or maybe ever, no matter what her mother and sister said. The therapist she had seen after Ian died, until recently, had told her that she was still rebelling at twenty-eight. Maybe so, but as far as Coco was concerned, it worked for her. She was happy in the life she had chosen, and the place where she lived. And the one thing she knew for sure was that she was never, ever going back to live in L.A.

As the sun rose in the sky, and Coco went back inside for another cup of tea, Ian's Australian shepherd, Sallie, sauntered slowly out of the house, fresh from Coco's bed. She gave a faint wave of her tail, and headed off on her own for a morning stroll on the beach. She was extremely independent, and helped Coco in her work. Ian had told her Australian shepherds made great rescue dogs, and were herders by instinct, but Sallie marched to her own tune. She was attached to Coco, but only to the extent she chose to be, and had her own plans and ideas at all times. She had been impeccably trained by Ian, and answered to voice commands.

She bounded off as Coco poured herself a second cup of tea and glanced at the clock. It was just after seven, and she had to shower and get to work. She liked to be on the Golden Gate Bridge by eight, and at her first stop by eight-thirty. She was always on time, and supremely responsible to her clients. Everything she had learned by association about hard work and success had served her. She had a crazy little business, but it paid surprisingly well. Her services were in high demand, and had been for three years, since Ian helped her set it up. And it had grown immeasurably in the two years since he died, although Coco diligently limited her clients, and would only take so many. She liked to be home by four o'clock every day, which gave her time for a walk on the beach with Sallie before dusk.

Coco's neighbors on either side of her shack were an aromatherapist and an acupuncturist, both of whom worked in the city. The acupuncturist was married to a teacher at the local school, and the aromatherapist lived with a fireman from the firehouse at Stinson Beach. They were all decent, sincere people who worked hard, and helped each other out. Her neighbors had been incredibly kind to her when Ian died. And she had gone out with a friend of the teacher's once or twice, but nothing had clicked for her. They had wound up friends, which she enjoyed too. Predictably, her family dismissed them all as "hippies." Her mother called them deadbeats, which none of them were, even if they seemed that way to her. Coco didn't mind her own company, and was alone most of the time.

At seven-thirty, after a steaming hot shower, Coco headed out to her ancient van. Ian had found it for her at a lot in Inverness, and it got her to the city every day. The battered old van was exactly what she needed, despite a hundred thousand miles on it. It ran fine, even if it was ugly as sin. Most of the paint was long gone. But it was still going strong. Ian had had a motorcycle they rode over the hills on weekends, when they weren't out on his boat. He had taught her to dive. She hadn't driven the motorcycle since he was gone. It was still sitting in the garage behind their shack. She couldn't bring herself to part with it, although she had sold his boat, and the diving school had closed since there was no one else to run it. Coco couldn't have, and she had a business of her own.

Coco slid open the back door of the van and Sallie jumped in with a look of excitement. Her run on the beach had woken her up and she was ready for work, as was Coco. She smiled at the big, friendly black and white dog. To those who didn't recognize the breed, she looked like a mutt, but she was a purebred Australian shepherd, with serious blue eyes. Coco closed the door, got in behind the wheel, and took off with a wave at her neighbor, who was coming back from his shift at the firehouse. It was a sleepy community, and almost no one bothered to lock their doors at night.

She followed the winding road at the edge of the cliff overlooking the ocean as she headed to the city, with downtown shimmering in the morning sunlight in the distance. It was going to be a perfect day, which made work easier for her. And just as she liked to be, she was on the bridge by eight. She would be right on time for her first client, not that it really mattered. They would have forgiven her if she was late, but she almost never was. She wasn't the flake her family made her out to be, just different from them all her life.

She took the turnoff into Pacific Heights, and headed south up the steep hill on Divisadero. She was just cresting it at Broadway when her cell phone rang. It was her sister, Jane.

"Where are you?" Jane said tersely. She always sounded as though there were a national emergency, and terrorists had just attacked her house. She lived in a constant state of stress, which was the nature of her business and suited her personality to perfection. Her partner, Elizabeth, was far more relaxed, and tempered her considerably. Coco liked Liz a lot. Liz was forty-three years old and every bit as talented and bright as Jane, just quieter about it. Liz had graduated summa from Harvard with a master's in English literature. She had written an obscure but interesting novel before going to Hollywood to write scripts. She had written many since then and won two Oscars over the years. She and Jane had met working on a picture ten years before, and had been together ever since. Their relationship was solid, and the alliance worked well for both of them. They considered themselves partners for life.

"I'm on Divisadero. Why?" Coco asked, sounding tired. She hated the way Jane never asked her how she was, she just told her what she needed. It had been the nature of their relationship since Coco was a child. She had been Jane's errand girl all her life, and had spent a lot of time talking to her therapist about it, while she was still seeing her. It was hard turning that around, although she was trying. Sallie was sitting in the passenger seat next to Coco and watched her face with interest, as though sensing Coco's tension and wondering why that was.

"Good. I need you right away," Jane said, sounding both relieved and harried. Coco knew they were going to New York soon, on location for a film she and Liz were coproducing.

"What do you need me for?" Coco sounded wary, as the dog cocked her head to one side.

"I'm screwed. My house-sitter just canceled on me. I'm leaving in an hour." Desperation had crept into her voice.

"I thought you weren't leaving till next week," Coco said, sounding suspicious, as she drove past Broadway, where her sister lived only a few blocks away in a spectacular house overlooking the bay. It was on what was referred to as the Gold Coast, where the most impressive houses were. And there was no denying that Jane's was one of the prettiest of all, although it wasn't Coco's style, any more than the Bolinas shack was Jane's. The two sisters seemed to have been born on separate planets.

"We have a strike on the set, sound technicians. Liz left last night. I've got to get there by tonight for a meeting with the union, and I have no one for Jack. My house-sitter's mother died, and she's got to stay in Seattle with her sick father indefinitely. She just called and bagged on me, and my flight's in two hours." Coco frowned as she listened. She had no desire to connect the dots of what her sister had just said. This wasn't the first time it had happened. Coco somehow always became the backup for everything that fell through the cracks in her sister's life. Since Jane believed Coco had no life, she always expected her to step up to the plate and fill in. Coco could never say no to the sister she had been daunted by for her entire lifetime. Jane had no problem saying no to anyone, which was part of her success. It was a word Coco had trouble finding in her own vocabulary, a fact that Jane knew well and took full advantage of, at every chance.

"I'll come in to walk Jack if you want," Coco said cautiously.

"You know that won't work," Jane said, sounding annoyed. "He gets depressed if no one comes home at night. He'll howl all night and drive the neighbors nuts. And I need someone to keep an eye on the house." The dog was almost as big as Coco's Bolinas house, but if need be, Coco knew she could take him there.

"Do you want him to stay with me until you find someone else?"

"No," Jane said firmly, "I need you to stay here." *I need you to,*

Coco heard for the ten millionth time in her life. Not *would you please . . . could you . . . would you mind . . . please, please, pretty please. I need you to.* Shit. This was yet another opportunity to say no. Coco opened her mouth to say the word and not a single sound came out. She glanced over at Sallie, who seemed to be staring at her in disbelief.

"Don't look at me like that," Coco said to the dog.

"What? Who are you talking to?" Jane asked in a rush.

"Never mind. Why can't he stay with me?"

"He likes to be at home in his own bed," Jane said firmly, as Coco rolled her eyes. She was a block away from her client's house and didn't want to be late, but something told her she was about to be. Her sister had a magnetic pull on her like the tides, a force Coco could never seem to resist.

"So do I like to be in my own bed," Coco said, trying to sound decisive, but she wasn't kidding anyone, least of all Jane. She and Elizabeth were going to be on location in New York for five months. "I'm not house-sitting for you for five months," Coco said, sounding stubborn. And films ran longer sometimes. It could be six or seven in the end.

"Fine. I'll find someone else," Jane said, sounding disapproving, as though Coco were a naughty child. That always got to her, no matter how often she reminded herself that she was grown up. "But I can't do that in an hour before I leave. I'll take care of it from New York. For God's sake, you'd think I was asking you to stay in the Tenderloin in a crack house. You could do a lot worse than stay here for five or six months. It might do you good, and you wouldn't have to commute." Jane was selling hard, but Coco didn't want to buy. She hated her sister's house—it was beautiful, impeccable,

and cold. It had been photographed for every decorating magazine, and Coco always felt uncomfortable there. There was no
place to curl up, to feel cozy at night. And it was so immaculate,
Coco was always afraid to breathe, or even eat. She wasn't the
housekeeper her sister was, or even Liz. They were neat freaks in
the extreme. Coco liked a friendly mess, and didn't mind a reasonable amount of disorder in her life. It drove Jane wild.

"I'll cover it for a few days, at most a week. But you have to line
up someone else. I don't want to live at your house for months,"
Coco said adamantly, trying to set boundaries with her.

"I get it. I'll do what I can. Just cover me for right now, please.
How fast can you pick up the keys? And I want to show you the
alarm system again, we've added some new features and they're
complicated. I don't want you setting off the alarm. You can pick
Jack's meals up at Canine Cuisine, they prepare them for him
twice a week, Mondays and Thursdays. And don't forget, we've
switched vets to Dr. Hajimoto on Sacramento Street. Jack's due for
a booster shot next week."

"It's a good thing you don't have kids," Coco commented drily
as she turned the van around. She was going to be late, but she
might as well get it over with. Her sister would drive her insane if
she didn't. "You'd never be able to leave town." Their bull mastiff
had become a child substitute for them, and lived better than most
people, with specially prepared meals, a trainer, a groomer who
came to the house to bathe him, and more attention than many
parents gave to their kids.

Coco drove up to her sister's house, and there was already a
town car waiting outside to take Jane to the airport. Coco turned
off the ignition and hopped out, leaving Sallie in the car, watching

out the window with interest. She was going to have a good time with Jack for the next several days. The bull mastiff was three times her size, and they'd probably break everything in the house as they chased each other around. Maybe she'd let them use her sister's pool. The only thing Coco loved about the house was the enormous projection screen in the bedroom, where she could watch movies. The bedroom was huge and the screen covered one entire wall.

Coco rang the doorbell, and Jane yanked open the door with a cell phone pressed to her ear. She was giving someone hell about the unions, and hung up as she stared at Coco. The two women looked surprisingly alike. They both had tall, spare frames and beautiful faces. Both had modeled in their teens. The most notice-able difference between them was that Jane was all sharp edges, with long straight blond hair pulled back in a ponytail. Coco's long, loose auburn hair and slightly gentler curves made her look warmer, and there was a smile in her eyes. Everything about Jane screamed stress. There had always been a sharp edge to her, even as a kid, but those that knew her intimately, knew that despite the razor tongue, she was a decent person and had a good heart. But there was no denying she was tough. Coco knew it well.

She was wearing black jeans, a black T-shirt, and a black leather jacket, and diamond studs in her ears. Coco was wearing a white T-shirt, jeans that showed off her long, graceful legs, and running shoes that she needed for work, and she had a faded sweatshirt tied around her neck. And Coco looked noticeably younger. Jane's more sophisticated style aged her a little, but both were striking women and looked noticeably like their famous father. Their mother was smaller and rounder, although she was blond like

Jane. Coco's coppery mane was a throwback to another genera-
tion, since Buzz Barrington had had jet black hair.

"Thank God!" Jane said as her enormous bull mastiff came running up to them and stood up on his back legs to put his paws on
Coco's shoulders. He knew what having her around meant, forbid-
den table scraps he would never get otherwise, and sleeping in the
king-size bed in the master suite, which Jane would never have allowed. Although she adored her dog, she was a firm believer in
rules. Even Jack knew that Coco was a pushover and would let
him sleep on the bed at night. He wagged his tail and licked her
face, which was a far friendlier greeting than she got from Jane.
Liz was by far the warmer of the pair, but she was already in New
York. And the relationship between the two sisters was always
tense. However good her intentions, and her love for her younger
sister, Jane never minced words.

Jane handed Coco a set of keys, and an information sheet about
the new alarm. She repeated the information about the vet, the
booster shot, and Jack's designer meals, and about fourteen other
instructions, all delivered like machine-gun fire at her younger
sister.

"And call us right away if Jack has any kind of a problem," she
finished.

Coco wanted to ask her "What about if I do?" but Jane wouldn't
have found it funny. "We'll try to come back for a weekend sometime to give you a break, but I don't know when we can get away,
particularly if we're having trouble with the unions." She sounded
harried and exhausted before she even got there. Coco knew
she managed the most minute details and was brilliant at what
she did.

"Wait a minute," Coco said, feeling weak, "I'm only doing this for a few days, right? Maybe a week. I'm not staying here the whole time," she repeated so they understood each other. She wanted no confusion about that.

"I know, I know. You'd think you'd be happy to stay in a decent house." Her sister glared at her instead of thanking her profusely.

"It's *your* 'decent' house," Coco pointed out. "Bolinas is my home," she said with quiet dignity, which Jane ignored.

"Let's not get into that," Jane said with a meaningful look, and then grudgingly, she looked at her sister and smiled. "Thanks for bailing me out, kiddo. I really appreciate it. You're a great baby sister to have." She gave Coco one of her rare smiles of approval, which had kept Coco trying to please her all her life. But you had to do what Jane wanted to get those smiles.

Coco wanted to ask her why she was a great baby sister. Because she had no life? But she didn't ask the question and just nodded, hating herself for agreeing so quickly to house-sit for them. As always, Coco had given in without a fight. What was the point? Jane always won anyway. She would always be the big sister that Coco couldn't beat at any game, couldn't say no to, and who loomed larger than life, sometimes even larger than their parents.

"Just don't leave me stuck here forever," Coco said in a pleading tone.

"I'll call you and let you know," Jane said cryptically, and then rushed into the next room to answer two phone lines that were ringing at once, and as she headed for them, her cell phone rang. "Thanks again," she called over her shoulder, as Coco sighed, patted the dog, and headed back to her van. By then she was twenty minutes late for her first client.

"See you later, Jack," Coco said softly, and closed the door behind her. And as she drove away, Coco had the sinking feeling that Jane was going to leave her stuck there for months on end. She knew her sister too well.

Coco was at her first client's house five minutes later. She took out a lockbox that she kept in the glove compartment of the van, twirled the combination, and extracted a set of keys with a tag on them with a numbered code. She had the keys to all of her clients' houses. They trusted her completely to come and go. The house she stopped at was a large brick house that was almost as big as Jane's, with neatly trimmed hedges outside. Coco let herself in the back door, turned off the alarm, and whistled loudly. Within seconds, a giant silvery blue Great Dane appeared and wagged his tail in frantic delight the moment he saw her.

"Hi, Henry, how're you doing, boy?" She clipped his leash on his collar, set the alarm again, locked the door, and led him out to the van, where Sallie was pleased to see her friend. The two dogs barked a greeting at each other, and jostled each other good-naturedly in the back of the van.

Coco stopped at four other houses nearby, and picked up a surprisingly gentle Doberman, a Rhodesian ridgeback, an Irish wolfhound, and a Dalmatian, all from similarly opulent homes. Her first run of the day was always with the biggest dogs. They needed the exercise most. She headed out to Ocean Beach, where she and the dogs could run for miles. Sometimes she took them to Golden Gate Park. And when necessary, Sallie helped her herd them back into a pack. She had been dog-walking for the rich and elite of Pacific Heights for three years, and had never had an accident, a mishap, or lost a dog. Her reputation was golden in the business, and even though her family thought it was a pathetic waste of her education and time, it kept her outdoors, she liked the dogs, and she made a very decent living at it. It wasn't what she wanted to do for the rest of her life, but for now it suited her just fine.

Her cell phone rang as she was dropping the last of the big dogs back at his home. She had a group of medium-size dogs to pick up next, and always took the small dogs out just before lunchtime, since most of their owners walked them before they went to work. And she did a last run of big dogs at midafternoon before she went back to Marin. It was Jane calling her. She was already on the plane, speaking quickly before they told her to turn off her phone.

"I checked my records before I left, and Jack's not due for that booster for two weeks, not one." Sometimes Coco wondered why her head didn't explode from all the minutiae she tried to keep track of. No detail was too small for Jane's attention, she micro-managed everything and everyone in her life, even the dog.

"Don't worry about it. We'll be fine," Coco reassured her, sounding relaxed. The run on the beach had mellowed her as well as the dogs. "Have fun in New York."

"Not with a strike going on." Jane sounded like a wire about to snap. But Coco knew that once she was with Liz again, she'd calm down. Her partner always had a soothing influence on her. They were a perfect match and complemented each other.

"Try to enjoy yourself anyway. Just don't forget to find another house-sitter when you can," Coco reminded her again, and she meant it, whether Jane cared or not.

"I know, I know," Jane said, and sighed. "And thanks for bailing me out. It means a lot to me to know that the house and Jack are in good hands." Her voice sounded gentler than it had all morning. They had an odd relationship, but they were sisters after all.

"Thanks," Coco said with a slow smile, wondering why it always meant so much to her to have her sister's approval, and hurt so much when she didn't. She knew that one of these days, she'd have to unhook from that and have the guts to turn her down. But she wasn't there yet.

Coco knew that as far as Jane and their mother were concerned, being a dog-walker didn't count. In the scheme of life, and compared to their achievements as a best-selling author and an Oscar-nominated producer, Coco's business was an embarrassment to them. In their eyes, it was as though she didn't have a job at all. And even Coco was aware that on the Richter scale of accomplishments she had been taught to demand of herself, as a dog-walker she didn't move the needle at all. But still, whether they approved of it or not, it was an easy, simple, pleasant life. And as far as Coco was concerned, that was enough for now.

Chapter 2

It was six o'clock as Coco headed back into the city again. She had gone home to pack a bag with sweatshirts, jeans, a spare pair of running shoes, clean underwear, and a stack of her favorite DVDs to watch on her sister's giant screen. She had just passed through the toll plaza when her cell phone rang. It was Jane, she had just gotten to the apartment she and Liz had rented in New York for six months.

"Is everything okay?" Jane asked, sounding worried.

"I'm on my way back to your place now," Coco reassured her. "Jack and I will have a candlelight dinner, while Sallie watches her favorite show on TV." Coco didn't let herself think back to the time, more than two years ago now, when she and Ian would cook dinner together, walk on the beach at night, or fish off his boat on the weekends. The time when she still had a life, and wasn't preparing designer meals for her sister's dog. But there was no point thinking of that now. Those days were gone.

They had been planning to be married the summer he died, and had wanted a simple ceremony on the beach, with a barbecue afterward for their friends. She hadn't yet told her mother, who would have had a fit over it. And they'd been planning to go back to Australia eventually, and open a diving school there. Ian had been a surfboard champion in his youth. Thinking about it made her wistful now.

Liz got on the phone while Coco was talking to Jane and thanked her profusely for staying at the house and babysitting their dog. Her tone and style were infinitely warmer than Jane's.

"It's okay, I'm happy to help out, as long as it's not for too long." Coco wanted her to hear it as well.

"We'll find someone, I promise," Liz said, sounding genuinely grateful for Coco's help. She never took her for granted, unlike Jane.

"Thank you," Coco said gratefully. "How's New York?"

"It'll be better if we avoid the strike. I think we may come to some agreement tonight." She sounded hopeful. She was a peacemaker at heart. Jane was the warrior of the pair.

Coco wished them luck as she pulled up in front of their house. She envied them their relationship sometimes. They got along the way married couples should and often didn't. Coco had grown up knowing that her older sister was gay, and accepted her lifestyle without question, although she knew that sometimes others were surprised. What bothered Coco about Jane was the way she steamrolled everyone to get what she wanted. Only Liz seemed able to humanize her, and even she couldn't manage it at times. Spoiled by their parents early on, and accustomed to adulation for her accomplishments, Jane was used to getting everything she wanted. And Coco had always felt second best, in her shadow. Nothing about that had changed. The only time it had felt different to her was when she lived with Ian. Maybe because she didn't care as much about what her sister thought then, or maybe because his presence protected her in some mystical unseen way. She had loved the idea of moving to Australia with him. And now, here she was, staying at her sister's house, and babysitting for her dog again. And what would have happened if Ian were still alive, and she had her own life? Jane would have had to find someone else, instead of using her baby sister like some sort of Cinderella to rush to her aid in every crisis. But what would it feel like not being there for her? Would it make her a grown-up in her own right, or the bad little girl Jane always told her she was when they were younger, and Coco didn't want to do what Jane said? It was an interesting question, to which she had not yet found the answer. Maybe because she didn't want to. It was easier to just do what she was asked, especially without Ian to protect her anymore.

Coco fed both dogs and turned on the TV. She lay back against the white mohair couch and put her feet on the white lacquered coffee table. The carpeting was white too, and made from the hair of some rare beast in South America, Coco vaguely remembered. They had used a famous architect from Mexico City, and the house was beautiful, but made to live in with perfectly combed hair, clean hands, and brand-new shoes. Coco felt sometimes as though if she breathed, she would leave a mark on something, which her sister would then see. It was a lot of pressure living there, and infinitely less cozy and comfortable than being in Bolinas in her "shack."

She went out to the kitchen eventually to find something to eat. Since they had left earlier than planned, neither Elizabeth nor Jane had had time to stock the refrigerator for the house-sitter. All she found in it were a head of lettuce, two lemons, and a bottle of white wine. There was pasta and olive oil in the cupboard, and Coco made herself a bowl of plain pasta and a salad, and poured herself a glass of white wine while she was cooking. Both dogs started barking insanely, standing at the windows, while she was tossing the salad, and when she went to see what was happening, she saw two raccoons strolling across the garden. It was another fifteen minutes before the raccoons finally disappeared as she tried to calm the dogs, and by then Coco could smell something burning. It smelled like an electrical fire somewhere in the house, and she ran all over, upstairs and down, trying to find it, and saw nothing. Her nose finally led her back to the kitchen, where the water in the pasta pot had burned away, with the pasta in a thick black crust at the bottom of the pan, and the handle of the pot partially melted, hence the evil odor.

"Shit!" Coco muttered, as she got the pot into the sink and poured cold water on it, and an alarm sounded somewhere. The smoke alarm had gone off, and before she could call the alarm company, she could hear sirens, and two fire trucks were at the front door. She was explaining what had happened, somewhat sheepishly, as her cell phone rang, and both dogs were barking at the firemen. When she answered, it was Jane.

"What's happening? The alarm company just called me. Is there a fire in the house?" She sounded panicked.

"It's nothing," Coco said, thanking the firemen as they got back on the truck and she closed the front door. She had to reset the alarm and wasn't sure she remembered how to do it, but didn't want to admit that to Jane. "It's no big deal. I burned the pasta. There were two raccoons in the garden and the dogs went crazy. I forgot I was cooking."

"Christ, you could have burned the house down." It was after midnight in New York, and the strike had been averted, but Jane sounded exhausted.

"I can always go back to Bolinas," Coco volunteered.

"Never mind. Just try not to kill yourself, or set the house on fire." She reminded Coco how to reset the alarm, and a minute later, Coco sat down at the island in the center of the pristine black granite kitchen and ate the salad. She was hungry, tired, and homesick for her own house.

She put the bowl in the dishwasher, threw away the pot with the melted handle, turned off the lights, and only when she got upstairs to the bedroom with both dogs following her did she notice that one of the lettuce leaves had stuck to the bottom of her running shoe. She lay on the floor of her sister's bedroom, feeling like a bull in a china shop, just as she did every time she came here, as inept as she always had whenever she was in her sister's orbit. She didn't belong here. Finally she got up, took her shoes off, and collapsed on the bed. As soon as she did, both dogs leaped onto it with her. Coco laughed as she saw them. Her sister would have killed her, but she wasn't there to see it, so she let them stretch out on the bed with her, as she always did.

She put a DVD in the player then, and lay in bed with the dogs, watching one of her favorite movies. The house still reeked of the pot she had burned beyond recognition. She'd have to replace it, and dreaming of Bolinas and Ian, she fell asleep halfway through the movie. She didn't wake until the next morning, and rushed out of bed to shower, dress, and get to her first client. She sailed past the kitchen on the way out, decided not to attempt tea, and took both dogs with her. And mercifully for once, her sister didn't call her.

After walking her usual round of dogs, in the Presidio, Golden Gate Park, and at Crissy Field, she was back at the house on Broadway at four o'clock, and sank into the Jacuzzi. She had already decided not to cook dinner that night, and while watching another of her favorite DVDs, she ordered Chinese takeout. Her mother called from L.A. as she was eating the spicy beef, and had just finished an egg roll. Jack was sitting eye level with the kitchen table, drooling, with Sallie right beside him.

"Hi, Mom," Coco said with her mouth full, when she saw her mother's number come up on her caller ID. "How are you?"

"Fine, and a lot happier knowing you're in a decent house and not that firetrap in Bolinas. You're very lucky your sister lets you stay there."

"My sister is very lucky I'm willing to house-sit for her on five minutes' notice," Coco snapped back before she could stop herself. Jack snatched an egg roll off the table, and Coco pulled the plate away while he wolfed it down whole. Her sister would have killed her for that too.

"Don't be silly," her mother chided her. "You have nothing else to do, and you're fortunate to be there. The house is gorgeous." There was no denying that, but it was like living on a stage set. "You should look for a place in the city. And a decent job, and a man, and go back to law school." Coco had heard it all before. Her mother and sister had a million opinions about her life, and never hesitated to express them. They were the arbiters of what was right. Coco the embodiment of all things wrong.

"So how are you, Mom? Everything all right with you?" It was always easier if she got her mother talking about herself. She was more interested in that anyway, and she had far more to say.

"I just started a new book," she said happily. "I love the subject. It's about a Northern general and a Southern woman during the Civil War. They fall in love, get separated, she becomes widowed, and her favorite slave helps her escape and gets her to the North to find him. She has no money left, the general is desperate to find her, and can't, and she in turn finds the slave's woman for him. It's kind of two stories in one, and it's fun to write," she said gleefully, as Coco smiled. She had been hearing those stories all her life. She liked her mother's books, and was proud of her, although as a very young child she had been embarrassed by her mother's success. All she had wanted as a kid was an ordinary mother who baked cookies and drove car pool, not a famous one. But she had grown into it over the years. She used to have fantasies about having a mother who was just a housewife, and her mother was about as far from that as anyone could get. She was always either writing or giving interviews when Coco was a child. By the time Coco was born, her mother was a major star. She had always envied people who didn't have famous parents.

"I see your last one is already at number one," Coco said proudly. "You never fail, do you, Mom?" She sounded almost wistful as she said it.

"I try not to, sweetheart. I like the sweet smell of success a lot better." She laughed as she said it. Her whole family liked that smell, not just her mother, but Jane, and their father. Coco often wondered what life would have been like growing up among "normal" people, like doctors and teachers, or a father who sold insurance. She hadn't had many friends like that growing up in L.A. The parents of most of her friends were famous, or one parent at least. Most of the children she had gone to school with had parents who were producers, directors, actors, studio heads. She had gone to Harvard-Westlake, one of the best schools in L.A., and many of the people she had grown up with were famous now too. It was like living among legends, and a lot to live up to. The majority were high achievers like her sister, although some of the kids she knew then were dead now, from drugs, or car accidents while driving drunk, or suicides. Those things happened to poor people too, but they seemed to happen with greater frequency to the rich and famous. They lived on the fast track and paid a high price for their lifestyles. It had never occurred to her parents when she was growing up that she would refuse to play, and simply bow out of the game. It made no sense to them, but it made a lot of sense to her.

"Maybe now that you're in the city, taking care of Jane's house, you could take some classes, and get ready to transfer down here and go back to school," her mother suggested, trying to sound casual about it, but Coco had heard that before too, and didn't answer.

"What kind of classes, Mom?" Coco finally asked, sounding instantly tense. "Piano? Guitar? Macramé? Cooking? Flower arranging? I'm happy with what I'm doing."

"You'll look a little foolish walking people's dogs when you're fifty," her mother said quietly. "You're not married, you don't have children. You can't just fill time for the rest of your life. You need to do something that has some substance. Maybe an art class. You used to like that." It was pathetic. Why couldn't they just leave her alone to do what she was doing? And why did Ian have to . . . but there was no point thinking about that either.

"I don't have your talent, Mom. Or Jane's. I can't write books or make movies. And maybe one day I will have kids. In the meantime, I make a decent living at what I'm doing."

"You don't need to make a 'decent living.' And you can't rely on children to fulfill you. They grow up and go off to their own lives. You need something to give you a sense of accomplishment of your own. Children are only temporarily time consuming. And a husband can die or leave you. You need to be someone in your own right, Coco. You'll be a lot happier when you find that out."

"I'm happy now. That's why I live here. I'd be miserable in the rat race in L.A." Her mother sighed as she listened. It was as though they were whispering across the Grand Canyon—neither of them could hear the other, nor wanted to. It was almost funny how Coco being a mere dog-walker made both her mother and Jane feel insecure. It didn't have that effect on Coco at all. Sometimes she felt sorry for them.

Talking to her mother depressed her. It gave her the feeling that she had never measured up and never would. She didn't care as much about it now, but it still bothered her at times. She thought about it after they hung up, and she ate another egg roll. In Bolinas, she lived on salads, and bought fresh fish at the local market. She was too lazy to go to the supermarket in San Francisco, and her sister's high-tech kitchen, which looked like the inside of a spaceship, intimidated her. It was easier to order out. She was still thinking about her mother when she went upstairs to her bedroom and put a movie on. Jack happily climbed into bed next to her, without waiting to be invited, and put his head down on the pillow, Sallie settled at her feet with a moan of pleasure. By the time the movie started, both dogs were snoring, as Coco snuggled into the comfortable bed to watch her favorite romantic comedy, with her favorite actor and actress. She had seen the movie half a dozen times and never got tired of it.

She noticed only after the movie was over that someone had sent her a text message on her cell phone. It was from Jane. Coco was expecting it to be something about the dog again. She had had several messages from her in the past two days, with reminders about the house, the dog, the gardener, the security system, their cleaning woman. Coco knew that as Jane got busier with the movie, she'd stop sending texts every five minutes. This one was slightly more involved than the others. It was about a friend of theirs who was apparently going to be staying at the house over the weekend. Coco wondered for an instant if she could ask her to babysit the dog, so she could go home to her place, but she had a feeling Jane would be mad if she imposed on their houseguest and escaped.

It said only, "Our friend Leslie hiding from psychotic, homicidal ex-girlfriend. Will probably show up tomorrow or Sunday to stay for a few days. Knows how to find hidden key and has alarm code. Thanks. Love, Jane and Lizzie." She couldn't remember meeting a friend of theirs called Leslie, and wondered if it was someone they knew from L.A. It sounded more exotic than most of their friends, who were intelligent and creative but generally a pretty staid group of middle-aged women, most of whom had been in long-term relationships like theirs, and not prone to psychotic homicidal lovers. Since the fleeing Leslie apparently had the alarm code and the key, she didn't need to worry about it. Coco put on another movie, and went to sleep around three A.M. She only had two dogs to walk the next day, and didn't have to show up until noon, so she was planning to sleep late.

She woke up to a brilliantly sunny day at ten A.M., and looked out to see a flock of sailboats on the bay, preparing for a regatta, and all she could think of was how much she wished she were in Bolinas. She was thinking about driving over to take the dogs for a run on the beach, and check her mail.

She stretched lazily, let both dogs out in the garden, and propped the door open so they could get back in. And then she went to the kitchen to make something to eat. She still hadn't had time to buy groceries in the two days she'd been there. She was trying to decide between the Chinese food from the night before, and some frozen waffles she'd found in the freezer, when she realized that she had left the Chinese food out. The containers were still sitting in the sink. So she opted for the frozen waffles and stuck them in the microwave. She found syrup in the fridge, and as she turned around to put it on the table, she saw Jack, standing, with both paws on the sink, happily eating the Chinese food. He had eaten most of it by the time she spotted him, and she had a feeling the spicy beef wasn't going to do him a lot of good. She shooed him away and he barked at her, and then sat down next to the kitchen table to watch her eat. Sallie sat next to him, looking hopeful too.

"You know, you guys are pigs," she said, addressing both dogs. Her long coppery hair hung straight down her back, and she was wearing her favorite flannel nightgown with the hearts on it, with pink wool socks because her feet were always cold at night. She looked like a kid as she sat there, with both dogs staring at the waffles as they disappeared into her mouth. "Yummm!" she teased, laughing at them as Jack turned his head from side to side. "What? The Chinese food wasn't enough? You're going to make yourself sick," she warned him. After she had finished the waffles, she walked back to the fridge to put the maple syrup away. Some of it had dripped down the sides, and she thought about wiping the bottle off, which was probably what Jane would have done, but Coco promised herself she'd do it another time. Jane wasn't coming home to check on her, and she wanted to shower and walk her two clients' dogs. She had almost made it to the fridge with the dripping bottle of maple syrup, when the scent of it overpowered Jack. He took a wild leap past Coco, and knocked the bottle from her hand. It spun across the granite floor, broke, and spilled the sweet-smelling syrup everywhere. Before she could stop him, Jack had leaped into it and was trying to gobble it up amid the broken glass, and she was pulling him away, as Sallie suddenly reverted to her shepherding origins and ran circles around them, barking. Coco was pulling Jack away by his collar when her socks slipped in the syrup and he knocked her down. She was sitting on the ground in a pool of syrup, fortunately with no glass in it, as Jack barked frantically at her. He wanted the syrup and she was determined to keep him away so he wouldn't cut himself on the glass. Her nightgown and socks were soaked by then, and she had even managed to get some of the syrup in her hair. She was laughing while both dogs barked, as she struggled to her feet and pulled the mastiff away. And as she did, she suddenly realized there was a man in the room watching them. In their excitement over the syrup, even the dogs hadn't noticed him, and they barked even louder as he took a step back, and Coco told them both to stay. It was a scene of utter chaos, and the man looked terrified of the dogs, and mystified by her.

"What are you doing here?" Coco asked sternly as she looked at him. He was wearing jeans, a turtleneck, and a black leather jacket, and he didn't look like a burglar, but she had no idea how he'd gotten in.

She was still standing in the maple syrup as she stared at him, and he was trying not to smile at the vision and the acrobatics he had just seen. She looked like a lion tamer, with her long, red hair wild around her head, her nightgown and socks soaked in maple syrup, and the huge dog barking in her arms, while the Australian shepherd ran rings around them, yelping frantically. He could smell the maple syrup and see it in her hair, glistening like spun glass. He couldn't help noticing that she was a very pretty girl and looked about eighteen.

"Did you have some sort of food fight?" he asked with a twinkle in his eye. "I'm sorry I missed it. I love that sort of thing. I think I'm meant to be a houseguest here for a few days, or a refugee." He held up the key to show that he entered the premises honorably, as Coco caught her breath. That couldn't be. Her sister had told her that a woman would be staying there. There had been no mention of him. Or had she also given access to someone else? And then suddenly, it all registered, the British accent, and as she stared at him, she nearly screamed. It couldn't be. This was impossible. She was dreaming it. She had watched him two nights in a row on her sister's enormous screen.

"Oh shit . . . oh my God . . . it can't be you . . . ," she said. But it all fit together now. Leslie. Not a woman. Leslie Baxter, the world-famous British heartthrob and movie star. How could her sister not warn her who it was? She blushed furiously as she looked at him, and his eyes laughed as he smiled, just as they did on screen. She had watched his movies a thousand times, and now he was here.

"I'm afraid it is me," he said apologetically, and then he glanced at the mess around her. "I suppose we ought to do something about this." She nodded, bereft of speech for the moment, and then she looked up at him again.

"Do you suppose you could get the dogs outside . . ." she asked, pointing to the open door to the garden, "so I can clean this up?"

"I would," he said hesitantly, "but I'm terrified of dogs actually. If you do the dog thing, I'll find a Hoover somewhere and clean up." She laughed at what he said, as much over the suggestion as the word. Ian had called their vacuum cleaner a Hoover too. Leslie Baxter was British, and no vacuum cleaner was going to suck up maple syrup.

"Never mind," she admonished him, and commanded both dogs to follow her, which very reluctantly they did, as he shrank away from them. Coco was back sans dogs a minute later. She picked up the glass in paper towels, and peeled off her socks so she wouldn't slip again. It was a miracle none of them had gotten hurt with the broken glass. Then she soaked up the gooey mess with her sister's pristine, spotlessly white, seemingly brand-new kitchen towels, while he helped. He got some of it on his good-looking brown suede shoes, and she had it all over her, as he smiled and tried hard not to laugh.

"I don't suppose you're the housekeeper," he said conversationally as they worked diligently to get it all up and the mountain of sticky towels grew. "Are you a friend of Jane and Lizzie's?" He had spoken to Jane and she hadn't mentioned anyone staying there, but clearly she wasn't a burglar either. Goldilocks maybe. Or an intruder who had spent the night in her funny nightgown with the hearts on it, and had decided to eat a hearty breakfast before ransacking the place.

"I'm dog-sitting for her," Coco explained, getting more of the sticky mess in her hair, as he tried to help her pull it back. It was impossible not to notice how beautiful she was as he struggled to keep a straight face. By then, the ancient threadbare nightgown was glued to her, and the effect was very appealing. "She sent me a text message that a friend called Leslie was coming. She never said it was you, and I thought it was one of her gay friends escaping a homicidal ex-lover." She looked up at him in embarrassment then, having said too much, and as she did, she noticed a nasty bruise on one cheek. "Sorry . . . I shouldn't have said that . . . I expected you to be a woman."

"I didn't expect you at all," he admitted, and by then he had some of the syrup in his hair too. He had dark brown, almost black hair, and startlingly blue eyes. He had already noticed that hers were green. "Well, you were half right. I am escaping a homicidal ex-lover, I'm just not one of their gay women friends." He looked apologetic again. And then he gazed at her with a curious expression and the words tumbled out of his mouth before he could stop them. "Are you?"

"Am I escaping a homicidal ex-lover? No, I told you, I'm dog-sitting. Oh . . ." She realized what he meant then. "No, I'm not one of their lesbian friends. I'm Jane's sister." As soon as she said it, he could see the resemblance, but their styles were so different that it hadn't occurred to him at first, and he had been so stunned to see her, particularly sliding around in a pool of maple syrup in a funny old nightgown, with two big dogs going berserk. He had been as startled by her as he had been terrified of the dogs. This was more than he had bargained for when Jane had told him he could use her empty house. This was not his definition of empty, by any means. It was anything but.

"How did you get lucky enough to be assigned as dog-sitter?" He was intrigued by her, and by then they had cleaned up most of the mess, although their feet stuck to the now-sticky floor like Super Glue.

"I'm the family black sheep," she said with a shy smile, and he laughed. She looked very young and very pretty, and he was trying not to look at the way the nightgown was glued to her.

"And what does a black sheep do? Drink to excess? Recreational drugs? A string of bad boyfriends? Drop out of school?" She looked like she was in high school, but he could tell she wasn't.

"Worse. I dropped out of law school, which is considered a capital offense, and I'm a professional dog-walker. I live at the beach. I'm considered a hippie, a flake, and an underachiever." She said it grinning, in the face of his good-humored assessment of her, and suddenly it didn't seem so awful saying it to him. It sounded funny instead.

"That doesn't sound so bad to me. The law school thing sounds very dreary. The dog-walker bit sounds quite terrifying, and very brave of you. I was a black sheep too. I dropped out of college to go to acting school, and my father was very nasty about it, but apparently I make more money now than I would have as a banker, so he's forgiven me. You just have to wait a while, they'll get over it. Perhaps you should threaten to write a book about them, and expose all their secrets. Or sell embarrassing photographs you've taken of them. Blackmail might be a useful thing. And I don't see what's wrong with living at the beach. People pay fortunes for houses in Malibu, and they're considered quite respectable, even enviable. You don't sound like a very convincing black sheep to me."

"I do to them," she assured him.

"I can't tell if you're a hippie, in that thing." He gestured toward her nightgown, and for the first time she realized how it was sticking to her and how much of her shape it revealed. "Perhaps you'd better take that off and change into your dog-walking clothes," he suggested discreetly. "I'll find a mop and try to get this stuff off the floor." He started opening closets and found one, as she turned toward him and smiled. He had a nice sense of humor, and he seemed almost shy as he looked at her. He didn't act like the movie stars she knew.

"Do you want anything to eat?" she asked politely, and he laughed.

"Presumably not anything that would require syrup. You seem to be fresh out. What was it, by the way?" he asked with interest.

"Waffles," she said from the doorway.

"Sorry I missed them."

"There's a half a head of lettuce in the refrigerator," she offered, and he laughed again.

"I think I'll wait. I'll pick up some food later. I'll get you some more syrup."

"Thank you," she said, as he poured water into a bucket, and then she scampered up the stairs, leaving sticky footprints all the way up to the bedroom. She was back a few minutes later, in jeans, a T-shirt, and running shoes. Her hair was still wet from the shower, and he had made himself some coffee and offered a cup to her, which she declined. "I only drink tea," she explained.

"I couldn't find any," he said, looking tired as he sat at the kitchen table. He looked like he'd had a rough couple of days, and the bruise on his cheek seemed fresh.

"We're out of everything. I'll pick up some stuff on my way home. I have to go to work, but I've only got two dogs to walk on Saturdays."

He looked fascinated, as though she had told him she was a snake charmer. "Have you ever been bitten?" he asked in awe.

"Only once in three years, by a crazed teacup Chihuahua. The big dogs are always sweet."

"What's your name, by the way? Since your sister didn't introduce us. You know mine, but I don't know yours."

"My mother named us after her two favorite authors. Jane was named after Jane Austen. Mine is Colette, but no one calls me that. I'm Coco." She held out a hand and he shook it, with a look of amusement. She was an enchanting girl.

"Colette would actually suit you," he said with a thoughtful expression.

"I love your movies," she said softly, feeling stupid as she said it. She had met hundreds of celebrities and famous people in her lifetime, many of them actors and important stars, but sitting across the table from him in her sister's kitchen, she felt awkward and shy, particularly since she watched his films so often and loved them so much. He was her favorite actor, and she had had a crush on him for years. She would have felt incredibly stupid if she'd admitted that to him. And now they were both staying in her sister's house. That wasn't the same thing. Now she had to treat him like a real person, instead of gawking at him on the screen.

"Thank you for saying that, about my movies," he said politely. "Some of them are awful, and some are all right. I never watch them myself. Too embarrassing. I always hate the way I look, and think I often sound ridiculous."

"That's the sign of a great actor," she said with conviction. "My father said that. The ones who think they're wonderful never are. Sir Laurence Olivier didn't like his performances either."

"That's reassuring," Leslie said, looking at her sheepishly as he sipped his coffee. The sleepless nights he'd had, thanks to his ex, were catching up with him, and he was dying to get to bed and sleep, but he didn't want to be rude to her. "Did you know him?"

"He was a friend of my father's." He knew who her father had been, and who her mother was, since he knew Jane. And he could see why they'd be upset that she was a dog-walker and lived at the beach, but he could also see why she would want that too. They were a lot for anyone to contend with, and he was fond of Jane, but she was a powerful woman. This girl with the auburn hair and green eyes looked like a whole different breed. She was a gentler soul. He could see it in her eyes and sense it in her manner.

She could tell that he was tired and offered to show him to his bedroom. He looked grateful when she said it, and she walked him upstairs to the main guest room, which was next to the master suite. She knew that Liz slept there occasionally when she was working late on scripts. It was a big, beautiful room with a spectacular view of the bay, but all Leslie could see was the bed, beckoning to him. He wanted to take a shower and sleep for the next hundred years, and he said as much to her.

"I'll bring back groceries in case you're hungry when you get up," she said kindly.

"Thank you. I'll just take a shower and go to bed. See you later then," he said as she waved and bounded down the stairs. She let the dogs back in as she left, ran out the front door, and got into her ancient van. She drove off a moment later as he watched her from the window and smiled. What a funny, lovely, unspoiled girl she was. And what a breath of fresh air to meet someone like her after the nightmare he'd just been through.

Chapter 3

Coco picked up the toy poodle and the Pekingese she always walked on Saturdays. After that she went to Safeway and stocked up on everything they might need. She could live on lettuce leaves and takeout food, and had been for two years, but with a man staying at her sister's house, she felt some obligation to supply more substantial fare. She figured that Jane would expect her to. So far Leslie Baxter seemed like a very nice person. She still couldn't quite get over his staying at the house with her, and wished her sister had warned her who was coming, other than an anonymous "Leslie" who was fleeing a psycho ex-girlfriend. Who knew it would turn out to be him? At least it would liven up the house for a few days while he was there, although given his phobia about dogs, she couldn't leave Jack with him and go home for the weekend, which she had hoped to do.

It was three o'clock by the time she came back with the groceries, an early edition of the Sunday paper, and some magazines for him. She suddenly felt obliged to play hostess and not just house-sitter, although she'd gotten off to a bit of a rocky start with maple syrup and broken glass everywhere. She was impressed that he'd been such a good sport, and had even helped her clean it up.

The house was strangely quiet when she walked in. She assumed that he was still sleeping, and the dogs had apparently tucked themselves in somewhere to do the same. So she unpacked the groceries quietly in the kitchen, and gave a start when he walked in. He was wearing a clean white T-shirt and jeans, with his very elegant, very English-looking brown suede shoes. Ian had only owned Tevas and running shoes. He didn't need anything else except hiking boots. Everything he wanted to do was involved with the outdoors, and she had shared that with him. All her mother had ever worn when she was growing up were four-inch heels. And they seemed to get higher every year.

"You're already awake?" she asked, as she put the last of the food away, and turned to look at him with a smile.

"I never went to sleep," he said ruefully, and she looked surprised.

"How did that happen?"

"Someone beat me to it." He beckoned her to come with him, and she followed him up the stairs to his room, faintly worried. Maybe Jane had invited someone else too, without telling them, and they had taken over his room. But she laughed as soon as she stood in the doorway to the guest room. Jack had sprawled out on the bed when Leslie was in the shower. He had his head on the pillow, was spread across the bed, and was snoring loudly. Sallie was nowhere to be seen, but Jack had made himself totally at home. "I didn't want to argue with him about it. I checked out your room, out of curiosity, and the other dog is asleep in there."

"She's mine," Coco explained with a grin. "This is the lord of the manor, it's his house. His name is Jack, although my sister doesn't let him sleep on the beds. He only does that when I'm here. He knows." She walked quickly toward the bed, patted the huge dog to wake him up, and pulled him off the bed. He looked very unhappy to be so rudely awakened, and headed toward the master bedroom to join Sallie. "Sorry." Coco looked at Leslie apologetically. "You must be beat."

"I dozed a little on the couch. But I have to admit, a real bed will feel good. I slept in my car last night. And hid out at a friend's the night before. L.A. is a little too small for both of us just now. She's nuts," he added, instinctively touching his cheek. "She's rather a big star, and she packs a hell of a punch. She does her own stunt work in action films." Coco knew who he'd been dating from the tabloids, but admired him for not saying her name. He seemed very polite. "I rented out my house six months ago, for a year. I've been living with her. I'm going to have to find an apartment, once I get my bearings. I've never been mixed up in anything so crazy in my life." He grinned at her sheepishly. "First time I've ever been slugged by a woman. Then she damn near killed me with her hair dryer, she threw it at me. When she threatened me with a gun, I figured it was time to leave. Never argue with a psychopathic woman with a gun. Or at least, generally, I try not to." He still looked a little shaken as he smiled.

"What got her so pissed off?" Coco asked cautiously. It was a lot more exciting than her life, or than she even wanted to imagine. Ian had been the gentlest man in the world, and their arguments had been brief, respectful, and harmless. She had had relationships that ended before him, but never badly. But she had heard plenty of stories from her father over the years of his famous clients being pursued by stalkers and psychopaths.

"I'm not sure," Leslie said in answer to her question. "She wanted to know which of my costars I'd gone out with, and then she got into a jealous rage about it, even though I explained that they were over. She kept insisting that I was going to get involved with the next one, and then she went nuts. She had a little problem with the bottle. It was all a bit over the top, to say the least. She called me on my cell and said she was going to kill me. I believe her. So I left town."

"Maybe you need to stay a little longer than a weekend," Coco said seriously, although it sounded typical to her of the madness she hated in Hollywood and L.A. She couldn't have lived like that herself. It was too high a price to pay for fame. "Guns and alcohol aren't such a great mix." He nodded. He hadn't figured out what he wanted to do yet. He had called Jane to tell her about it, since Jane knew her and had worked with her, and he had wanted her assessment of just how crazy the woman was, and how dangerous she might be. Jane had suggested he get out of Dodge, and go up to their place in San Francisco. It seemed like a good idea at the time. He didn't want to run into this woman anywhere right now, and in Los Angeles, he might. Jane thought she was even more dangerous than he feared.

"I've never had anything like this happen," he said, looking embarrassed. "My past relationships have always ended on good terms. I'm friends with all of them. None of them ever wanted to kill me, or at least not that I know of." He sounded incredulous as he said it.

"Did you call the police?" He shook his head in answer.

"I can't. If I do, it will be all over the tabloids and that will make it even worse."

"My father had a death threat once, from a crazy client, when I was a little girl. He called the police and they gave him guards around the clock for a while. I was terrified the actor was going to kill him. I had nightmares about it for years," Coco confessed.

"Yes, but she probably wasn't an ex-girlfriend. This is the kind of stuff the tabloids love. I don't want to be involved in a mess like that, or cause it. I've got a break between films now. I'd rather just stay away for a while. I might go to New York for a few months. I don't have to work again till October, so I've got time."

"She'll probably find out you're there. And my sister and Liz aren't coming back for five or six months. You can stay here while you figure it out, and maybe she'll calm down."

"I think it'll take a lobotomy for that to happen. I'm hoping she gets obsessed with someone else. In the meantime, I'm planning to lie low, and she'll never figure out that I'm here. I haven't been to San Francisco in twenty years. I always see Jane in L.A. We worked on a picture together." Coco remembered that, although she had never met him with Jane before. But she was aware that they were friends.

"Well, you'll be safe here. And now that Jack is out of your bed, get some sleep," she said with a friendly smile. It sounded like a nasty story, and he looked shaken up by it.

Leslie thanked her for rescuing him, and as she headed to her own room, he closed his door. She closed hers too. Both dogs were asleep on her bed, and she put the TV on with the sound low. She dozed off for a while herself, and around eight o'clock she went downstairs to make herself dinner. She took some sushi she had bought out of the fridge and made a salad. She was eating it and reading the Sunday paper when he walked in, looking sleepy, and more rested than he had before. He yawned and stretched as he sat down. They were like two shipwrecked people on a desert island. The house was quiet, and it was easy and pleasant. It was Saturday night, and neither of them had obligations or plans.

"Would you like some?" She pointed at the sushi, and he nodded as she got up to get more out of the fridge. And he was instantly on his feet to help her.

"You don't have to wait on me. I'm the interloper here. Thanks for buying food today. I'll get the next round." They were like two roommates who had wound up sharing a house, and good manners prevailed. He was very English and obviously very nicely brought up. He helped himself to some sushi, and she gave him a plate, and made him a salad, as he thanked her.

"What part of England are you from?" she asked as they ate their dinner, and Jack sat watching them with interest. Sallie had smelled the fish and gone back to bed.

"A little town just outside London. I never got to London till I was twelve. My father was a postman, and my mum was a nurse. I had a very middle-class upbringing, and a very normal home life as a kid. My parents were horrified I wanted to be an actor, and embarrassed by it actually, at first anyway. My dad wanted me to be a teacher, or a banker, or a doctor. I faint at the sight of blood. And I thought teaching was too boring. So I took acting lessons and started out doing Shakespeare. I was bloody awful." He grinned at her. "Good salad. No syrup?" he teased her.

"I bought more." She laughed at him. "And waffles."

"Perfect. I'll make them tomorrow. And what did you want to be when you grew up?" he asked her, looking as though he cared about the answer.

"I was never really sure. I just didn't want to be my parents. Or in film like my sister, she was so intense about it. She's that way about everything she does, but it didn't look like a lot of fun. I always hated writing. For about five minutes, I wanted to be an artist. But I don't have a lot of talent. I do watercolors once in a while, but nothing terrific. Just beach scenes and still lifes of flowers and vases. I studied art history in college. I probably would have liked teaching, or research of some kind. And then my father talked me into law. He said it was a good starting point for anything I'd want to do later, like go into his business and be an agent. I didn't want to do that either, and I hated law school. The teachers were mean to everyone, the students were nasty and competitive and neurotic. Everyone was trying to put everyone else down. I was terrified for two whole years and cried all the time. I was scared to death I'd flunk out, and then my father died and I quit."

"And then what?"

"I was relieved." She smiled at him across the table. "I was living with somebody then. My parents didn't approve of him either. He had dropped out of law school too, in Australia. He loved the outdoors, and he ran a diving school, so we moved to the beach, and I was never happier in my life. I came up with the dog-walking idea, just to tide me over for a while, and three years later I'm still doing it. It works for me. I'm living at the beach, and it's what I want to do for now. My whole house is smaller than this kitchen. My mother calls it a 'shack,' and I love it."

"And the Australian with the diving school?" Leslie asked her with interest as he finished his salad, and sat back in his chair, looking at her. She looked like a normal, happy woman, except when she talked about law school. "Is he still around too?"

"No, he isn't," she said, shaking her head quietly.

"That's too bad. Your eyes lit up when you talked about him."

"He was a great guy. We lived together for two years, and then he had an accident and died." Leslie looked at her more intently as she said it. She looked sad about it, but not distraught. She seemed as though she had made her peace with it a long time before. But he was startled by what she'd said, and sorry for her. She didn't look sorry for herself.

"Car accident?"

"Hang gliding. A gust of wind blew him into a cliff, and he fell. It was a little over two years ago. It was very hard at first. But I guess those things happen. It was rotten luck for us. We were planning to get married, and go back to Australia to live. I think I would have liked it."

"You might." Leslie nodded. "Sydney looks a lot like San Francisco."

"He said that too. That's where he was from. We never got there. I guess we weren't meant to." She sounded philosophical about it, and he admired her for it. There was nothing maudlin about this girl.

"Has there been anyone since?" He was curious about her.

She smiled at Leslie Baxter sitting across the table from her in her sister's kitchen. It was so weird, it made her laugh. Leslie Baxter was asking about her love life. Who would have thought?

"Just a lot of bad blind dates with boring guys. I tried for a while about a year ago, just so my friends and family would shut up. It just wasn't worth the effort, or maybe I wasn't ready. I've kind of given it a rest for the last six months. It's hard starting again with someone new. We got along really well."

"You don't look as though you'd be difficult to get along with," he said matter-of-factly. "I was involved with a woman like that once. She was fantastic." He looked dreamy as he said it.

"What happened?"

"I was stupid, and young. My career was just starting, and I wanted to stay in Hollywood and play for a while. She was in England and she wanted to get married and have babies. By the time I figured out that she was right, she had given up on me and married someone else. She waited for about three years, which was more than I deserved at the time. She has five kids now and lives in Sussex. Nice woman. I had another very good woman in my life. We never married, but we have a daughter. Monica got pregnant around the time the relationship had run out of gas, and she decided to keep the baby. I was pretty leery of the whole idea at the time. As it turned out, she was right. The relationship was shot, but my daughter Chloe is the best thing that ever happened in my life."

"Where is she?" Coco looked surprised. He had a very Hollywood life, with women trying to kill him, broken romances, and a child with a woman he'd never married, but he seemed very normal and down to earth at the same time. Or maybe that was just an act he put on. She had met a lot of crazy actors through her father in her youth. Some of them seemed like normal people, but they weren't. In the end, they were as crazy and narcissistic as the others. Her father had warned her never to go out with an actor. But Leslie seemed different. He seemed real, and for the moment at least, not self-centered or arrogant, or impressed with himself. He seemed very willing to admit to his own mistakes, and wasn't trying to blame anyone else, except for his recent disaster, which didn't sound like it was his fault anyway. Lunatics did happen, particularly in his world.

"Chloe lives in New York, with her mother," he explained. "She's a serious actress on Broadway, and a surprisingly good mother. She keeps her out of the limelight, and Chloe comes out to see me two or three times a year. I go to New York to visit her every chance I get. She's six, and the sweetest little elf on earth." He beamed with pride when he spoke of the child. "Her mother and I are the best of friends. Sometimes I wonder if it would have lasted if we got married. I don't think so though. She's a very serious person and a little dark. She got involved with a married politician after we broke up. Everyone knew about it, but they kept it very quiet. And there have been a number of very rich, powerful men since. I was too boring for her. And too immature at the time. I'm forty-one, and I think I've only just started to grow up. It's embarrassing to admit, but I think that defines late bloomer. I think actors tend to be very immature. We're spoiled." The way he admitted it so openly touched her.

"I'm twenty-eight," she said shyly, "and I still haven't figured out what I want to be when I grow up. I wanted to be an Indian princess when I was a kid, and once I figured out that that wasn't going to happen, I haven't been able to come up with anything else equally appealing since." She looked faintly disappointed and he laughed. "I enjoy my life the way it is. The dog-walking thing works for now. And even if it doesn't make sense to my family, I'm content the way things are."

"That's all that matters," he said gently. "Does your family pressure you about it?" But knowing Jane and who her mother was, it seemed obvious to him that they would.

Coco laughed out loud in answer. "Are you kidding? They think I'm a total flop and a disaster. They all have high-powered careers. My sister got her first Oscar nomination at my age. She's been a huge box-office success since she was thirty. My mother's been writing best sellers since she was in diapers. My father founded the agency himself, and represented every major star in Hollywood. And I walk dogs. Can you even imagine what they think of that? My mother got married at twenty-two. She had Jane when she was twenty-three. Jane and Liz have been together since Jane was twenty-nine. And I feel like I'm fifteen years old and in high school. I don't even care if I get invited to the prom. I'm happy living with my dog on the beach." He didn't remind her that she would have been married by then if Ian hadn't died. And Coco was aware of that too. "I come from a family of overachievers, who knew what they wanted the moment they were born. I swear I was switched at the hospital at birth. Somewhere out there is a nice normal family who lives in a beach community, and would think it's great that I walk dogs, and wouldn't care if I never get married. And they probably wound up with a kid who wants to be a rocket scientist or a brain surgeon or a Hollywood agent, and they don't know what hit them. Meanwhile, every time I'm around my family, or even talk to them, I don't know what hit me." It was the most honest she had been with another person since Ian, particularly one she had just met, not to mention a movie star, and it worried her a little that Leslie was Jane's friend. He could see it in her eyes.

"I'm not going to say any of this to Jane, you know. So you don't need to look so worried." He seemed to be able to read her thoughts, as though he understood.

"We just have nothing in common," Coco said with tears in her eyes, and then felt silly about it, and embarrassed. "I get so tired of their telling me everything I do wrong, and everything I'm not. And in a funny way, it works for them. It makes them feel important, and my sister has been using me as her minion all my life. If I had a life, it might actually not be quite as convenient for them. Jane is a good person and I love her, but she's very tough," Coco explained and he nodded.

"I know. Maybe you just need to say no," he said softly, and Coco laughed again and wiped her eyes with her T-shirt, while he tried not to notice her pink bra when she did. She was completely unaware that she had exposed it, and it made him smile. In some ways, she really was a kid, and he liked that about her. She was so honest and so real, so gentle and so kind.

"I've been trying to say no to them all my life. That's why I moved to Bolinas. At least it puts a bridge between us. But you'll notice who's babysitting the house and the dog."

"One of these days you'll surprise yourself and put your foot down," he said kindly. "You'll do it when it's time and feels right. And Jane's not easy to turn down, even for me. She's a strong woman, and hard in a lot of ways, although I like her a lot, and she's so incredibly smart. Liz is too but she's a much gentler person. She mellows Jane out a lot, or at least she tries."

"Jane's a lot like my dad. She's very blunt and direct. My mother is more manipulative to get her way. She cries a lot." And then

Coco laughed at herself as she looked at him across the table. "I guess I do too. I'm sorry. You didn't come here to listen to my sad stories about running away from a famous family in Hollywood to live in a shack at the beach. It's a pretty easy life."

"Your stories don't sound so sad to me," he said honestly, "except for your Australian friend. That's sad for him, and for you. But you're young, you've got years and years and years ahead of you, to figure out what you want to do, and find the right person. And it sounds like you have a good time and a good life in the meantime. That's pretty enviable, if you ask me. I think you're doing better than you know. And they don't have to approve of what you do. My parents still worry about me. They think I missed the boat on marriage and kids, and they may be right. They love Chloe, but they'd love to see me married, with four kids, and back in England with all of them, where they think I belong. That's their assessment, not mine. This Hollywood thing comes at a high price. Sometimes you wind up giving up the wrong things. I've figured that much out myself."

"It's not too late," Coco reassured him. "You could still wind up married with ten kids, and probably will. There's no one to set the rules about when that has to happen."

"It's a lot more complicated when you're famous," he said thoughtfully. "The good ones are wary and figure you must be some kind of freak, or a player at best. And the ones that come like moths to a flame are the weirdos and groupies and some really bad people, like the one I'm running away from. Once you're famous, you stand out like a beacon in the darkness to them. And those are the ones that make me run like hell. Although this time, I didn't see this one coming. She hid her game pretty well at first, I thought she was a genuinely nice girl, and I thought maybe it would be easier because she's famous too. Big, big mistake. She turned out to be everything I don't want."

"So you'll try again," Coco said, smiling at him, and then got up to clear the table. She offered him some ice cream, and when he accepted with delight, she handed him a Dove bar from the freezer. She had bought half a dozen flavors for him that afternoon, since she didn't know what he liked. They were in effect strangers, and yet they were sharing their deepest secrets, regrets, and fears with each other, and they both felt comfortable about it.

"I get tired of trying again sometimes," he admitted as the ice cream dribbled down his chin, and he looked like a kid himself.

"I felt that way when people were trying to set me up. That's why I stopped for a while. I figured if it's going to happen, it'll just happen by itself. And if it doesn't, I'm fine the way I am." He laughed at that.

"Miss Barrington," he said formally, "I can assure you that, at twenty-eight, it's not over, and you're not going to wind up alone. It may take you a while to find the one you want. But any man would be fortunate to have you. And I promise you, the right one will come along. Just give it time."

She smiled at him then, "I am going to make you the same promise, Mr. Baxter. The right one *will* come along. I promise. Just give it time," she repeated his own words back to him. "You're a terrific guy, and if you stay away from the psychos, a nice woman will find you. And that's a promise." She stuck her graceful hand across the table, and he shook it. They both felt better for having talked to each other, and winding up in Jane's house at that time had turned out to be a blessing for them both. They each felt as though they had a new friend.

"What happens in this town on a Saturday night?" Leslie asked her with interest, and she laughed.

"Not much. People go out for dinner, and by ten o'clock everyone is off the streets. This is a small town, not like New York or L.A."

"At your age, you should be out having fun on a Saturday night, not sitting around talking to an old fart like me," he chided her, and she laughed again.

"Are you kidding? I'm sitting here talking to the biggest movie star in the world, in my sister's kitchen. Every woman in the country would give their right arm to spend Saturday night like this," she said admiringly. It was heady stuff, even for her. She hadn't been around her parents' world in years, or even her sister's. "Not to mention what Saturday night is like in Bolinas, where I live. There would be ten old hippies sitting at the bar, if that. Everyone else would be home in bed by now, and me too, watching one of your movies." They both laughed at that. He helped her put their dishes in the dishwasher, turned off the lights on the main floor, and he walked slowly upstairs behind her, as the dogs followed. It still made him nervous to be around the bull mastiff. Sallie was smaller and less imposing, and seemed less ominous to him. Jack could have knocked him down in seconds, although Coco knew he wouldn't do that. He was even gentler than Sallie. But he weighed more than Leslie did.

They said goodnight to each other on the landing, outside their respective bedrooms. Leslie asked what she was doing the next day, and she said she had no plans. She never worked on Sundays, although she would have loved to go home for the day, and was thinking about it.

"I wouldn't mind seeing that funny little beach town where you live," he said hopefully. "How far is it from here?"

"Less than an hour," she answered, smiling at him. She would have loved to show it to him.

"I'd like to see that shack of yours, and walk on the beach. There's always something so restorative about the ocean. I had a house in Malibu for a while. I was really sorry after I sold it. Maybe we can take a drive over to Bolinas tomorrow," he said, stifling a yawn. Now that he was relaxing and felt safe again, he realized that he was exhausted. "I'll make you waffles when we get up," he promised, and then kissed her on the cheek. "Thanks for listening tonight." He really liked her. She was such a decent, honest person, and there was nothing she wanted from him. Not fame, not fortune, no press or publicity, she didn't even want dinner. He felt surprisingly comfortable with her, considering he had only met her that morning. One sensed easily that she was someone to be trusted, and she felt the same way about him.

He heard his cell phone ring as he walked into his room. The number that showed on his caller ID was blocked, but he was almost sure it was the psycho bitch from hell, trying to stalk him. He let it go to voice mail, and a minute later he got a text message from her, threatening him again. She had lost it. He deleted it and didn't answer. He closed his door, took off his clothes, and got into bed. He lay there for a long time, thinking about Coco and the things they'd said to each other. He loved her openness and honesty about herself. He had tried to be equally so with her, and thought he had been. He let his mind wander when he turned off the light, but he couldn't sleep.

An hour later, he decided to go down to the kitchen for a glass of milk, and saw that the lights were still on in her bedroom. He knocked softly on her door to ask if she wanted anything, and she called out and said to come in. She was lying between both dogs in a pair of faded flannel pajamas, watching a movie. He glanced at the screen and looked into his own face. It was like seeing himself in a giant mirror, as he stared at it in amazement, and Coco looked embarrassed to have been caught watching his film.

"Sorry," she said, looking sheepish, and like a little girl again, "it's my favorite movie." He smiled then. It was quite a compliment from a woman he had come to admire in a single day. She wasn't trying to flatter him. If he hadn't come in, he wouldn't even have known she was watching his movie.

"I liked that one too although I thought I was awful in it," he admitted casually, grinning at her. "I'm going downstairs. Do you want anything?"

"No, thanks." It was nice of him to ask. They felt like two kids at a pajama party, in Jane's very sophisticated house. Coco had left her clothes all over the floor of the bedroom. It made it look homier to her. Everything was so neat when Jane was around. Coco thought her mess added humanity to it, although her sister wouldn't have agreed.

"See you in the morning. Enjoy the movie," Leslie said to her, as he closed the door, and went downstairs for the glass of milk he had wanted and another ice cream. He half hoped that Coco would come down and join him, but she was too engrossed in the movie. He went back upstairs after he finished the milk and ice cream. And this time, when he went back to bed, he fell into a sound sleep within minutes, and didn't stir until morning. He felt as though he had left all his worries behind in L.A., and he had found just what he had wanted when he came here. A safe place, out of harm's way, far from people who wanted to hurt him. And in the safe place, he had found something even more rare. He had found a safe woman. He hadn't felt that way since he had left England and come to Hollywood. And he knew that, tucked away in this house in San Francisco, with this funny girl and the two big dogs, nothing bad could ever touch him here.

Chapter 4

It was another perfect sunny day when they both woke up the next morning. The weather was warm, and the sky was a brilliant blue. Leslie came downstairs before she did, and had already made bacon to go with their waffles. He poured himself a glass of orange juice, and put the kettle on to make tea for both of them. He was pouring the water into two mugs when Coco walked into the kitchen. She had just let both dogs out into the garden. She was going to take them for a long walk after breakfast.

"Smells delicious," she said, as he handed her a mug of green tea that he had found in the cupboard. He had helped himself to some English Breakfast tea, and drank it without milk or sugar. And a moment later he set a plate of waffles down on the table for her. The maple syrup was already on the table. They both laughed as they remembered the scene of utter chaos when he had walked into the kitchen the day before. "Thank you for making breakfast," she said politely as he sat down across from her, with his own plate of waffles and bacon.

"I'm not sure I trust you in the kitchen," he said, teasing her, and then glanced out at the bay through the enormous window. "Are we going to the beach today?" he asked, looking at the sailboats already gathering in race formations. There was constant activity on the bay, and an endless flock of boats.

"Would that be all right with you?" she asked cautiously. "I can go by myself if you don't want to. I need to pick up some things, and I should check my mail."

"Would you mind if I go with you?" He didn't want to overstep his bounds with her, or be a nuisance. She probably had things to do, or might prefer some peace and privacy at her cottage, or even a chance to see friends.

"I'd love it," she said honestly. And how painful could it be spending a day in Bolinas with Leslie Baxter? "I want to show it to you. It's a crazy little village, but it's terrific." She had told him about there being no signs, so no one could find them.

An hour later, they got in her van with both dogs, wearing jeans, T-shirts, and flip-flops. She warned him that it could get chilly if the fog rolled in, so they had both brought sweaters. And there was no sign of anything but blue skies as they drove down Divisadero toward Lombard, and joined the flow of traffic heading north to the Golden Gate Bridge. They chatted easily as he told her about growing up in England, and he admitted that sometimes he missed it. But he also confessed that it was different now when he went home. His fame had even changed the way people treated them there. No matter what he did to convince them otherwise, the ordinary people he had known growing up now acted as though he were special or different in some way, no matter how ordinary he still felt.

"Tell me about Chloe," Coco said, as they drove across the bridge, and up the hill to the rainbow tunnel in Marin.

"She's delicious," Leslie said, and his face lit up the moment he thought about her. "I wish I saw her more often. She's very smart, and extremely adorable. She takes after her mother." He said it with a look of deep affection, not only for the child, but also for the woman who had been his girlfriend long before. "I'll show you pictures of her when we get to Bolinas." He always kept a batch of them in his wallet. "She wants to be a ballerina or a truck driver when she grows up, apparently she thinks they're interchangeable and equally interesting professions. She says truck drivers get to dump things all over the road, which she thinks is extremely entertaining. She takes every imaginable kind of lesson. French, computer, piano, ballet." He looked proud and happy whenever he talked about his daughter. He said his relationship with her and her mother was easy and straightforward and always had been. "Her mother had a serious boyfriend for a while recently, and I thought she was going to get married. I was a little worried. He was Italian, and Florence would have been even harder for me to get to than New York. I was relieved when they broke up, although Monica deserves to have someone in her life too. To be honest, I was jealous of him with Chloe. He got to see more of her than I do. I don't think her mother's seeing anyone right now," he said as they took the Stinson Beach turnoff and drove through Mill Valley.

"Would you ever go back to her, because of Chloe?" Coco asked him with interest, and he shook his head.

"I couldn't, and neither could she. The trail is cold on all that now. It's been too long, and there's too much water under the bridge. It was really over for us before Chloe was born. She was just a wonderful accident that happened. Chloe is the best thing that ever happened to either of us. She makes everything worth-while."

"I can't even imagine having children," Coco said honestly, "at least not now." And even when Ian had been alive, she had felt too young to think about having kids, even with him. "Maybe when I'm in my thirties," she said vaguely as they drove along. He admired the way she handled the curves in the road with the ancient van. It made some pretty scary noises, but it chugged along. Leslie mentioned that he loved working on cars. It was a boyhood passion he had never outgrown. He was impressed by the hairpin turns that followed the cliffs along the coastline, which she negotiated with ease. She seemed competent and calm and in control of her life to him, no matter what her mother and sister thought. He felt certain they were wrong. And the closer they got to the beach, the happier Coco was.

"I hope you don't get carsick," she said, glancing over at him with concern.

"Not yet. I'll let you know." The weather was gorgeous and the scenery fantastic. Both dogs were sound asleep in the back of the van, and after twenty minutes of sharp turns, the road dropped down to Stinson Beach. Half a dozen shops sat haphazardly next to each other on either side of the road. An art gallery, a bookstore, two restaurants, a grocery store, and a gift shop. "This has to be one of the lost wonders of the world," Leslie said, looking amused at the quaint town, if you could call it that. It was over in two blocks, and they rounded a turn, passing some narrow roads with falling-down shacks.

"There's a gated community over there." She gestured vaguely past a lagoon. "And a bird preserve on our right. It's pretty un-spoiled here." And then she smiled broadly. "Wait till you see Bolinas. It's a time warp and even less civilized than all this." He loved the ruggedness of it, and the simplicity. This was no fancy beach town, and it felt as though it was a million miles from any city. He could see why she lived here. The feeling he had as they drove along the unmarked road was one of ease and peace. It was as though one could leave one's burdens far behind just by coming here. Even the harrowing drive over had relaxed him.

Coco took an unmarked left turn ten minutes later, and they rose onto a small plateau. There were houses that looked more like old farms, huge ancient trees, and a tiny church.

"I'll show you the town first," she explained, and then laughed as she said it, "although that's somewhat euphemistic. It's even smaller than Stinson Beach. Our beach isn't as good, this is more rural, but that keeps the tourists away too. It's too hard to find and too hard to get here." As she said it, they drove past a ramshackle restaurant, a grocery store, the head shop, and the ancient dress shop with a tie-dyed dress of some kind in the window. Leslie looked around with a broad grin.

"This is it?" He looked vastly amused. The stores were tiny and from another era, but everything around them was pretty and green. There were big, solid old trees, and they sat on a slight ele-vation above the sea. It looked like country more than beach.

"This is it," Coco confirmed. "If you need incense or a bong, that's the place to go." She pointed, and he chuckled.

"I think I can manage without, just for today."

She drove past the cluster of stores then, and down the road dotted with old-fashioned mailboxes, picket fences, and the occasional wrought-iron gate. "There are a few really lovely houses here, but they're a well-kept secret and tucked away. Most of the homes are just cottages, or old surfer shacks. In the old days, a lot of the hippies used to live in broken-down school buses near the beach. It's more respectable these days, but not much," she said with a look of peace on her face. It felt good to be back.

She left the van parked outside her house, let the dogs out, and they followed her and Leslie through the weather-beaten wooden gate. Ian had built it for them. She unlocked the front door and walked inside, as Leslie came in cautiously behind her and looked around. She had a perfect view of the ocean from her living room, although the windows were old and not particularly large, unlike the floor-to-ceiling picture windows in Jane's house in the city. Nothing here had been built for show, it was just a cozy place to live, and Leslie could see that. It looked like a dollhouse to him. There were books stacked up on the floor, old magazines on the table. One of her watercolors was propped up on an easel in the corner, part of the curtains had come unhooked. But despite the friendly disorder that resulted from her living alone, the place was inviting and looked well lived in. She used the fireplace every night.

"It's not much, but I love it," Coco said happily. There were some framed watercolors on the walls, and pictures of her with Ian on the mantelpiece and on the shelves of the overstuffed bookcase. The kitchen was open and slightly in disarray but clean, and behind the living room was her tiny bedroom with a cozy comforter on the bed, and a faded old quilt she had found at a garage sale.

"It's wonderful," Leslie said, his eyes lighting up. "It's not a shack, as you said, it's a home." It had a hundred times the warmth of her sister's elegant digs on Broadway, and he could see easily why Coco preferred it. He glanced at a photograph of her and Ian looking happy and young in wet suits on his boat, and then he walked out onto the deck behind her. She had an extraordinary view of the ocean, the beach, and in the far distance the city. "I think if I lived here, I'd never leave," he said, and meant it.

"I don't, except to go to work." She smiled at him. It was a lifetime away from the mansion in Bel-Air where she had grown up, and now this was all she wanted. She didn't need to explain it to him, he understood it, and looked down at her with a gentle smile. He felt as though she had just shown him her secret clubhouse, her hidden garden. Being in the house with her was like looking deep into her soul.

"Thank you for bringing me here," he said softly. "I feel honored." As he said it, the dogs came bounding up to them, already dusted with sand, and Jack had a branch with some leaves on it tangled up in his collar. The big dog looked elated to be there, and so did Sallie, as Coco smiled up at Leslie.

"Thank you for understanding what this means to me. My family thought I lost my mind when I moved here. It's hard to explain to people like them." Leslie found himself wondering if she would have stayed there if Ian were still alive, or someplace like it in Australia, and he suspected that she would. Coco was someone who wanted desperately to let go of her origins, the values she found fault with, and all the trappings of that world. This was the outer manifestation of all she had rejected when she came here. The falsity, the obsession with material goods, the fight to get ahead, the sacrifice of people for careers. "Would you like a cup of tea?" she offered, as he let himself down into one of the two faded deck chairs.

"I'd love it." He noticed the old statue of Quan Yin then, which Ian had given her. "The goddess of compassion," he said softly as she handed him a mug of tea a few minutes later and sat in the deck chair next to his. "She reminds me of you. You're a kind woman, Coco, and a fine one. I saw the photographs of your man. He looks like a good man," he said respectfully. Ian was a tall, handsome blond, and the couple looked carefree and happy in the photo. For a moment as he walked by the smiling images, Leslie felt envious of them. He suspected that in his entire life he had never had what they had shared.

"He was a good man." She looked out to sea and then turned to smile at Leslie. "Everything I want in the world is here. The ocean, the beach, a quiet, peaceful life, this deck where I watch the sun come up every morning, and a fire at night. My dog, books, people I care about in houses nearby. I don't need more than this. It works for me. Maybe one day I'll want something different, but not now."

"Do you think you'll ever go back, to the 'real' world, I mean? Or perhaps I should say the unreal one, where you used to live?"

"I hope not," she said firmly. "Why would I? None of that ever made sense to me, even when I was a child," Coco said as she closed her eyes and turned her face toward the sun. Leslie watched her closely. Her hair shone like freshly polished copper, and both dogs had gone to sleep at their feet. It was a life one could get used to, an absence of complication and artifice. But he could imagine that it would get lonely too. It was a life for the most part without people, or strong attachments for her right now.

But his was no better. He was hiding from a woman who was try-ing to kill him. Without question, this made more sense. Leslie loved everything he was seeing here, but he wasn't sure he could live here. Although thirteen years younger than he was, Coco seemed to have found herself long before he did. He was still look-ing, though closer to knowing what he wanted than he had been in years. At least he knew what he didn't want. Coco had figured that out sooner too.

"I have to admit . . ." He chuckled softly as Coco opened her eyes and looked at him again. Everything about her was centered, solid, and peaceful. She was like a long drink of pure water from a mountain stream. "I can't see your sister here." Coco laughed at that too.

"She hates it. Lizzie likes it more than she does, but it's not their thing. They are women of the city. Jane thinks San Francisco is a village. I think they both prefer L.A., but they love their house here, and Lizzie says it's easier to write here than there. There aren't as many distractions."

Leslie was still smiling. "I remember when I met Jane. I thought she was the most beautiful woman I had ever seen. She was in her mid-twenties and she was a knockout. She still is. I had a huge crush on her for about a year, I kept taking her out, and she kept treating me like a buddy. I couldn't figure out what I was doing wrong. I fi-nally lost it completely and kissed her one night after we had din-ner, and she looked at me like I was insane and told me she was gay. She said she had done everything she could think of to let me know, including wear men's clothes from time to time when we went out. I just thought she was eccentric and it made her look sexy. I felt like the biggest idiot you can imagine, but we've been great friends ever since. And I really like Liz. They're perfect for each other. Liz softens her somehow. Jane has mellowed a lot over the years."

"That's a scary thought," Coco commented. "She's still pretty tough. On me, anyway. As far as she's concerned, I never measure up. And I don't think I ever will." The secret was to stop trying, but Coco knew better than anyone that she hadn't gotten there yet. She still tried too hard to win her sister's approval, even if she lived in Bolinas.

"She probably wants the best for you, and worries about you," Leslie said reasonably, as they sipped their mugs of tea. Coco liked sitting next to him, staring out at the ocean, and talking about life.

"Maybe. But not everyone can be like her. I don't even want to try. I'm headed in the opposite direction. Away from all that. My mother doesn't understand it either. I'm just different. I always was."

"I think that's good," he said peacefully, relaxing in the deck chair.

"So do I. But it scares most people. They think they have to be the same as everyone else, and accept lives and values that don't fit. Theirs never fit me, even when I was little."

"I can see that in Chloe, even now," he said thoughtfully. "She doesn't want to be an actress, like me or her mother. She'd rather drive a truck. I think that's her way of saying she's who she is, and she's not us. You have to respect that."

"My parents never did. They just ignored it, hoping it would go away. You're way ahead of the game if you already respect who she is at six." Coco smiled as she thought about it. "My mother wanted us both to be debutantes. Jane had recently come out and was militantly into gay rights. She got off the hook because I think my mother was afraid she'd show up in a tuxedo instead of a dress. She got a lot more pissed off at me eleven years later. I said I'd rather cut my liver out with an ice pick than make my debut. I thought it was wrong and elitist, a throwback to another era where the whole purpose of it was to find a husband. I went to South Africa for Christmas that year instead, and helped build a sewage system in a village. I had a lot more fun than I would have had at the cotillion. My mother had hysterics and wouldn't talk to me for six months. My father was cooler about it. But he wouldn't have been when I dropped out of law school. I guess they each had their dreams for us. Jane doesn't quite fit, but they overlooked it because she's a big success, which was always the gold standard for them. I never bought into that and I never will," she said, sounding sure of herself in a way that he admired.

"Your family will get used to it eventually," Leslie said in a quiet tone, but from what she'd said to him so far, he wasn't sure they would. Coco was not someone who wanted to meet another person's expectations if they felt wrong to her. She was totally true to herself and all that she believed, whatever the cost to her. He respected that in her immensely. "I like your watercolor on the easel, by the way. It looks very peaceful."

"I don't do those much anymore," she admitted. "I usually give them away as gifts. They're just fun to relax with." He could sense that she was talented at many things, and enjoyed them all, even if she hadn't yet discovered her final goal. In some ways, he envied her the exploration. He got tired of acting sometimes, and all the craziness that went with it.

They sat for a while in silence, lost in their own thoughts, and finally he dozed off. She took their mugs inside, and packed a few things to take back to the city with her. And when she came back out on the deck, he woke up.

"Does anyone ever swim here?" he asked, feeling lazy and sleepy in the sun.

"Sometimes." She smiled. "There are shark attacks occasionally, which discourage the faint-hearted, and the water's pretty cold. It's better with a wet suit. I have one about your size if you want." Ian was about the same height as Leslie, and a little broader and more athletic. She still had his old wet suits in the garage, and his diving gear. She had thought about giving them away, but never did. She liked seeing his things there, it felt less lonely that way, and he seemed less gone, as though he might come back and use them.

"I think the 'occasional shark attacks' just did it for me," he chuckled. "I'm a devoted and confirmed coward. I had to dive with a shark in a picture once. It was supposedly trained and sedated. I opted to use a stuntman for everything except the love scenes. I was trained and sedated for those myself." She laughed at what he said.

"I'm not very brave either," she confessed with a shy look, and he instantly disagreed.

"Are you serious? I think you're extremely brave. About important things. You've flown in the face of tradition with your family, you've bucked the system. In fact, you've walked away, and done it with courage and grace. No matter how much pressure they've put on you, you've done what's right for you, and what you believe. You loved a man and lost him, and you're not lying here whining—you've gone on. You've stayed here. You live alone in a funny little community. You're not afraid to live alone, or be alone. You've created a job that works for you, even if those you love insult you for it. All of that takes courage. It takes a lot of courage, Coco, to be different. And you do it all with dignity and poise. I'm full of admiration for you." They were lovely things to say, and she appreciated his recognizing who she was, without telling her everything she was doing wrong. Instead he was validating the decisions she had made and the life she had chosen. She smiled warmly at him after what he said.

"Thank you. I admire you too, Leslie. You're not afraid to admit it when you're wrong, or made a mistake. You're amazingly humble given who you are, what you've accomplished, and the world you live in. You could be a real jerk with all of that, and you aren't. You've managed to stay real in spite of it."

"My family would disown me if I didn't," he said honestly. "Maybe that's what keeps me true to myself. I have to face them, and myself at some point. It's very nice being a movie star, and having people fall all over themselves to give you what you want. But at the end of the day, you're still only a human being, a good one, or a bad one. It's embarrassing in my business to see people act like fools, and a lot of people do. I don't have a lot of patience with it. And most of the time, when I look at myself, I see all the things I do wrong, not the ones I do right. Maybe in that sense," he said, looking at her seriously, "being extremely insecure on a long-term basis is a good thing." They both laughed at what he said. "I'm impressed that you don't seem insecure."

"I am. I'm just very stubborn." She sighed then. "I'm always trying to figure out who I am, and what I want to do. I know how I got here, and why. I just can't seem to figure out where I want to go from here. Or maybe in the long run this will be what I want. I haven't decided yet."

"It'll come to you. At least this way you have a lot of options. All doors are open to you."

"I like the ones I've opened so far. I'm just not sure which ones I want to open next."

"We all feel that way at times. Everyone else looks as though they have the answers. They're just faking it. They don't know any more than we do. Or they've kept their worlds very small. It's easier for them that way. If you're willing to look out in the world, it's a lot more exciting, but sometimes it's scary as hell." He seemed very humble as he said it, and not afraid to show her his fears and uncertainties as well.

"You're right," she agreed. "It is scary. What about you? What are you going to do now? Find an apartment and go back to L.A.?" And start all over again, looking for a new woman? She didn't ask the question, but it was on both their minds. She wondered how many times you could start again, meeting people, singling one out, giving fate a chance, moving forward, and then ultimately being disappointed and ending it again. At some point that had to get old. Even after two wonderful years with Ian, she was having trouble getting up the courage to try again. She wondered if it was harder for her because everything with him had been so right. But if you wound up with the wrong woman every time, how many times could you start again? She could only imagine how many failed romances Leslie Baxter had had. At forty-one, starting over had to seem like a very, very old game to him. It was precisely what he was thinking when she asked.

"I'll find something temporary, I guess. I get my house back in six months, and I start a picture in four. I'm going on location in Venice for that. The tenant will be out of my house by the time I get back. I could stay at a hotel now, but there isn't a lot of privacy there. And it would be a lot easier for Miss Psycho Ex to get to me in a hotel, if she even cares two weeks from now. My guess is that she'll find someone else to torture fairly fast. She's not one to be without a man for long. As far as all that goes"—he answered the question she hadn't asked but he had understood—"I'm more inclined to wait for a while. I need a bit of a break after all that. It was something of a shock, to have misjudged someone so totally and been so wrong." Unconsciously, he rubbed his bruised cheek as he spoke. He had left his cell phone at the house in the city, in order to avoid her text messages for a while. Leslie never wanted to speak to her again, although he knew that eventually, in their world, their paths would inevitably cross. He wasn't looking forward to that. "I don't need romance in my life. Not for a while anyway. I'm beginning to think I want the real thing, or nothing at all. This passing fancy stuff, for a while, is a lot of work, and always turns into a mess. It's fun for about five minutes, and then you spend a hell of a lot of time cleaning it up. Rather like the maple syrup disaster when we met." She smiled at what he said. "Cleaning up after a bad romance is like that, but not nearly as much fun. And a lot harder to clean up." His ex-girlfriend had already told him that she was going to destroy everything he had left at her house. The text message after that had said she had. Nothing he had left there couldn't be replaced, but it was still a giant nuisance and a hell of an affront. He laughed then at his next thought. "I suppose I'm homeless, then. That's a novel experience for me. I don't usually live with women, and certainly not at their place. I was a bit too overconfident about this. She played an awfully good game at first. It turns out that she's a *much* better actress than I thought. She should be up for an Oscar for our first three months. It's a hell of a lesson to learn at forty-one. I guess one can be a fool at any age."

"I'm sorry it worked out that way," she said sympathetically. She felt sorry for him. She had never had an experience like that. And she hoped she never would. In his Hollywood life, given who he was and the target he was inevitably, it was more commonplace. She remembered how many times her father told them stories of high drama among his clients, broken romances, assaults, people ripping each other off, cheating on each other openly or secretly, attempted suicides. It was all part of the life she didn't want and had fled, although bad things happened to people in the real world too, but not as publicly, and not as often. It was part of the territory for someone like Leslie Baxter. Movie star romances were usually short-lived, ephemeral, went up in a public display of fireworks, and ended in a mess. She didn't envy him. And even if he brought it on himself with the women he chose, it had to be discouraging for him. From the sound of it, he could have wound up with a lot worse than a bruised cheek.

"I'm sorry too," Leslie said quietly, "sorry I was such a fool. And I'm sorry you lost your guy. You look happy in the photographs with him."

"I was. But sometimes even good things come to an end. Fate." It was a healthy way to look at it, and Leslie admired her for that too. There was nothing he didn't admire in her so far. She was an amazing woman, and he was glad he had sought refuge at Jane's.

He might never have met her otherwise, particularly as she was the self-declared black sheep of the family, and Jane had barely spoken of her over the years. She was far more interested in herself. In Leslie's eyes, Coco was like a small, white peaceful dove in a family of hawks and eagles. He could only imagine how hard it must have been growing up in their midst. But Coco seemed to have come out of it unscathed. She wasn't bitter to have been set down in the midst of them, just surprised. And ultimately, she had flown away. She still had ties to them, but the threads that bound her to them seemed to be getting thinner every day. It was the impression Coco gave, not incorrectly, although she had nonetheless gotten tangled up in house-sitting for Jane. And Leslie was extremely glad she had, otherwise they might never have met.

They lay on the deck in the sun for most of the afternoon, and only spoke once in a while. Leslie slept and Coco finished reading a book. They made sandwiches from what she had left in the fridge and packed up the rest to take to the city with them, so it didn't go to waste. And after they locked up the house, she drove him to the public beach at Stinson, so he could see the spectacular stretch of smooth white sand. It went for miles, with smooth sand and shells spread out near the water's edge. There were birds wading in the surf, seagulls flying overhead, and small interesting rocks that Coco picked up and slipped in her pocket as she always did. They walked the length of the beach, sat at the point and looked at the ocean coming into the lagoon, and saw Bolinas just ahead of them across the narrow inlet, and then they walked back to the van, with the dogs running far ahead and then coming back to them. Twice, horses galloped past, and there were very few people on the beach. Leslie was surprised when Coco told him it was always that way. Only on rare days of intense heat did people bother to come to this beach. Most of the time there were only a handful of people on it, spread out over several miles. It was the perfect getaway, and Leslie felt as though he had had a week's vacation as they drove back along the cliff again. The sun was just setting, and it had been an extraordinary day.

"I heartily approve," he said as she handled the hairpin turns expertly again, this time on the outer edge of the cliff, which impressed him even more. She even managed to avoid the potholes and many places where the road was in bad shape, which kept most people from coming there. It was spectacular, but far from an easy drive.

"What do you approve of?" Coco asked. The dogs were sound asleep in the back, utterly worn out from their long run on the beach, particularly when they chased after the horses. Sallie had tried desperately to herd them, but they had gotten away. She had had to content herself with chasing birds, while Jack lumbered after her. He was so tired he could hardly walk by the time they left, and he was snoring loudly now. It made a soft, steady purr from the back of the van.

"I approve of your living here," Leslie said comfortably. "In case you need to hear that from someone. In fact, I envy you." She smiled at what he said. It was nice to hear.

"Thank you." She liked knowing that he saw the beauty of it, and the value of the life she lived. He didn't think she was a hippie or a freak, and he didn't think her home was a dump. He had experienced it like a warm embrace, and loved seeing that piece of her. All the pieces of her fit seamlessly. She was just totally different from Jane, which was too difficult for her family to accept. They all fit into a single mold, Coco didn't, and she seemed far better to him for that.

They drove through Mill Valley quietly, and onto the Golden Gate Bridge in Sunday night traffic. She got off the ramp after the bridge into Pacific Heights, and asked him if he wanted to stop somewhere to pick up food. He really didn't. He was totally sated from the good feelings of the day, and relaxed after their long walk on the beach. He had even dozed in the car on the way home, as Coco drove in silence. In spite of who he was, which no longer impressed her as it did when she first met him, and the shock of seeing him in her sister's kitchen, they were totally at ease with each other. She was surprised at how comfortable she was being with him, and he had noticed the same thing and commented on it during their walk on the beach. He said that it was rare for him, and he usually protected himself from strangers. But she was no longer a stranger. They were already friends, even after two days.

"How about if I make you an omelette? I'm rather good at those, if I do say so myself. You could make one of your lovely California salads," he said hopefully, and she laughed.

"I'm not much of a cook," she confessed. "I live on salads, and the occasional piece of fish."

"You look it," he said as a compliment. She seemed healthy, strong, trim, and very thin. He could tell even in her T-shirts that she had a lovely body, but so did her sister, who was a good decade older. Leslie had to try harder, went to the gym every day, and worked out with a trainer intensely before every film. His livelihood depended on it, and so far so good. He didn't show his age, and his body hadn't changed in ten years. But it wasn't easy. And his penchant for ice cream was a curse.

"The omelette sounds delicious," she said as the ancient van labored up the hill on Divisadero. They barely made it to the crest on Broadway, and the dogs were still asleep when they got out. "Everybody out!" she called to rouse them, as Leslie picked up the groceries they'd brought back with them, and she carried in the big straw bag full of clean clothes. They looked no different than the rest of what she had at Jane's. She always wore the same things, in different colors, and more often than not white T-shirts and jeans. She had a closet full of them, and since losing Ian, she never bothered to dress up. There was no one to see or care what she wore. All she needed was to be clean, warm, and have decent running shoes for work. It was a simple life, and far, far less complicated than his. Every time he went out, he had to look like a star. He had mentioned that he had a whole wardrobe to replace now, and didn't really care about that at the moment either, since no one was seeing him, and he wasn't going anywhere. It was a relief not to have to think about it, and a blessing not to have to worry about paparazzi in L.A. No one knew he was in San Francisco, except Coco and her sister and partner. As far as the rest of the world was concerned, Leslie Baxter had disappeared. It defined freedom to him, which was what Coco cherished in her life too. Freedom and peace. It was almost like a blessing he was catching from her, and he liked it. It was an easy way to live.

While Coco turned off the alarm Leslie turned on the lights in the house. She left her tote bag at the foot of the stairs, and they put the groceries away together in the kitchen, while the dogs stood around waiting for dinner. She fed them, and then set the kitchen table with some of Jane's impeccable French linen place mats and elegant silver, while Leslie got out the ingredients for their omelette. And Coco made the salad he had asked for. She made a Caesar dressing, and half an hour later, she lit the candles, and they sat down to a simple dinner. As promised, the omelette was delicious.

"What a terrific day," he said, looking happy, as they chatted about nothing in particular. The day at the beach had been great for both of them, and they finished the meal with Dove bars again.

"Do you want to watch a movie?" she asked as they rinsed the dishes and he looked pensive.

"I think I'd like to take a swim. I checked the pool yesterday and it's very warm. I have to work out every day in L.A., but I'm too lazy to do it tonight," he said with a grin. Jane had a very professional-looking gym, where she worked out daily with a trainer. Coco never bothered, nor did Liz, who always complained about ten extra pounds but did nothing about it. Jane was a perfectionist in all things, including her appearance.

"I get my exercise walking the dogs every day," Coco said.

"After looking at the ocean all day, I really fancy a swim." She smiled at the expression. Now and then he reminded her of Ian, with his very British expressions, that were the same as the Australian ones Ian had used. They were comfortable and familiar, and a little nostalgic for her. "I trust there are no sharks in the pool."

"Not lately," Coco reassured him, and he invited her to join him. She usually didn't bother to use her sister's pool, but it sounded like fun with him. "Okay," she agreed.

They left the kitchen, went to their bedrooms, and five minutes later met at the pool, while Coco turned the lights on. It was spectacular, and indoors, since the weather in San Francisco was usually chilly. She knew that Jane swam in it daily, and occasionally Liz.

They swam together for nearly an hour. Coco swam laps while Leslie watched her, and then not to be outdone, he swam laps alongside her. He was winded long before she was, but she was younger and in better shape.

"Good lord, you have the endurance of an Olympic swimmer," he said in admiration.

"I was captain of the women's swimming team at Princeton," she confessed.

"I rowed in my youth," he volunteered, "but if I tried it now it would kill me."

"I was on the crew team for a year, sophomore year, I hated it. Swimming was easier." They were both relaxed and tired as they got out of the pool. He had worn plain blue swim trunks, and she wore a simple black bikini that showed off her figure, but there was nothing overtly seductive about her. She was a pretty woman with a good body, but she never flirted with him. She was coming to value their friendship.

They both put on the thick terrycloth robes Jane kept at the pool, and went back to their bedrooms to shower, dripping water on the carpet. He came to her bedroom a few minutes later, showered and clean, wearing the robe from the pool. She had on her flannel pajamas, and had just started a movie, not one of his this time, so as not to embarrass him. She knew it made him uncomfortable to see himself on screen, from what he had said the night before. "Want to watch? It's a chick flick. I'm addicted to them." It was a well-known romantic comedy that she had already seen many times and loved. He said he had never seen it, and she patted the bed beside her. Jack hadn't taken his favorite place yet, and was passed out on the floor with Sallie. They had worn the dogs out totally that day, which Leslie considered a blessing. They still made him a little nervous when they got lively, particularly the bull mastiff, however gentle Coco said he was. He was still a two-hundred-pound dog.

At her invitation, Leslie settled back against the pillows to watch the movie with her. She disappeared for a few minutes and came back with a bowl of popcorn. She giggled and he smiled. It felt like being children again. Her cell phone rang as soon as she sat down. It was Jane. And he could hear Coco's end of the conversation. Yes, everything was fine. She gave her a full update on the dog. She assured her sister she wasn't bothering him, and Leslie suddenly realized that Jane was inquiring about him. It intrigued him to note that Coco did not tell her that they had gone to Bolinas, nor that they were comfortably ensconced on her bed, watching a movie together. The conversation was brief and more like an interrogation. There were no warm, intimate exchanges between the two sisters. Coco said yes about six times to what were obviously instructions, and hung up with a glance at him.

"She wanted to make sure I wasn't annoying you. Tell me if I am," Coco said, looking hesitantly at him, and Leslie leaned over to kiss her cheek chastely to reassure her.

"I've just had the two nicest days I've had in years, thanks to you. If anyone is being annoying, it's me, intruding on you. And I really like this movie," he said, grinning. "I usually stick with sex and violence. It's kind of sweet watching these two silly people bumbling around and falling in love. Do they wind up together in the end?" he asked hopefully and Coco laughed at him.

"I'm not telling. Wait and see," she said, turning off the light, as they watched it on the enormous screen. It was like being in a theater, on a bed in pajamas. It was the perfect way to see a movie, as they shared the bowl of popcorn.

The movie turned out just as they wanted it to, as Coco knew it would. She loved seeing it again and again. It never bored her. The happy ending was always reassuring. She preferred those kinds of movies.

"Why can't life turn out that way?" he sighed, as he lay back on the pillows, thinking about the movie. "It makes so much sense, it's so reasonable and so simple. A few kinks to work out, a few minor dilemmas that can be resolved when everyone figures out what they have to do. They don't act like assholes, they're not mean to each other, no one is hopelessly screwed up by an abusive childhood, they're not out to get each other, they like each other, they fall in love, and they live happily ever after. Why is it so goddamn hard to have that happen?" He sounded wistful as he said it.

"Because people are complicated sometimes," she said gently. "But maybe it can happen. It almost did to me. It happens to others. I think you just have to be smart going in, keep your eyes open, don't kid yourself about who you're getting involved with, be honest with them and yourself, and play fair."

"It's never that simple," he said sadly. "Not in my world anyway. And most people don't play fair. They're obsessed with winning, and if one of you wins, you both lose." She nodded agreement.

"Some people do play fair. Ian and I did. We were very good to each other."

"You were babies, and nice people I guess. And then look what happened. If we don't screw it up for ourselves, destiny does."

"Not always. I know a number of couples in Bolinas who are happy. They don't lead complicated lives. I think that's part of the secret. In the world you live in and I grew up in, people complicate things, and most of the time they're not honest, particularly with themselves."

"That's what I love about you, Coco. You are, and so straightforward. Everything about you is clean and good. It's written all over you." He smiled at her as he said it.

"You strike me as honest too," she said warmly.

"I am, but I fool myself about who I'm getting involved with. I think I did with this woman I'm running away from now. Maybe I knew she was wrong from the beginning and I didn't want to see it. It was easier to close my eyes, and much harder later to keep them closed. And now look at the mess I'm in, hiding in another city, while she sets fire to my clothes." The image of it made them both smile, and he didn't look unhappy in his San Francisco bunker. In fact, he looked relaxed and totally at peace. He was a different man than the exhausted, stressed, anxious one who had arrived the day before. Their time in Bolinas had done him a world of good, and Coco as well. It had felt wonderful to be at home, on her own turf, for a few hours, particularly with him. He had appreciated everything it was about.

"Next time you'll be wiser and more careful," Coco said quietly. "Don't beat yourself up. You learned something from it. We always do."

"What did you learn from your Australian friend?" he asked gently.

"That it's out there, it happens. You just have to be lucky enough to find it, or have it find you. And it does."

"I wish I had your faith in that," he said, looking at her intently.

"You need to watch more chick flicks," she recommended seriously, and he laughed. "They're the best medicine there is."

"No," he said softly, never taking his eyes off hers. "I've found an even better one."

"And what's that?" she asked innocently, with no suspicion of what was coming, as she looked right into his eyes.

"You. You're the best medicine there is. The best person I've ever known." And as he said it, he leaned toward her and kissed her, and held her in his arms. She was so startled she didn't know how to react at first, but he didn't let go of her, and she found herself with her arms around his neck, holding on for dear life and kissing him back. Neither of them had expected to do that, or planned it, and he had promised himself when he saw her in the bikini that he wouldn't make a pass at her. He respected her, he liked her, he wanted to be friends with her, and suddenly he wanted so much more than that. Not only from her, but he wanted to give her everything she had ever dreamed of, because she was such a good person and she deserved it. And for the first time in his life he felt as though he did too. There was nothing seamy or wrong about this, and he didn't give a damn that he had only known her for two days. He was falling head over heels in love with her, and she looked stunned when the kiss ended and she looked at him again. She didn't want this to be just sexual, but she had never wanted anyone so badly in her life. Leslie Baxter was in bed with her, and kissing her, but suddenly he wasn't the famous movie star, he was just a man, and their attraction to each other was so powerful that she had no desire to resist.

"Oh." She made a tiny sound of surprise, and he kissed her again, and before either of them knew what had happened to them, their clothes were off, tossed onto the floor, and they were making passionate love. There was no way that either of them could have stopped. They didn't want to. It had been two years since Coco had made love to anyone, since Ian, and as he was making love to her, Leslie wondered if he had ever been in love before. He knew he was now with her.

They lay side by side breathless afterward, and Coco rolled over even closer to him and looked into his eyes. "What was that?" she whispered. Whatever it was, she knew she wanted more of it again. But not just yet. She had never experienced anything like it with any man, not even Ian. Their lovemaking had been easy and peaceful and comfortable. What had just happened with Leslie was earth-shattering and passionate. She felt like they'd just gone through a tornado together. The world had turned upside down and bells went off in her head. And the emotions they shared were so powerful that she felt as though she had been swept away on a tidal wave with him. And he felt the same.

"I think, my darling Coco," he whispered back, "that was love. The real deal. Until now, I wouldn't have recognized it if it bit me on the ass, but I think it just happened to us both. What do you think?" She nodded in silence. She wanted it to be love, but she wasn't sure. It was so soon.

"And then what happens?" she asked, looking worried. "You're a movie star and you go back to your world, and I'm a beach bum in

Bolinas, and I wind up alone here." It was too soon to worry about it, but the handwriting on the wall was clear, and he had already admitted that he didn't look or think carefully enough going in. She did. It had taken her three months to sleep with Ian. And exactly two days to sleep with Leslie. "I've never done anything like this in my life," she said, as a tear crept out of the corner of her eye. She was deeply moved by what had happened to them, and she didn't regret it. She was just scared.

"Neither have I, without meaning to anyway." He had slept with lots of women the first time they went out, if they were willing. But he had never been taken by surprise like that before, and grabbed by the heart so fiercely that he was pulled along by forces he hadn't planned and couldn't resist. It was the most powerful feeling of his entire life. "And as for the movie star–beach bum story, it isn't really quite like that. You're not some poor little orphan who knows nothing about my world. And as for how the story turns out, we'll just have to 'watch and see,' as you said. Maybe this is one of those chick flicks you love . . . darling, I hope it is," he said, and meant every word.

"I know about your world," she whispered back to him, "and I hate everything about it . . . except you," she said sadly.

"Let's just take it one day at a time," he said wisely. But she was more afraid that they were on borrowed time. She didn't want to get attached to him, and then have to tear herself away when he went back to his world, and sooner or later he would. This was just a fantasy, a dream. But she wanted it as much as he did. And she wanted to believe that dreams do come true. Hers almost had before, and maybe this time they would. She wanted to believe that was possible, but this had happened so suddenly, and given who he was in real life, she didn't know what to think. "Will you promise me not to worry too much, and just trust this and me for now? I won't hurt you, Coco. That's the last thing I want to do. Let's give this, and us, a chance and see where it goes. We'll figure it out." She didn't say a word to him, she just nodded like a five-year-old and burrowed deep into his arms. He held her that way for a long time, and then with all the gentleness of his tender emotions for her, he made love to her again. And the tornado they had felt for each other before hit them both for the second time.

Chapter 5

When Coco woke up the next morning, she wondered if she had dreamed everything that had happened the night before. She was alone in the bed. There was no sight of Leslie anywhere, and as she lay there, staring at the ceiling, thinking of him, he walked into the room, with a towel wrapped around his waist, carrying a breakfast tray for her, with a rose from Jane's garden in his teeth. She sat up in bed and stared at him.

"Oh my God, you're for real!" Or at least she hoped he was. There was nothing in the world she wanted to believe more. "And we weren't even drunk."

"That would have been a poor excuse," he said as he set the tray down over her legs. He had made her cereal, orange juice, and toast. And had even slathered the toast with butter and jam. "I would have made you waffles, but I figured Jane would kill us if we did the maple syrup trick again in here." They both laughed at the memory of when they had met, and how. It would be a private joke between them forever. And Coco was relieved to see that it was only seven A.M. She had an hour to spend with him before she went to work. She wished they could spend the day in bed.

"Thank you," she said, looking mildly embarrassed by the breakfast he had made for her, the lavish service, and what had happened between them the night before. He could see all of it in her eyes.

"I just want to say something to you, before you scare yourself to death. Neither of us knows what this is just yet. I know what I want it to be, and what I hope it is, and even though I've only known you for two days, I think I know who you are. I know who and what I've been, and who I want to be when I grow up, if I ever do. I've never lied to anyone intentionally. I don't mislead people. I may be a jerk at times, but I'm not a shit. I'm not trying to sweep you off your feet, twirl you around for a while, and then go back to Hollywood with another notch on my belt. I've had enough of those. I don't need another one, and especially not you. That's not who I want you to be in my life. I'm in love with you, Coco. I know that sounds crazy after two days, but sometimes I think you just know when it's right, and when it's for real. I've never felt that way before, or been this sure. I think I want to spend the rest of my life with you, and that sounds as crazy to me as it does to you. I just want us to give this a chance. We don't need to panic. There's no fire raging out of control here. We're two good people falling in love with each other. Let's turn this into a chick flick for our viewing pleasure, and hope it stays that way. Can we do that?" he asked, as he held a hand out to her, and she slowly extended hers toward him. He gently took her fingers in his and kissed them, and then he bent down and kissed her on the lips. "I love you, Coco. I don't give a damn if you're a beach bum, a dog-walker, or the daughter of the most famous agent in Hollywood and a best-selling author. I love *you* and everything you are. And with any luck at all, maybe you'll learn to love me," he said, as he sat down next to her on the bed, and she turned to him with the same look of astonishment that had been in her eyes since the night before.

"I already do, not because you're a movie star, but in spite of it, if that makes any sense."

"That's all I want. We'll figure the rest out, one day at a time," he said, sounding humble to her again. He had never been as happy in his life.

He shared the toast with her, and half an hour later, he got in the shower with her, and looked like a mother hen as she left for work. She told him she'd be back for lunch, and he had calls to make that morning. He wanted to call his agent and tell him what had happened with the woman in L.A. and where he was now, and he needed to warn his PR man that she might pull some stunts. And he had realtors to call to find a new apartment, furnished, until his own house was free in six months. He had enough to do to keep him busy until she got back. And later on, he wanted to do some exploring around the city and get his bearings. He thought it might be fun if they went out to dinner that night. He had already told her he wanted to go to Bolinas for the weekend. He smiled to himself as he showered and dressed. This was a very, very nice life, particularly with Coco in it.

Coco felt as though she were in a daze as she walked her clients' dogs that morning. She loved everything he had said, and all that they had done. But in her rare moments of clarity and sanity, it was hard to believe that anything this wonderful could last, especially with him. He was Leslie Baxter, after all. Eventually, he would have to go back to Hollywood and make another picture. The tabloids would eat him up, and them. Famous actresses would fawn all over him. And where would Coco be in all that? In Bolinas, waiting for him to come home? And there was no way she would live in L.A. again. Not even for him. She took a deep breath as she returned the last of the morning's dogs to their homes and reminded herself of what he had said. One day at a time. It was the best they could do for now. And as he said, they'd figure it out. But she also didn't want to lose someone she loved again. And a happy ending at the end of this wouldn't be so easy to pull off, given the cast.

When she got home, with sub sandwiches she had picked up for them, he was still on the phone. He was talking to a realtor about a furnished house in Bel-Air that was available for six months, while a famous actress finished a film in Europe. Coco looked worried as she listened, and Leslie laughed when he got off the phone.

"Don't panic yet," he reassured her. "She wants fifty thousand a month for it." He had been thinking about her all morning, and how things might work out in the long run. "You know, maybe eventually I could live here. Robin Williams and Sean Penn do. It seems to work for them." She nodded, still in a state of shock over what was happening to them. The cleaning woman had just left as she walked in. They forgot about the sub sandwiches and went back to bed, and made love until she had to go back to work, to walk the next group of dogs. She could hardly tear herself away from him. And when she came back at four, he was sound asleep on her bed. His agent had promised that morning to send him several scripts, and for now he was going to stay in San Francisco with her. Jane had told him he could stay as long as he wanted, and that afternoon they agreed not to say anything to her yet. They wanted to keep this miracle to themselves.

He got a call from his press agent late that afternoon. The actress who was stalking him had released a statement to the press that she had dumped him, and in thinly veiled terms, implied he was gay. Leslie said he didn't care. There was plenty of evidence to the contrary, and it just sounded like sour grapes. He was relieved in fact that she was telling the press she had dumped him. It could mean that she was ready to move on and stop torturing him. But he didn't trust the message yet. He wanted to wait and see before going back to L.A.

He had asked Coco to make a reservation for them at a quiet restaurant, under her name. She had chosen a simple little Mexican place in the Mission where she was hoping no one would recognize him. For sure, no one would expect to see him there. And after making love again in the shower, they managed to put their clothes on and get out of the house by eight.

He loved the restaurant when he saw it, and no one paid any attention to them, until he paid the check. The woman at the cash register had been staring at him all night. He paid in cash, so there were no credit cards involved, and she sent over a request for an autograph with his change. He tried to play dumb, but within minutes, people at several other tables had turned around, the waiter was chattering excitedly in Spanish, and without signing the autograph, which would have confirmed his identity, they tried to look nonchalant as they left, and then ran for the van.

"Shit," he muttered as Coco started the van and then drove away. "I hope no one calls the press." It was an element of life that Coco had never dealt with firsthand before. Life was complicated for him, and it meant that they couldn't go anywhere, or had to be extremely careful when they did. If he was recognized that easily in the Mission, he would be recognized anywhere, and neither of them wanted sightings reported all over San Francisco. They stayed home for the rest of the week, and Leslie went on long walks on the beach with her. And on Saturday after she walked her last dogs, they left for Bolinas, and spent the weekend there. They had no problem with anyone at the beach, and when Leslie ran into Jeff, the fireman who lived next door, when they were both taking out the trash, he stared at Leslie and then nodded, smiling broadly. He held out a hand and introduced himself and said that he was happy to see that Coco had a friend staying with her. He seemed to think the world of her. They saw him again on Sunday morning on the beach, with his dog, and he talked easily to both of them, and made no obvious sign of recognition or comment about who Leslie was. It was a community where people minded their own business, but still managed to look out for each other. Leslie said he had been a volunteer fireman in England when he went to college, and they talked about fires, equipment, and living in Bolinas. And from there, they somehow segued to fire engines, and then to cars. They discovered that they both loved to work on cars and rebuild engines. Leslie seemed to fit right in, and both men enjoyed talking to each other. Leslie and Coco were happy and relaxed when they drove back to the city on Sunday night. And Leslie mentioned again how much he had enjoyed chatting with her neighbor.

Coco was always a little worried that the fragile bubble of their hidden life would pop, but so far no one was bothering them. Jane knew he was still there, and didn't seem to mind it. She regularly

admonished Coco to leave him alone and not to bother him, and
Coco assured her that she wasn't.

It was the end of their second week of living together when
Leslie's realtor in L.A. insisted that there were several houses and
apartments that he had to see. He didn't even know if he wanted
to bother, but he thought he should see his agent too, and just
show his face in L.A. so no one thought he had gone into hiding
over the rumors of his being gay. His ex was still at it, and the
tabloids had run a couple of headlines that were no more shocking
than their usual fare.

"Do you want to come down with me on Saturday?" he offered.
"We could spend the night at the Bel-Air." The hotel had always
been extremely discreet, and no one knew who Coco was anyway.

"What'll we do with the dogs?" She had not only Sallie but her
sister's dog, and she knew Jane would be furious if she left.

"What about one of your neighbors in Bolinas? Could we leave
them at your place there?"

"Jane would strangle me if she knew," Coco said, looking guilty,
but she wanted to go with him. "Maybe we could. I'll call and ask."
In the end, both her neighbors agreed to look out for them, feed
them, walk them on the beach, and one of them even agreed to
drop them off on Sunday night when they came to a birthday
party in the city. Everything was set, just as he had said. One day
at a time. It all worked out. And they were getting along like two
peas in a pod.

In the end, just to be cautious, they flew to L.A. on two separate
flights, were met at the airport by two cars, and agreed to meet at
the hotel. Just in case. It was a little bit like being in a spy movie,
and they told no one they were coming down. Leslie took an

earlier flight, and saw the apartments the realtor had for him before Coco arrived. He didn't like any of them, and his interest in
renting anything in L.A. had waned since meeting her. He was
happy in San Francisco for now. And Coco was relieved when he
told her that at the hotel.

They had a beautiful suite at the Bel-Air Hotel. And Coco's presence was never acknowledged. The staff was used to handling sit-
uations like that with the utmost discretion. They went to dinner
at a dive he knew in West Hollywood that had delicious Cajun
food, and were happy and relaxed when they got back to the hotel.
It was nearly midnight as they walked slowly back to their room
through the gardens, and saw a couple holding hands and kissing
near the swans that swam in the little stream that wended through
the grounds. Coco smiled when she saw the couple kissing and
thought there was something familiar about them, but everyone
in L.A. always looked familiar to her. They were either well-
known stars, or people who wanted to look like them. It was funny
at times. The woman was a good-looking, well-dressed blonde
with a good figure in a black cocktail dress and high heels, whom
they could only see from the back, and the man with her was
handsome and young in a well-cut black suit. They stopped and
kissed again for a long time as Leslie and Coco approached, and
moved away at the last minute on the secluded path that led to
their suite. And as they did, the woman turned. Her face was lit by
the subtle lights on the grounds, and she turned her face up to the
man she was with. And then Coco gasped.

"Oh my God!" she said out loud, clutching Leslie's arm.

"What's wrong? Are you okay?" She shook her head and stood

rooted to the ground. There was no question who the woman was, and once Coco realized who she was, she ran to their room, while Leslie followed with a worried look. Coco looked absolutely panicked and she was crying as she stood in the living room of their suite. Leslie came to put his arms around her, and didn't understand what had happened. It was just a couple kissing as they watched the swans. They were obviously staying there too, and looked very much in love. But Coco looked as though she'd seen a ghost.

Coco sat down with a thunderstruck look. She was in shock.

"What's going on?" Leslie asked as he sat down next to her with an arm around her. "Tell me, Coco. Do you know that man?" He wondered if it was an old love. The only one he knew about was Ian.

She shook her head in answer to his question, as tears rolled down her face. "It's not him ... that woman is my mother," she said, staring at Leslie, and he was so startled for a moment, he didn't know what to say.

"That's your mother? I've never seen her in person. She's very beautiful." Coco looked nothing like her, although she was beautiful in her own right.

"He's half her age." She was stunned.

"Not quite," Leslie tried to reassure her, but there was no question, he was a lot younger than she was, and they had appeared to be very much involved. She had looked at her companion adoringly when she turned her face, and he looked very taken with her. He was a nice-looking guy, stylishly dressed in the manner of L.A., with relatively long hair, and a handsome face. He could have been an actor or a model, or almost anything for that matter. For a minute, Leslie didn't know what to say. "I take it, you didn't know about him."

"Of course not. She always says she could never be with anyone after my father. You see what I mean!" she said, suddenly in a rage. "Everyone is full of shit here. Everyone lies, everyone's fake, even my mother, with all her holier-than-thou righteous crap about everything on the planet. She calls me a hippie and a flake, and what is *she*?" The implication in Coco's voice was not pleasant, and Leslie winced.

"Maybe a lonely woman," Leslie said gently, trying to calm her. "It's not easy being alone at her age." He assumed she was at least sixty, given Jane's age, but she didn't look it. She had looked closer to fifty in the light, and the man with her was clearly younger, but it hadn't shocked him. They looked nice together, and happy. If it gave them some joy and comfort, what harm was there in that? But he didn't say that to Coco, who looked as though she were about to have some kind of attack. He had to admit, he wouldn't have enjoyed seeing his own mother in that context either, and she was older and not as well preserved, and she was still married to his father, although they complained good-naturedly about each other and always had. But Coco's mother was younger, sexier, expensively dressed, widowed, and famous. She was fair game.

"She's sixty-two years old, and she's had more plastic surgery than a goddamn burn victim. It's just not right. How can she tell me how to run my life when this is what she does when nobody's looking? My father would never have done that to her." But even as she said it, she knew that wasn't true. Her father had been a handsome man, with an eye for the ladies, and he and her mother had had their share of battles over his young, attractive clients. Her mother had kept an eagle eye on him, and a short leash. And if he had been the one to survive them, Coco suspected even now that he might have had someone too. She had just never expected it of her mother, and certainly not with a man that age.

"Maybe your father would too. Why do they have to be alone, just because it makes us uncomfortable to think of them as sexual? I hate to say it to you, but she has a right to a life too."

"And what do you think a guy that age is after? Sex, at her age? He's after her money, power, connections, all the fallout from her fame."

"Maybe," Leslie said reasonably. She had calmed down a little, and she was no longer crying. But she still looked stunned. It had been a hell of a shock to see her mother kissing in the moonlight, and not even with a man her own age. Seeing that had rocked Coco's world, and not in a good way. "You left out one thing," Leslie reminded her gently. "Love. Maybe she's in love with the guy. It may be more wholesome than it looks, despite their age. Men do it all the time, fall in love with women a lot younger than they are. I'm thirteen years older than you, and no one would be shocked by us. Why do we have to be so stereotypical about relationships? You don't seem to have a problem with your sister living with another woman and you respect their relationship, we all do. Why not your mother and a younger man?"

"I don't like to think of my mother that way," Coco said, always honest with him and herself. She looked seriously upset.

"I probably wouldn't either," he said, equally honest. "Why don't you ask her about it and see what she says?"

"My *mother*? Are you kidding? She *never* tells the truth. At least not about herself. She lied about having plastic surgery for years. First she got her tits done, when my father was still alive. Then her eyes. Then she had a face-lift. Then she had another one three weeks after the funeral, 'to cheer herself up,' she said later. Christ, maybe she was already seeing *him*!"

"Maybe not. Maybe he's just the end result. I just think you should reserve judgment until you talk to her. That seems more fair. The guy may be an asshole, and he may be after her fame and money, but maybe he isn't. At least hear what she says. They certainly looked in love."

"She's just oversexed," Coco said, glaring at him, and he laughed.

"I think that could be genetic, and I'm not complaining. If you look as good as she does, at her age, I'll be happy as a pig in shit. And you don't ever have to get a face-lift for me. I'll love you just the way you are, even if you melt." Coco was a far more natural beauty than her mother, and more likely to age better, but there was no denying that her mother looked remarkable for her age. And if the old adage was true about seeing a woman's mother before you fell in love with her, he had done well.

Coco was still stewing about it when they went to bed that night, and at breakfast the next morning. It irked her even more to realize that she couldn't question her mother, as Leslie suggested, or tell her sister, since she was in Los Angeles in secret with him. If she told Jane, she would know they had left her dog, and her mother would want to know immediately why Coco was in L.A. and hadn't called. There were far too many secrets in the family these days, especially her mother's. She and Leslie had nothing to hide, except to protect him from his psychotic ex-girlfriend, and to stay out of the tabloids for as long as possible themselves, which would be no mean feat when the time came. But for now Coco's lips were sealed and her hands were tied. She had to keep this gigantic tidbit about their mother to herself, and it was eating her alive.

They flew back to San Francisco again on different planes, and went to Jane's house in separate cars. But it was the first thing they talked about as soon as Leslie walked in. He could tell this was a very, very big deal to her. She had taken a lot of heat from her mother for her life choices, and now Coco wanted a serious explanation for what she'd seen. She didn't approve of anything she had observed or could imagine. Neither the kisses, the romance, and most especially the age of the man her mother was with.

Jane happened to call her that night, and could hear all of it in Coco's voice. "What are you all wound up about?" she asked her immediately. Coco sounded as though she had been fighting with someone, or wanted to, and Jane was instantly suspicious.

"You're not picking fights with Leslie, are you? Don't forget he's my guest."

"And what am I, other than just the house-sitter and dog-walker? Chopped liver?" Coco snapped at her, and Jane looked stunned at the other end.

"Well, pardon me. Just don't take that attitude out on my house-guest, Coco. And don't get smart with me. He may want to stay there for a while to get away from that lunatic and the press. So I'll thank you not to make his life miserable by acting like a brat!" She always treated Coco like a kid, and Coco almost laughed at her sister's remark.

"I'll try not to make his life miserable," she said haughtily, faking it this time. She had their secret to cover too. Her mother wasn't the only one in the family with a secret now, and theirs was a lot more wholesome than her mother's. But neither she nor Leslie wanted to tell Jane yet. They wanted to protect the privacy of what they had, without dealing with other people's reactions to it, or opinions. As she thought that, she wondered if her mother was doing the same thing, and when she was planning to share it with them, if ever. If it was only sexual, she wouldn't, but if it was serious, she would in time. Maybe it was what she and Leslie were thinking too. "I hardly see him anyway," Coco said pointedly, referring to Leslie, to throw her sister off the scent.

"That's a good thing. He needs peace and quiet. He's had a very rough time. First, she tries to kill him, and then she tells the tabloids that he's gay."

"Is he?" Coco asked innocently, and almost laughed. She had had ample and constant proof that he wasn't in the last two weeks, and was enjoying it immensely. They were having a great time, both in bed and out.

"Of course he's not gay," Jane snapped at her. "You're just not his type. He goes for very glamorous, sophisticated women, usually his costars but not always. I think there have been a number of British marchionesses and European princesses thrown into the group. Hell, he's the biggest male movie star there is. And he sure isn't gay," she repeated. "He even tried to jump me once. The guy would screw anything that moves." But not you, was the implication, which wasn't lost on her younger sister. In fact, Coco was depressed about it when she got off the phone.

"Did you tell her?" Leslie asked her, and Coco shook her head.

"I couldn't, because of the dog. She said you screw anything that moves, especially and almost always your costars, and far more glamorous and sophisticated women than me." Coco looked as though she'd been slapped, or spanked.

"She said that?" He looked shocked. "What brought that on?"

"I asked her if you were gay, to throw her off the scent."

"Terrific. And that was her answer? Yes, I have slept with some of my costars, but not in a long time. That's a younger actor's game. I've tried to be involved with real women, not just starlets. And you are the only woman I have ever really loved. And no, I am not gay."

"Prove it to me," she said, pretending to pout at him, and he burst into laughter.

"Well, if you insist," he said, stopping as he unpacked his suit-case and advancing toward her on the bed. "Your wish is my command, and if you want me to prove to you that I'm not gay, I will." And within minutes after that, he did. Again and again and again.

Chapter 6

By the end of June, Leslie's ex-girlfriend had stopped giving interviews to the tabloids about him, and issuing statements on *Entertainment Tonight*. She was even seen on the dance floor in an L.A. nightclub making out with a well-known rock star. It looked like Leslie was off the hook. He didn't want to push his luck, but she hadn't bothered him in weeks. He had to go back down to see his agent in L.A., to discuss some business with him, and he left for two days. As soon as he did, Coco slipped into a funk. It reminded her of what life had been like without him, how much she loved him, and how devastating it was going to be when he went back to his real life for good. Their fantasy life couldn't last forever. He was who he was, and she lived in a world far removed from his. She was reminded again that they were living on borrowed time. She was still depressed about it when he got back.

"What happened? Did someone die?" he teased her the night he came home. He could see how sad she was. He wondered if it had something to do with her mother. She had kept the secret to herself, and was still upset about it. It never occurred to him that she was upset about him.

"No, you went away. And it made me think about what it's going to be like when you leave." He was touched by what she said, and he felt the same way. He thought about it constantly, and how they could make their future work. He wanted it to, more than anything.

"There's no rule written in stone that you can't come to L.A. with me. We could live together there." She vehemently shook her head.

"My mother would drive me insane, the paparazzi would eat us alive, people would be going through our garbage, I know what all of that is like. I remember the stories about my father's clients. I can't live that way."

"Neither can I," he said, looking worried. He knew he'd never get her to live in L.A., and he needed to be there, at least some of the time.

"But you do live that way. It goes with the territory for you."

"Then we can live here, and I'll commute when I have to. I'm on location half the time anyway. You can come with me there."

"The paparazzi will drive us insane on location too," she said miserably.

"What are you saying to me, Coco?" he asked, looking frightened. "That you don't want to share my life with me? That it's too hard to deal with paparazzi so you'd rather give this up?" He seemed panicked, and she shook her head.

"I don't know what to do. I love you, but I don't want all that garbage to ruin our life."

"Neither do I. Other people get through it. You just have to put some thought and effort into it. At least you're not in the business too. That ought to help. And no one's bothering us right now, so we might as well enjoy it while it lasts." They had been very lucky so far, and extremely careful about where they went. He didn't go downtown shopping, or turn up in local shops more than once. They bought groceries at Safeway late at night, with him wearing a baseball cap and dark glasses, and they spent every weekend in Bolinas, hiding out, and took long walks on the beach with no one around. He didn't have the luxury of being able to go out in public. It was a fact of his life. He had come here to hide from one woman, and was now hiding with another, trying valiantly to protect her and shield her and their love story from public view. Undeniably, it was a challenge, but he knew the drill, and as long as no one figured out that he was living in San Francisco with her, everything would be fine. As he said to her frequently, so far so good. But they both knew it couldn't last forever, and sooner or later they'd have to face the music and the fallout of his being a big movie star in love with a woman. It was all of that that Coco dreaded and abhorred, no matter how much she loved him.

"I just don't want this to end," she said sadly, "I mean the way it is now."

"It may not be quite like this in future, but we can manage to lead a very private life. And it won't end if we don't want it to," he said sternly. "That's up to us." And with that, he kissed her and told her again how much he loved her. The last thing he wanted was for their romance to fall apart. He wanted to be with her for the rest of his life and hers. Of that he was sure. How they were going to do it was another story. He was determined to work it out, whatever it took.

He never bothered to rent a furnished apartment in L.A. He had decided to stay in San Francisco with Coco until mid-September, two and a half months from now. He was starting his next film in October and he had to be back for pre-production and costume fit-tings in September. He had ten days of shooting scheduled in L.A., and after that he was going to be in Venice for at least a month, and by the time he got back his house would be vacant again. He didn't need a place in L.A. for now. All he needed was Coco and the life and house they shared.

He suggested they spend the week in Bolinas over the Fourth of July, and asked if she could get a replacement for her dog-walking, so they could spend the whole week at the beach. She gave all her clients two weeks' notice, and found one of Liz's young gay friends who was happy to fill in for her with the dogs. Erin was a nice woman, needed the work, and spent a week following Coco around to learn the job. It was going to be the first time Coco went away for a week in two years. And they were both looking forward to it. Once they were in Bolinas, Leslie settled in as though he had always lived there. He even borrowed Ian's wet suit and went swimming in the ocean, although he was terrified of sharks. But the weather had been hot and gorgeous and he couldn't resist. It was an odd feeling for Coco watching him come out of the water in the familiar wet suit. His body was slightly different and she knew it wasn't Ian, but until he took the mask off, her heart flut-tered a little. And the minute she saw Leslie's face, smiling at her, it soared. She realized then how much she loved him, and that she had put Ian in a special place. It was Leslie who owned her heart now. They lay together on the sand for hours, looked for shells, collected rocks, went fishing, cooked dinner together, read, talked, laughed, played cards, and slept for hours.

He spent some time working on her van, and much to her amazement, got it purring like a kitten. Jeff came out and consulted with him on it several times. And Coco laughed when Leslie came back into the house. His face was streaked with grease, and his hands were black. He looked thoroughly delighted like a small boy who'd been playing in the dirt all day. Leslie looked like a happy man.

Her other neighbors invited them to a barbecue on the Fourth of July, and Leslie wanted to go.

"What if people recognize you?" she asked, looking worried. They had been so wise and careful so far, and it had paid off. They were living an idyllic life of total anonymity and peace.

"Your neighbors already know who I am. They've been very discreet about it." He sounded confident and sure, a little too much so for her.

"The rest of the neighborhood may not be."

"If it feels weird or gets out of hand, we can leave. It might be nice to be part of the local pageantry for a change." In the end, she agreed.

They went late, so it was dark, and slipped in quietly, helping themselves to two beers. Leslie sat down on a log and started talking to a little boy who was about the same age as Chloe. Eventually, his mother came up to retrieve him and stared in astonishment the moment she saw Leslie. Word spread quickly among the group after that. Jeff made no comment, but there were about fifty people there. They reacted to the newsflash that Leslie Baxter was drinking beer in their midst, but no one asked for autographs, no one annoyed him, and finally their fellow guests settled down again. Leslie had a very pleasant conversation with three men about fishing, and children seemed to love him. He had a nice way with them. Jeff looked at her and winked, and then sidled up to her for a chat.

"I like him," he said simply in a soft voice. "The first time we met at the trash cans, I was a little taken aback. But he's a nice, normal, regular guy. He's not full of himself the way you'd expect him to be. You look happy, Coco. I'm glad for you." Jeff looked genuinely pleased for her and was enjoying his friendship with Leslie, conducted in the backyard.

"Thank you," she said, smiling at him. He hadn't seen her like that in years, and she had never felt this way in her entire life. So sure, so confident, so comfortable in her own skin, and of what she was doing and who she was with. It was a very grown-up feeling, and she loved it a lot.

"Are we going to lose you to L.A.? I hope not," Jeff added, and she shook her head.

"No. I'm staying here. I think he might commute." Jeff nodded, hoping that would work for him.

Leslie had talked about buying a house in the city at some later date, once word would be out about them and they figured out what they were doing. Nothing as fancy as Jane's, he had promised Coco, but something simple and cute, like an old Victorian. But he still wanted to spend time with her at the beach. It would just be an easier commute for him from L.A. to the city. It was too soon to tell, but he was keeping that option in mind. He was open to anything that would work. He was willing to invest a lot of time, effort, and money into loving her. All he needed was a little compromise in exchange from her, about his movie star life and its downsides, and the time he might have to spend in L.A. Coco still felt a little dazed.

The rest of the Fourth of July week went smoothly, and after the barbecue, a few people greeted him on the beach when they walked their dogs. No one focused on him unduly, tried to take his picture, or called the press. They were more respectful than that, and he just disappeared into the woodwork in Bolinas like everyone else. If he had looked for a place to hide out, he couldn't have found a better one.

Jane and Liz had been in New York working on their movie for six weeks, when Liz had to go out to L.A. to do some work. They still hadn't found a replacement house-sitter by then. They never mentioned it, and Coco suspected Jane hadn't even tried. But she was happy living with Leslie, so she no longer said anything about it either. Liz was planning to be in L.A. for a few days, and Jane couldn't leave the set. Liz called them from L.A., but had no reason to come to San Francisco, so she didn't. She knew that Leslie was still there, which was fine with them. It was company for Coco, if they even spoke to each other, which Jane doubted. She thought he was unlikely to befriend a girl her age, and there was no question in Jane's mind that she wasn't dating fodder for him.

Liz had suggested otherwise once or twice. They were, after all, both good-looking, intelligent, nice people, living in the same house. Jane had laughed.

"Stop inventing stories for screenplays and sitcoms," Jane chided her partner, making fun of the idea. "Leslie Baxter isn't going to get involved with a dog-walker, even if she is my baby sister. Trust me. She's not his type." Jane was so adamant about it that Liz backed off. But it struck her odd that now that his ex-girlfriend was living with a rock star and no longer threatening him, Leslie was still staying at their house. And she had more respect for Coco than Jane did. To Jane, Coco was still a child, and a rebellious one at that. Liz knew what lay beneath the surface. Jane never tried to find out. Maybe Leslie had. The thought had crossed Liz's mind.

And as she always did, Liz visited who she referred to as her "mother in love" when she went to L.A. It was a duty call, out of respect for her partner's mother, but one that she always enjoyed. And she was happy to find Florence in excellent form, and looking better than ever. It had not gone unnoticed by Liz, however, that as she arrived at the house in Bel-Air, a young man had left. He had smiled at Liz as they passed each other, and he looked about Jane's age. He got in a silver Porsche parked outside and drove off. Liz had no idea why, but she had the odd feeling that the young man was planning to come back as soon as she left. And there was a man's cashmere sweater hanging on the back of the door when she used Florence's bathroom, and two toothbrushes in the cup. She told herself she was too suspicious but teased Jane's mother about it anyway, over champagne in the garden, a ritual with her. Her new face-lift had finally settled in, and she looked fifteen years younger than she was. Her figure was better than ever.

"Is that your new beau I saw driving off in the Porsche when I arrived?" Liz teased her, and was stunned when she saw Florence go visibly pale and choke on her champagne.

"I . . . of course not . . . don't be silly . . . I . . . I . . ." She stopped talking in midsentence as she looked at Liz, and bowled over the younger woman as she started to cry. "Please don't tell Jane or

Coco . . . we've been having such a nice time. I thought it was just a passing thing, but we've been together now for almost a year. I know it doesn't make sense. He thinks I'm fifty-five. I told him I had Jane at sixteen, which sounds awful, but I didn't know what else to say. He's thirty-eight years old, and I know it must sound disgraceful, but I love him. I loved Buzz while I was married to him, but he's gone. And Gabriel is a lovely man. He's very mature for his age." Liz had to remind herself to close her mouth as she tried not to stare at her mother-in-law. Liz had always been more sympathetic and gentler than Jane, and Florence had often confided in her, but never about anything like this.

"If it makes you happy, Florence," she began cautiously, not sure what to say, or what the man's motivations were for being with someone that much older. Liz was understandably worried about that. And she knew that Jane would have a fit, and more than likely Coco too. "What does he do? Is he an actor?" He looked like one, and was handsome enough to be, which made Liz suspicious of him too.

"He's a producer-director. He makes independent films." She mentioned two that had enjoyed considerable success, so at least he wasn't a gigolo, only after her money. "We have a wonderful time together. It's lonely now that Buzz is gone, and the girls don't live here anymore. I can't write or play bridge all the time. Most of my friends are still married, and I'm always the odd man out." Liz had understood for a while that it was hard, harder than Florence's older daughter wanted to admit. And Florence was still young enough to want companionship, and even sex, although it startled Liz a little to think about. And she knew Jane would want to hear nothing about that. "Are you going to tell Jane?" Florence asked her with a look of panic, as Liz thought about it.

"Not if you don't want me to." Florence wasn't committing a crime, or doing anyone any harm. She wasn't mentally incompetent, or risking her health. She was having an affair with a younger man, twenty-four years younger in fact. But in the end, Liz thought to herself, why the hell not? Who were they to tell her she was wrong? Or that she couldn't? Or make her feel bad about it? Still, she was afraid that Jane would do all of the above. She could be very tough. Liz loved her anyway, but she was well aware of her weaknesses, flaws, and quirks, and acceptance of her fellow man had never been one of her strong suits. "I think you should tell the girls yourself," Liz said gently.

"You do?"

"Yes, I do," Liz said honestly. "When you think it's the right time. If it's a passing thing, it's none of their business. But if he's planning to stick around, you have a right to feel loved and accepted by your family. It's nice for them to know what's going on in your life."

"I think Jane will have a fit," her mother said miserably.

"So do I," Liz said honestly. "She'll get over it. She has no right to tell you how to run your life. I'll remind her of that, if that helps."

"Thank you," Florence said gratefully. Liz had championed other causes for her before, successfully. But they both knew that this was going to be tough.

"I wouldn't worry about Coco," Liz added. "She's a gentle soul, and not as critical as Jane. They both want you to be happy."

"But they probably don't want me to have a young lover. There's no money involved," she said, to reassure Liz, and indirectly Jane. "I told him he needs to get married and have children. But he's already been divorced and has a two-year-old. And we're very happy. I don't think we'd ever get married," she said apologetically, as though she were doing something awful.

"You know, if you were a man," Liz said, sounding suddenly angry on her behalf, and feeling sorry for her at her obvious embarrassment and shame, so much so that she had been lying to her daughters. "If you were a man, you'd be showing off a girl half his age at every party you could go to, you'd have her strutting her stuff at the pool at the Beverly Hills Hotel, and bragging to your children, your barber, and your neighbors. You'd be married by now, and having a baby. In fact, if you were ten years older, and he were ten or twenty years younger, if your sexes were reversed, that's exactly what would happen, and everyone would stare at you with envy. Now *that* is what's disgusting, that double standard that makes you feel you have to slink around and lie and hide, and makes a man in exactly the same position feel he should shout it from the rooftops. Florence, this is *your* life. We only go around once. Do what makes you happy. I was married before I met Jane, and I probably could have stayed that way forever. I didn't want anyone to know or think I was gay. I was so busy being respectable and being who everyone wanted me to be that I was absolutely miserable. The best thing I ever did was leave my husband and move in with Jane. I finally have the life I always wanted. And you know, if Buzz were still alive, I'm sure he'd be doing exactly the same thing with an even younger woman." She raised her glass of champagne in honor of the woman who was her mother-in-law by love if not by law. "To you and Gabriel, Florence. Long life, and only happiness ahead." They both cried as she said it, and sat in a hug for a long time. And a moment later, Florence called him on his cell phone and told him. She wanted to introduce him to Liz, but Liz felt that it wouldn't be fair if she met him before Jane did. That smacked of a conspiracy to her, and she knew it would to Jane, although she could have reassured her. She promised to meet him next time, once Jane and Coco knew about him.

She left a little while later, and the two women embraced on the doorstep.

"Thank you," Florence said, looking gratefully at her. "You're such a kind, decent person. My daughter is very lucky."

"So am I," Liz said, smiling at her, and got back into the town car that had brought her there. They headed down the driveway, as the Porsche was returning. Liz lowered her window as he passed them, and she smiled and waved, as he looked at her in amazement, and smiled back.

"Welcome to the family," Liz thought to herself, as they headed toward the airport. She could only begin to imagine the explosion it was going to be when Florence finally got up the guts to tell Jane. Liz would do whatever she could to soften the blow, but she knew Jane. There was going to be hell to pay. For a while anyway.

Chapter 7

It was the end of July, two weeks later, when Florence finally got up the courage to call Jane. She decided to tell her first. And predictably, Jane went insane.

"You what?" Jane sounded incredulous. "You have a boyfriend? When did that happen?"

"About a year ago," Florence confessed, trying to sound calmer than she felt. She had had three glasses of champagne before she called. "He's a very nice man."

"What does he do for a living?" Jane growled.

"He produces and directs films."

"Do I know him?" Jane was still shocked that her mother had called to tell her she had a beau. "What's his name? I assume he has his own production company." At her age that was obvious. He was probably someone important in the business, whom they had all known for years. But it still seemed a little strange. Jane didn't like to think of her mother that way.

"Gabriel Weiss." Jane thought about it for a minute and nodded. There had been nothing too frightening so far. The name was respected in the business. "I know his son by the same name. He's made a couple of very good films. I didn't know his father was a producer too."

"He isn't. His father was a neurosurgeon, and he died ten years ago. We're talking about the one you know." Florence felt suddenly braver than she had before. The moment of truth had come, and the champagne had kicked in. Gabriel had told her that day that no matter what happened and what they said, he loved her, and there was nothing wrong with what they were doing. Loving someone, despite a considerable age gap, was not against the law. She reminded herself of that now. She was sixty-two, but Gabriel still thought she was fifty-five. She didn't have the guts to tell him the truth.

"Wait a minute, Mom," Jane said, sounding confused. "The Gabriel Weiss I know is twelve years old."

"Not quite. He's your age. He'll be thirty-nine next month."

"And how old are you?" she said cruelly. "Sixty-two? Almost sixty-three? Isn't that a little ridiculous? In fact, I'd say it's downright disgusting for a woman your age to be dating a man his age. What's wrong with him? Does he need money for his next film?" Liz had just walked into the room and felt sick as she listened. She hated it when Jane got like this, going in for the kill. She had heard her do it to Coco too, and others. Underneath it all, Jane was a good person, but she decimated people. Liz loved her anyway, and didn't put up with it from her. But the others did. "I think this is the most embarrassing, revolting, shameful thing I've ever heard. I hope you come to your senses very, very soon."

Her mother startled her then. "And I hope you find your manners again soon. Gabriel is a respectable man. He doesn't need my money. And I'm a respectable woman. I'm your mother. And I'm doing you the honor of telling you myself before you hear it from someone else. We're not doing anything wrong, and we're not doing anything any man wouldn't do, given half a chance. Gabriel is twenty-four years younger than I am, and if we can deal with it, maybe you can too. I'll talk to you soon," she said, and hung up while Jane was still spluttering at the other end. She couldn't believe what she'd just heard, and her mother had hung up on her. It was a first. And long overdue. The two were usually an even match, but this time Jane had gone too far. And her mother felt some allegiance to Gabriel too.

Jane turned to Liz in disbelief. "My mother has Alzheimer's," she said with an agonized look.

"How did you come to that conclusion?" Liz asked, trying to keep a straight face.

"She's having an affair with a guy my age. Gabriel Weiss."

"Is he a bad guy?" Liz asked evenly.

"What do I know? He's a good producer. But he can't be a good guy, if he's screwing my mother, who's nearly twice his age."

"She doesn't look her age," Liz reminded her, "and guys her age and older do it all the time, with girls half his age." It was not what she wanted to hear from Liz.

"She's my mother, for chrissake!" She had tears in her eyes as Liz sat down next to her and put an arm around her.

"What if she'd reacted like that when you told her you were gay?"

"She did!" Jane laughed through tears. "She threatened to kill herself. For about two days. And then she told my father, and he was wonderful about it. I think they were disappointed, but they were always very supportive after that. You're right, I guess. But shit, Liz, why does she have to do this? What if the guy is just after her money and is making a fool of her?"

"What if he isn't? And even if he is, what if he makes her happy for a while? It's not easy getting older. She's all alone in L.A."

"She has millions of fans. She sells a zillion books every time."

"Her fans don't keep her warm at night, or hold her when she's sad. What if we didn't have each other?" Liz said pointedly as Jane wiped her eyes.

"I would die. My life would be a wasteland without you, Liz. You're all that matters in my life. You're my family."

"Try imagining life without that. Your father was her whole world. She doesn't have that anymore. Now she has him. Maybe he's a bad guy or maybe he's a good one. Either way, she has a right to figure that out, not to be alone, and to share her life with whoever she chooses."

"What makes you so wise at such a young age?" Jane asked, and blew her nose on the tissue Liz handed her as she laughed.

"She's not my mother. But she's a good woman, and I love her. I want the best for her too. Let's give her a chance on this. I think she deserves it." Jane hung her head as she thought about it, and then put her arms around Liz and hugged her.

"I think my mother is a nutcase, but you're terrific." Liz smiled at her. The bond between them was growing stronger every day.

"Okay. So now you get two days to tell her you're going to commit suicide over this, like she did when you came out. But maybe after that, you can suck it up, for her sake. See what you think."

"I'll think about it," Jane said quietly, and then she called Coco. It was one of those times when sisters needed each other and blood was thicker than water.

Coco had been laughing hysterically with Leslie when the phone rang. He had been telling her a story about a series of mishaps on the set of one of his first movies. She loved those stories, and he told them well. She was still laughing when she answered and heard Jane at the other end, with the voice of doom.

"Our mother has gone insane" was how she opened. And Coco instantly suspected what was coming next since she had seen it with her own eyes. "She's having an affair with a man my age." Coco was relieved to hear that he was no younger. She had been afraid, after seeing him, that he was closer to her own age.

"Who told you?" Coco asked calmly.

"She did. You don't sound surprised," Jane said accusingly.

"I suspected something like that might be going on." She'd been pretty happy for a while. And lately, she'd been leaving Coco alone. She hardly ever called. That was new. In the past, she had called several times a week to tell Coco everything that was wrong with her, and her life. Recently, her calls had been rare and brief and very superficial.

"So what do you think?" Jane asked her.

Coco sighed, thinking about it. "I don't know. Part of me thinks she has a right to do what she wants. Another part of me thinks it sounds crazy and all wrong. What do I know? I live like a hippie in a shack in Bolinas because it suits me. I almost married a diving in-structor and moved to Australia. You're gay, and practically mar-ried to a woman. What right do we have to tell her what's right for her? Maybe the guy is okay. She's smart enough to figure it out if he isn't. Our mother is nobody's fool."

"When did you get so grown-up and philosophical?" Jane asked, sounding suspicious. "Did she put you up to this?"

"No. This is the first I've heard about it, from you. But who knows, maybe Daddy would have done the same thing with someone younger, maybe even a real bimbo. Once people that age are alone, they do that kind of thing. No one wants to be alone," she said, and smiled at Leslie as he gave her a thumbs-up.

"You don't seem to mind it," Jane said with an edge to her voice. "And at her age, you wouldn't think it would make a difference."

"Why would that be? Why would she want to be all alone after all those years with Daddy?"

"Why would she want to be with a much younger man at her age and make a fool of herself?" It didn't make sense to Jane.

"Maybe it makes her feel young. I think she's lonely."

"We should visit her more often," Jane said, frowning.

"That's not the same. You know that. I don't know, Jane. I don't like it either. But it's not a crime."

"It's in incredibly bad taste. And mortifying for us."

"She never says that about your being gay." Coco scored a point with that one, and Jane fell silent for a moment. "She's always been supportive of how you live."

"It's not a choice. It's what I am."

"She could object anyway, and she doesn't. She's always been proud of you." And not of me, Coco wanted to say, but didn't. Neither her mother nor her sister had been supportive of her, and yet she was willing to champion them. It wasn't fair, but it was the way their family worked.

"She's proud of you too," Jane said softly, sensing what her sister was thinking, and suddenly embarrassed by her own criticism of her. Coco never did that to them.

"No, she isn't," Coco said simply, with tears in her eyes. "And neither are you. That's not a secret. But I think we owe her something now. Some kind of respect, or at least acceptance of what she's doing." For a long moment, Jane didn't answer. She was thinking of all the times she had told Coco everything that was wrong with her, and what a failure she was. It made her feel terrible, and want to share something with her now.

"I have something to tell you too," Jane said, as she glanced at Liz, and her partner nodded. "I'm twelve weeks pregnant. I got inseminated before we came to New York. We didn't want to tell anyone till we were sure it would stick. We did it last year and I had a miscarriage, but this time everything is fine." Coco was stunned. They hadn't told her last time, and Coco had had no idea that was their plan. But when she thought about it, she remembered that Liz had always wanted kids. It seemed ironic to Coco that Jane was having the baby, when Liz was by far the warmer and more maternal of the two, but Jane was a few years younger so maybe that was why.

"Congratulations!" Coco said, smiling and still surprised. "When's it due?"

"Beginning of February. I still can't believe it's happening. It doesn't show yet. I'll be six or seven months pregnant when we come home, depending on when we do."

"I can't wait to see that!" Coco laughed. And then she thought of something. "So maybe you should be a little nicer to Mom. If you can have a baby with a woman. And I can drop out of law school and live like a 'freak,' according to all of you. Maybe she has a right to have a boyfriend your age. Who are any of us to judge each other and tell each other what to do?" Jane knew in her heart of hearts that what her sister said was true. There was a long silence at her end as she thought about it, and she reached out and took Liz's hand. Liz ran her other hand gently over Jane's belly, and their eyes met and held.

"I'm sorry," Jane whispered to Coco and meant it, "for all the stupid things I've said. I love you, and I hope this baby looks just like you," she said as tears rolled down her cheeks.

"I love you too," Coco said. And for just a minute Jane was the big sister she had always dreamed of and never had.

They hung up a few minutes later and Coco wiped her eyes and looked at Leslie with a wistful smile.

"I'm proud of you," he said gently, and took her in his arms.

"She apologized to me. She found out about my mom, and she was furious about it."

"You said all the right things," he praised her, which meant the world to her.

"So did she, in the end." And then she looked up at him with a smile. "She's having a baby."

"That's interesting. Maybe motherhood will mellow her a little."

"It sounds like it already has," Coco said, thinking of the sweetness of her sister's words. And with that, Leslie kissed her and she closed her eyes.

"I'd like to have a baby with you one day too," he whispered, and she nodded. She liked that idea too, although she never had before. It was hard to absorb all of it sometimes. So much had happened in such a short time.

Chapter 8

Both Coco and Jane spoke with their mother several times in the next few days. Jane was still upset about her so much younger lover, and although both Liz and Coco had convinced her that her mother had a right to go out with whomever she wanted, Jane still thought it was incongruous and mortifying that her mother was involved with a man Gabriel's age. And she still wasn't totally convinced he wasn't after the money. But she agreed to at least meet him and give him a chance when she and Liz got back to the West Coast. It wouldn't be for several months. Jane hadn't told their mother about the baby yet. She said there was still plenty of time. Liz finally convinced her a few days later and she relented, and told her that there was a grandchild on the way. Florence was thrilled and amazed.

"You know, one of the things that upset me, when you told me you were gay," she admitted, "was that I thought you'd never have children. It never occurred to me that you'd do it this way. Does it bother you," she asked candidly, "not knowing who the father is?"

"Not really. We selected the sperm donor from some very thorough profiles. We know his family history, national origins, health history, education, personal quirks. He and his father both went to Yale." Like her parents, Jane was an academic snob, and wouldn't have selected anyone who hadn't gone to college, and even graduate school. He was a medical student, healthy, young, of Swedish origin. They knew everything about him but his name.

Jane told her mother that she was planning to do amniocentesis, to make sure that the baby was genetically healthy, and it would be fun to know the sex. She and Liz were both hoping for a girl. Florence couldn't believe she was going to be a grandmother. And when she thought of it, she wondered if Gabriel would feel any differently about her. Her daughters had shaken her up badly in the last few days.

Coco was easier on her, but it was obvious that she was upset too. She had had a little more time to get used to the concept of her mother being involved with a much younger man, since she had seen them at the Bel-Air.

"Thank you for not being angry at me," her mother said softly. In the end, as she always was, Coco had been kind to her.

"I'm not angry. I just worry about you," Coco explained. It felt strange to have a parental role with her mother now. And Florence seemed more inclined to confide in her now than in Jane, which was odd too. Her mother and older sister had been much closer to each other over the years. It was partially due to Jane's age, and that Florence and her elder daughter had enjoyed the relationship of mother and only child until Coco was born. As a result, Coco had always felt that Jane had a head start on her, and that they shared a bond that rarely, if ever, included her. They just wouldn't let her in. Their way of thinking was similar, they were equally critical, opinionated, and shared many of the same ideas. Even as a child, Coco had been different from either of them. She had felt like an outsider in their midst almost since birth. As long as she could remember, her mother and Jane had been best friends.

Jane had left for college when Coco was six, and instead of becoming the favored only child after that, Coco had remained an outcast, brought up and entertained by nannies, while her mother worked. Florence had been far more interested in writing her books than in spending time with her younger child. It was Jane she would always drop her work for, whom she spent time with, went on trips with, who was more interesting as an adult. Somehow, whatever the time or the season, Coco always felt as though she never made the grade. And now, for once, it was the always perfect, irreproachable, knowledgeable about everything, arbiter of right or wrong, famous Florence Flowers, who felt as though she was in disgrace. It was an unfamiliar feeling for her. And she was leaning on her far gentler daughter for comfort.

"How did you meet Gabriel, Mom?" Coco asked her in one of their lengthy conversations about him. As long as he seemed to be firmly entrenched in her mother's life, she wanted to know everything there was to know. Florence mistook it for approval, and was grateful to her. She had been very hurt by the things Jane had said. And even if she had apologized later, you can't unring a bell. She had accused her of being senile, having Alzheimer's, being a foolish old woman who was being taken advantage of by a man who wanted nothing more than to exploit her money and fame. Coco realized that could still be true, but she had been more cautious about what she said. Although her relationship with her mother was difficult, she was basically a profoundly kind person and didn't want to hurt her.

"I sold one of my books to Columbia for a movie last year, and Gabriel was assigned to produce and direct. We worked closely together on the script, although I don't think it will be shooting till next year. We had a lot of fun collaborating. He's a very interesting, sensitive man." She sounded suddenly shy then, which startled her daughter. It was an unfamiliar tone for her. "And he says the same thing about me. He was involved with an older woman in college, though not this old," she admitted. "He had a thirty-year-old girlfriend when he was eighteen." He clearly had a thing for women who were older than he was.

"I look forward to meeting him," Coco said quietly. It was true, for a number of reasons. Although she didn't say it, she was still extremely suspicious of him. It didn't seem right or normal for him to be with a woman twenty-four years older than he was, although admittedly her mother didn't look her age, and he didn't know the full truth about Florence's age. But he still thought there were seventeen years between them, which was a lot. She wondered if her mother had had something like this in mind when she had the second face-lift right after Coco's father died. Probably not, but it did occur to her now. And she had had a tummy tuck and liposuction then too. Florence had always been very vain. It was all part of what Coco had rebelled against, as part of the Hollywood life she knew. Jane was vain too, though not as much so as their mother, and Coco knew that she had been getting Botox shots for the past several years. Coco couldn't even remotely imagine doing any of it. That kind of vanity and self-absorption was totally foreign to her.

"He wants to meet you too," Florence said in response to what her daughter had said. Just hearing her say it was a relief. She had been terrified that they might both stop seeing her. Jane had thought about it, but had been considerably calmed down by Liz.

"So what do you think of the baby?" Coco asked her idly. She couldn't imagine that becoming a grandmother was what her mother had in mind these days. It would surely be awkward for her.

"I think it's nice for them. I always thought you'd be the one to have children. It never occurred to me that they'd do something like this. It's a little strange not knowing who the father is." But what her mother was doing was a little strange too.

"Jane says she didn't want the complications of doing it with a friend. This way the baby only belongs to her and Liz. I can see her point. It would probably feel weird having the baby of someone she knows. It still seems a long way off." It was six months away. "I suppose we'll all be used to the idea by the time it arrives."

"I'm not sure I will," Florence said honestly. "I have other things on my mind right now. And I'm starting a new book." The shock and humility had already begun to fade from her voice. She rarely if ever lost sight of who she was, although Jane's fury at her had taken her down a notch or two, at least for a few days. She almost felt as though becoming a grandmother now, with a younger man in her life, was Jane's ultimate revenge on her. There was no question in the minds of anyone who knew her that for the most part Florence Flowers was all about herself. And the only person she occasionally let into her private world was Jane. She was sad to realize that with a baby now, that would change. Jane's allegiance would lean more toward her own child and Liz. And suddenly

Florence felt left out. It brought her even closer to Gabriel than be-fore.

She talked about her daughters with him that night. He knew she had told them about him, and he was nervous about it. He couldn't imagine their approving of him, and he was right.

"Are they both still upset?" he asked nervously, when they had dinner on the terrace of the Ivy that night. Florence was wearing white jeans, high-heeled gold sandals, and a turquoise silk shirt. She looked better than ever, and it was hard to believe she had been unnerved by them at all as she looked adoringly at him.

"They'll get over it. They already have," she reassured him. "Coco was startled by it, but she's a very sweet girl. She said she just wants me to be happy, and she's looking forward to meeting you the next time she comes down. She can't come at the moment. She's house-sitting for her sister right now." She didn't say a word about the baby, and didn't intend to until she had no other choice. She didn't want him to start thinking of her as a grandmother. The age difference between them was bad enough, without adding that. It hadn't seemed that monumental to her for the last year, but it clearly was to Jane. "My older daughter is harder," she said to him, as he ordered champagne for both of them. They had something to celebrate now—they could come out of hiding and stop worrying about her daughters finding out. Florence had been worried about the press too. She was a major celebrity, and their romance was a juicy story that would eventually wind up in the tabloids and fan magazines. They had been lucky and careful so far.

"Was Jane very angry at you?" Gabriel asked, looking worried, as he toasted her with the champagne. He was wearing a T-shirt and white jeans, with brown alligator loafers and no socks. The

shoes had been a gift from Florence months before. She liked seeing them on him. He wore them a lot when he was with her. She
had bought him black ones too.

"She was at first," Florence said honestly about her oldest
daughter. "I don't think it ever occurred to her that something like
this could happen. I think it shook them up because of their dad.
You're the first man in my life since he died." That wasn't entirely
true, but she thought it would sound better to him. She had had
two brief affairs in the year after Buzz died, which she had never
mentioned to her girls. They had been very dull men, and she
hadn't been in love with either of them. But she was madly in love
with Gabriel Weiss, and had fallen head over heels for him the day
they met. He claimed to have felt the same for her. And their romance had been quick and hot, and still was. "I think it's an adjust-
ment for them. Jane has a very sweet, very intelligent partner.
When I last saw her, she promised to try and make it right with
Jane for me. And I think she did. Liz wasn't shocked about us at
all." He smiled at her, looking sympathetic about her daughter.
From everything he knew of her himself and had heard in the business, Jane Barrington was hell on wheels.

"My age must have come as something of a shock," he said simply. "I never think about it when I'm with you." He smiled at her,
and kissed her neck, well aware of her cleavage in the silk shirt,
which was hard to ignore. He loved the way she dressed, and how
sexy and elegant she was at the same time. She was the most seductive woman he had ever known. "I always feel like we're the
same age." He said all the right things, and Florence believed
them. Maybe it was crazy, but she was sure he was sincere. And Liz

was right. If she were a man, no one would care, in fact they'd approve and envy her.

"Jane will be fine," she reassured him again. "She has other things on her mind right now. She's up to her ears in headaches and union problems on location with a film. Our little romance is going to be the last thing on her mind." Not to mention the baby, which he knew nothing about, and hopefully wouldn't for a long time. They might even be married by then. Gabriel had been talking about it all summer, and Florence loved the idea. The only stumbling block they'd had to overcome was the girls. And she wasn't about to upset them even further by talking marriage. She wanted them to get to know him, and hoped they would calm down.

For the rest of dinner they talked about the movie he was working on. She had been going over scripts with him for months, and had given him excellent advice. They worked well as a team. In fact, they were a great match at everything they did. She noticed a few people glance at her enviously as they finished dinner. Other women looked at her, stared at Gabriel, then back at her with open admiration, or so she thought. No one had ever referred to him as her son. And he looked slightly older than he was. The difference between them looked more like ten years than twenty-four. And a woman with a man ten years younger was fairly common these days. Demi Moore and Ashton Kutcher had forged the way for couples such as theirs. She was to be envied, or so she thought, not criticized or shunned.

They went back to her place afterward, as they usually did. He stayed with her most nights now, and had for the past several months. And once in a while, when they wanted to do something special, they spent the weekend at the Bel-Air Hotel. When they stayed there, Gabriel always paid. He never let Florence pay for anything for him, except random gifts. He had given her a diamond bracelet for their six-month anniversary, and he was hoping to give her an engagement ring sometime in the next year, but she didn't know about that yet. He had already picked one out. He was hoping her daughters would have met and approved of him by then. He didn't want to tear their family apart, but he was madly in love with their mother, for better or worse. He thought she was terrific.

Gabriel stretched out on her bed as though he owned it, and by now, he did, just as he owned her. Discovering sex with him had been an experience like no other in her life. It had never been this good in her thirty-six years with Buzz, even when they were young. Gabriel was an incredible lover. He had recently told his own mother about their affair, and she had been just as upset as Jane. But she was also beginning to understand that there was nothing she could do about it. Gabriel said he was in love with her and had made up his mind. And she knew her son well. She knew that nothing she could do would sway Gabriel from what or whom he wanted. He was the most persistent man in the world. He had been that way with Florence too, when she resisted him at first. But she didn't for long. She had given in and abandoned herself to the myriad pleasures they shared. Sex wasn't the most important on that list, although it mattered, but he loved talking to her, laughing with her, listening to her, holding her for hours on end after they made love. He loved everything about her, her mind, her body, her style, her strength, her fame, her reputation, and her

enormous talent. She was a woman like no other, beyond com-
pare. He had expected to feel insignificant with her, but instead
she pulled him up to her level in so many ways. He was learning so
much from her, about writing, discipline, talent, humor. Thanks to
her, his writing had already improved immeasurably, as had his di-
recting. He could tell, and Florence noticed it too. He felt as
though he were worshipping at the feet of the master, and in many
ways he was.

As he lay in bed with her that night, he took off her sexy gold
sandals and tossed them to the floor. The white jeans and turquoise silk shirt were next. She was wearing a thong and a lacy
pale blue bra, and he smiled as he looked at her.

"There isn't a sexier woman alive," he said, admiring her. Her
body was still slim and tight. She worked out with one of the best
trainers in town now every day. Making love with Gabriel every
night gave her motivation. And she had taught him things he
never knew.

She slowly peeled his clothes off then, in her slow sensual way
that drove him insane, and moments later they were lying naked
in each other's arms. She let the help go home at night now, and
on warm nights they made love in the pool. But tonight, they were
content to stay in her bed. It was a huge four-poster with a pink
canopy, and for the past year it had been home to him.

She covered his lips with her own, slid on top of him, and began
to ride him, and within seconds, Gabriel began to moan. She
stayed that way, alternately teasing and pleasing, tantalizing him,
and then slipped off him again, and went down on him with her
mouth. He returned the favor and slowly the tides turned, and
Gabriel was in control, and he drove her as crazy as she had him.

It was a long time before they were sated and it was over, and afterward she lay in his arms, looking pleased. Gabriel looked spent and exhausted, and then laughed as he held her. He didn't know what her daughters thought of him, and at the moment he didn't care. He had never loved a woman like this. And minutes later, they were sound asleep in each other's arms. For both of them, the rest of the world just didn't exist.

Chapter 9

In mid-August, Leslie got a call from Chloe's mother. She had been invited on a yacht in the South of France for two weeks. She'd been spending weekends in Southampton with Chloe, and had been working on the same play on Broadway for a year.

"I'm sorry to do this to you, Leslie," Monica apologized. She usually gave him more notice. "I need a vacation, and I may not get another chance for months. They have a good understudy for me, and I'd love like hell to get to Saint-Tropez on a boat. Could you take Chloe for me for a couple of weeks?" Normally, he would have leaped at the chance, but he had no idea how Liz and Jane would feel about having a child in their house. They were expecting their own now, but that was different. A six-year-old was more of a presence than a newborn, to say the least. He wanted her to get to know Coco anyway, so he hoped they would allow it.

"I think I can," he said, sounding awkward. "I'm actually house-sitting at the moment, camping out at friends'. I have to ask them if they're okay about having a little girl here. I suppose if not, I could go to a hotel." But he would lose his anonymity there, and everyone would know he was in town. He wanted to stay under the radar with Coco for a while. They didn't need the headache of the press. "I'll call you back," he promised, and immediately called Jane. Instead he got Liz, who was keeping her cell phone for her while she was on the set. He explained his dilemma to her, but said he'd go to a hotel with his daughter if they preferred.

"Don't be silly," Liz assured him. "We'd better get used to having kids in the house. We're having one of our own." She wasn't sure if Coco had told him, or was friendly enough with him to do so. She knew that Coco had been telling Jane they hardly saw each other, which Liz didn't entirely believe.

"So I hear. Congratulations, to both of you. And I really appreciate your letting me have Chloe here. She's a lamb, and very well behaved. Like a small adult. Her mother takes her everywhere." But apparently not on a yacht in the South of France, Liz mused. "I can hardly wait to show her San Francisco, and I thought Coco and I could take her to the beach."

"I'm sure she'd love that," Liz said with interest. What he said didn't quite support Coco's claims to her sister that they rarely met. "How are you and Coco getting along, by the way?" Liz asked innocently, fishing a little. She couldn't resist. For some strange reason, she loved the idea of them together. She had a lot of respect for Jane's younger sister, far more than Jane did herself. Unlike Jane, she didn't think Coco was a hopeless case, just different from her hardcore ambitious sister, and she knew Ian's death had hit her hard. Liz had always been very fond of Leslie too, and in spite of being an actor and a major star, she thought he was a good man, with good values.

"We're getting on like a house afire," he admitted, sounding faintly sheepish. "She's an amazing woman. She's her own person, and profoundly good and kind and decent." He sang her praises, although he didn't need to, to Liz.

"It sounds like you two have been talking," Liz said with a tone of approval.

"Yes, when she's not out with the 101 Dalmatians. It's a bit of an odd job, but her clients seem to keep her very busy, and she's happy doing it for now." He didn't think her current job was a life-time commitment, and he didn't see why her mother and sister were so upset about it. It was lucrative and respectable, after all, and she did it well. It was a profitable little business.

"They love her," Liz confirmed. "She's the Pied Piper of dogs."

"I suspect she will be with children too. I'm sure my daughter will love her. And thank you again for letting me have her here. I appreciate it a lot. Do I need to add to my security deposit for that? I feel like I should be paying rent." He had been there for ten weeks. And Liz laughed.

"It's good company for Coco. I feel guilty as hell that we haven't found anyone to let her off the hook. We both tried, but everyone had summer plans, or they're going back to school in the fall. At least she's getting to live with a handsome movie star. That ought to make up for having to stay at our house." Liz realized then, as she talked to him, that Coco hadn't complained in months, or begged to be relieved of her duties. That alone made Liz suspicious of what was going on. And Leslie sounded friendly and enthusiastic about her, but he didn't say they were head over heels in love with each other either. Maybe they were just friends, although Liz still didn't believe it, or they were being discreet. That seemed more likely. Or possibly nothing major had happened yet, and never would. Little did she know that they had made mad passionate love on his second night there, in their bed. There were some things she didn't need to know, so Leslie kept his tone light. Coco always said that Jane never asked, and it probably didn't even occur to her that they had gotten involved. She had already told Coco long since that she wasn't his type.

"Give my love to Jane," he said as they were about to hang up, "and congratulations again about the baby. That'll be a big change for you both."

"Jane says she's going to take six months off. I'll believe it when I see it. I'm going to stay home for a year, if I can. I write at home anyway. I've wanted this all my life." She had always wanted children, but not with the man she was married to, which told her how wrong it was. It felt perfect to her now. She could hardly wait for the birth of their child. She was only sorry she wasn't carrying it, but their doctor had preferred that Jane do it, so Liz had deferred to her. Jane was in better shape, and the four years between them made a difference, in the hope of avoiding a miscarriage. They didn't want that to happen again. And there was no sign of it this time. "Say hi to Coco for me. Is she doing all right after all the excitement about their mother?" She hadn't spoken to her a lot since, although Jane had. And she had tried to leave all the conversation between the two sisters. At her end, she had calmed Jane down as best she could. Fairly effectively, she thought, although Jane was still grumbling about it. But she wasn't insanely angry the way she had been when she first heard the news. And Coco had calmed her down too. Liz knew she would. Coco was far more tolerant of human foibles than her sister.

"I think she's fine about it. She was a bit upset at first. But she realizes that her mother has the right to lead her own life, with whomever she chooses. And these days, that kind of thing happens. Age no longer matters the way it once did, even for an older woman."

"That's pretty much what I said to Jane too. It didn't go over quite so well here," Liz confessed with a sigh. But fortunately being pregnant and thinking about the baby had also mellowed Jane a little.

"No," Leslie said pensively, thinking of Liz's partner, whom he knew well, "I imagine it wouldn't. It sounds like Jane is pretty tough on Coco too," he said, revealing more than he should. It hadn't gone unnoticed by Liz, but she wasn't going to say anything to Jane about it. She had enough on her plate, without getting wound up about that too, and she might. She was very possessive about her friends, and Liz sensed instinctively that she wouldn't want Coco getting involved with Leslie. It was an odd kind of rivalry between sisters. She wanted Leslie to be her friend, not Coco's.

"Did Coco tell you Jane is hard on her?" Liz asked with interest. It was something that had always bothered her and never seemed fair to her. Coco needed the support and understanding of her family, not the kind of raking over the coals she sometimes got, both from Jane and her mother.

"Not really," Leslie said, trying to back off, and fearing he had already said too much. Liz was nobody's fool, and she would figure it out if he wasn't careful, if she hadn't already. "I just guessed, from bits and snips she's said."

"If she said that to you, she's right. Just as a frame of reference," Liz said honestly. "They've been giving her a hard time for years, since she dropped out of school and even before. They gang up on her, and she's no match for them. She's much too nice about it, but that's the way she is." Leslie almost said that that was why he loved her, but caught himself in time.

"Maybe they can beat up Florence's boyfriend now instead," Leslie said, and laughed. "It's been nice talking to you. I haven't seen you in ages. I feel a bit guilty staying here, but I love it. No one knows I'm in town. I've got to go back in September. I'm starting a picture in October. It's the icing on the cake now to have Chloe come out before I leave."

"Have fun," Liz said cryptically. He thanked her again and they hung up. And he called Monica right back.

"No problem. I can have her here," he said with delight. "How soon do you want to send her?"

"Would tonight be too soon?" Monica asked, sounding sheepish. "I can catch a ride to Nice on a friend's plane tomorrow. The boat is in Monte Carlo, and going from there to Saint-Jean-Cap-Ferrat and Saint-Tropez." They were the fanciest watering holes in Europe.

"You lead a hard life," he teased her.

"I earned it," she said firmly. "I've been working my ass off on Broadway without a vacation for a year. Two weeks isn't too much to ask. Thanks for taking Chloe."

"I'm delighted," he said, and meant it.

"I'll text you the flight."

"I'll call you as soon as I pick her up," he promised. They worked well as tag-team parents, taking turns with their child. It had proved to be a blessing for them both. They were still good friends long after their relationship had died, which was nice for their daughter. Chloe loved it when Leslie came to visit them in New York. And he could hardly wait to have her with him for two weeks.

He told Coco as soon as she got home. "Tonight?" She looked stunned. She hadn't expected to meet Chloe so soon. "I hope she isn't upset that I'm around," she said, looking worried. "She might not be happy to share her dad."

"She's going to love you," he said with a look of conviction, and then kissed her. "I had a nice chat with Liz when I called to ask about having Chloe stay here."

"Does she suspect anything?" Coco asked with interest.

"I couldn't tell. But Liz is pretty sharp."

"More than my sister." Coco grinned. "Jane is so self-absorbed, I don't think it crosses her mind."

"I have a feeling you're right," he said, and then went to check the refrigerator. They had bought groceries two days before, so they were well stocked and had all the things Chloe liked. Cereal, waffles, frozen pizza, peanut butter and jelly. They even had croissants, which she loved. He had seen his daughter eat snails on more than one occasion, in fancy French restaurants. Her mother took her everywhere with her and treated her like a grown-up companion. But left to her own devices, Chloe still preferred the foods and pastimes of any kid.

They shared a salad that night before they left for the airport, and Leslie could see Coco was nervous. It was a big deal to her to meet his child.

"What if she hates me?" she asked, looking anxious, as they put the car in the airport garage. They had driven Jane's Mercedes station wagon, and not Coco's disreputable-looking van. There would have been no seat for Chloe if they had, since she had taken all but one passenger seat out, to make room for the dogs.

"She's going to love you," he said again. "And don't forget that I do," he reminded her, and gave her a hug.

The plane was ten minutes early, and they arrived just in time to meet Chloe as she came through the arriving passengers' gate. A member of the ground crew was with her, and they delivered the enchanting-looking little girl into her father's hands as she leaped into his arms with delight. She peeked over his shoulder as he held her and smiled at Coco. She had huge blue eyes and long blond braids, and she was wearing a pink smocked dress and carrying a battered-looking teddy bear. She looked like the poster for the perfect child. She had her mother's coloring and Leslie's astonishing good looks. You could already see that she was going to be a knockout when she grew up.

Leslie set her gently down on her feet and held her hand as he introduced her to Coco. "This is my friend Coco," he said simply, as Chloe looked up at her with interest. "We're staying at her sister's house. It's very pretty and I think you'll like it. And they have an indoor pool, and it's very warm." He gave her all the pertinent information, and Coco suddenly realized that she wouldn't be able to sleep with him while Chloe was there. They hadn't talked about it before she arrived, but she didn't want to shock his child, and she was sure he wouldn't want to either.

"All right now," Leslie said, sounding very official, "let's get your bags. You must be very tired," he said, as they walked toward the baggage claim area hand in hand, as Coco followed. Chloe kept glancing up at her, as though she was trying to figure out who she was.

"I slept on the plane," she informed them, "and we had hot dogs and ice cream for dinner."

"That sounds very good. We have ice cream at the house for you too. And two big dogs, but they're very nice. One of them is very big." He was trying to warn her about Jack so she wouldn't be frightened when they arrived at the house. Coco thought Leslie had a very nice way with his daughter. He suddenly seemed very grown up, as she saw him acting like a dad. It was obvious that Chloe was crazy about him and thrilled to be there. She never let go of his hand.

"I like dogs," she said simply, looking up at Coco. "My grandmother has a French poodle. It doesn't bite."

"Neither do ours," Coco explained. "Their names are Jack and Sallie. Jack is as tall as your dad, when he stands up." Chloe laughed.

"That sounds very silly," Chloe said, as Leslie got both her bags off the turntable and set them down next to Coco.

"I'll go and get the car," he announced, and suddenly took off, leaving Chloe with Coco. She wasn't quite sure what to say to her, but Chloe chatted with her with ease.

"My mom is an actress on Broadway," she explained, while they waited for her father. "She's very good and the play is very sad. Everyone dies. I like musicals better, but my mom doesn't play in those, just sad ones. She gets killed at the end. I was there on opening night." She was exactly what Leslie had said, both enchanting child and small adult. "Are you an actress too?" Chloe asked her pleasantly.

"No. I walk dogs." Coco felt silly as she said it. It was harder to explain to a child. "I walk people's dogs for them while they're at work. It's kind of fun."

They chatted easily for a few minutes until Leslie returned. He was pleased to see that Chloe looked completely at ease with Coco. He carried the bags out to the car, strapped Chloe into the backseat, put her suitcases in the back, and a moment later they drove off.

"What are we going to do here?" Chloe asked as they drove into the city. "Is there a zoo?"

Coco answered for Leslie, since she knew the city better. "Yes, there is. And there are cable cars, and there's a place called Chinatown. And we can go to the beach."

"Coco has a lovely cottage at the beach that I think you'll love," Leslie filled in, as Coco smiled at him. She realized then that this was going to be like playing house, with his child. They had been living together for two and a half months, and suddenly they were a family. Or he and Chloe were, and she was tagging along. This was his real life. It was a taste of reality for both of them. It scared her a little, but she liked it.

When they got to the house, Leslie opened the door with his keys and turned off the alarm, and then turned to Chloe with a broad smile. "Welcome home for the next two weeks," and then he walked her into the kitchen and offered her ice cream. She was still holding on to her bear. She had told Coco at the airport that his name was Alexander. It was a handsome name for a very raggedy old bear. All three of them sat down at the kitchen table, and Coco got out the ice cream. And then much to her horror, Leslie told his daughter about the scene with the maple syrup when they met. Chloe let out big belly laughs as he explained it to her, while she dribbled ice cream down her chin, and so did he. It warmed Coco's heart to see them both. Chloe looked as though she should be part of his everyday life. Being a father seemed to come so naturally to him.

When the three of them finished their ice creams, Coco introduced Chloe to the dogs. She made Jack hold out his paw to shake her hand, and Chloe giggled. She wasn't afraid of him at all, and Sallie ran circles around them, while Coco explained that Sallie used to herd sheep in Australia. And then they all went upstairs. Chloe was going to sleep with her father in the guest room that night. He winked at Coco over his daughter's head, and she got the message that he'd come in to visit when Chloe fell asleep.

Coco unpacked her bag for her, and Leslie watched while she brushed her teeth. She washed her face and put on her pajamas, and then Coco helped her unbraid her hair. It was fair and long and fine and wavy from the braids. Chloe got into the big bed then, and Coco kissed her goodnight and went back to her own room, while Leslie sat with her until she fell asleep.

He wandered into the master suite twenty minutes later, with a happy smile as he flopped down on their bed.

"She's adorable," Coco said, smiling at him, as he leaned across the bed and kissed her. "She looks just like you, in blond."

"So I'm told," he said proudly. "She thought you were very nice and very pretty. She wanted to know if I love you, and I said I do. I'm always honest with her. She said I could sleep in here if I wanted to. I left her door open, and the light on in the bathroom. And we can leave our door open too, if you don't mind."

"This is so grown up," Coco giggled, looking like a kid herself, and he laughed.

"Yes, it is, isn't it? Fatherhood always does that to me. She makes me feel very responsible. I wish I saw her more," he said wistfully. "She's such a great kid."

"Yes, she is," Coco agreed, as he got under the covers next to her. "Are you sure it's all right if you sleep in here?"

"She said it was," he said comfortably. "She's a pretty savvy little kid." He liked that she felt at ease with Coco too, and he liked the way Coco talked to her. She had a gentle, kind way with dogs and children, and with him too. He loved her even more now after seeing her with his daughter. It was wonderful for him having two people he loved under one roof. He was looking forward to the next two weeks with both of them. He pulled Coco into his arms then, and they lay side by side, talking for a while, in whispers, although Chloe couldn't hear them from the next room, and she was sound asleep.

Half an hour later, he and Coco had fallen asleep too. The dogs were downstairs, asleep in the kitchen. Coco had left them there so they didn't bother Chloe or climb up on her bed.

The house was quiet while all of them slept, and the next morning, when Coco rolled over before her alarm went off, and opened one eye, she found herself looking at Chloe, who was smiling at her. She had climbed into their bed when she woke up. Leslie was still sound asleep, and Coco laughed when she saw her.

"Are you hungry?" Coco whispered, as Chloe nodded with a broad grin. "Let's go downstairs and get something to eat." They tiptoed out of the room so as not to wake her father. Coco let the dogs out, and Chloe sat down at the kitchen table as though she'd lived there all her life. "What do you like to eat for breakfast?" Coco asked her as they smiled at each other.

"Cereal and a banana, and toast, and a glass of milk."

"Coming right up," Coco said as she got it all together and put the kettle on for tea. "Did you sleep okay?" Chloe nodded happily, and then looked at Coco more intently.

"My dad says he loves you. Do you love him too?" she asked with a serious expression.

"Yes, I do," Coco answered as she put the breakfast in front of her. "Very much. And he loves you a lot too, most of all." She wanted to reassure her.

"My mom lets me watch his movies whenever I want," Chloe informed her as she dug into the cereal, and then had some juice.

"I like to watch them too," Coco confessed as she sat down across from her. "There's a big, big screen in our room here, if you want to watch his movies, or some other ones. It's fun to watch them on such a big screen."

"My dad doesn't like watching them," Chloe informed her, and Coco nodded.

"I know. We can watch other stuff with him."

"What are you two up to?" They both jumped as Leslie walked into the kitchen. They hadn't heard him come in on bare feet.

"We're talking about watching your movies on the big screen," Coco explained, as Chloe shoved too much of the banana into her mouth and then tried to talk. Leslie imitated her and they all laughed, and then the dogs wandered in and out again. It was everything a family should be.

"Why don't we take Chloe to the beach today, when you finish at noon?" he suggested. It was Saturday, and sounded like a great idea to all three of them.

"Can we swim?" Chloe asked, looking excited, and Leslie told her it was too cold to swim there. He didn't tell her about the sharks, and he said they could swim at home, in the pool.

He took her to see the pool while Coco tidied up the kitchen, and then went upstairs to dress. And when Chloe and her father came back, Coco offered to do her braids for her before she went to work. It was fun taking care of her and being there with them. She ran a bath for Chloe before she left, and promised to be back soon. Chloe waved from the window while Coco drove off in her van. It was nice knowing they'd be there when she got home. This was a whole different life than the one she'd had for years now in Bolinas, solitary for the past two years. She loved playing house with Leslie and his daughter.

Coco was back in time to have lunch with them, and immediately after, they left for the beach. Chloe watched with interest as they drove along, asked questions, and told her father what she'd been doing in the Hamptons all summer. She said her mother had a new boyfriend and he had a boat, and she was going to Saint-Tropez with him after joining him in Monte Carlo. Coco tried not to smile as she listened. Chloe made comments about the people in her life, and more than likely would be telling her mother about Coco when she went back.

"He's kind of funny-looking," Chloe said about Monica's new boyfriend. "He has a big stomach and he's bald, but he's very nice. And Mom says his boat is very big." Monica had never been one to ignore material benefits from the men she dated, Leslie thought, as Chloe described him. But if it worked for her, why not? He could see that Coco was trying not to laugh. "He's old too," Chloe added. She had brought her bear with her, and held him up to look at the sea as they drove along the cliffs. And then she turned her interest to Coco. Leslie was driving this time. "Why aren't you married, and have children?" she asked, looking curious. She had told her father again that morning that she thought Coco was nice.

"I haven't met the right man yet," she answered honestly. "My mom asks me the same thing."

"Do you have brothers and sisters?" Chloe wanted to know everything and wasn't afraid to ask.

"I have a sister named Jane. She's eleven years older than I am."

"That's old," Chloe said, looking sorry for her, as they drove down the hill to Stinson Beach. There was a haze of fog on the ocean, but the sky was blue and the weather was still good. The climate was always unpredictable in August, and cold and windy in the city. The locals were used to it, and tourists were always disappointed, but Chloe didn't seem to care. She was just happy being with her father and Coco. She didn't seem to mind sharing him with a woman. She had met a lot of his girlfriends over the years. She had informed Coco of that over breakfast, and Coco just nodded as she listened. "Is your sister married and has kids?" Chloe asked hopefully. She liked playing with other children, but she was comfortable alone with grown-ups too, just as Leslie had said. She seemed totally at ease in her world, and even someone else's. She had been exposed to a very sophisticated life in her six years.

"No, she's not married either," Coco said apologetically, "and she doesn't have any children. She lives with a friend, kind of a roommate. Her name is Liz."

"Is she gay?" Chloe asked with wide-open eyes, and Coco nearly fell off her seat. She turned to look at the child with a cautious smile, and Leslie chuckled. He'd survived many interrogations of that sort at his daughter's hands. It was all new to Coco.

"What does gay mean?" Coco asked, feigning ignorance, to see what she would say.

"Don't you know? That means when boys live with boys and girls live with girls, and they kiss sometimes. And they can't have babies because only boys and girls can do that. Do you want to hear how people make babies? My mom told me about it," she announced with a knowing look and then hugged her bear. She was the oddest mix of child and adult, adorable pixie and tiny woman. Coco had never met anyone like her, and already loved her. It was hard not to. She was the funniest little girl.

"I don't think I need to hear how people do that," Coco said quickly. "My mom told me too. I was a little older than you when she did," like about fourteen, and by then Coco had already heard the essential mechanics from Jane.

"It sounds weird, doesn't it?" Chloe commented, as they drove past the tiny town of Stinson Beach heading toward Bolinas. "I don't want someone sticking their penis in me when I'm older. That's disgusting," she said, looking incensed, and then she turned wide eyes to Coco again. "Does my dad do that with you?" she asked clearly as Leslie choked and glanced at Coco, who was stumbling over her words.

"Errr . . . uh . . . no, he doesn't," she lied, but she was not about to admit it to her. Some things were impossible to admit to a six-year-old, no matter how well informed she was.

"That's why you don't have children," she said matter-of-factly. "You'll have to do that one day if you want to have a baby. My mom did it with my dad." She said it like something silly they'd done a long time ago, or a trip they'd taken. She obviously didn't understand the full meaning of what she'd been told, or the implications, although she had the mechanics right.

"Well, I'm very glad they had you," Coco said blithely, trying to recover from the conversation, as Leslie took the turnoff to Bolinas, and they continued down the bumpy narrow road until they reached her house. "Here we are," Coco said, ready to get out of the car, before Chloe could embark on any more delicate topics. Coco hadn't been ready for that.

All three of them got out of the car, and Coco unlocked her tiny house, as Chloe bounced in behind her. The dogs who had been cramped in the back of Jane's station wagon bounded off to the beach.

"Oh, it's so pretty!" Chloe said, clapping her hands, with her bear tucked under her arm. She set him on the couch and looked around the cottage. "It looks like where Goldilocks lived, or Snow White." Coco laughed in answer. They had gone from sex to Snow White in under five minutes. Chloe walked out onto the deck then, as Leslie grinned at her.

"That's my girl," he said in a whisper. "I told you she's very adult. Her mother treats her like one. But she's still very much a child at the same time. You handled that very well. And I promise never to do that disgusting thing to you again that she mentioned, unless we want to have a baby." Coco laughed out loud, and they followed his daughter out to the deck.

"Can we play on the beach?"

"Of course, that's why we came here. Do you want to build a sand castle, or just run around?" Coco asked her.

"A castle!" she said, clapping her hands again. In answer, Coco took a series of pans and mixing bowls out of a cupboard, and a little pail to carry water in. And a moment later, after taking off their shoes, all three of them headed down to the beach.

Coco carried the water for them, and Leslie did most of the building. Chloe decorated the castle with rocks and shells and little bits of driftwood and sea glass. She was very creative. And by the time they were finished, it was a very impressive castle, and all three of them were pleased. It was late afternoon by the time they went back to the house.

Coco had two frozen pizzas in the freezer, and enough lettuce to make a salad for all of them. Coco and Chloe toasted marshmallows on the stove before dinner, and Coco promised to make s'mores for her for dessert. They ate dinner at the battered old kitchen table, and afterward they sat out on the deck and ate the s'mores at dusk.

After dinner, Leslie told stories about how funny Chloe was as a baby. She had heard them all, but loved hearing them again. And then they put her to bed in Coco's bedroom. Coco had volunteered to sleep on the couch that night, although Leslie insisted he would, but she thought he should sleep with his child, and she didn't mind. The living room was cozy and warm with a heater. And they lit a fire after Chloe went to bed. Coco had gone in to kiss her goodnight, and she had held up her bear for Coco to kiss too.

"Thank you. I had fun today," she said, yawning.

"So did I," Coco said, smiling at her, and almost as soon as she left the room, the little girl was fast asleep.

"She is the funniest kid," Coco whispered to Leslie, as they sat on the couch together.

"I know," he said proudly. "I just love her to pieces. I never would have thought it, but Monica is actually a very good mother. A little too modern for my taste at times, the sex education and all that, but I think Chloe is a very well-adjusted child. No thanks to me, I fear. I would spoil her rotten and keep her home from school every day to play with." He smiled happily, and Coco nestled close to him on the couch.

"You're a very good father." He was patient, and kind and loving, just as he was with her.

"That was a very handsome sand castle we built," he said, smiling at her. "You should have been an architect."

"I'd rather be a beach bum." She grinned.

"You do that very well too," he said as he kissed her, and then ran a hand under her sweatshirt to touch her breasts.

"You're not going to do that disgusting thing to me that Chloe talked about, are you?" she teased him, and he looked mock serious as he fondled her.

"Never! I would never do a thing like that, especially not with Chloe asleep in the next room . . . but under other circumstances I could be talked into it . . . if you ever want a baby . . ." His voice drifted off and she smiled mysteriously.

"Maybe one day." She had thought of it several times recently. And the thought of having a little girl like Chloe was strangely appealing.

They lay together on the couch until midnight, talking, and then walked out on the deck to look at the sky. There were a million stars shining brightly, and a big, beautiful moon above them. They sat on the deck chairs and talked for another hour, about nothing in particular, and then reluctantly Leslie left her in the living room and went to bed with his daughter, while Coco settled in to a sleeping bag on the couch.

All three of them woke up bright and early. Leslie made breakfast. He made Mickey Mouse–shaped pancakes with bananas in them, which Chloe said were her favorites, and afterward he went next door to help Jeff work on his car. He had seen him tinkering with it all morning and was dying to lend a hand. Coco smiled as she watched him from the window while she and Chloe cleaned up the kitchen, and afterward she read her stories on the deck.

Leslie joined them two hours later, his hands covered with grease, with a look of delight, and said they had fixed Jeff's car. It had been a perfect morning for him, under the hood of Jeff's car.

After that, they drove to Stinson, and went for a long walk on the beach with the dogs. They came back to Coco's place in time for lunch. Leslie and Chloe played checkers, while Coco watched, and afterward, they all ate sandwiches and chips, and eventually lay on the deck chairs in the sun. They were all sorry to leave the beach that evening, after they ate hot dogs and toasted marshmallows. Chloe slept in the car on the way back. It had been a perfect weekend.

The three of them watched *Mary Poppins* on the huge screen in their bedroom that night, and when Chloe fell asleep, Leslie carried her to her own bed in the guest room. Coco had promised to take her to Chinatown the next day, where they were going to have dinner at a Chinese restaurant, "with chopsticks," Chloe insisted. And they were planning to go to the zoo later that week, and ride on a cable car for sure before she left.

"Thank you for being so sweet to her," Leslie said as he climbed back into bed with Coco.

"It's not hard to do," Coco said, looking happy. And with that, Leslie got up again and locked their bedroom door. "What are you doing?" she asked, as she nestled under the covers and smiled at him. She was loving these precious days with both of them.

"I thought we might have a few minutes of privacy. It's not easy with a child in the house." They had gotten spoiled by being alone till then. But they both loved having Chloe with them.

Leslie turned off the lights, and took Coco in his arms. He was delighted to discover that she was already naked and had taken her pajamas off while he put Chloe to bed. He took his boxer shorts off, and within seconds they were lost in their love for each other once again. It almost seemed as though Chloe's visit had brought them even closer. And Coco realized that she had never felt anything was missing before, but now she felt complete.

Chapter 10

In the two weeks Chloe spent with them, they managed to do everything they had promised her and more. They went to both the Oakland and San Francisco zoos and the wax museum at Fisherman's Wharf, which Coco thought would be too scary for her, and Chloe loved. They went to Chinatown twice, and wandered around Sausalito. They went to the movies, rode the cable car, went back to Bolinas for the weekend, and made another castle, an even bigger, more elaborate one this time. And Coco took her to a toy factory she'd read about, where they let Chloe design and stuff her own teddy bear. Alexander had a friend, a girl bear this time with a pink dress, whom Chloe named Coco, the ultimate compliment. She showed it to her father proudly, and on her last night, they all swam in the pool, and Coco cooked dinner. She even made a cake with pink icing and candy sprinkles on it. It was lopsided, but Chloe loved it anyway. Coco had spelled out her name on it in M&Ms.

Chloe asked them both over dinner if they were going to get married, and her father looked vague. He and Coco hadn't gotten that far yet, although they had touched on the subject of having babies. He was still trying to talk her into coming to live with him in L.A., and had gotten no commitment from her yet. She had an aversion to the city where she'd grown up, and the lifestyle of the people in it. They had a number of hurdles to get over before the subject of marriage could be discussed, but it had crossed his mind. He didn't want to say anything to Chloe about it, for fear of disappointing her later, if things didn't work out. She was in love with Coco, which was mutual, and she even liked the dogs.

"I think your sister might be gay," she had said pensively to Coco one afternoon, "to have a dog like that. Girls have things like poodles or Yorkies, or little tiny fluffy dogs. Only boys have dogs like Jack."

"You could be right," Coco had said noncommittally. "I'll have to ask her." She didn't want to lie to Chloe, but she wasn't ready to answer her either. She didn't want her going back to her mother and announcing that Coco had a lesbian sister. She might think she had said too much to the child, although Monica didn't seem to hesitate to discuss anything with her daughter. But Chloe was her child, so she had that right. Coco wanted to keep firmer boundaries than that, and Leslie was very proper and more traditional too. They seemed to have similar ideas on that and every subject.

They had only one small mishap during Chloe's entire stay. On her very last night, Chloe burned her finger toasting marshmallows with Coco over the stove. She got too enthused and touched the red-hot fork, trying to get the melted mass of marshmallow off. She let out a yelp and burst into six-year-old wails and tears immediately as the finger came up in a blister. Coco acted quickly and ran it under cold water, as Leslie ran into the kitchen when he heard Chloe cry.

"What happened?" he asked, looking panicked, as tears rolled down his daughter's cheeks. "Did she cut herself?"

"She burned her finger," Coco said, holding Chloe close to her and the wounded finger under the stream of cold water in the sink.

"Did you let her play at the stove alone?" he asked accusingly, and Chloe instantly turned to her father and the tears stopped.

"It's *not* her fault!" she said fiercely in defense of Coco, having heard the tone of accusation in her father's voice. "She told me not to touch the fork, and I did anyway," Chloe said, leaning into the warmth and safety of Coco's arms. "It's better now," Chloe said bravely, as all three of them examined the small, raised white blister. Coco put ointment and a Band-Aid on it, as Leslie looked at her apologetically.

"I'm sorry. That was stupid of me. I was just afraid she was badly hurt." He felt terrible to have implied that Coco had been neglectful in any way, but when he had heard Chloe's anguished cries, it had gone straight to his heart. But he could see that Coco was just as concerned, and had done a great job with first aid.

"Don't worry about it," Coco told him reassuringly as she lifted Chloe off the stool where she had sat her next to the sink.

"I love you, Coco," Chloe said, throwing her arms around Coco's waist and squeezing her tight as Leslie smiled at them both.

"I love you too," Coco whispered and bent to kiss the top of her head.

"Can we make more marshmallows now?" Chloe asked, smiling at them, holding the injured finger in midair.

"No!" both adults said in unison and then laughed. Leslie still felt terrible for his comment to Coco, but she had taken it in stride, and knew it was only due to fear and concern for his child.

"How about ice cream instead?" Leslie suggested, and Coco looked relieved. It had frightened her when Chloe got hurt and she felt badly about it, but the child was happy and fine again by the time they left the kitchen, and she lay in bed cuddling with both of them, watching TV as all three of them savored their last night. Coco realized how much she was going to miss her. Chloe had lodged herself deep into Coco's heart.

And all three of them looked sad as Leslie drove them to the airport. Chloe was carrying both her old bear and her new one, and Coco almost cried when she said goodbye to her, and they handed her over to the ticket agent who was going to walk her to the plane for New York.

"I hope you come back to visit soon," Coco said, as she hugged her. "It won't be the same without you." She meant it, and Chloe nodded in answer, and then pulled away to look at Coco with a serious expression.

"Will my dad be here if I come back to visit?"

"I hope so. Sometimes. You can both come back anytime."

"I think you and my dad should get married." She echoed the same opinion she'd voiced earlier, not long after her arrival. The bond between Coco and Chloe had been almost instantaneous and had gotten stronger every day.

"We'll talk about that sometime," Leslie said, and hugged her tightly. "I'm going to miss you, you little monkey. Say hi to your mom for me, and call me tonight."

"I promise," she said sadly.

"I love you," he said, hugging her for a last time, and then called it out again, as she went through security and turned to wave at them, smiling brightly. She was waving to both of them, and Coco blew her kisses and touched her heart and then pointed at her. They stood there until she disappeared into the crowd at the airport and headed for the gate, holding the ticket agent's hand.

They stayed until the flight took off, in case it was delayed for some reason, and once it was in the air, they went back to the garage to get the car. They were both silent for the first few minutes, thinking about Chloe, and how empty the house would seem now.

"I already miss her," Coco said sadly, as they drove away from the airport. She had never lived with a child for two weeks before, and now she couldn't imagine life without her.

"So do I," he said with a sigh. "I envy people who live with their children. Monica is so lucky she has her all the time." But he couldn't imagine being married to her either, and never had. "If I ever do it again, I want to stick around. It breaks my heart when she goes, or I do, every time." He looked mournful as they drove back to the city, and they decided to go to a movie, to keep from going back to the empty house. They felt like two lost souls.

The movie was violent and action-packed, which kept them both distracted, and by the time they got home, Chloe was halfway to New York.

Coco went to swim laps in the pool, and Leslie sat in the study making notes on a script he'd been reading to decide if he wanted the part they were offering him. They met in the kitchen later, and sat staring sadly at the cake Coco had made for Chloe the night before. It was hard to shake the mood of loss as they sat there, and then finally Leslie made them both a cup of tea and sat down with a smile.

"I think this means her visit was a success," he said, looking a little better. "We all had a good time."

"How could you not have fun with her?" Coco said, sipping her tea. "I hope Jane and Liz's baby is half as cute six years from now." She was excited about that too.

"What do you think of Chloe's suggestion, by the way?" he asked nonchalantly. "The thing about getting married." He looked boyish and nervous as he asked, like any other normal mortal, and not a famous movie star. "I thought it was a rather intriguing idea myself," he said, pretending to be more self-confident than he felt. At times he sounded very British, and it made Coco smile. His self-deprecating style and humility were part of his huge appeal on the screen, and also in real life. She had loved that about him from the first day she met him with the maple syrup.

"Definitely interesting," she said softly, smiling at him, with love in her eyes. "But possibly premature. I think we have to figure out where we would live first and how we'd work it out." It was not a negligible point to Coco. They had lived together at Jane's for three months by then, which was a good start. And she had never gotten along with anyone as well or as easily in her life, not even Ian. But her big concern was still about his fame, and what kind of life they would have, constantly pursued by the press, particularly if they lived in L.A. She wanted a much more private life than that or it might ruin what they had. And they hadn't come up with a solution for the problem yet, and maybe never would.

Other than that very major issue, she and Leslie had had only one very minor disagreement, about the dogs, one night when they came in wet from the pool and jumped on the bed, for what Leslie claimed was the fourth time in a row. With the exception of that minor mishap and Chloe's burned finger the night before she left, they were doing great, and had been for three months. They loved being together, living together, she was interested in his work, and he loved hearing her opinions on the scripts that came in for him. And he was always open to what she had to say on any subject. He was respectful of her in every way. And she loved his daughter. Their only nemesis was his fame and what it might do to their life.

There were things they still didn't know about each other, what kind of people they each liked or what it would be like sharing a social life with each other, since they were living in seclusion. They had never traveled together, or faced a crisis, and she hadn't experienced what Leslie was like when tired and stressed, making a film. But for the ordinary elements of everyday life living under one roof, so far all the pieces fit more than comfortably. They were both kind, considerate people who respected each other and had a good time together. They enjoyed each other's sense of humor. All that remained to be seen was how they would stand the test of time. The only thing that seriously worried her about him was that he lived in L.A., and the life he led there, but he appeared to be flexible about that too. He had suggested San Francisco and Santa Barbara as alternatives, and had offered to spend time, whenever he could, in Bolinas. He was even willing to consider New York. He was a reasonable person, with sensible ideas, and he was willing to compromise with Coco. He seemed like an ideal candidate as a husband, and he had long since decided that Coco would be the perfect wife for him. She just wanted a little more time to think about it. Three months didn't seem like long enough to her to make a decision that would affect them for the rest of their lives. And his stardom presented unavoidable challenges they would have to face.

"I'm not sure where we live is the important issue," Leslie said quietly. He didn't want to push her, but he was already convinced. Chloe had just helped to spur him along with her question the night before, and seeing Coco with her, and now he wanted to discuss it with her. "You can't stop loving a man, or leave him, because you don't like the city he lives in," he said sensibly.

"It's not about the city, it's about the lifestyle that comes with your work," she said, looking worried. It was her only concern. "I don't know what it would be like to live with a major movie star, and all that goes with it. That's scary, Leslie. The press and paparazzi and all that pressure and public exposure ruin people's lives. I need to try that on for size first. I don't want to screw up your career, or my life. I love what we have here, but this is fantasyland," she said honestly. "We're hiding out. When we come out of the closet, it's going to create an explosion that will be heard around the world. That scares the shit out of me. I don't want to lose you, because other people screw things up for us, and they could."

"Then let's start telling people and see how it feels. Why don't you come on location with me to Italy? I'll be in Venice for at least a month, maybe two. You could stay there with me, if you can find someone else to walk the dogs. Will you think about it? And maybe we should go to L.A. for a few days before that, and try that on for size too." He was ready to announce to the world he was in love with her. In fact, he was dying to be seen with Coco, and share his happiness with the entire planet. "I love you, Coco," he said gently. "And whatever happens, and however the press handles it, I'll be right there with you." She smiled at him with tears in her eyes.

"I guess I'm just scared. What if they hate me, or I do something stupid, or I screw things up for you? I've never been in the public eye before. I know what they used to do to my father's clients. I don't want that happening to us. Everything is so simple now, but it will never be like this again once people find out about us." But she knew they only had two weeks left of the idyllic life they had shared. He was going back to L.A. to start the picture in two weeks. All they had left were days. After that, it would be open season on them. And Leslie knew it too. He couldn't deny it. And he worried about it for her. She was a very private, retiring person, and he lived in a very public world, where privacy was hard to come by and anonymity unheard of. They had been unusually lucky and extremely careful for the past three months. But once he went back to Los Angeles and on location in Venice, every move they made would be in the tabloids and the press. Coco needed to at least see it and taste it, before she agreed to a steady diet of it forever.

"Just take it one day at a time," he said as her cell phone rang. It was Jane, just checking in. Ever since the explosion with their mother, she had been calling a little more often. It had cleared the air for them somewhat. Leslie got up, came around the table, and kissed Coco before leaving the kitchen. He hadn't had a satisfactory answer to his question about marriage, but he knew it would take time for Coco to adjust to the realities of his life. She seemed less frantic about it than she had in the beginning, but he hadn't convinced her yet. He wasn't ready to give up by any means, and he left her to talk to her sister. He had every intention of bringing up the subject again. Coco was grateful that he wasn't pressuring her about it. She was upset enough that he was going to be leaving San Francisco soon.

Coco asked Jane how her pregnancy was going, and she said it was fine. She said that she and Liz were excited about it, and it was still hard for them to believe that in five months there would be a baby in their house. Coco couldn't believe it either, and the thought of it still seemed odd to her. She had never in a million years thought of Jane as a mother, and still couldn't. She knew her too well, or maybe not well enough.

"At least I can tell you that your house works perfectly for a six-year-old. Leslie's daughter was here for two weeks, and she loved it. We had a ball." There was a brief silence at the other end as her sister listened and didn't comment.

"How was that, by the way?" Jane asked coolly.

"Great. She's the cutest kid you've ever seen. I hope you have a girl, just like her."

"Sounds like she was a big hit," Jane said, sounding cautious. "I hope she didn't break anything."

"Of course not. She's beautifully behaved." Her sister's tone of voice made Coco faintly nervous, particularly after the conversation she had just had with Leslie, and she could feel herself saying too much to cover her discomfort. "We took her everywhere, the zoo, the cable car, Chinatown, Sausalito, the wax museum. We had a great time with her."

" 'We'? Is there something you haven't told me, Coco?" She still couldn't believe that Liz's suspicions were right, but what she was hearing suddenly concerned her. "Is something going on with you and Leslie?" she asked bluntly, and there was a long pause at Coco's end. She could have lied to her, and had before, but this was all part of what she and Leslie had been talking about. It was time for them to come out. And it made more sense to do it with family first. As a trial balloon, she decided to make a clean breast of it with Jane.

She said it in a single word. "Yes." She had no idea what would come next. Astonishment probably, but maybe approval since he was Jane's friend. For once, Jane couldn't tell her that he was unsuitable and from a different world, as she had with Ian and everyone else. But Coco was wrong again.

"Are you insane? Do you have any idea who he is in the real world? He's the biggest star on the planet. The media will eat you alive. You're a dog-walker from Bolinas, for chrissake, have you considered what they'll do with that?"

"I'm also Buzz Barrington's daughter, and Florence Flowers's, and your sister. I grew up in that world."

"And dropped out to become a hippie. He's been linked to half the sophisticated women in the world and every movie star alive. They'll eat you for lunch and spit you out. You'll be an embarrassment to him. How could you do anything so stupid? I ask you to live in my house and take care of my dog, and you wind up fucking my houseguest who just happens to be a world-renowned movie star. What were you both thinking of?" She was as mean and thoughtless as ever as she barreled down on Coco, as she always had. Coco sat listening with tears in her eyes.

"Actually, we were thinking we fell in love," Coco said quietly, hating her and everything she said, and worse yet, fearing she was right.

"How could you be so stupid? That's the dumbest thing I ever heard. He'll forget you in five minutes when he goes back to work. He'll be sleeping with his costar, all over the tabloids, and all you'll be is a joke, and another notch on his belt. Believe me, I know Leslie well." He wandered back into the kitchen at that precise moment and saw the look of devastation on Coco's face. And he knew instantly that her sister had just done it to her again. It never failed. Being friends with Jane was one thing, but Leslie knew she could be a raving bitch, especially to her kid sister. He ran a hand over Coco's shoulders and she turned away from him, which worried him. She had never done that before.

"We'll have to see how it shakes out when he goes back," Coco said cryptically as Leslie walked out of the room again. He didn't want to intrude on them. He was always polite, respectful, and discreet.

"It's not going to shake anywhere," Jane said cruelly, "trust me, it will be over the day he leaves. It already is. You just don't know it yet. There's no future in this for you. I'm sure he's a great lay, but that's all you're ever going to get out of this. You'd be an embarrassment to him in his own world." Coco wanted to tell her that they'd just been talking marriage, but she didn't dare. And listening to what Jane had said, she felt sick. Jane was right. She was deluding herself if she thought she could hold her own in Leslie's world. "I hope you get a grip, and wake up and smell the coffee, Coco. At least don't humiliate yourself by hanging on to him. When he leaves, let it go with grace. You never should have gotten involved with him while you were staying at the house. I thought you were smarter than that, or had a little more self-respect than to be a piece of ass for a hottie like him." What she said was cruel, but given the opportunity, Jane often was. To Coco anyway. She always had been. Pregnant or not, nothing had changed.

"Thanks very much," Coco said, choking on her misery. All she wanted was to get off. "Talk to you soon," she said, and hit the red button on her cell phone, as tears slid down her cheeks. She didn't want to give Jane the satisfaction of hearing her cry. Leslie looked at her as he walked back in.

"What the hell happened? What did she do to you now? I used to like her, and I swear I've come to hate her ever since I met you and see what she does to you. She's always been a good friend to me, but she treats you like shit and I hate it," Leslie said, looking unhappy.

"It's a sister thing," Coco defended her. She could reduce Coco to rubble in minutes. It made him want to do the same to her, so she could fight with someone her own size.

Coco was choking on sobs when he took her in his arms to comfort her.

"She's right," she said, crying all over his sweater as he held her. "She says I'm a slut and a lunatic, and I'd be an embarrassment to you, and I'm just a notch on your belt, and you've been with the most glamorous women in the world, and the media will eat me up and spit me out and it's over between us the day you leave." It was one long run-on sentence that spilled all the hurt her sister had inflicted on her, all over both of them. Coco was inconsolable and looked heartbroken, and there was fury in Leslie's eyes.

"I swear, I'm going to kill that woman. What the hell does she know about what the press will do? And who goddamn cares? You're a gorgeous, beautiful, intelligent, dignified, gracious woman, and I would be proud to be at your side. I deserve to be at your feet. Your sister isn't fit to shine your shoes, and she's a nasty, cruel bitch. She's jealous of you. You'll always be younger than she is. I don't give a damn what shit she said to you, Coco. None of it is true. And it's not over when I leave. It's just beginning for us when I leave here. I want you to come with me, and I'm going to tell the world how lucky I am to be with you. And they'll fall in love with you too. And anyone who doesn't is a fool. Ask Chloe," he said, smiling down at her as he held her, "she knows. And you can't fool a kid, certainly not mine." Everything he said was right, and was just what she needed to hear, but the meanness of what her sister had said had wounded her very soul.

"You're wrong," Coco insisted, but there was less force to it now. Leslie had dulled Jane's barbs just enough. "It'll hurt your career." She sounded like a wounded child, which, whenever she got near her older sister, she was.

"No, losing you would hurt my career, because I would turn into a hopeless drunk." She giggled through her tears, but Jane had worried her severely, and it was everything Coco was afraid of and didn't want to hear. "She's a monster," he said soundly. "Don't talk to her again. She owes both of us an apology. I love you, and that's that." And a moment later, he gently led her upstairs and pulled her onto their bed. It took another hour to calm Coco down, but at least she told him all of it and vented. And he was more furious by the minute. He thought of calling Jane back himself and telling her what he thought of her vicious, senseless attack on her sister and her disrespect for them. But he decided she wasn't worth it and concentrated on Coco instead. He didn't give a damn what Jane thought of them.

And finally, with his gentle words and his kisses, Coco started to relax. He smiled at her, and gently took her clothes off, as she looked up at him. She remembered all too clearly her sister calling her his piece of ass.

"What are you doing?" she said softly, as he kissed her on the neck and sent a shiver down her spine.

"I thought I'd try that disgusting thing again. I want to be sure I get it right. It takes a lot of practice to do something like that," he said, and Coco laughed. And by the time he had finished undressing her, she no longer cared what Jane had said. Leslie was the love of her life.

Chapter 11

Once Chloe left, the last two weeks of Leslie's stay in San Francisco went by much too fast. They tried to cherish every moment and were together constantly. He had a lot to do to get organized before starting his next film, and he stayed with Coco until the last minute. He was only going to be in L.A. for ten days before he left for Italy on location, and he wanted Coco to come down and visit. She promised that she would for a few days.

She didn't speak to Jane again for several days after her attack. Jane tried calling her the next day, and Coco didn't answer. She'd heard enough from her, and had no need or desire for more of the same. Jane told Liz about it the next morning before leaving for the set, and Liz wasn't startled to hear about the romance between Leslie and Coco, but she was disturbed by Jane's reaction.

"Why are you so upset about it?" Liz asked as she poured them both coffee.

"He's my friend, not hers," Jane said, almost visibly pouting, as though she felt left out or out of control.

"He may be your friend," Liz reminded her, "but now he's her boyfriend. That's a different relationship and a special bond. He's a nice guy and a serious person, and I don't think he plays around as much as you think. I don't think he'd be irresponsible with her, he's an honorable man."

"He used to play around all the time," Jane insisted.

"So did everyone," Liz said, looking at her partner with worried eyes. She could only imagine the things Jane had said and how hurtful they must have been. "Is that what you're afraid of? That he's just fooling around with her? Are you protecting your sister, or is it that you don't want her involved with your friends? If that's the case, it's not fair to her. She did us a favor, and if we let him stay at the house, what happened between them after that is really their business, not ours."

"He's going to make a fool of her," Jane said, glowering at Liz.

"I don't agree with you," Liz said staunchly. "I don't think it's fair of you to assume that. They're both adults, they know what they're doing and what they want. Just like we do."

"Why are you always on everyone else's side? My mother, Coco. Every time they do something stupid or outrageous, you champion their cause," Jane said petulantly.

"I love you, but I don't always agree with you. And in this case, I think you're wrong."

"What does he want with her? She's just a dog-walker, for God's sake."

"Don't be such a snob. She's a lot more than that, and you know it. And even if she weren't, he has a right to fall in love with her. I think he'd be good for her, if she can handle what goes with his success."

"She can't," Jane said, sounding convinced. "She doesn't have the guts. She ran away from L.A., and she dropped out of law school. She's a quitter."

"No, she's not!" Liz said firmly. "And whatever they decide to do is up to them."

"He's going to drop her like a hot brick the minute he starts his next film, which is in about two weeks, I think. How long do you think it'll last after that? He'll be sleeping with his leading lady, and he'll forget all about Coco, living like a hippie at the beach."

"Maybe not. Maybe this is for real," Liz insisted. For some reason, she had the feeling that it was. They had been so careful to protect their secret that it made her think that they were serious about each other. She hoped that was the case. She was very fond of them both. "She has the right to find out for herself what this is all about and means to both of them. If he's not serious about her, she'll figure it out soon enough."

"And so will half the world when they read about it in the tabloids. They don't need that headache, and neither do we. I love Leslie, but I don't need to read about my sister being his latest fling."

"I think she must be more than that to him. He cares about you too, and he wouldn't take advantage of your sister and have a fling just for the hell of it."

"They're both crazy if they think this would ever work. Take my word for it, it won't, even if they're serious about it now. The kind of pressure he's under is way too much for Coco to handle. She's going to collapse like a house of cards."

"I think you should give her more credit than that. She didn't fall apart when Ian died."

"No, she just became a recluse for the last two years. And what happens when the tabloids start stalking our house and hers? Who needs it? She lives in a dream world, Liz, and so does he if he thinks she can be part of his real life. The press will make fun of her."

"Maybe not. She can get it together if she wants."

"She'll never go back to live in L.A. And he can't live in that shack at the beach with her. He has a major career, even bigger than ours."

"Let's see what happens," Liz said quietly. "And I think all of that is beside the point. If she's going to try and do this, she needs our support. She doesn't need you beating her up."

"I didn't beat her up," Jane growled at her partner, but they both knew she had. Liz could see it in her eyes. There was guilt all over Jane's face. "I just told her what I thought."

"Sometimes, with you, that's the same thing. You don't know how much your words can hurt. You can be very sharp."

"All right, all right. I'll call her," Jane promised as they got ready to leave the apartment they had rented. The film they were making was going well, and they were going home sooner than planned. In the end, Coco had house-sat for them for the entire time, but it had worked out well for her too. And now they knew why.

But when Jane called Coco later that morning on her cell phone, Coco didn't answer, nor later in the afternoon. Two days later, Jane had understood that Coco didn't want to speak to her. She felt bad by then and had calmed down. She decided to call Leslie then to see what he had to say.

His voice was ice cold when he answered his phone and recognized her number on caller ID.

"What's up?" he said tersely, sounding even more British than usual. Jane recognized in his reaction how much she had hurt her sister, and it made her feel defensive.

"Coco tells me you've been having a hot romance all summer," Jane said, trying to make light of it, which was what she still believed it was. A summer fling. No matter what Liz said.

"I wouldn't call it that," he said bluntly. "I fell in love with your sister. She's an extraordinary woman, and a nice one. She's been doing you a favor for the last three months, and I've been the benefactor of it, thanks to your hospitality. There was no need to say the things you did to her. I find it inexcusable. I don't know what bug you've got up your ass, Jane, but I suggest you get a grip on yourself. If you ever speak to her that way again, you can forget me as a friend. I have no use for people like you, who hurt people for the hell of it. What is it? Kind of a sport with you? You live with one of the nicest women in the world, and your sister is another one. I suggest you take lessons from both of them." He had hit his mark, and Jane felt like she'd been slapped, which was exactly what he had intended. He didn't want Jane upsetting Coco, or telling her he would dump her, forget her, or cheat on her the moment he left. He had never been in love like this in his life.

"I don't need you to tell me how to talk to my sister. I told her what I thought, and I still do. Don't bullshit me, Leslie. You're going to be in bed with your costar the minute you start the movie, and you won't give two shits about Coco, or remember her, by next week." They had known each other for a long time.

"Thank you for the vote of confidence," he said angrily. "There's no need to be rude to me, or to Coco. I have nothing more to say to you until you learn some manners, or buy yourself a heart. Maybe Liz can lend you half of hers since it's twice the normal size. There are only two big things on you, Jane. Your talent and your mouth. I respect the former immensely, but I want nothing to do with the latter. Just leave Coco alone."

"Why? Because I told her the truth? You wouldn't be this angry at me if that weren't the case. It sounds like I spoiled your game."

"There is no game here," he said quietly. "I'm in love with your sister. And if I have any luck at all, I'm hoping to convince her to live with me in L.A."

"Don't count on it. She's phobic about L.A., and everything it represents. She had some kind of childhood trauma, growing up around famous, successful people. She hates all of us, and eventually that will mean you too. She can't handle it. And if I know Coco, she won't even try."

"I give her more credit than that," he said coolly, praying Jane was wrong. She had a way of cutting close to the bone.

"You'll be disappointed by her, Leslie," Jane said, quieter now too. They were an even match, which wasn't the case between the two sisters, as they both knew. Coco was no match for Jane. She was neither mean nor tough. "We're all disappointed by her. She may have started this with you, but she won't finish it. She'll drop out. She doesn't have what it takes to see it through, or live your way of life. That's why she's a dog-walker instead of an attorney, and she lives where she does, among surfers who dropped out of the real world forty years ago. That will be her one day. It already is." There was bitterness in her voice.

"Why does it bother you so much that she's a dog-walker and dropped out of law school?" he asked, hitting the nail on the head. Jane was such an overachiever, obsessed with performance and success that she couldn't deal with what Coco had chosen to do. "It doesn't bother me in the least. I respect her for having the courage not to compete with all of you. It's not a fair race for her. She's not as tough as the rest of you. Or as mean, thank God. She's a gentle person who has found her own way."

"Thank you for your analysis of my sister. Believe me, I know her better than you. I love her, but she's a flake. And she's been lost all her life."

"I think I know her better than you do now. She's a much better person than you or me. She doesn't sell out. She follows what she believes, and she lives it."

"If you have her believing she can handle the kind of heat you take on a daily basis, you're kidding yourself and her. She'll collapse like a soufflé the first time the cameras go off in her face, or she sees you in some star's arms. She'll run like hell."

"I'll do everything in my power to see that that doesn't happen," he assured her sister, but he was worried about that too. And so was Coco. It wasn't an easy life being a star, or loving one. And Coco knew that well.

"Good luck," Jane said, sounding sarcastic, and they were both annoyed when they hung up. He hated the way Jane treated her sister and the things she said about her. She was so uncharitable and so merciless in her assessments and attacks. Jane gave no one a break. And Jane hated the fact that he was defending Coco. Who did he think he was? She was still angry when she told Liz about it that night. But at least Liz knew that Leslie could hold his own. Unlike Coco, who was wounded by her sister's razor tongue every time.

Leslie told Coco about the call from Jane when they went for a walk on Crissy Field that afternoon with Sallie and Jack. She said nothing as she listened, and he had censored some of their exchange so as not to injure Coco further, but he wanted her to know that he had stuck up for her. He thought it was time someone did. They were holding hands as they walked.

"You didn't have to do that for me," she said softly. "I can defend myself." But not as well as he, Leslie thought, remembering the things Jane had said. No one could survive that barrage. He thought it a mercy that Jane had already left the house when Coco was growing up.

"You shouldn't have to defend yourself against your sister. That's not what family is about. Or it shouldn't be."

"They were all like that," Coco said, thinking of her parents and sister. "I couldn't wait to leave."

"I can see why. I hate the things she says to you, the assumptions she makes. I can't bear the fact that she thinks I was just playing with you, that this was just a passing affair, for either of us. You're the woman of my dreams," he said, and leaned down to kiss her. They stood there for a long moment, kissing on the path, as people jogged and walked around them, smiling at the handsome young couple in each other's arms, and then they walked on. No one recognized him in Coco's arms.

Liz called them both that night and apologized for Jane. She said she had been stressed during the whole time they were on location, and being pregnant was a big change for her. But she was sorry that she had been hard on them. Leslie assured her that he was serious about Coco, and Liz said she understood and wished them well.

It was just one more thing to think about and deal with in their last days together in San Francisco. He took her out for a nice dinner the night before he left. He had asked for a quiet table in the back and made the reservation in Coco's name.

They were both depressed. They had shared a magical three and a half months, and they both knew it would never be quite the same again. Real life was about to intrude, possibly in a very big way. It frightened Coco more, but he was worried too. About how she would react to it, but also being away from her for several months now was going to be very hard for them both. He was dreading the separation as much as she was, and he hated the idea of being so far away once he left for Venice in ten days.

"When can you come down to L.A.?" he asked for the hundredth time.

"I've got Liz's friend Erin to cover me for three days at the end of this week." He looked relieved as she said it. Jane had worried him. He had been afraid Coco wouldn't come at all. "She'll walk Sallie and Jack too. Jane doesn't want her staying at the house."

"I'll try to keep my schedule as free as possible, but I'll have to be on the set some of the time. You can be there with me if you like." He didn't want to be away from her for a minute, and hoped the producer and director didn't want too much of his time. He was going to do as much of it as he could before she arrived.

"See how it goes once you start. I can wait at the hotel." They were going to be at the Bel-Air, where they had spent the night when she had gone to L.A. with him before. "I can visit my mother if she's not too busy or working on a book." Coco knew that if she was writing, she wouldn't see anyone at all. "I'll call her once you know your plans. You're my priority while I'm there, not my mom," she said, smiling at him, and his heart melted again.

Their last night together was sweet and tender. They made love several times, and Coco lay in bed awake at dawn, watching the sun come up, as Leslie slept in her arms. She couldn't imagine being there now without him. It was going to be so lonely, and even the house in Bolinas wouldn't be the same. He was part of everything now, and had become inextricably woven into the fabric of her life. But she also knew that his life was far bigger than hers. He had other things to do. The time they had shared in the house on Broadway had been a precious gift. She was grateful to Jane for that, even if she had little faith in what they meant to each other, or what would happen next. She had sent Coco a text message apologizing for shooting her mouth off, as she always did. And Coco had responded, thanking her, but they hadn't spoken to each other again. Her conversation with Leslie had the effect he wanted from it for Coco. Jane had backed off, which was easier for them at least. He didn't give a damn about what Jane thought, only about what she said to Coco. He didn't want Jane upsetting her anymore. And Liz had suggested she let it rest for a while too. Jane was busy anyway finishing up in New York.

Coco had helped Leslie pack the night before. And the car and driver came much too soon. He had production meetings on the set that day and had stayed with her until the last minute. He was catching a nine A.M. flight, and had to leave the house by seven-thirty. He stood in the doorway kissing her for a last time.

"Take care of yourself," he said, smiling at her. "I'll see you soon. I'll call you later, when I have a break. And you'll be in L.A. in a few days." He said it to reassure himself as much as Coco. He hated leaving her.

"I love you, Leslie," she said simply, suddenly aware that he no longer belonged just to her. He was going back to his own world, where others owned him too. Producers, directors, film companies, fans, agents, friends. Like it or not, she had to share him now.

"I love you too," he responded, kissed her one last time, and hurried toward the car. He couldn't miss his flight. The producer had offered to send a plane for him, but it seemed unnecessary and he had said he would take a commercial flight, just like everyone else. And since Coco wouldn't be with him, he didn't have to worry about protecting her from prying eyes.

She waved as the town car drove away, and he stuck an arm out the window and blew her kisses as they headed toward Divisadero, turned right, and disappeared.

She walked back into the house, wanting to cry. She went upstairs and lay down on their bed, which she would be returning to her sister and Liz soon. It wouldn't be the same without Leslie now anyway. She got up finally and put on a sweatshirt and jeans. She had to go to work. All she could think of now was him. She felt as though someone had ripped half her heart away.

He called her from the airport while she was walking the big dogs. She was out of breath from running, and he was about to board the plane.

"Don't forget I love you!" he reminded her.

"Me too," she said, smiling. They talked for a few minutes until he was seated in first class, and the flight attendant told him to turn off his phone.

She went through all the motions of what had once been her life, and now seemed like nothing without him. She wondered how only four months before she had thought this was enough. It no longer was.

She walked all the dogs on her schedule, and went downtown

at four o'clock. She had shopping to do. If she was going to meet him in L.A., she had to look respectable. It had been years since she owned clothes like that. She stayed downtown until the stores closed, and returned with a van full of shopping bags. She had even bought two suitcases to put them in. When she met him in L.A., she was going to make him proud.

Chapter 12

The plane took off from San Francisco airport at ten A.M. She was landing at LAX at eleven, and Leslie was meeting her at the Bel-Air Hotel at noon. He was sending a car and driver to the airport for her. He was hoping to spend two hours with her at lunchtime between meetings, and then he had to go back. They were planning to stay in that night. But the next day he was going to a dinner the producer was giving for the whole cast and major stars. Leslie was taking her with him. It was at the producer's home. It would be their first glimpse of the cast of the movie they were making, and there was a star-studded cast, of which Leslie was the biggest of all. It was going to be Coco's debut, going out with him in an important way. She had bought a sexy black cocktail dress to wear and gorgeous new high heels.

The car and driver were waiting for her at LAX as promised, and picked up her bags. They sped to the Bel-Air Hotel while she tried not to think of what might happen the next day, and concentrated on seeing Leslie instead. She wondered if he'd be different here.

Maybe even in the past few days, everything would have changed. What if Jane was right? It was Coco's worst fear.

They had an even bigger suite at the Bel-Air this time, and the same swans were there, swimming in the stream, and wandering the grounds. The hotel was peaceful, and the room was spectacular. She was still looking around after they set down her bags, when she heard the door open and turned to see Leslie beaming at her. He had been terrified she'd change her mind and cancel at the last minute, and he took her in his arms with such force he knocked the breath out of her. They were like two long-lost children who had found each other after a war. The past four days had been agony for both of them.

"I thought you'd never come!" he said, squeezing her tight, and then holding her away so he could look at her. She looked very grown up. She was wearing jeans with a soft white sweater that showed off her figure, a suede jacket, and sexy high heels. Her hair was brushed long, and there were tiny diamond earrings on her ears. He had never seen her that dressed up, and was impressed to see what good taste she had and how well she put herself together. Even when they had gone out to dinner in San Francisco, they had both been casual. He had never seen Coco look that way before. "Wow!" he said with admiration. "You're a knockout!"

"I feel like Cinderella at the ball. I may turn into a pumpkin any minute."

"Well, if you do, you're my pumpkin, and I will chase you all over the kingdom with the glass slipper." Her shoes were Louboutin and worthy of any star. As a connoisseur of stylish women, he recognized the signature red soles. "I like the ones you're wearing, by the way." He was full of admiration and praise of her. And he looked wonderful to her too. He was wearing one of his perfectly tailored custom-made English shirts, jeans, and alligator loafers, with a cashmere sweater over his shoulders. He'd had a haircut, and they had put a rinse in his hair to cover the few wisps of gray. It was even darker than before. He looked like the Leslie Baxter she had seen on the screen a hundred times before. But his eyes told her he was hers. That was all she wanted to know.

She complimented him on the fancy room, which he said was courtesy of the producer. "He said we can use his house in Malibu for the weekend. We should be private there. It's in the Colony, so we'll be secluded." He had thought of everything to make her happy and keep them safe from prying eyes. He poured them each a glass of champagne. "To our future," he said happily and then kissed her. She helped herself to a giant strawberry and fed one to him, and ten minutes later they were in bed. It seemed like centuries since she had been in his arms, and they both wanted to make up for lost time. They never got around to ordering lunch, and he had to rush back to the studio for another meeting to address the director's changes in the script. Coco got into the bath as he left, and he promised to be back by six.

She called her mother that afternoon, and her secretary told Coco that she was writing a new book. Coco didn't say she was in L.A., and she spent the rest of the afternoon walking around the grounds and reading a book she had brought with her. The weather was warm, and Leslie came back an hour late at seven. They stayed in the room that night and ordered dinner, watched TV, and talked about his meeting. He liked the cast and the producer, he knew the director and said he was difficult but usually got great results. He had worked with him before. They weren't starting in earnest until they got to Venice. He complained a little about one of his costars, and he commented that Madison Allbright, the female lead, who Coco knew was a megastar, was a very pretty girl.

"Should I be worried?" she asked, as they lay on the couch in the living room of the suite, with his head in her lap. She was stroking his hair, and he looked like a sleepy cat as he lay there, nearly purring with pleasure. He had missed her incredibly in the past four days.

"You don't need to worry about anything or anyone," he reassured her. "I'm the one who should be worried, the way you looked when you arrived." She had hung all her new clothes in the closet, and had sent the cocktail dress out to be pressed, so it would be impeccable for the producer's party the following night. Leslie hadn't told her yet that there would be press at the party. He didn't want to scare her. But there was no reason to worry. As far as they knew, she was just a date. It was only after they'd seen her a few times that they would catch on that this was a hot item, and she was his new romance. His psychotic ex-girlfriend was already engaged, so that was ancient history and of no interest anymore. Their brief alliance had been typical of Hollywood romances that came and went, even though it had been more troublesome than most, but at least he had managed to keep that out of the press, despite her statements and accusations that he was gay. Everyone had forgotten that by now.

They went to bed early since he had an early meeting, and Chloe called them before they fell asleep. She was up late with a babysitter, she said, her mother was out. She had started school that day and told them all about it. She was in first grade, and said she already had lots of friends. She reported to Coco that the pink bear named after her was doing well. For Coco, it was a taste of their summer idyll to talk to her again.

They both slept like tired children in the comfortable bed, and the operator woke them at seven the next morning. Leslie had to be at the studio no later than eight that morning, and he had a long day ahead. He told her with regret that he wouldn't be able to meet her for lunch as they were working straight through till six or seven, to address all of the director's notes for them. The party they were attending was scheduled to start at eight. Leslie was coming back to change and pick her up. And she said she'd be dressed by then. She was planning to get her hair done that afternoon.

"Will you be all right today?" he asked, looking worried as he finished breakfast. He had a cup of coffee to wake him up, while she drank tea.

"I'll be fine." She smiled at him. "I'll do some shopping and go to the museum." It had once been her city, and she knew it well. There were old friends she could have seen, but she didn't want to. She came here so seldom now that she had lost touch with most of them. And her life was very different than her classmates who had turned into Beverly Hills housewives, or were in the entertainment field now themselves, either acting or producing. She was one of the few who had fled. Most of them loved L.A.

Leslie kissed her goodbye when he left, and told her that he had ordered a car and driver for her. She showered and dressed and left the hotel herself at ten. No one paid any attention to her since there was nothing to link her to Leslie yet. She was still an anony-mous civilian as she wandered in and out of shops on Melrose, ate lunch at Fred Segal, and went to the L.A. County Museum of Art.

She was at the hairdresser at the hotel by four o'clock, and back in their room by six. She had just enough time to bathe, do her makeup, and dress, before Leslie walked in promptly at seven. He looked exhausted and was carrying his dog-eared script with a million jotted notes on it. They were getting new scripts the next day, which would include all the changes they'd just made. He had a lot of complicated lines to learn.

"How was your day?" he asked when he kissed her. It was a thrill for him to see her when he finished work. She was the peace and haven he came to, to seek refuge from the pressures he lived with when he was working. He loved having her be part of his normal life. It was everything he had hoped for when they talked about it, and he had never dared to dream.

"It was fun," Coco said, looking relaxed and happy, as he smiled admiringly at what she was wearing. She had on a thong, a black lace bra, her earrings, and high-heeled shoes, and her hair looked long and smooth. She was going to put her dress on at the last minute so she didn't crease it before that.

"Nice dress," he teased her, admiring her long shapely legs and perfect figure. He thought she looked fantastic. She had had a manicure and pedicure at the hairdresser too. Even before she put her dress on, she looked beautiful and sophisticated. The dog-walker he'd fallen in love with in San Francisco had transformed into a swan. He loved the original version, but he had to admit, he liked this one too.

He rushed into the bathroom to shower and shave, and he emerged a few minutes later, freshly shaven, with wet hair, buttoning an impeccable white shirt. He put on black slacks, a black cashmere blazer, and black alligator loafers, and while he was dressing, she put on the black cocktail dress. It was both sexy and demure, just low enough to reveal a hint of cleavage, but covered enough to be discreet. She looked so beautiful she took his breath away, and they stood admiring each other with a look of pleasure. It was the first night they were going out in public together in Leslie's world.

"You're the most beautiful woman I've ever seen," he said, looking dazzled by her as they left the room. She had a small black satin clutch under her arm. Everything she'd bought had been chic and enhanced her looks to perfection. He tucked her hand in his arm as they walked to the driveway to the car waiting for them, and a photographer snapped their picture. Coco looked startled for a moment and then recovered as they got into the car. She didn't comment, and Leslie patted her hand gently, and they chatted all the way to the producer's house which was nearby in Bel-Air.

When they got there, it was a palatial mansion and there were valet parkers. It was obviously a bigger party than they'd expected, but there were a lot of big-name stars associated with the film. There were no paparazzi outside, and Leslie whisked her in, relieved that there weren't, and a moment later they were standing in a marble hallway with a grand staircase and an art collection worthy of the Louvre. There were two Renoirs, a Degas, and a Picasso, and as they walked into the living room, a crowd of people stood among beautiful antiques and priceless art. The producer greeted them warmly and kissed Coco's cheek.

"I've heard a lot about you," he said, smiling warmly at her. "I knew your father. He was my agent for many years. I know your mother and sister too. You come from a bloodline of Hollywood legends, my dear." As he said it, Leslie smiled at a spectacular-looking woman who approached them, and Coco realized instantly who she was. It was Madison Allbright, his leading lady in the film.

"Maddie, I'd like you to meet Coco," Leslie said as he brought the two women together and their host disappeared into the crowd as other guests continued to arrive.

"He hasn't stopped talking about you all week," Madison said, smiling at her. She was wearing jeans, high heels, and a loose rhinestone-studded top. She had an incredible figure and a mane of long blond hair. She was the same age as Coco and looked about eighteen, with huge eyes and flawless skin.

The two women chatted for a few minutes as Coco tried not to be overly impressed by the people she was meeting. She reminded herself that she had met people as important as they were in her parents' home, but it had been a long time since then. She was more nervous than she seemed. But Leslie never strayed from her, he introduced her to everyone and kept an arm around her waist most of the time. He wanted her to feel his support. He knew this wasn't easy for her.

And before dinner was served, members of the press emerged from the crowd, seemingly out of nowhere, and began taking pictures of all the major stars. Leslie was top of their list. The first reporter looked inquiringly at Coco and raised an eyebrow. She looked straight into Leslie's eyes and asked the question his fans would want to know: "Someone new?"

"Not so new," Leslie answered, laughing. "We've known each other for a long time. I've been a family friend for years," he said, keeping a firm arm around her waist. He could feel Coco tremble, and took her hand in his.

"What's her name?" the female reporter asked him.

"Colette Barrington," Coco answered for herself, using her full name.

"Are you one of Florence Flowers's daughters?" she inquired, scribbling hastily on her pad.

"Yes, I am."

"I read all her books. And I love your sister's movies," she said with a barracuda-like smile. Coco knew the type well. "Whose dress are you wearing?"

She wanted to say "mine," but knew she had to play the game. If she had agreed to come with him, she had to do this right for Leslie. She owed him that at the very least. "Oscar de la Renta."

"Very pretty," she commented, jotting that down too, and then turned back to Leslie, as a photographer took their picture with his arm around her. "So, Leslie, is it serious or what?" "What" being just another pretty face.

"Miss Barrington was kind enough to join me this evening, which is a huge imposition for any civilized person," he said, flashing his dazzling smile at the reporter. "I don't think we need to destroy her reputation quite yet." The reporter laughed at what he said, and it seemed to satisfy her for the moment.

"When do you leave for Venice?" she asked with interest.

"Next week." He knew all the pat answers and how to fend off what he didn't want to address.

"Are you excited about working with Madison Allbright?"

"Extremely," he said with an exaggerated look of delight, and the reporter laughed again. "I mean, look at the shirt she's wearing. All those rhinestones would dazzle any man, or blind them." He looked serious then. "She's a wonderful actress, and I'm honored to be working with her. I'm sure she'll do a fantastic job."

"Good luck with the film," the reporter said, and moved on to someone else. She asked the same kinds of questions to everyone, as did half a dozen others who had been invited into the inner sanctum of the producer's home. They had been carefully chosen as to the publications that would do them the most good. Leslie whispered to Coco under his breath that it was a cattle show. A dozen photographers were there as well, taking pictures of everyone. They all got a turn with Leslie and Coco, they took some shots with her and others with him alone, and three of them wanted photographs of him and Madison. They cooperated fully with the press, and then the reporters and photographers were ushered out, and dinner was served at tables around the pool. There were orchids on every table and hundreds in the water. Leslie looked at her carefully when they sat down.

"Are you all right?" She had done a fantastic job with the press, just the right amount of pleasant and polite, a warm smile, and no information about anything but her dress. It was such a relief to be with someone who hadn't crawled all over him or kissed him, or draped herself on him like a snake, which most of the actresses he went out with did, to further their careers. She wasn't fighting him for the limelight or pretending a relationship they didn't have, although in their case they did. But she was so elegant and poised that you couldn't really tell if she was just a date for the evening, or something more. He was grateful for her discretion. And he could tell as he watched her that she had experienced this kind of thing before, and she did it well, better than she knew.

"I'm fine," she said, smiling at him. It would have been a perfect evening without the press, but that couldn't be avoided. She had suspected they might be there but didn't dare to ask. She hadn't wanted to scare herself more than she already was.

"You were splendid," he whispered, and then introduced her to everyone at their table, most of whom were actors in the film, and their significant others.

It was a beautiful evening, and they thanked the producer and his wife when they left. They were among the first to leave. Leslie had had enough, he had sung for his supper, and he could see that Coco was tired too.

There were four photographers waiting outside to take photographs of the guests as they left, and they leaped toward Leslie as he smiled at them and didn't flinch, and held Coco's hand. "What's her name?" one of them shouted at him.

"Cinderella!" Leslie answered. "Be careful or you'll turn into one of the mice," he quipped as he slipped gracefully into the car and pulled Coco in beside him just as quickly. They closed the door and drove away, as Leslie heaved a sigh of relief and looked at her. "It may please you to know, my darling, that I hate those evenings too. They're a bloody lot of work. I feel like my face may fall off if I smile one more time."

"You were fantastic," she said, smiling proudly at him.

"So were you. Did you hate every minute of it?" he asked, looking concerned.

"No," she said honestly. "In a weird way, it was fun. Though a little goes a long way. Madison is gorgeous," she commented, trying not to look worried, but she was. She remembered everything her sister had said about him and his costars, and so did he.

"I think you're far more beautiful than she is. She looked vulgar in that shirt. And her new breasts are about four sizes too big. I swear they've doubled since I last saw her. You looked far prettier and more elegant than she did. I was very, very proud to be with you," he said, and obviously meant it. "Thank you for putting up with it."

"I loved being with you," she said honestly. She hadn't even minded the press as much as she thought she would. "If it never gets any worse than that, I can deal with it."

He looked unhappy to admit it to her, but he wanted to be honest. "It gets a lot worse than that. They were all on their best behavior tonight, or they would have been tossed out on their ears, or worse." He smiled at her again, as they arrived at the hotel, and walked quickly back to their room in case one of the photographers had followed them, but no one did. He used bodyguards to accompany him at times, but not tonight. Everything about the evening had been well controlled and very tame.

Leslie took his jacket and shoes off and sprawled out on the couch, and then he remembered something the producer had given him, and fished it out of his pocket to show her. "I have the keys to the house in Malibu. We have it for the weekend," he said victoriously, and tossed them on the table. It was Friday night, and he was planning to take her there in the morning whenever they woke up, hopefully not soon.

Coco took her dress off and hung it up, and followed him into the bedroom. The evening had been a success, and she had survived it. It was exciting being with him, and she had felt how proud he was of her. She was equally so of him. And a few minutes later they both slipped gratefully into bed. As nice as it had been, it had been exhausting for him, and even for her, and they were both glad it was over. Now they could play for the rest of the weekend. Leslie was so tired, he was asleep before she could turn off the light. She kissed his cheek gently, and he didn't even stir. He was dead to the world. It had been a long day for him.

They ordered room service the next morning when they woke up, and Leslie carefully perused the paper. Without comment, he handed it to her. It was there, a large photograph of them talking to Madison Allbright. Coco's name appeared below the photograph, but it made no further comment. It looked totally appropriate.

"Well done," Leslie said, looking pleased.

Half an hour later they walked out of the hotel, and left for Malibu. They found the producer's house easily. The refrigerator had been stocked with everything they might need, and the house was spectacular, right on the beach in the Colony. Coco felt like Cinderella again. It was a fairy-tale life with him.

"It's not exactly Bolinas," she commented with a grin. It was an enormous house, designed by a famous architect and decorator, everything was white and pale blue, and there was a gigantic four-poster bed in their room.

It was the perfect weekend. They walked on the beach, slept in comfortable chairs on the deck, played cards, watched movies, made love, and talked about a thousand things. It was exactly the break they needed, and he promised to come to Bolinas the following weekend. He was planning to leave for Venice from San Francisco. It was more complicated for him, but he wanted to be with her until he left.

"What about coming over to see me once I settle in?" he asked lazily as they lay on the deck after a long walk on the beach.

"I don't think I can until Jane and Liz come home. And I'm not sure I can get coverage for that long, but I'll try. You'll be working hard anyway," she said sensibly, and he looked disappointed. He didn't want to wait to see her until he came back from Italy.

"I have to go back to the hotel at some point. And you can hang out on the set, or discover Venice. It's a lovely city." But more important, Coco thought he was a lovely man.

"I'll try. I promise. Liz said they'd be home in about two weeks." A week after he left. "I'll see if I can get Erin to cover for me." She was working for Coco that weekend, and she seemed to like the money and the work, which was a blessing for them. Coco had the feeling she might be using her often, if Erin was willing. She had another part-time job, and they still had to work it out.

"I'm going to go crazy without you," Leslie said, looking sad. "I hate being away from you," he confessed, but she didn't like it either. It had been an agonizing four days without him when he left San Francisco. And this was only the beginning. He went on location a lot, often for many months of the year.

"I'm going to miss you too," she said, trying not to think about it. But at least he was coming to Bolinas the next weekend before he left.

He wanted to ask her if she was feeling any better about moving to L.A. to be with him, but he didn't dare. He knew it was too soon. And things were not always going to go as smoothly as they had the night before. That had been a carefully orchestrated dog and pony show. At other times, left to their own devices, the press got out of control, and a feeding frenzy occurred. He knew just how much Coco would hate that, and he did too. But it was part of the territory for him, and not for her. She didn't have to put up with it, he did. And at its worst, it was insane, and no way for a sane person to live.

They went back to the hotel on Sunday afternoon. There was a lone photographer waiting outside, and he took their photograph as they got out of the car. Coco could see that Leslie was annoyed, but he flashed the camera a brilliant smile. His philosophy was that if they got you, at least look good and not like an ax murderer about to strike. It was why she had almost always seen him looking smiling and pleasant in the press.

They hurried to their room and he didn't follow them. Paparazzi were not tolerated on the grounds of the Bel-Air. And they stayed in their room with the shades drawn until she left. They made love and slept for a while, and reluctantly, he woke her, and she packed, took a shower with him, and dressed. She was taking the last plane back to San Francisco. Erin couldn't cover for her any longer. They'd had three days, and Leslie had to work long hours all week on final meetings.

Leslie carried her bags himself so they didn't have to call a bellman, and he handed them to the driver, and as he turned to say something to Coco, a series of flashes went off in their faces. It was the staccato of strobes, and Coco was temporarily blinded as she felt someone shove her, and the next thing she knew she flew through the air into the car before she knew what hit her. Leslie landed on top of her, and he was shouting to the driver to pull away, and they sped off. She was breathless as she turned to look at Leslie as he settled back against the seat.

"What was *that?*" she asked in amazement.

"Paparazzi. A whole flock of them. My darling, there goes your reputation. You will no longer be considered just a date for an evening. Now the fun begins." He looked resigned as he said it. He had been through it a thousand times before, but this was her first taste of what lay ahead. "Did I hurt you when I pushed you?" he asked with a look of concern, and she shook her head.

"It all happened so fast I didn't know what hit me. I didn't know if they pushed me or you did."

"I didn't want them swamping you completely. They would have. There were about ten of them. I suppose the word has gotten out, or they were just checking. They got what they wanted, so now they'll be hot on the trail. I'm glad you're leaving tonight. It would be annoying for you." And they would have no idea where to find her in San Francisco, which was a blessing. Leslie looked unruffled, and Coco took her cue from him and tried not to let it upset her. But there was no question, their secret was out now. Welcome to Leslie's world. And he was right, it was not always as tame as the night before. This had been somewhat rougher, although he had protected her quickly, with the instincts born of experience and practice.

He walked her to the security line in the airport, and kissed her. There were no photographers there. Only people who glanced at him, and then started as they recognized him, and then whispered to each other. And it was only after he kissed her and walked away that someone stopped him for an autograph. He waved at her, and she smiled at him, and then went through security. She already missed him, and she could feel the coach turning into a pumpkin as she walked to the gate alone.

Chapter 13

Much to Coco's amazement, her mother called her at eight o'clock the next day just before she left for work.

"Good lord, now what are you up to?" She had no idea what her mother meant. She had overslept after getting in late the night before, and she was rushing to pick up her first set of dogs.

"I'm on my way to work. Why?"

"Well, you must be doing more than that these days. There's all sorts of gossip about you and Leslie Baxter in this morning's paper. It says you spent the weekend with him at the Bel-Air and you're his latest fling. When did that happen?" her mother asked with interest.

"Over the summer," Coco said cautiously. She didn't want to discuss it with her mother, or hear the kind of comments she'd gotten from Jane. Her mother had been taken down a notch or two over her affair with a much younger man, but she was still the same person she had always been. And she had never approved of any man in Coco's life. If she did this time, it would be a first, and Coco didn't think it was likely. Some things never changed.

"Don't you think he's a bit racy for you?"

"He's a pretty normal person, when he's not in L.A."

"They all are, or most of them, when they're somewhere else. But Coco, he's a very, very big star, and you aren't. In the end, he'll go back to his own kind. You're probably a breath of fresh air for him, but that won't last," her mother warned her, echoing more politely what her sister had said.

"Thank you for the vote of confidence," Coco said tersely. "I can't talk about it now, I'm late for work."

"Well, have fun with him, but don't take it seriously."

"Is that how you feel about Gabriel?" Coco asked.

"Of course not. Why would you say a thing like that? We've been together for a year, and we have great respect for each other. It's not just a summer fling," she said, sounding offended.

"Well, maybe this isn't either. We'll see what happens."

"You'll get your heart broken when he leaves you for some famous actress. Besides, he's too old for you." Coco rolled her eyes as she listened.

"I can't believe that you of all people are saying that to me. I've got to go, Mom."

"Well, just be careful. Enjoy it while it lasts." They both hung up, and Coco was upset about it as she got into her van. Why did everyone think he was just going to play with her and dump her? Why couldn't a movie star fall in love too, or be a real person, or want more than just a quick affair with a costar? Why did everyone believe that she meant nothing to him? It was a statement of what they thought of her, even more than what they thought of him. That she was so insignificant that she would mean nothing to him, and it would end, because she didn't deserve him. She was depressed about it all day, and she couldn't talk to Leslie until late afternoon, because he was in meetings. He finally called her at six o'clock and sounded drained.

"Hi, sweetheart. How was your day?" he asked, and she immediately told him about the call from her mother. She had also had a call from Jane, but didn't take it.

"It's all so stereotypical," she ranted at him. "The movie star and the dog-walker. My mother acts like all I'm good for is a piece of ass, and only a temporary one at that."

"Don't underrate yourself," he said seriously. "I think you would make a great piece of ass long term."

"Oh shut up," she said, and smiled for the first time all day.

"Don't let it get to you. There was a lot of stuff in the papers today. Including a great shot of me with both hands on your bottom shoving you into the car. I think that one was my favorite."

"What are they saying?" Coco asked, sounding worried.

"One of the papers said you are my 'latest beauty.' Another one calls you my new mystery girlfriend. It's all pretty standard stuff. We didn't do anything wrong. You weren't falling-down drunk, neither was I. We didn't have sex in public, although we could try that. It just says you're my new hot date, or my current fling or whatever. After we've been around together for a while, it'll calm down. Right now, it's hot news and everyone wants to know where you live and who you are. And you don't live here, and I'm going away, so you're fine." But what if she did live there, and with him? They'd be all over them every day. It was exactly why she didn't want to move to L.A. "Don't worry about it. It was bound to happen sooner or later. Now we're out in the open and it's done. It's kind of like losing your virginity to the press, it only hurts the first

time, and as long as we behave decently in public, we'll be fine."
She thought he was being overly optimistic, but she didn't want to
argue with him about it. It was still very much on her mind that
night when her mother called her again. Coco almost didn't answer, but in the end she did. She called to tell Coco that some
reporter had called her asking where her daughter lived. She
wondered if it was the reporter at the party who had asked if she
was Florence Flowers's daughter. One of the papers had reported
on that fact, according to Leslie. And her mother had had her secretary tell them that she lived in Europe and was only in L.A. for a
few days.

"That was clever of you, Mom. Thank you." She was grateful for
that at least, even if her mother thought she wouldn't hold Leslie's
interest for long.

"It'll throw them off the scent for a while. When are you seeing
him again?" Her mother was curious about them now.

"This weekend. In Bolinas. He leaves next Monday for Venice on
location, he'll be gone for a month or two."

"That may end it between the two of you. He'll be working with
his costars all the time, and you'll be six thousand miles away.
Hollywood romances don't usually survive that. Absence makes
their hearts fonder of the people they're working with, not the
ones they leave at home. Kind of like a cruise."

"Thanks for the reassurance," Coco said glumly. It was more of
what she'd heard before.

"You have to be realistic about it, if you're going to date someone like him." Coco wanted to ask her how realistic she was about
her twelve-year-old boyfriend, but she didn't. She was always more

respectful of her mother than Florence was of her. "Who's in the movie with him?" Florence asked with interest.

Coco reeled off the names of his costars, among them Madison Allbright. "She'll probably be the one," her mother said. "She's a gorgeous girl. It would be hard for any man to resist her."

"Thank you, Mom," Coco said, sounding depressed again, and after thanking her mother for covering for her with the press, she got off the phone. She lay in bed awake for hours, thinking about what she'd said. And by morning Coco was in a total panic over Leslie's costar. She was too embarrassed to even say it to him, but she was seriously worried about it, and had a miserable week as a result. She never once mentioned Madison's name to him when they talked. And it was all she could do not to burst into tears when he walked into the house on Friday night. He let himself in with the keys he had kept, and found Coco in the bathtub with her freshly washed hair wrapped in a towel. He took one look at her, burst into a broad smile, took off his clothes, and got into the tub with her, as she grinned.

"Now this is what I call a homecoming," he said with obvious delight as he kissed her. And within minutes of getting into the tub with her, they made love. And in spite of all her fears during the week, it was a perfect night. It was as though he had never left to go back to L.A. Everything felt as right as it always had.

They left for Bolinas with the dogs the next morning, and the weather was glorious. It was typical late-September weather and hotter than it had been all summer. The nights were warm and balmy, which was rare. And they had never been more in love with each other. There was no sign of his having fallen for Madison

Allbright. But then again, they weren't in Venice yet. But Coco was no longer as worried. There was no doubt in her mind, as she lay in his arms on the deck under the stars, that he was as in love with her as she was with him. He said it to her over and over again, and she believed him. There was no reason why she shouldn't. He had begged her again to come to Venice, and she had promised him she would.

He had brought all the press clippings about them from that week. They had run a number of photographs of them, and there was no question now, the media were hot on their trail.

They talked about it over breakfast on Sunday morning.

"We knew it would happen sooner or later," Leslie said philosophically. "Any new face on the scene snags their interest. They have nothing better to do than look for gossip and juicy stories."

"I'm not very juicy," Coco said as she glanced at their photographs again, in every paper, and sipped her tea. "Wait till someone tells them I'm a dog-walker. That'll really do it for them." Instead they had latched on to who her mother was, which made her more interesting. She had already told him that they had called her mother.

"You're very juicy!" he assured her, and leaned over to kiss her. "What do you think Jane will say if they call her?"

"That I'm a hippie and a flake and a complete zero, or something equally charming," Coco said, looking sad about it.

"If she does something like that, I'll kill her," Leslie said with fervor. "You know, I really think it boils down to jealousy with her," he said, looking pensive, as he glanced at the ocean and then at Coco. "I think she's pissed off that you're beautiful, do what you want, and you'll always be eleven years younger. I think she's just narcissistic enough to consider that an insult. Maybe she was always jealous of you as a little kid, and you just didn't know it. I don't think this has anything to do with your dropping out of law school, or moving to Bolinas. I think that's her excuse.

"I think, bottom line, she's mad at you for what you are and she's not, starting with younger. You're soft, kind, gentle, compassionate. People love you. Jane is tough as nails, she's had to be to get where she is. The only thing warm and fuzzy about Jane is Liz. She'd be unbearable without her. Everyone likes Liz better, and you. That must be tough for her to stomach. And on top of it, she was an adored only child until you came along when she was eleven. And you fucked it all up for her. I think underneath all the bullshit she talks about and accuses you of, she hasn't forgiven you for that yet. She always puts you down, and treats you like a five-year-old." What he said had a ring of truth to it, even to Coco, and it shed light on her sister's negative attitude toward her, as long as she could remember. His theory certainly explained it.

"The worst part of it is that I act like I'm five years old when I'm around her. She scared me to death when I was a kid. She was always threatening to get me in trouble with Mom or Dad, or treating me like her slave. She still does." Coco sighed then. "And I let her do it. I don't know what she's so pissed off about. She's always been Mom's favorite, and Dad thought she walked on water, especially when she started producing. And even before that, he was thrilled when she went to film school at UCLA. I don't think my going to Princeton impressed him half as much. He thought it was stuffy. I redeemed myself when I got into law school at Stanford. I don't think I even wanted to. I just did it to make him happy, and then I hated every minute of it. I set myself up to fail. All I really wanted to do was get a master's in art history and work in a museum. He said I'd never make a dime at it, and it was stupid."

"Why don't you do that now then?" Leslie suggested, his eyes lighting up at the idea. "Either that or become a vet," he teased her. She loved every dog she walked and treated them like children. But he knew she had a passion for art too. Her tiny house was crammed with art books.

"What would I do with that now? It's a little late to go back to school."

"No, it isn't. And if it makes you happy, why not? You could go to UCLA, if you come down there to live with me. Or Stanford or Berkeley, if we move up here." He was still trying to convince her to live with him. It would be easier for him in L.A., but he was open to moving to San Francisco for her.

"Maybe," she said, looking pensive. "I've always been interested in art restoration. I took a class on it in college, and I thought it was fascinating." She had never admitted that to anyone but him. Ian wasn't interested in art, only the outdoors, and she was younger then and it suited her too. And her father had thought that any kind of academic pursuit other than law school was a waste of time.

"Why don't you spend some time learning about it? You can decide what to do with it later. Maybe nothing, but I agree with you. I think it would be interesting to know." She was an entirely different creature than her family, and it was obvious even to Coco that he respected that, and they didn't. He made her feel good about herself. And his theories about Jane's anger toward her struck a chord with her too. "Venice might be particularly fun for you, if you're interested in restoration. They've been fighting to keep the place from falling apart for years. It's an absolute gem of a city."

He had been there before, she hadn't. She had been to Florence and Rome, and Pompeii, and Capri once on a yacht with her parents, but never Venice.

"I'm not going there to see the art." She smiled at him. "I'm coming to see you."

"You can do both. I'll be working a lot of the time anyway. And if you're into churches, there are about ten million of them, one more beautiful than the next." It sounded exciting, and she had promised him she would come when Liz and Jane got back. They hadn't solved the problem of where they would live eventually, or even if they would live together, but little by little they were making plans together, and Coco thought the rest would unfold, if it was meant to be. If she left San Francisco, she would have to close her business. Her father had left her enough to live on comfortably, but she always felt guilty if she wasn't earning a living on her own. And her dog-walking business had proved to be more lucrative than she'd expected, and supplied all her needs. It allowed her to save and invest the rest, which provided a nest egg for her future. She didn't want to be dependent on him. Her mother and sister were both big earners and made a fortune at their careers. Coco had never made a lot of money, but she had a far more modest lifestyle than either of them.

He pressed her several times that afternoon about when she was coming to Venice. All she could tell him was soon, hopefully in a few weeks. Jane and Liz hadn't given her the exact date of their return yet, but she had already warned Erin that she'd be needing her services to cover for her when she left. She wanted to stay with Leslie in Italy for a week or two, although he was hoping to convince her to stay longer.

They went back to the city just after sunset. Leslie drove and Coco looked at the cliffs and the ocean view she loved, thinking about how lucky she was to live there. She didn't feel ready to leave that yet. She'd been happy in Bolinas for the past three years. It would be a sacrifice for her to leave her comfortable, safe haven at the beach. No one bothered her, or intruded on her. There was no press to worry about when she was at the beach cottage with him. It was totally, completely peaceful. But she knew that she would be lonely there now without him. Leslie had become part of everything she did. And his world was light-years away from this. She wondered if maybe, in the future, they could still spend time here when he was between films. He had loved being at the beach with her that summer, but he was used to bigger cities, and a much bigger life. She knew that to some degree, she would have to adjust her life to his. It was inevitable, since he had the more demanding career. For now, she had none at all, just a job.

They spent the night watching an old movie she had never seen before, and loved it. Leslie said it was a classic and he was right. He was knowledgeable about practically every movie ever made. And Coco loved learning about them from him. He wasn't just a handsome actor appearing in commercial hits, he had a profound interest and passion in his trade, and had studied both important and obscure films and what made them great. He had admitted to her once that he wanted to be Sir Laurence Olivier when he grew up, but knew he never would. But he at least wanted to be as good as he could be, in the kind of films he did. Producers tended to cast him in films that capitalized on his looks and charm, but he was a good actor nonetheless, and always had an eye out for more serious parts. He was an excellent performer despite the sometimes lighter roles he played. Jane had said as much about him too, and had a deep respect for his work. He loved doing comedy too, and had a knack for it. He brought his own flair for humor into play, and audiences loved the funny movies he did. But his heart always longed for something deep. Inevitably he had been lured by the fortune to be made doing commercial films. It was hard to resist that kind of money, and they paid him well.

They stayed up late that night, eating ice cream in the kitchen, and talking about the part he was going to play in the current film. He was trying to bring something more to it, and tried out several ideas on Coco, some of which sounded very good to her. She was impressed by how much thought, preparation, and study he put into his roles. She wondered if all actors did that, and Leslie laughed when she said it. "No. Only the good ones." He admitted to being worried about working with Madison. He had heard from others who had worked with her before that she never knew her lines. It would make it harder for him, and he and the director had already had several arguments about how Leslie viewed his part. They attributed different motivations to the character, and so far the screenwriter was backing up Leslie, which didn't sit well with the director. He had a big ego, and wanted everyone to agree with him. It was going to be challenging for Leslie in Venice. And he was anxious for her support when she came over.

It was two in the morning by the time they got to bed, and he had to get up at seven, in order to leave by eight. They made love hurriedly when they woke up, and took a shower together. He ate a hasty breakfast, kissed her frantically before he left, and promised to call her when he arrived, as she wished him luck with the movie. The house seemed shockingly silent the moment he was gone, and even more so when she came home for a break at lunchtime. She hated knowing that he was going to be far away, but she knew that if she was going to exist in his life, she had to get used to it. He was away on location a lot. Either that, or if she stayed with him, she would have to go with him, which meant she could no longer have a job or even a life of her own. She was afraid of giving up her life for him and living in his shadow, but he had insisted for months that that wasn't what he wanted. He wanted a partnership with her, not a groupie, a handmaiden, or a slave. Unlike her sister, who thought her main purpose in life was to take care of all her minor needs, as though she were a lesser person, which in Jane's mind Coco was. Coco thought Leslie was right the day before when he said that Coco's arrival in their family had upset the applecart for her, and she hadn't forgiven her younger sister for it yet, and maybe never would.

The house was agonizingly quiet that night. Coco watched one of Leslie's old movies, a favorite of hers, hoping to feel less lonely, and instead it only made her miss him more. She sat in her sister's bed, staring at his face on the screen, as it hit her just who she was in love with. "Oh my God . . . ," she said out loud. She was madly in love with one of the most successful actors in the world. He may not have been Laurence Olivier, but in the eyes of his fans, he was even bigger. She could suddenly hear in her head all the things her sister had said, and wondered what she was thinking, and what he was doing with her. She was nothing and no one, she was just a dog-walker who lived in a shack in Bolinas. Maybe Jane was right. She was overwhelmed by a wave of terror, and cried herself to sleep that night. The only thing that consoled her was a call from Leslie in the middle of the night when he arrived in Venice. He sounded exhausted after two long flights, one of which had been delayed in Paris.

Coco tried to explain to him everything she had felt when she went to sleep that night, the raw terror of realizing who he was and who she wasn't.

"That's total garbage," he said, after listening to her. "You're the woman I love, and don't you forget it." But all she could think of after they hung up was the question that was dancing in her head and had been after watching his movie. For how long? And if Jane was right, what gorgeous, glamorous movie star would replace her? Coco shuddered at the thought.

Chapter 14

Jane and Liz returned the week after Leslie had left for Venice. Coco moved back to Bolinas the night before, and she came by to drop off the keys on her way to work on Monday morning. She had left everything as neat as possible, made sure the kitchen was scrubbed, and the sheets and towels in the master suite were changed, and had even left flowers for them. Liz had called to thank her when they got home on Sunday. And Coco was stunned when Jane opened the door on Monday when she dropped off the keys. Jane was wearing black leggings and a tight black sweater, and there was an enormous bulge in her middle. She was five months pregnant. The rest of her was as thin as it had always been, but she looked as though she had a basketball in her leggings. In comparison to the rest of her, her belly seemed huge. Coco laughed the moment she saw it.

"What's so funny?" Jane asked testily, as Coco smiled at her.

"Nothing. You just look really cute." She pointed to her niece or nephew as Liz walked up behind Jane with a broad smile.

"Pretty impressive, don't you think?" Liz asked her proudly and then hugged Coco. The two sisters exchanged a cursory hug and kiss, and her belly bumped into Coco as she did.

"It looks great," Coco confirmed as she handed the keys to her sister.

"Thanks for bailing us out for four and a half months," Liz was quick to say. They were home a month earlier than planned. The filming had gone well.

"It worked out for me too," Coco said, and then blushed. "I mean . . . well, anyway . . . I enjoyed it."

"I'll bet you did," Jane said crisply. "Where's Leslie?"

"In Venice. He'll be there till Thanksgiving, or maybe even Christmas."

"That'll give you both time to come to your senses," Jane said unkindly. "Mom sent me all the clippings. You started a hornets' nest when you went down to L.A. It'll only get worse if you two stay together. I hope you're ready for it," she said bluntly.

"We're taking it one day at a time," Coco said, echoing his words.

"Do you want to come over for dinner tomorrow?" Jane asked her.

"I can't. I'm busy," Coco said without hesitating for a second. She had no desire to get beaten up by her sister, or listen to her say how quickly Leslie would dump her after he fell in love with his costar in Venice. She didn't want to hear it. She was worried enough about that herself.

"Another time, then. We need you to stay here again next weekend, by the way," she said offhandedly as the three of them stood at the front door. It didn't even occur to her to ask Coco if it was convenient. She just assumed she'd do it. She always had before.

"I can't," Coco said, savoring the unfamiliar words. It was hard for her to get them out, but she did. Jane would always be the domineering, slightly scary older sister to her. There were too many years between them for Coco to feel like an adult, with needs of her own, when dealing with her.

"You have to. We're going to L.A. to set up post-production. We have to see a couple of houses to rent, and I want to meet Mom's boy toy. I take it you haven't met him yet." Jane gave her an inquiring look, prepared to pounce on her if she had and failed to tell her.

"No, I haven't," Coco confirmed. "Mom was working on a book when I went down to see Leslie, so I didn't see her." They both knew that their mother didn't take calls or see visitors when she was writing. They wondered if those rules applied to Gabriel too. Maybe they did. In any case, they applied to them. And Jane said their mother had just finished her book, so she had agreed to see them.

"Anyway, I need you to stay with Jack for the weekend. You can take him to Bolinas if you really have to. Once we rent a house, we can take him with us." Coco knew they would be in L.A. for post-production for several months. "But we're flying this weekend, so we have to leave him here."

"I won't be here," Coco said simply, looking her sister in the eye. It was the truth.

"Why not?" Jane looked stunned. She couldn't remember when Coco had ever said no to her. This was a first. It had taken Leslie to free her. Liz didn't say a word but wanted to cheer, and smiled at Coco over Jane's shoulder, to give her courage.

"I'm leaving for Venice on Friday. I'll be there for a couple of weeks. I'm sure Erin can walk him for you. She's covering my clients for me. I was going to ask you if I could leave Sallie here, but I guess I can't."

Liz was quick to answer for her. "Yes, you can." She wanted to validate the bold move she had made. "Erin can walk them both, and Jack won't be so lonely if Sallie is here with him." The two dogs had just lived together for four and a half months and got along well. Jane didn't say a word, she just stared at Coco in disapproval and disbelief. Errand girls and slaves didn't just get up and leave, and make their own plans. This was going to require some serious rethinking for Jane.

"Have you thought about what it's going to be like dealing with the paparazzi in Venice?" Jane asked coolly. It was as though she wanted to punish Coco for her independence.

"Yes, I have," Coco said quietly. "We'll do the best we can. We're going to try and go to Florence for a few days, during a break."

"That sounds fabulous," Liz said enthusiastically, and Jane just looked at her, wondering who and what her sister had become. The change in Jane was more obvious, and physical. The one in Coco was far less visible, and ran deeper. So far motherhood didn't seem to have softened Jane's heart. She was as tough as ever.

"We got the results of the amnio," Jane suddenly volunteered. "The baby's fine." She looked faintly disappointed for just an instant. "It's a boy." They had both wanted a girl, but Liz said she didn't care as long as it was healthy. "That's going to be a lot harder to deal with. Boys are not exactly my thing." She smiled as she said it, and Coco laughed.

"I think you'll do just fine." And Coco privately thought that she was much too tough to be the mother of a girl. In fact, she couldn't see her as a mother at all. This had been an interesting choice for her, and a big surprise to them all. Their mother hadn't recovered from it yet. The prospect of being a grandmother didn't thrill her. It just made her feel old, and she had never been enamored with babies, even when she was young and they were hers. She was even less so now, particularly with a man twenty-four years younger in her life. "What are you going to name him?" Jane and Liz had talked about it a lot, and were leaning toward naming him after Jane's father. Liz's father had been named Oscar, which neither of them liked.

"We'll probably name him after Dad. We want to see him first and see what he looks like."

"I can't wait to see him myself," Coco said sincerely. It was still hard for her to believe that they were going to have a baby. It was the most unlikely turn of events she could imagine. "You look great, by the way. The only thing different is the basketball under your shirt."

"The doctor says he's pretty big," Jane said, looking anxious for a minute. She wasn't looking forward to the birth. The thought of it terrified her, but Liz would be there coaching her. More than once she had wished that they had impregnated her instead. "His father was six foot five, so he should be pretty tall." Jane was quite tall herself, and Coco was the same size, although in her mind's eye, Jane was always much taller, since she had been when she was a child. That was the memory that had stuck with her.

Coco left them to go to work then, and she dropped Sallie off at their place on Thursday afternoon. They were leaving for L.A. the next day, and Coco was flying to Venice via Paris. She was already packed and wildly excited about it. She and Leslie were talking two and three times a day, and he was thrilled that she was coming.

When she dropped Sallie off, Jane was out, and Liz invited her in for a cup of tea. Coco had just finished work, and she was leaving at the crack of dawn the next morning.

"How are things going with Leslie?" Liz asked her as they sipped their tea.

"Unbelievably well," Coco said, beaming at her. "I still can't believe it happened, or figure out why he wants me."

"He's lucky to have you," Liz said with a look of conviction. She had always hated the way Jane gave her such a hard time. The dynamic between the two sisters pained her, and she had always hoped that Coco would break the ties that bound her one day. But Coco hadn't gotten there yet. The age difference between them, and their history, had always done her a disservice.

"We seem to have gotten off pretty lucky with the press so far," Coco said cautiously. "It scares me, but hopefully they won't get too crazy over us. I know Jane thinks they'll eat me alive, but it's not like I just got out of jail or am a drug addict or something."

"Dropping out of law school, living in Bolinas, and running a dog-walking business are not felonies, the last time I checked," Liz said wisely, "contrary to the impression your sister may have given you. You're a respectable person, work for a living, and you're a terrific woman. They can't do much with that," Liz reassured her, and Coco sighed.

"Jane thinks he's going to dump me for someone else in a hot minute. And I worry about that too," she confessed. "There's a lot of temptation in that business, and he's human like everyone else."

"He seems to be a human who's very much in love with you," Liz reminded her. She had heard from Jane about the dressing-down Leslie had given her, which Liz thought was a good sign of his love for Coco. "There are plenty of solid relationships and good marriages in this business. You just don't hear about them, because the tabloids would rather talk about the bad ones. Have a little faith in yourself, and in Leslie. He's a good guy." Coco basked in the warmth of what she was saying and visibly relaxed.

"I can't wait to see him in Venice," Coco said with a happy smile.

"You deserve a break. I can't remember the last time you took a vacation." Not since she had gone on vacation with Ian three years before, as far as Liz could recall. It was about time she came back to life again, and it was obvious that she had. "I can't wait to hear about it when you get back."

They talked about the baby then, and how excited Liz was about it. She said Jane was too, and was getting used to the idea that it was a boy. She said they were turning the guest room into a nursery, and planned to interview baby nurses in L.A. Coco was excited about it too. She had never expected to have a niece or nephew, and Chloe had reminded her that summer of how great kids could be.

She was leaving just as Jane returned, and for once Jane looked happy and relaxed in an outfit that showed off her protuding belly. Coco couldn't help smiling at it and told Jane she had just dropped Sallie off to stay with Jack.

"Have fun in Venice," Jane said, sounding gentler for a change. She was in good spirits and said she had just seen the doctor again. Everything was fine, and the baby's heartbeat was strong. She had already started an album with pictures from their sonograms, which sounded funny to Coco. The sentimental gesture was so unlike her, she wondered if she'd be a good mother after all. Neither of them had a strong role model on that score, since their own mother had been anything but maternal. She was competent and responsible, but much more interested in her career and her relationship with her husband than she had ever been in her children. She had forged a relationship with Jane ultimately, as she grew up, but had never managed it with Coco. They had too little in common. Coco had always been the odd man out. She had come along too late, and was too different from all of them to ever feel welcome in their midst. "Call us when you get back!" Jane said as she left, and Coco drove back to Bolinas, thinking about Leslie and Venice and everything they would do there together. She couldn't wait to see him on the set, and to take a few days traveling around Italy with him. He had already promised her a gondola ride under the Bridge of Sighs, which, he had been told and reported to her, would ensure that they would be together forever. It sounded good to her.

Her mother called her that night and invited her down for the weekend, since Jane and Liz were coming, and Coco explained that she was going to Venice to see Leslie.

"Are you sure that's a good idea?" her mother asked her, sounding suspicious. "You don't want to run after him, dear. It might make him feel like you're stalking him."

"I'm not stalking him, Mom," Coco said, rolling her eyes as she listened. "He *wants* me to come. He said so."

"All right. If you're sure. But he must be very busy if he's making a movie. Men don't like it when women hang all over them. It makes them feel smothered." Coco wanted to ask her if Gabriel felt "smothered" by her, but she didn't. She didn't want to get upset fighting with her mother. Besides her mother and Jane always won.

"Thank you for the advice," Coco said tersely, wondering what she had ever done to deserve them. Her sister thought she was just a notch on his belt, and not a very attractive one, soon to be replaced by someone more glamorous and better-looking. And her mother thought she was stalking a movie star, who didn't really want to see her. Why was it that neither of them could imagine that she was worthy of him, and he truly loved her? "How's Gabriel?" she asked, to change the subject.

"Wonderful!" she said, sounding radiant over the phone. Her romance interested her a great deal more than Coco's, and she had no trouble imagining that he adored her. It was much harder for her to imagine that Leslie was equally in love with Coco. "We're having dinner with Jane and Liz this weekend." She was a little apprehensive about it, knowing how tough her older daughter could be, and how critical, but she was excited to have Gabriel spend time with them, and share their happiness with them. Coco thought she was being naive, and Jane would use every opportunity to find fault with him and turn it against their mother later.

"Have fun," she said to her mother as they hung up. And she was annoyed with herself later when she realized that her mother had scored a hit again. She was suddenly worrying that maybe she was forcing herself on Leslie and he didn't want her there as desperately as he said.

"I will *not* listen to them," she said to herself, as she zipped her suitcase closed at midnight. "Mom and Jane are full of shit. They hate me, they have always hated me, and I don't care what they say. He loves me, and I love him, and that's all I need to know. He *wants* to see me, and we are going to have a wonderful time in Venice." She said the whole speech out loud, and was proud of herself. And as Coco walked out on the deck and looked up at the stars, she prayed that everything would be all right when she got there. After that, she walked back inside and went to bed, and reminded herself that twenty-four hours later she would be in Venice, with the love of her life. It didn't get better than that, movie star or not. She wasn't going to question it, or dwell on what her mother had said. She was going to fly to Italy and have the time of her life.

Chapter 15

Coco made the same trip that Leslie had made almost two weeks earlier. The only difference was that he had made it in first class, and she flew in coach. Leslie had offered to buy her a first-class ticket too. But Coco liked to pay her own bills, and had refused. It was a long, eleven-hour cramped flight from San Francisco to Paris. She had slept fitfully on the flight, and she arrived feeling rumpled and dirty. She was too excited to fall into a deep sleep, and had watched four movies. She had a three-hour layover in Paris, where she managed to take a shower in the public bathroom, and have something to eat at an airport café. And she was starting to get seriously sleepy when she boarded the plane to Venice. She dozed off right after takeoff, fell into a heavy sleep, and the flight attendant had to wake her when they landed. It was the middle of the night for her, and she felt as though she had been traveling for days.

She had gone through customs in Paris, so all she had to do in Venice was walk off the plane, and get her passport stamped by immigration on the way out. She brushed her teeth, washed her face, and combed her hair before getting off. She had worn an old sweatshirt on the flight to Paris, but had changed into a new black sweater and black leather flats before disembarking in Venice. And as she left the plane, carrying a large tote bag, she saw Leslie waiting for her on the other side of immigration. It was lunchtime in Venice and the late October sun was very bright. But brightest of all was the look of joy in his eyes. He was thrilled to see her and swept her into his arms immediately, took the heavy bag from her, and walked her out of the terminal to a waiting limousine. He handed the driver her baggage stubs, and he went to claim her luggage while Leslie kissed her passionately in the car and told her how glad he was to see her. They both acted as though they hadn't seen each other in months, although it had been two days shy of two weeks.

"I was so afraid something would happen and you wouldn't come," he admitted to her. "I can't believe you're here!" He looked ecstatic.

"Me neither. How's the movie going?"

"We have two days off. And I think they're giving us next weekend off too." It was perfect. "I booked us into a hotel in Florence next week," he said, beaming. He could hardly keep his hands off her as the driver appeared with her bags, put them in the trunk, and got back in the car. They were riding in a stretch Mercedes, which the producer had brought in from Germany, specially for him. He said the film was going well, although he and Madison had had some problems, but he didn't go into detail. All he wanted was to concentrate on Coco now that she was here.

It was a relatively short drive from the airport to the enormous parking lot, where they had to leave the limousine, and from there he had rented an enormous *motoscafo,* a speedboat, to take them to the Gritti Palace, where he was staying. The rest of the crew and some of the stars were staying at other smaller hotels, but he and Madison had been given suites at the Gritti, which was considered the most luxurious hotel in Venice. Madison had wanted to stay at the Cipriani, but the producer had insisted that it was farther and too complicated for transportation every day. And the director had taken refuge at the Bauer Grunwald, which he insisted he preferred. Leslie was delighted where he was.

The *motoscafo* took them rapidly down the Grand Canal, as Coco looked around her with awe. As they left the parking area, the city began to reveal itself before them. Churches, domes, basilicas, ancient palazzi, and eventually St. Mark's Cathedral and the square were dazzling in the October sun. It was easily the most beautiful place she had ever seen. And Leslie smiled at the look of wonder on her face.

"Beautiful, isn't it?" he said, and then pulled her into his arms and kissed her. He couldn't think of a better place to share with her than this. He had already rented a gondola for that night to take them under the Ponte dei Sospiri, the Bridge of Sighs, on their way to dinner, if she was still awake by then. There were a thousand things he wanted to do with her and show her. This was only the beginning. And he was grateful to have time off to be with her that weekend. They had been working hard.

When they arrived at the Gritti Palace, they were instantly whisked inside, and Leslie took her to their rooms. She had expected him to have a suite, but instead they had given him several suites, joined together, to form a palatial apartment just for him. It was in his contract, but more elegant and luxurious than anything Coco had ever seen. And the view from his windows was spectacular, looking across the canal at other palaces, many of them private and still owned by noble Venetians. It was a remarkable and unique city.

Several of the hotel's formidable staff were bowing and scraping to Leslie, as two maids disappeared to unpack her bags, and a liveried waiter arrived carrying an enormous silver tray with food for her, and a perfectly chilled bottle of Louis Roederer Cristal champagne.

"One gets a little spoiled on location," Leslie whispered to her with a sheepish grin.

"I'll say," she said, trying to remind herself that she was here for only a week or two. And when she left, the royal coach she was traveling in with him would turn into a pumpkin again. She had to remind herself of it constantly. Being with Leslie was a totally Cinderella experience, and without a doubt, he was the handsome prince. It was hard to believe that the glass slipper would really fit her in the end. That only happened in fairy tales, but clearly this was one.

They settled onto an enormous yellow satin couch as the waiter poured her tea for her, and served her a plate of exquisite little sandwiches, and then discreetly left the room.

"I'm not sure if I'm Cinderella or Orphan Annie," she said, looking at Leslie in disbelief. "Last time I looked, I was in Bolinas. How did I ever wind up here?" She hadn't expected anything like this. All she had thought about was being with him again, it never occurred to her what his life would look like on location, or the lengths to which producers went to, to make things comfortable for him. This was way beyond comfortable. It was opulent in the extreme.

"It's not a bad life, is it?" He smiled mischievously. "But it was miserable until you got here. It was no fun without you," he said, and showed her through the rooms. There was a gigantic, palatial bedroom, all done in exquisite antiques, with a frescoed ceiling, two sitting rooms, and a private dining room big enough to entertain two dozen friends. He had a small office, a library, and there were so many vast marble bathrooms in the suite that she lost count when he showed them to her. There were fresh flowers in every room, and he had picked out a pink marble bathroom for her, with a spectacular view of Venice.

"I think I'm dreaming," she said as she followed him, and then without further ceremony, he pulled her onto their enormous canopied bed. It was fit for a king, but there she found the Leslie she knew and loved again. Despite the elegance of their surroundings, he was as loving and playful as he had been in Jane's house and Bolinas with her. One of the beauties about Leslie was that he enjoyed his life and everything that went with it, but he wasn't full of himself. And all he wanted now was to be with her.

They made love and slept through the afternoon, and then they took a bath in the enormous pink marble bathroom. He told her to put on jeans. He wanted to take her for a walk, and show her some of the wonders of Venice. They scampered quickly through the hotel lobby, and his private *motoscafo* deposited them in St. Mark's Square. From there, they wandered through some of the narrow back streets, walked into churches, bought gelato from a street vendor, and strolled over tiny bridges that covered the smaller canals. She totally lost her sense of direction as she walked with him, but neither of them cared. He was learning a little bit of the city, but being lost in Venice was never ominous. Wherever you went it was beautiful, and somehow you wound up back in the right place in the end. They saw other lovers like them walking everywhere, and most of them were Venetians at that time of the year. The weather was cool and sunny, and as the sun disappeared finally, they went back to the *motoscafo,* which deposited them back at the hotel.

Back in his palatial rooms again, she stood looking out at the city, and then turned to Leslie with all the love she felt for him in her eyes. "Thank you for inviting me here," she said softly. It was almost like a honeymoon, being there with him, and the most romantic place she'd ever been.

"I didn't invite you," he reminded her, with a look that mirrored hers. "I *begged* you to come. I wanted to share this with you, Coco. It was just a job until you came." She couldn't help smiling at the term. It was an awfully nice place to work.

They talked about the movie then, and how it was going. He poured her a glass of champagne, and eventually they went to dress for dinner. He was concerned that she might be too tired to go out, but she had slept just enough that afternoon to revive her. She didn't want to miss a minute of the time with him, especially while he didn't have to work.

This time, when they went downstairs, there was no sign of his *motoscafo,* and a huge gondola was waiting for them. The gondolier was wearing a striped shirt, a short navy blue jacket in the evening chill, and the traditional flat hat worn by all the gondoliers. The boat itself was a wonder of shining black trimmed in gold, and looked just as all the gondolas had for hundreds of years. As promised, they slid under the Bridge of Sighs on the way to dinner, as the gondolier sang to them. It was right out of a dream.

"Hold your breath and close your eyes," Leslie whispered to her, and with eyes wide at first, she did, as he kissed her gently on the mouth, holding his breath too, and as they came out from under the bridge, he told her she could breathe again. She opened her eyes and smiled at him. "Okay, now the deal is sealed," he said, looking delighted. "According to legend, we will be together forever. Hope you don't have any objection." She laughed as he settled into the seat next to her again. What was there to object to? The most romantic, loving man on the planet? Or the most beautiful city she'd ever seen? It would have been hard to imagine anything to object to in any of it, and she didn't.

"I want to come here on our honeymoon if we ever have one," she whispered, as they slipped under another bridge and she was swept up in the mood. It would have been impossible not to be, especially with him. "If we ever get married, I mean."

"Now you're talking," he said, looking elated, as they stopped at some small stone steps, with a cheerfully lit restaurant at the top of them. The gondolier handed them out, and Leslie walked into the restaurant with his arm around her. "The concierge at the hotel said this would be quiet and discreet. A lot of the locals come here. It's not fancy, but he said it's very good."

The restaurant was small and only half full. The headwaiter led them to a small cozy table at the back of the restaurant. No one paid any attention to them, and they dined like everyone else, without intrusion or interruption. Leslie said the press had been fairly good here so far, and hadn't bothered them. Madison had caused something of a stir when her press agent called the fan magazines with some absurd stories, but they had only been bothered on the set, and nothing had come of it since, much to everyone's relief. It hadn't gotten the European press going. Leslie didn't tell her what the stories were, only that they were insignificant and annoying and typical of her. He said she liked to be the queen bee on the set of every movie she made, which didn't bother him, as long as she learned her lines, showed up on time, and didn't slow things down in any way. He was enjoying Venice, but he was hoping to come home as soon as possible to her. And he said the movie was on schedule so far. They were going to be shooting in St. Mark's Square that week, and inside the basilica, which had taken endless permits, but their Italian production assistant had been a genius at getting them everything they needed.

They chatted all through dinner, and now and then Coco felt a wave of drowsiness come over her. Her time zones were completely out of whack, but she enjoyed the evening thoroughly, and a walk in St. Mark's Square afterward. And then they went back to the hotel in their gondola. She was yawning when they returned to their rooms. She could hardly keep her eyes open by then. It was midnight in Italy, and she'd been up for many hours. Somewhere along the way, she had lost a whole night's sleep, but it was for a good cause, to say the least.

Coco was sound asleep before Leslie could even make love to her, and he lay there watching her as she slept, with a smile on his face, and then cuddled up next to her. Having her there was like a dream come true for him. And together, they slept until almost noon the next day. They awoke to the sun streaming into their rooms, and got up to start their day after they made love.

He took her to Harry's Bar for lunch, which was an old favorite of his. She had Risotto Milanese as only they could make it, with lots of saffron, and he had lobster salad as they discussed what to do that afternoon. He had hired a gondola for her again, as it was more romantic than the faster, more practical *motoscafo* that took him to work every day. They were in no hurry, and spent the afternoon visiting the Doge's Palace, and admired the Campanile, the bell tower of the basilica. They strolled through the Royal Gardens, and then wandered in and out of several beautiful old churches before going back to the hotel. It had been another perfect day. They decided to order room service, since he had a six A.M. call on the set to get his hair and makeup done. She had promised to come with him, at least for the first day. After that she was going to explore Venice a little on her own. For a tiny city, there was so much to see, and she didn't want to bother him while he was working on the film.

Leslie traveled very simply, and never took an entourage with him. He said he didn't need an assistant as long as the concierge was good, and the Gritti Palace was known for their remarkable staff. He used the hair and makeup people on the set and never brought his own. For a major star, he was surprisingly undemanding and without pretension. He said he preferred less fuss and attention. Unlike Madison, who had brought her own hairdresser, two makeup artists, her sister, two assistants, and her best friend with her. She was known for giving producers long lists of her personal needs and demands before signing a contract for a film. She traveled with a personal bodyguard and a trainer too, and she had demanded that all of them be put up in the same hotel with her. It didn't win her friends on any set where she worked, but she was the biggest female box-office draw in the world at the moment, so no one argued with her. They just gave her what she wanted to keep her from making a scene, which she never hesitated to do.

"It's a little wearing to be around all that," Leslie admitted to Coco, as they left for the set the next day. Coco was wearing a warm sheepskin jacket in the cool morning air before the sun came up, and a favorite old pair of cowboy boots. She looked fresh and young and beautiful with no makeup on, her big green eyes, and her mane of copper hair. She was everything he admired in a woman, honest, simple, natural, undemanding, without putting on airs. Her goodness and integrity shone from within, which enhanced everything about her. They made a handsome pair as they strode onto the set, and walked into the trailer that had been set up for him, under the arches around St. Mark's Square. She couldn't imagine how they'd gotten it there, but it gave him a place to be, and relax or study between scenes.

The hairdresser and principal makeup artist were waiting for him. They had been hired locally, but spoke good English, as Leslie chatted easily with them and sipped a cup of steaming coffee, and Coco sat quietly in a corner, watching the scene.

Despite the early call, they didn't start shooting until nine o'clock. Breakfast had been brought in for all of them, and finally, there was a knock on his dressing-room door to say that they were ready for him. They had been setting up the lighting till then with a stand-in who took his place for him, a young Italian of similar size and coloring. Leslie was wearing a well-cut black suit and turtleneck for the scene, with black suede shoes. He looked sexy and beautifully put together as he left the trailer in full stage makeup, which hardly showed. He never let them overdo it, and his hair had been meticulously done and sprayed.

Coco watched in fascination as the other actors in the scene appeared. The director took his place next to the cameraman and instructed him. He knew exactly what camera angles he wanted, and spoke to the actors quietly. Coco had been on sets before with her sister, but there was a seriousness and intensity about this, which was new to her. The actors in this film were the biggest stars in the business. No one took it lightly, and they didn't want to miss a shot. There was a fortune to be made if it was a success, and Oscars to be won for extraordinary performances. That was obviously on everyone's mind. There was no fooling around here.

She stood quietly where she'd been told to stand, so as not to disturb anyone, and she watched Leslie carefully as he rolled through the first take of the scene. Madison wasn't in it and it was another hour before she appeared, in a sexy red cocktail dress she was only half-wearing, with a coat over it, with her famous cleavage and her long spectacular legs, and sexy high heels. She went right into the scene with him and had to run across the square. Someone was trying to kidnap her, and Leslie was running after her, trying to rescue her, although she was supposed to have no idea who he was. It was a complicated, intricate plot, and Coco knew the story from reading the script, and helping him learn his lines. She remembered the scene, but it was different here, with actors giving electrifying performances and a tension you could feel. Carabinieri were helping to keep the portion of the square clear that they were using, and someone silently gave Coco a fold-ing chair so she could sit down. She nodded her thanks, and a few minutes later a woman with blond hair sat down in a chair next to her. Coco had no idea who she was, other than that she was someone in Madison's entourage.

"She's good, isn't she?" the woman said to Coco, during a break. "I would kill myself if I tried to run in those heels." Coco laughed in response.

The woman didn't ask who she was or why she was there. There were so many people on the set that no one bothered to ask. Like the other woman, and everyone else on the set, Coco had a pass on a cord around her neck, which meant she was part of the crew or cast, or someone's entourage. "They look good together, don't they?" the woman said, watching them more closely, as Coco studied them too. She hadn't really thought about it, but they did. Leslie had his arms around Madison in that scene. She was out of breath from running in the scene before, and melted slowly against him when he finally caught her. It made Coco faintly uncomfortable to realize they did look good together, which was why they had been cast for their parts. "Did you see the piece about them in the magazines last week?" the woman asked casually, glancing at Coco again. "They looked hot. Stories like that get interest going in the film. And who knows what will happen by the time they leave here?" The woman grinned. Coco gave her a weak smile, and looked slightly confused as the woman obligingly took a fan magazine out of her enormous tote bag and handed it to Coco to read.

Coco gulped as she saw the picture on the cover. It was a picture of Leslie and Madison kissing, with a headline that ran above it and said, "Too hot to handle. New romance for Leslie and Madison begins in Italy." Coco didn't want to read it, but was mesmerized by it, and flipped the magazine open to the right page. There were several more photographs of them, two of them kissing, and one where they were both looking startled, as though they'd been interrupted doing something they didn't want to be seen doing. Her stomach turned over as she read it. The article said that he'd broken up with his last girlfriend in May, who'd accused him of being gay. And it went on to say that he looked anything but while diving into a hot romance with Madison Allbright on the set of their new movie, being filmed on location in Italy. The article said nothing about Coco, and her appearance with him in L.A. She handed back the magazine to the woman a few minutes later and thanked her. Coco was feeling sick.

This was what her sister had meant. This was what it was like being in love with a major star, who slept with his costar in every film. They had been there for two weeks. It hadn't taken him long. And there was no denying what she'd just seen in the pictures in the fan magazine. He was clearly kissing her. She felt wooden as she sat there, watching him with Madison now, wondering how he could have had the bad taste and cruelty to invite her to Venice, when he was having an affair with his costar. Admittedly, he had invited her before he left the States, but he could have stopped her from coming if he had any heart at all. And he had made love to her for the past two days. What kind of man would do a thing like that? Apparently, a movie star. It killed Coco to admit it, but Jane was right.

She sat feeling like a robot, watching him do his scenes for the next three hours. All she wanted was to go back to the hotel and pack her bags. To hell with Leslie Baxter. There were tears in her eyes as she watched him. All she wanted now was to go home to Bolinas and cry.

Leslie came to find her when they were finished working, and walked her back to his trailer, where the caterers would serve them lunch. She noticed that he said something to Madison that made her laugh as they left the set, and he put an arm around her and gave her a hug. Coco wanted to throw up as she watched them, but she said nothing as she walked back to the trailer with him, nor once they got inside.

"How did it look?" he asked her, as he took off his jacket and sprawled into a chair with a smile at her. "It felt like shit in the beginning, and I still think the running scene looks stupid, but the director won't give it up. I liked the scene under the arches a lot better. It would look better too if they could get her tits under control." Coco couldn't believe he was saying that to her after what she'd just read. He had suddenly become someone she didn't know. "I take it you didn't like it," he said, looking worried, misinterpreting her silence as criticism of his performance, which upset him even more. He was a perfectionist about his work.

"I thought the scenes were fine," she said quietly, sitting down in a chair across from him. She didn't know whether to tell him what she thought of him now, or wait until they got back to the hotel after work.

"Then what didn't you like?" Her face was suddenly white and drawn. He valued her opinion now, just as he had when he asked her to read the script.

"Actually, what I didn't like a hell of a lot," she said, deciding to

get it over with now and not wait, so she could go back to the hotel and leave before he finished work that night, "was the article
someone just handed me on the set."

"What article?" He looked blank, which disturbed Coco even
more. He had always been honest with her, or so she thought, and
now he was playing dumb.

"I can't remember the name of the magazine, I don't usually
read that kind of crap. It was an article about the affair you and
Madison are apparently having on the set. You might have mentioned that before I came over. It would have saved me the trip."

"I see," he said, as he dropped his head and stared at his feet,
and then he stood up with a serious look. "I can imagine how you
feel about it. If you don't mind, I'd like you to come with me for a
minute. Am I assuming correctly that the person who gave you the
magazine was one of the lovely people in Miss Allbright's entourage?"

"I think so. She never introduced herself. But I saw her arrive on
the set with her."

"Wonderful. That would be either her sister, one of her fourteen
assistants, or her best friend from high school, all of whom arrived
by private jet from their favorite trailer park." He had opened the
door to the trailer then and gestured for Coco to follow him. She
hesitated for a moment, but he looked so ominous suddenly that
she didn't argue with him. She walked down the steps and under
the arches to a similar trailer nearby, considerably larger than his.

He knocked on the door, and without waiting for an answer, he
opened the door, and pulled Coco in behind him. The trailer was
full of people, and reeked of cheap perfume and smoke. There

were people laughing, others on cell phones, wigs on stands, and she noticed the woman who had shown her the magazine, who smiled at Coco as they walked by her. Leslie walked through them to a room at the back, where he knew Madison hung out to get away from the others. He knocked, and at the sound of her voice, he yanked the door open, and stood glaring at her. She was sitting on a couch with a man wearing an undershirt and jeans, and his arms and chest were covered with tattoos. She looked up in surprise when she saw Leslie.

"Hi there," she said with an innocent look. "Something wrong?" He had been fine on the set with her that morning.

"You could say that. One of your girlfriends showed Coco that disgusting piece in the fan magazine you invited here last week in order to fuck our lives up."

"I didn't invite them," she said innocently. "My press agent did. I can't control who he contacts."

"The hell you can't." He turned to Coco, looking absolutely livid. "Miss Allbright, or her press agent, as the case may be, issued an invitation to the sleaziest fan rags in the business to come over here and take our pictures. And someone in the process, we don't know who of course, mentioned to them that Madison and I are having an affair, in order to make them more interested in making the trip over. As it so happens," he said, turning his furious gaze from Coco to his costar, "I am not having an affair with her, never have, and don't intend to, in spite of her remarkable figure and fabulous implants and extraordinarily beautiful legs," he said, spitting the words out. "As it so happens, she is married to her hairdresser, who is this gentleman here"—he pointed to the man with the tattoos for Coco's benefit—"who works on every movie with her because it's in her contract, and he keeps a firm and loving eye on her. And furthermore, although it is meant to be the darkest secret on the set in order to keep her sexy image hale and hearty, at my expense in this case, she happens to be five months pregnant. And coincidentally, it's an equally dark secret that she's happily married. Now that we've cleared that up, and you've screwed my life up with that bullshit you fed to the press, perhaps you'd like to explain to my friend here that what I'm saying is accurate. And by the way . . ." He turned to Coco again. "The photographs they took of the two of us kissing were from a scene we shot last week. I don't know who the hell they paid to get on the set, unless it was one of your people," he said nastily to Madison. "But I don't need that kind of publicity at the moment. I happen to be in love with this woman, and neither she nor I needs or wants the headache from that kind of rumor." There was practically steam coming out of his ears as Madison looked at him uncomfortably, and her hairdresser husband cleared his throat and walked out of the room. He didn't look the least bit jealous of Leslie, and apparently he had nothing to add to what he'd said. He smiled at Coco on the way out, and went to join the flock of hangers-on in the other room. Fights between costars were commonplace, and Madison got in a lot of them. Her husband preferred not to get involved and kept a low profile since their marriage was a secret. She handled her battles herself.

"Now come on, Leslie. You have to admit, that kind of thing always spikes interest in a film." Madison smiled at Coco and saw the look of amazement in her eyes. Coco had never been in the midst of anything like it. "And if you tell anyone I'm pregnant, I'll kill you," she said to Coco in an even tone. It was why she had worn a coat over the tight red dress. The only person who was supposed to know was the woman handling wardrobe. Madison had signed the contract to do the film before getting pregnant, and she didn't want to lose the part. Instead, Leslie had almost lost Coco.

"Do me a favor," he said to Madison as he glared at her, "we have to work together for the next few months. This is a job for both of us. Try not to destroy my personal life for me while we do it. I won't screw with your life. Don't screw with mine."

"All right, all right," she said, getting up from the couch, and Coco could see the faint bulge under her dressing gown. She was wearing a tight corset under her dresses, but she took it off whenever she was in the trailer. "Just don't tell anyone that I'm married and pregnant. It's bad for my image. Sex symbols aren't supposed to be married *or* pregnant."

"How are you going to explain the baby when it comes?" Leslie asked, fascinated by her lies, and Coco could see he didn't like her. It was easy to see why.

"All the world needs to know about the baby is that it's my sister's," Madison said coolly.

"And where are you planning to have it? Under a cabbage leaf somewhere?"

"That's all worked out," she said, as she looked at Coco. Madison was beautiful, but Coco realized now that there was nothing nice about her. All she cared about was her career. And who she rolled over in the process was of no interest to her whatsoever. "Honey," she said to Coco, "take him back to the trailer and give him a blow job. He needs to relax before our next shot." With that, Leslie propelled Coco out the door before she could say a word, and through the mob at the front of the trailer. Coco followed him back to his own trailer, and looked at him with deep regret in her eyes. It had been an awkward scene for both of them. Nothing would have embarrassed Madison Allbright, or ever had.

"Leslie, I'm sorry," she said mournfully, "I just thought . . . when I saw that magazine . . ."

"I know. Don't worry about it," he said, sitting down heavily in a chair. He still looked upset. "There's no way that you could know that was all manufactured bullshit. That bitch would sell out her own mother, if she ever had one, to make a buck, and hype a film." It was an ugly side of the business that Coco had never experienced firsthand. "But you also have to know," he said, giving her a warning look, "that I'm sure that's not the last time it will happen. Madison is a sneaky little bitch, and she'll pull another stunt like that again. It can happen on any movie, innocently or intentionally. You just have to know that I'm not going to do something like that to you. I have too much respect for you to do that, and besides, I love you. If I get involved with another woman, or want to, I'll tell you about it, and get out of your life. You're not going to be reading about it in fan magazines or the tabloids. As badly behaved as I may have been in the past, I've never done anything like that to anyone, and I certainly don't intend to start now. I'm sorry it upset you," he said, reaching out to her, and pulling her down on his lap. Coco looked mortally embarrassed.

"I'm sorry I made such a stink. I didn't mean to cause a problem between the two of you." It wasn't going to make it any easier for him to work with her, but in a way, he was glad he had made things clear to her. If Madison was going to start rumors about having affairs on the set, she was going to have to start them with someone else. He had no intention of blowing his relationship with Coco over her.

"I love you. And why on God's earth would I want a bimbo like that?" She had suddenly looked like what she was, in the midst of all her sleazy assistants and sidekicks. She looked like a cheap tramp. "That's the kind of thing that happens in this business, Coco. It's a constant rumor mill, and most of the people you work with will climb all over you or stab you in the back to get ahead. It's very rare to work on a film with decent people who won't sell you out whenever they get the chance. You may have to get used to that."

"I'll try." It had been an eye-opener to see what kind of operator his costar was, and how Leslie had handled it. And then suddenly he laughed.

"I guess I kind of lost it for a minute there." They had both noticed how her husband had slithered out of the room. "I did think the suggestion about the blow job was rather good though. What do you think?" He glanced at his watch and then back at her. "Do we have time?" He was only teasing, and they both laughed. And then he looked at her more seriously. "Round one. You've just had your first trial by fire. Welcome to show business."

"I think I flunked abysmally," Coco said, still looking somewhat shaken by it. She had been ready to walk out on him when she thought he was having an affair with Madison. What if she had left Venice without talking to him? She had learned a valuable lesson.

"On the contrary," he said, looking proudly at her. "I think you did surprisingly well. We survived it, and I don't think the evil little witch will screw with us again." Leslie made them sound like a team against the world. But they both knew that Madison might not, but sooner or later someone else would. Coco was beginning to understand that it was the nature of his business. People used each other at every chance, in every way they could.

They ate lunch together quietly in the trailer, talking about the film and the things Coco wanted to see in Venice, and as they did, she suddenly realized that her sister had been wrong. She had come up against just the kind of thing Jane had said she would. And contrary to what Jane had predicted, she hadn't collapsed like a house of cards, and Leslie had stood by her and been true. She'd been shaken by it, but was not destroyed. Better yet, the fan magazine had been wrong too. So far so good.

Chapter 16

Coco spent several hours on the set watching Leslie film every day. And she had noticed tension between him and Madison several times. Sometimes it increased the electric atmosphere of the movie, and at other times, it made their love scenes almost painful, and surely not easy for him. He didn't like her and it showed. But they had to work together anyway, and neither of them wanted it to impact the film. It made Coco realize again that this was acting, it wasn't love. Leslie was astonishingly good at what he did. More so than his costar, who constantly forgot her lines.

And when Coco got tired of watching them film, she spent hours wandering around Venice. Leslie teased her that she had been in every church in the city. She went to the cloisters of San Gregorio, Santa Maria della Salute, and Santa Maria dei Miracoli. She spent hours exploring the Accademia di Belle Arti, the La Fenice Theatre, and the Querini Stampalia Gallery. She had seen every inch of Venice by the end of the week and could tell him all about it when he got back to the hotel at night. He was tired after long days of shooting, arguments with the director, and the stress of working with Madison. But no matter how worn out he was, he was always thrilled to find Coco waiting for him at the hotel. And they were both looking forward to their weekend in Florence. He had rented a car and planned to drive them there himself.

It was the night before they left that he complained there had been paparazzi on the set. Some of them had come from Rome and Milan. He suspected Madison, or her press agent, of tipping them off, although he admitted that it was bound to happen. Everyone passing through St. Mark's Square that week had seen them filming. It was hardly surprising that the press had shown up, with major American film stars making a movie in their city.

"I'm glad you weren't there today. I don't want them crawling all over you too." He said the carabinieri had kept them off the set, but there had been a dozen of them waiting for him at the trailer. And if Coco had been there, they would have besieged them both. As far as Leslie was concerned, the British and Italian paparazzi were the worst and the most persistent. He had always found the French press more respectful when he made movies there.

He got out a map that night, and they planned their route to Florence. He wanted to take her to the Lido too, but they hadn't had time yet, since it was twenty minutes away by boat. He had been busy working, and she had walked all over Venice on foot.

They were planning to stop in Padua and Bologna on the way to Florence. She wanted to see the Scrovegni Chapel in Padua, with the Giotto paintings she had once studied, and told Leslie about, and the thirteenth- and sixteenth-century walls that surrounded the city, and the cathedral. In Bologna, she wanted to see the Gothic Basilica of San Petronio, and the Pinacoteca Nazionale Gallery, if they had time.

They planned to get to Florence in the late afternoon, and there was so much they both wanted to see there. The Uffizi Gallery, the Pitti Palace, the Palazzo Vecchio, the Duomo. There was no way they would be able to see it all. And when they set out in the morning from Venice, it was a glorious day. His *motoscafo* took them to the giant parking lot where their rented car was waiting. He had rented a Maserati, and he grinned as they roared off in the powerful car.

The road to Padua and Bologna was beautiful, and then they got on the Autostrada to reach Florence. He had reserved a suite for them at the Excelsior Hotel, and Coco insisted they stop at the Uffizi Gallery first. She couldn't wait to see it. She had been there years before with her parents, and Leslie had never seen it at all. He was discovering a whole new world with her. They were relaxed and happy when they checked into their hotel.

They had dinner at a restaurant the hotel had recommended that night and then walked around the square. They ate gelato and listened to street musicians, and then walked back to the hotel. It was a whole different set of wonders from Venice. And Coco said she was sorry they couldn't get to Rome as well.

"Stay until I finish the movie," he teased. "Then you can see it all." She wanted to see Perugia too, and Assisi. But they both knew she had to go back. She couldn't just abandon her clients and her business, and Erin could only cover for her for two weeks. But they were both sad to realize that they wouldn't see each other again until he returned to L.A. It would be at least another month, maybe two, if Madison didn't start remembering her lines. It was becoming increasingly stressful working with her, and Leslie didn't want her to ruin the film. She had promised the director to spend the entire weekend studying the script. Leslie hoped she would. Her cleavage wouldn't be enough to carry the film.

Coco and Leslie spent a peaceful night in their elegant suite. Just as they were about to leave the next day, they were startled by the hotel manager when he appeared at their door. He was deeply apologetic and had no idea how it had happened, but someone had informed the press that Leslie was there. There were a flock of paparazzi outside the hotel, waiting for them. The security had managed to keep them out of the lobby. But there was no way they would be able to leave without being mobbed. It was big news that Leslie Baxter was in town. When he heard it, Leslie looked at Coco with an unhappy frown. Fortunately, the hotel had put their car in the garage.

The manager made the only suggestion he could think of, to spirit them out the service entrance in the rear. He said that perhaps if they disguised themselves, with dark glasses, hats, whatever they had on hand, they could escape before the paparazzi saw them leave. He bowed low as he expressed his regrets, which told Leslie that someone in the hotel had squealed.

A bellman came to get their bags, as Coco put on dark glasses and a scarf over her head. They weren't looking for her, they wanted Leslie, they both knew, but if they got him, they would discover her as well. And having seen her in Los Angeles with him, if she turned up in Italy too, everyone would know that this was a serious affair. Leslie was hoping to spare them that kind of heat for a while. And once they knew who she was, if they discovered where she came from, they would besiege her in Bolinas too. He didn't want that to happen to her. It was bad enough that he had to live with it, but for the moment, he wanted Coco protected from the press.

They took the elevator to the basement, and exited through the garage. Leslie was wearing dark glasses and a golf cap the manager had unearthed somewhere, and they quickly got into the car, and drove out the back entrance behind a laundry truck and a van from a local florist. They were gone long before the paparazzi discovered that they had checked out. They drove peacefully back to Venice, congratulating themselves on having outfoxed the press.

"Well done," Leslie said, smiling at her. Thanks to the manager's warning, their exit had been extremely smooth. Both he and Coco were relieved.

They got back to Venice early enough to take a boat to the Lido, and have a drink at the Cipriani. It was a spectacular hotel, with an incredible view of Venice. And then they went back to the Gritti, to dine privately in Leslie's rooms. It had been a perfect weekend. Coco was thrilled that she still had another five days with him. She loved living with him again. They were golden days for both of them. Before they went to bed, they called Chloe. She reported on everything she was doing at school, and had won the prize for best costume on Halloween. She asked when she was going to see him. Leslie had promised to spend Thanksgiving with her and her mother in New York, if he finished the film in time. He looked apologetically at Coco after he hung up.

"That was stupid of me, wasn't it? I should have asked you what you were doing first. I just usually try to spend the holiday with her." Coco knew he hadn't seen her in two months, and it would be another three weeks before he did.

"Don't worry about it," Coco said, smiling at him. "I always spend it at my mother's in L.A. We usually do Christmas there too, but this year we're doing it at Jane's. She'll be too pregnant to travel by then." It felt weird to say it. The idea of Jane being pregnant and having a baby still seemed totally foreign to her.

"I'll come to see you right after Thanksgiving," he promised. "Hopefully, we'll be finished here by then. And we'll get a break while they set up in L.A. We should get a decent hiatus over Christmas too. I'll spend every minute I can with you. I promise." She leaned back into his arms with a blissful look.

They tried to be together that week as much as they could. She watched him on the set for hours, and in her spare time she went back to the churches she liked best, and discovered some new ones. She could find her way easily around Venice by then. Leslie was impressed. She knew the city far better than he did, but he rarely got time off, except at night.

They went out to dinner on her last night, to a small, funny restaurant on a back street. A gondola took them there, a different one than they'd had before. He took them to one of the ancient landing blocks, and from there they walked down an alley and around a corner to the restaurant. Coco had no trouble finding it, after her extensive explorations of Venice. It was charming when they walked in. It had a small garden, although it was too cold to sit outside. And the food was delicious, the best they'd had so far. They shared a bottle of Chianti, and were in good spirits when they left, although both of them were sad that she was leaving the next day. But with luck, he'd be home in a few weeks. The shooting had gone well that week, better than the week before. Madison had actually remembered her lines. A weekend of studying the script had paid off.

Leslie stopped on the street outside the restaurant and kissed

Coco. Her stay in Venice had been perfect for both of them, almost like a dream come true. And better yet, it was real.

"Do you have any idea how much I love you?" he whispered to her and kissed her again.

"Almost as much as I love you," she answered when she caught her breath and smiled into his eyes. And just as she did, there was an explosion of flashes everywhere, a sense of people shoving them, and before either of them could understand what had happened, they were surrounded by pushing, aggressive paparazzi who had lain in wait for them and jumped them. It was an ambush. Someone had tipped off the press, and it was not just a handful, it was a mob. And Leslie and Coco had a good distance to cover to get to the boat. Leslie wanted to pull her out of the crowd and protect her but had no idea how. He didn't even know which way to turn, and their only escape was via the gondola. There were at least thirty photographers between them and the boat.

Coco was looking up at him in shock and confusion, and he shouted to her, asking her which way to go. He had gotten totally turned around, and a half bottle of wine didn't help.

"That way!" She pointed over the shouts of the crowd. They were pushing and shoving Coco and Leslie to take their pictures. The photographer closest to them had a cigarette pressed between his lips, and he was so close that the ashes from it dusted her coat, as Leslie shoved him back.

"Come on, boys," Leslie said firmly in English, "that's enough . . . *Basta!* . . . No!" he said, shouting at one of them who was pulling at their coats, trying to hold them back, and as he did, the whole crowd seemed to turn around, like a writhing beast, and pinned them both against a wall. And as they did, Coco slammed against it hard. Leslie was starting to panic. He had been in paparazzi attacks like this before, mostly in England, and inevitably someone got hurt. He didn't want it to be her, but he couldn't get her through the crowd. "No!" he suddenly shouted at them, shoving them hard, and with that he yanked Coco by the arm, and dragged her through the press of men, who hadn't stopped taking their pictures since they found them. It was an agonizing journey to the boat, which seemed to take forever. The gondolier was waiting for them and looked frightened when he saw them. There were three *motoscafi* standing by in which the paparazzi had come, and suddenly Leslie realized that he could hear British voices in the crowd, French ones, and some German. They were a group of international paparazzi who had joined forces to attack them. There was strength in numbers. He and Coco didn't have a chance. He didn't mind them getting photographs, but the mob mentality was out of control, which was clearly dangerous for them.

Two of the paparazzi jumped into the gondola ahead of them, and nearly tipped the boat. Reacting to them as though they were pirates, the gondolier hit them with his oars, and they both fell into the canal amid outraged shouts. Leslie realized that they wouldn't have minded at all if it had been him and Coco. She crouched down on the seat as he protected her and shielded her with his body, as the gondolier set off, and the ragtag press corps jumped into their *motoscafi,* and tried to head them off to stop them. The gondolier started shouting insults at the drivers of the motorboats, who shrugged and made obscene gestures. They had been paid to do a job, and what happened after that was not their problem. They didn't want to know.

"Are you okay?" Leslie asked, shouting over the noise of the paparazzi and the boats. The flashes were still going off, and they almost overturned the gondola as they reached the Grand Canal. Coco looked terrified. She felt as though they were going to be killed. And there was very little that Leslie and the gondolier could do to protect them. He was praying they'd see one of the police boats, but none appeared. They steadily made their way back to the Gritti Palace as fast as they could go, surrounded by the paparazzi in the *motoscafi*. The paparazzi reached the dock nearest the Gritti before Coco and Leslie arrived in the gondola. Leslie pressed three hundred euros into the gondolier's hand, preparing to make as quick an exit as they could. It was only a short dash to the hotel from the dock, but the rabid photographers weren't going to make it easy. He almost wondered if it would help if they stopped and posed for them, but they were too far gone for that. A mob mentality had taken hold, and they were egging each other on in a feeding frenzy. Leslie wanted Coco out of it and away from them as fast as he could.

He got out of the gondola first and pulled her out, but there was already a wall of photographers between them and the hotel, and Leslie knew he would have to break through it to get her to safety. She was just stepping onto the dock, when one of them reached out of their boat and grabbed her ankle and pulled hard to stop her. She screamed and fell back into the gondola, and nearly fell into the water. Leslie looked down at her in desperation, stepped back into the boat himself, lifted her out, and ran to safety with Coco in his arms. His years of rugby as a young man served him well, he broke through the barrier of bodies and ran into the hotel with the paparazzi on his heels. The doorman and a fleet of security and bellmen tried to stop the crowd following them, and there was a melee of bodies and fists in the lobby as Leslie literally ran up the stairs with Coco in his arms. One of the security men followed with a look of grave concern.

"Are you all right, sir?" he asked as Leslie looked at Coco and gently set her on her feet outside his suite as the security guard let them in. They were both out of breath and Coco was shaking violently from head to foot, and there was blood all over her coat and Leslie's jacket. She had cut herself when one of them had grabbed her ankle and she fell back into the boat.

"Get a doctor!" Leslie said tersely as the security guard left the room immediately to find one. Before he left, he assured them that there would be guards outside their room all night, and he would call a doctor and the police. He said he was very sorry.

Leslie gently led Coco to a chair and ran into the bathroom to get a towel. He gently helped her take off her coat as she winced, and saw that her arm was at a nasty angle. He didn't say it, but he was sure that it was broken.

"Oh God, darling...I'm so sorry...I never thought...we should have gone somewhere else...or stayed here..." He was almost in tears, and she was crying. He took her in his arms and held her as she shook violently and said not a word. He could tell from the look on her face she was in shock. He just sat there and rocked her as she cried, and told her he loved her, until the doctor came. Leslie explained to him what had happened, and the doctor examined her as gently as he could. There were the beginnings of a nasty bruise on her back where she had been slammed into the wall before they reached the boat. The cut she had gotten on her hand needed seven stitches, and her wrist was broken. Leslie felt sick when the doctor told him.

He gave Coco a shot to numb her hand before he stitched it up, another shot to sedate her, and a tetanus shot. She was groggy when the orthopedic surgeon came, and set her wrist in a small fiberglass cast. Neither doctor wanted to risk taking her to the hospital and exposing her to the mob again. The orthopedist said he had seen several paparazzi lurking outside, although there were none in the lobby. The security had thrown them out. The doctors said that her wrist and hand would hurt for a few days, but they cleared her to travel. Leslie wanted her out of there now. He didn't want to risk having them pay someone to get into their room at the hotel. The hunt was on. The sharks would smell blood in the water and refuse to leave them alone from now on. Their Venetian idyll had ended in disaster. It was time for her to go home.

Leslie lay awake all night watching her, stroking her cheek and her hair as she dozed. He propped her arm up on a pillow, and she woke once or twice when he put ice packs on her hand, but the drugs had taken effect, and she was too sedated to say anything more than that she loved him, and thank him before she fell asleep again. She finally came out of it enough to talk to him at six o'clock in the morning, and then started to cry again.

"I was so scared," she said as she looked at him with panic in her eyes. "I thought they were going to kill us."

"So did I," he said miserably. "It happens that way sometimes. They drive each other into a frenzy." He had never felt so defenseless in his life. He had wanted a last romantic gondola ride for her, and they had been totally unprotected. They had no escape. "I'm so sorry, Coco. I never wanted anything like that to happen to you. Someone must have tipped them off at the restaurant or here. They get paid for that, and you never know who does it. The poor gondolier didn't know what hit him." He had made a hell of a tip for the experience, but Leslie doubted it was worth it to him. He had been terrified too, although he had probably made more from Leslie's tip than the snitch who had sold them out to the paparazzi.

"What happened to my wrist?" She stared down at it. She remembered nothing of the doctor putting on the cast the night before. She had been heavily sedated.

"It's broken," Leslie said in a hoarse voice. There were circles under his eyes, and beard stubble on his face. "They said you should have it looked at when you get home. They didn't want to take you to the hospital last night, and risk it happening again. You had seven stitches in your hand," he said with a look of anguish. "They gave you a tetanus shot. I didn't know if yours was current." He had taken wonderful care of her, but he hadn't been able to protect her from the paparazzi nightmare, and he bitterly regretted that. It was everything she was afraid of in his life, and her only reason for hesitating about living with him. He had enlisted in that kind of life when he became an actor. She had done all she could to run away from it.

"Thank you," she said softly, and then looked at him with broken eyes. "How can you live like that?" It had scared her to death.

"I have no choice. They would pursue me now even if I stopped working. It's the downside of my job." And in her eyes, it was a big one.

"What if we have children? What if they go after them like

that?" Everything she thought about it was in her eyes. What Leslie saw there was raw terror, and he didn't blame her. It had been a terrifying night, one of the worst he'd been in. And he hated that it had happened when he was with her, and she had been the one to get hurt. He felt like a monster for putting her in a situation where it could happen.

"I've always been very careful with Chloe," he said quietly. But he had been careful with her too. It was just rotten luck that it had gotten so out of hand, and they'd been in such a vulnerable place. "I don't take Chloe to public events with me," he explained. But this had only been dinner in a hole-in-the-wall restaurant in a back alley in Venice. They both knew it could happen anywhere. "I'm sorry, Coco. I truly am. I don't know what else to say." She nodded and lay silently in their bed for a while, and then finally she spoke again. All she could think of was the moment when one of them had yanked her ankle and she fell back into the gondola headfirst and tried to break her fall. She knew she would remember it forever.

"I love you. I truly do," she said sadly. "I love everything about you. You're the best, kindest man in the world. But I don't think I could live like that. I'd be terrified to go anywhere, and I'd be worried sick for our kids, and for you."

"It was a hell of a way to start," he admitted ruefully. If ever she had needed confirmation of her fears, she had gotten it the night before.

She burst into tears as he took her in his arms again. "I love you so much, but I'm so scared," she sobbed in anguish. She kept remembering all those awful men out of control.

"I know, baby, I know," he crooned as he held her. "I understand." He didn't want to, but he did. And he wanted to convince

her otherwise but felt it wouldn't be fair to her. She had been very
brave. But it was a lot to ask of anyone. Dealing with the paparazzi, and surviving them, was part of his life, but it didn't have
to be part of hers. She had a choice. He didn't. And he only
prayed now that she would still choose a life with him, when she
calmed down and recovered.

"Let's just get you safely on the plane to Paris now. We can talk
about this again when I get home." He didn't want her making any
final decisions about him in the state she was in. He worried that
the decision would be to end it with him. And she might get to that
anyway.

He called the director and told him what had happened the
night before, and asked him to shoot around him that morning.
The director said how sorry he was and asked if there was anything he could do to help. Leslie asked him to send over one of the
hairdressers with an assortment of wigs in anything but Coco's
color. He called the manager of the hotel after that, and asked for
several security guards to accompany her on the *motoscafo,* and a
police guard if necessary. But the hotel manager thought they
could handle it themselves.

Leslie got her into the shower. They had given her a cast that
could get wet as long as she didn't soak it. He held her in his arms
to make sure that she didn't stumble, slip, or faint. And then he
helped her dress. He had already made a decision not to leave the
hotel with her. He didn't want to do anything to draw attention to
her. They would recognize Coco now, but most of all, they would
be looking for him, or shots of them together. He didn't want to set
her up for that, and was going to say goodbye to her at the hotel,

and let her leave alone with the security guards from the Gritti. It was a sad end to their trip. And he couldn't help wondering if he'd ever see her again as he helped her dress. She had packed her bags the night before, so there was nothing for her to do except put on her jeans, a sweater, and her sheepskin coat.

The hairdresser from the set arrived as soon as Coco was dressed. Leslie sat her down at the dressing table and saw her eyes in the mirror. He could see that she was still in shock.

The hairdresser had brought several long blond wigs she had on hand, and a short black one. It was stylishly cut and full enough to cover all of Coco's long copper hair. She pinned it up for her, put a stocking cap on the way they did for films, and slipped the wig on her head. It was a shock seeing her with black hair, and in spite of himself Leslie smiled. She looked incredible, and it totally transformed her, which was what he wanted. She was unrecognizable in the black wig.

"You look like a very young Elizabeth Taylor." Coco only nodded. She didn't care what she looked like. She was heartbroken to be leaving him, and she hated what she had learned about his life. They had survived the rumors in the fan magazine, and the bogus affair with his costar. But it was much harder to overlook the nightmare she had lived through with him the night before.

Leslie thanked the hairdresser and she left, and he stood looking at Coco. "What can I say to you? I love you, Coco. But I don't want to ruin your life. I know how much you hate all this."

She smiled sadly at him. "One day at a time, I guess," she said, feeding his own words back to him, and he smiled.

"I wish I could leave with you. Please don't run away from me now. We'll deal with this together." He knew she had every reason to end it with him now, and he wouldn't blame her if she did. But he desperately hoped she wouldn't. He had changed her ticket home to first class as a gift from him. He wanted her to travel back in comfort, and had been startled that she had traveled coach on the way over. At least now she could sleep all the way home. He felt it was the least he could do for her.

"All I know is that I love you. I need to think about the rest," Coco said sadly, and he nodded, knowing it was the best they could do for now. She still looked badly shaken, and he knew her arm must hurt. It had been a terrifying experience for both of them, especially for her. And she was the one who had gotten injured. The thought of it made him feel sick.

There was a knock at the door, and the security guards were outside, waiting for her. There were four big burly men, and a bellman to carry her bags. He took them downstairs to the motorboat waiting outside the service entrance. She was going out the back way, as they had done in Florence. Leslie had to do that often.

He took her in his arms then and held her there, and for a moment he said nothing. He just wanted to feel her warmth against his chest, and remember every minute detail of her face. "Just know that I love you, and I understand whatever happens." He was afraid that it was over with her. It was written in her eyes as she looked back at him and nodded.

"I love you too." And then she added awkwardly, "I'll never forget Venice . . . I know that sounds ridiculous after last night. But I've never been so happy in my life. It was perfect until last night."

"Hang on to that," he said, daring to be hopeful, in spite of his fears. "Take care of your wrist, and don't forget to have it looked at when you get home." She nodded, and kissed him ever so gently on the lips.

"I love you," she said one last time, and then walked out of his suite and closed the door behind her. Leslie felt as though someone had just ripped his heart out and broken it to bits.

Chapter 17

Coco felt numb and dazed all the way back to San Francisco. She thought of calling him from Paris between flights, but she knew he'd be on the set by then, and working, so she didn't. And the flight back to San Francisco seemed endless. Her wrist ached, and she had a headache from the night before. Her whole body felt as though it had been jolted badly. Her back was sensitive from the bruise. And all she wanted to do was sleep. She didn't want to think about anything or talk to anyone. And every time she fell asleep, she had nightmares. Not just about the paparazzi, but about Leslie. She knew she couldn't share his life with him. It was just too frightening and overwhelming. And twice when she woke up, she was in tears. She felt as though she had lost not only the man she loved, but her dreams. It was a terrible feeling.

With the time difference, it was two o'clock in the afternoon when she got to San Francisco. It was eleven o'clock at night in Venice by then, but her cell phone was dead and she didn't call him.

She got a porter to help her through customs and walked into

the terminal almost blindly. She was going to take a cab back to
Bolinas. She was too worn out to take a shuttle. And as she looked
around on the sidewalk, she saw Liz hurrying toward her. Her
flight had come in early, and it never occurred to her that Liz was
there for her. Coco was still too dazed to think.

"Hi. Are you going somewhere?" Coco looked at her blankly, as
Liz looked her over with worried eyes.

"Leslie called me. He told me what happened. I'm sorry, Coco."

"Yeah, me too," Coco said, as tears filled her eyes. "Jane was
right. It's just too scary."

"It would be for most people," Liz said compassionately. "He un-
derstands that. He loves you, and he doesn't want to screw up your
life." She didn't tell her that Leslie had been crying when he called
her. He was terrified he had lost her forever. And from what Liz
could see in her eyes, she had a strong suspicion that could be the
case.

"Why did that have to happen?" Coco said miserably. "Everything was so perfect before that. We had a wonderful time. I've
never been happier in my life, and he's such a good person."

"I know he is. But this is part of his life too. Maybe it's better
that you saw it. Now you know what you'd be dealing with." It
would help her make the right decision, one she could live with.

"It's a terrible way to live," Coco said, thinking of the moment
the night before when she had fallen back into the boat. She
couldn't get it out of her mind, and was completely shaken by it.

Liz told her to sit on a bench and wait for her while she went to
get the car, and she was back a few minutes later. Coco still looked
dazed as the porter put her bags in the back of the car. "What did
Jane say?" Coco asked glumly as they drove away from the airport.

Liz glanced over at her from the driver's seat and then back at the road. "I didn't tell her. It's up to you what you want to say. She doesn't need to know about this, if you don't want her to." Coco nodded, grateful to Liz for her kindness and discretion. "Being scared of paparazzi attacks doesn't make you a bad person. Any sane person would hate living like that. I'm sure he does too. It just happened to him. He doesn't have much choice in the matter." Coco nodded. She knew it was true.

"It's a terrible reason not to stay with someone you love," Coco said, feeling guilty. She loved him. But she hated what came with his success and his life. She didn't want to be hiding and running and wearing wigs as she sneaked out the back door for the rest of her life. It was a miserable existence. And the furor in the eyes of the paparazzi the night before had been the most frightening thing she had ever seen. "I was afraid they were going to kill us," she explained, and Liz nodded as Coco started to cry again. Liz realized that she was traumatized by what had happened.

"Apparently so was Leslie. He feels terrible about it."

"I know," Coco said softly. "He was wonderful to me after."

"We're going to the doctor, by the way."

"I don't want to. I just want to go home," Coco said, sounding exhausted.

"Leslie says you have to. They set your wrist without doing an X-ray. They were afraid to take you out of the hotel again. The paparazzi were still outside. So you have to get the wrist looked at and checked." Coco nodded. She was too tired and upset to argue with her. Liz had made an appointment at an orthopedist she knew.

They went to Laurel Village for the appointment. And the orthopedist confirmed that it was broken, and said they had done a fine job of setting it in Italy. He replaced the cast with an identical one, and an hour later they were on their way to the beach.

"You don't have to take me home," Coco said miserably, and Liz smiled at her.

"I could let you walk, I guess, or hitch-hike. But what the hell, it's a nice day. It'll do me good to go to the beach." For the first time in hours, Coco smiled.

"Thank you for being nice to me," she said softly, and then she remembered. "How's the baby?"

"Growing every day. Jane looks fabulous, but it looks like it's going to be a big baby." She was six months pregnant by then, although Coco was in no hurry to see her. She would see immediately that something terrible had happened on the trip, and Coco didn't feel up to discussing it with her. Only with Liz. Liz was more like the big sister she wished she'd had, and never did.

Coco fell asleep in the car on the way to the beach, and Liz woke her gently when they were outside her cottage. Coco started, looked around, confused for a minute, and then looked at her house sadly. She wished she were back in Venice with him, and that the end had been different. For the first time ever, she didn't want to be in Bolinas. And she was afraid she could no longer be with him. It was a terrible situation for her.

"Come on, I'll take you in." Liz carried her bags, and Coco unlocked the door. They hadn't stopped to pick up Sallie, but Liz had said she didn't mind keeping her for a few more days. Coco had enough to cope with right now with her wrist. All Liz had said to Jane was that she'd had an accident in Italy and broken her wrist.

"Thank you for picking me up at the airport," Coco said as she hugged her. "I was a mess. I guess I still am."

"Get some sleep. You'll feel better tomorrow. And don't try to figure it all out now. You'll know what to do." Coco nodded, and Liz left.

Coco walked into her bedroom and put on her old faded pajamas. It was five o'clock in Bolinas and two in the morning in Venice. All she wanted to do now was sleep. She didn't even want to eat. It was too late to call Leslie, but she didn't want to anyway. She didn't know what to say to him. And maybe Liz was right, she thought to herself, as she got under the covers. She could figure it out later. Right now, all she wanted to do was try to forget what had happened and sleep.

Chapter 18

Leslie called Coco the day after she got home, to see how she was, and check on her wrist. He didn't tell her, but he had already called Liz the night before after Coco got back, at four in the morning for him. She told him they'd been to the doctor and they'd put another cast on. She said that Coco looked dazed and beaten up, but she was doing all right. She suggested he let the dust settle a little and give it some time. But he wanted Coco to know that he was thinking of her, so he called her the next day himself, from his trailer on the set. He said he missed her terribly and apologized again for what had happened.

"It's not your fault," Coco tried to comfort him when he called her. But he could hear something different in her voice, as though she had already backed away. "How's the movie going?" she asked, trying to change the subject. She felt worse after the flight, but had gotten up anyway. Erin couldn't work for her that day, and she didn't want to let her clients down. The doctor said she could work if she felt up to it, but he didn't recommend it.

"It went pretty well today. Madison blew all her lines yesterday.

But so did I, so I guess we were an even match." He couldn't think straight after Coco left. His heart and mind had left with her. "I'm still hoping we make it home by Thanksgiving." They would have been there for seven weeks by then. He wanted to come and see her after that, but he didn't dare say it. He could hear how shaken she still was, and so was he. There were pictures of them all over the European papers. He looked like a madman, trying to protect her, and she looked wide-eyed and terrified. There was even one of her as she fell back into the boat, headfirst. He could hardly stand looking at the photographs, and it just made him miss her more. So did talking to her. "Try to take it easy for a couple of days. You had a hell of a jolt to your system the other night." And he suspected she'd be shaken up for a while, and have post-traumatic stress.

"I'm fine," she said, feeling like a robot. It tore her heart out to talk to him too. She was more in love with him than ever after the trip to Italy, but the paparazzi attack had convinced her that she wasn't strong enough to deal with what he went through. It was no way for her to live. "I'm on my way to work," she said, as she crossed the bridge while talking to him. Their time together in Venice felt like a lifetime away to her, and to him too.

"Call me when you want to talk to me," he said sadly. "I don't want to pressure you, Coco." He wanted to give her time to breathe. Liz had suggested it would be a good idea. The trauma had been severe for Coco.

"Thank you," she said, as she took the turnoff to Pacific Heights, wishing they were back at Jane's house again, back at the beginning, instead of at the end. "I love you," she whispered, but she could no longer see any way to make it work, unless she wanted to live the same crazy existence he did, and she didn't. But she couldn't bring herself to say it to him. He knew.

"I love you too" was all Leslie said.

She went to pick up Sallie then, before she picked up the other dogs. Jane came to the door and told her she was sorry about her wrist. Coco smiled when she saw her. She was huge.

"You're getting bigger," she commented, and Jane rubbed her hands over her round stomach. She was wearing tights and a sweater, and she looked prettier than ever. There was something slightly softer about her face.

"Three more months," Jane said, looking apprehensive. "It's hard to believe." They were commuting to L.A. by then, doing post-production on their film. Liz had said they'd be finished by Thanksgiving, which was a good thing. It would give Jane two months to take it easy and get ready for motherhood. "Are you and Leslie coming to Mom's for Thanksgiving?" she asked offhandedly, and Coco shook her head.

"I am, but he'll be in New York with his daughter." Coco didn't want to get into it with her and quickly changed the subject. "How was Gabriel, by the way?" She remembered that Jane had met him in L.A. and she hadn't talked to her since. Jane laughed at the question.

"Young. Jesus, is he young. And Mom looks like she feels sixteen. It's a little unnerving, to say the least. He's a decent guy, I guess. I don't know what he's doing with a woman her age. It can't last, but at least she's having fun." Coco was shocked to see that Jane had relaxed about it. She had expected her to be on a mission of destruction, and instead she didn't seem to care. "Whatever works. I guess we all have our crazy moments, and the right to make decisions about our own lives, whatever everyone else thinks. How was Italy, by the way?" Coco almost shuddered at the question, but she had steeled herself for it.

"It was great," she said with a broad smile and prayed her all-seeing sister didn't see through it. "Except for my wrist."

"That was shit luck, but at least it was your left wrist." Jane didn't say a word about Leslie, and as Sallie followed her to the van a few minutes later, Coco wondered if Jane had relaxed about him too. The whole time they were talking, she'd been rubbing her belly, the way pregnant women did. Coco was wondering if something had changed. They were going back to L.A. until Thanksgiving, and Coco hoped that by then she wouldn't feel as though her own life had come to an end. She had lived through it when Ian died, and survived it. She could go through it again now, after Leslie, and knew she'd survive this too.

She went to pick up the big dogs, and the ones in Cow Hollow after. She followed her usual route, and did everything she had to do. She went through the motions, and went back to Bolinas every afternoon, but she felt as though everything inside her had died. Leslie didn't call her for the next three weeks, and she didn't call him. He didn't want to push her, and she was trying to get over him and the best way to do it, she knew, was not to talk to him at all. She didn't want to hear his voice and fall in love with him all over again, and she knew she would. And then the same thing would happen again. She couldn't. It was too scary.

Coco didn't talk to anyone until she left for L.A. on Thanksgiving, three weeks after Venice. She left Sallie with Erin, and she was only planning to go down for two days. Liz had invited her to stay at their rented house. And Gabriel was going to join them for Thanksgiving dinner. It was the first time she was going to meet him, although she had caught a glimpse of him that night at the Bel-Air when she saw her mother with him.

Liz picked her up at the airport in L.A., and drove her back to the house where Jane was waiting. It was the night before Thanksgiving, and the three of them were going to have a quiet dinner. Liz didn't ask her about Leslie, and Coco didn't mention him. Coco was wondering if he had made it to New York for Thanksgiving with Chloe and her mother. He hadn't called her, and she had no idea if he had left Venice. She thought it was best to just leave things the way they were, to drift away. The die had been cast on their last night in Venice, and her decision had been made. He knew it from her silence, and she knew from his that he understood. They still loved each other, but there was no doubt in her mind now. It could never be.

Jane was sprawled on the couch when she and Liz got back from the airport, and she waved when Coco walked in. She looked like a beach ball with arms and legs and a head, and Coco smiled as she walked over to give her a hug.

"Holy shit, you're *huge*!" Her belly looked as though it had doubled in size in three weeks.

"If that's a compliment, thank you." Jane grinned at her. "If not, screw you. You should try wearing this." Coco almost winced as she said it. She had put the idea of marriage and babies behind her, and hearing her say it made her think of Leslie instantly. "I don't even want to think about how big this kid is going to be in two months. It scares the shit out of me."

They talked and laughed over dinner. Liz and Jane had finished

their film, and were moving back to San Francisco for good the following week. They were halfway through dinner and a good bottle
of wine when Jane suddenly turned to her and asked how Leslie
was. She suddenly realized that Coco hadn't mentioned him all
evening.

"Fine, I guess," Coco said, trying to brace herself for what would
come next. She gave a quick glance at Liz, who obviously hadn't
said anything, and Coco was grateful for that. She had needed the
last three weeks to compose herself before telling Jane.

"Is everything all right with you two?" Jane asked, frowning.

"Actually, no, it's not," Coco said quietly. "It's over. You were
right. We had a couple of minor brushes with the paparazzi, and
on my last night in Venice, they ambushed us. And as you predicted," she said stoically, "I folded like a house of cards. They
scared the hell out of me. I wound up with seven stitches and a
broken wrist, and I figured that was enough for me. I can't live like
that. So here I am, alone again. Just me." There was a long silence
after she made her brief speech, and she was waiting for a barrage
of "I told you so"s, and instead Jane leaned over and touched the
cast on her wrist. By then, the stitches had been taken out, and the
wound on her hand had healed. There was only a small scar to
show for it, which was nothing compared to the condition of her
heart. She felt as though it had been shattered.

"The paparazzi broke your wrist?" Jane said in disbelief. She
looked both sympathetic and stunned.

"Not intentionally. I was getting out of a gondola at the dock at
the Gritti, and one of them grabbed my ankle and tried to yank me
back, so I fell back into the boat headfirst, and when I tried to
break my fall, I cut my hand and broke my wrist. They ambushed

us leaving a restaurant before that and smashed my back into a wall. We finally made it to the gondola, they jumped in with us, and nearly overturned the boat. There were about thirty of them and they followed us in three *motoscafi,* and then tried to keep us from getting out of the boat. It was pretty nasty."

"Are you kidding?" Jane said in astonishment. "What I meant was that they would follow you around and invade your privacy, and you're such a private person, I knew you would hate that. I never meant that they were going to beat the crap out of you, smash you into walls, try to knock you out of boats, cut you up, and break bones. Where was Leslie in all that?" She wanted to know if Leslie had left her to the wolves, and if so, she was going to call him and rip his head off.

"He was with me. He did what he could, but there was nothing much either of us could do. We were in a back alley in Venice, and we couldn't even get to the boat at first. There were about thirty of them, and only two of us. It was pretty rough stuff."

"Christ, I'd have folded like a house of cards over that too. Did you end it after that?"

"More or less. He knows how I feel. That's not how I want to live," she said, trying to sound matter-of-fact about it, but there was a catch in her voice that her sister understood, and so did Liz. She was still in love with him, but she had made a decision, and she was determined to stick to it, no matter how hard it was. She thought staying with him and living like that would be worse. But losing him was awful. Leaving Leslie was the hardest thing she'd ever done.

"No one would want to live like that. He must have felt terrible about it." Jane looked horrified by everything she had just heard, and the look in Coco's eyes broke her heart, as Jane leaned over to give her a hug.

"He did. He was wonderful to me after. After I fell back in the boat, he just grabbed me, picked me up, and ran through them. I had to leave through the service entrance, in a black wig, with four bodyguards the next day."

"Christ, that's awful. I've heard of a few attacks like that over the years, but not many. Mostly they just push and shove and get in your face. I'm surprised he didn't kill one of them."

"He was too worried about me. I was bleeding all over the place by then."

"Why didn't you tell me when you got back?" Jane asked, looking distressed. She had glanced at Liz, who did not say a word.

"I was too upset." Coco sighed and looked at her sister honestly. "And I was afraid of what you'd say. You warned me in the beginning, and you were right."

"No, I wasn't," Jane said, looking embarrassed. "I shot my mouth off, and Leslie gave me hell for it, and he was right. Liz gave me hell too. I don't know, I was just worried that you'd gotten in over your head or he was using you for a summer fling. I always think of you as a little kid. He leads such a big Hollywood life, and I couldn't imagine you being part of it. But you love each other, Coco. What happened to you in Italy is extreme. He can get bodyguards for you if he has to. I'm sure he would. You can't give up someone you love when the going gets tough." She felt terrible now about everything she'd said before, and she hoped she hadn't influenced her to give up. Leslie had impressed her when he'd called her and read her the riot act. She had no question in her mind now that he was deeply in love with her, and she could see that Coco still was too.

"I'm not cut out for that life," Coco said simply. "It would drive me insane. I'd be scared to go anywhere, scared to take my kids out, if we had any. What if one of our kids got hurt by one of those lunatics? What if your baby was in danger of that every day?"

"I'd find a way to protect him. But I wouldn't give up Liz," she said quietly. "You love him, Coco. I know you do. That's a lot to lose."

"So is my life. They could have killed one of us that night. And afterward I kept thinking about all of Dad's horror stories about his clients. I never wanted to be one of them when I grew up, and I still don't." She said it as tears rolled down her cheeks, and she brushed them away. "Leslie has no choice. He has to live that way. I can't." The life went out of her eyes as she said it.

"I'm sure after what happened, Leslie would see to it that it never happened again," Jane tried to reassure her. Coco didn't answer, she just looked down at her plate and then back at her sister again and shook her head.

"I'm too scared," she said sadly as Jane reached out and touched her hand. Liz was proud of her when she did, and of everything she had said. She had a lot to make up for, and she had finally come through. Impending motherhood had done a lot to soften her sharp edges recently.

"Why don't you give it some time?" Jane said quietly, still holding her hand. "When is he coming back?"

"I don't know. I haven't talked to him in three weeks. Sometime around now, I think, if they're not running behind."

"You can't let those bastards run you off. You can't give them that too." But she already had. Coco felt there was no turning back. This wasn't how she had wanted it to turn out, but after the paparazzi attack, Coco was afraid for her life if she stayed with him. Leslie knew that, which was why he hadn't been more forceful about trying to convince her otherwise. He loved her enough to let her go, if it was best for her.

Coco helped Liz clear the dishes then, and Jane went to sit on the couch to watch TV. "What have you done to her?" Coco asked Liz in a whisper in the kitchen. "She was *nice.*"

Liz laughed at what Coco said. "I think the hormones are finally kicking in. That baby may make a human being out of her yet."

"I'm impressed," Coco said, as they put the last of the dishes in the dishwasher, and went back to join Jane on the couch. They didn't mention the paparazzi attack again, and a little while later, they went to bed. They had to be at their mother's for lunch the next day, which was always a formal, traditional affair. And as Jane put it with a grin, this time the Boy Wonder would be there.

They all got up late the next morning, and at one o'clock they drove to Florence's mansion in Bel-Air. Jane was wearing the only decent dress she had that still fit. It was a pale blue silk tent that looked pretty on her with her long blond hair. Coco was wearing a white wool dress she had worn in Italy, and Liz was wearing a well-tailored black pantsuit. And when she opened the door, Florence was wearing a pink Chanel suit that looked spectacular on her. And as they all stood hugging and kissing each other in the front hall, a handsome man in a gray double-breasted suit and Hermès tie approached them. Coco knew instantly who he was.

"Hello, Gabriel," she said with a warm smile, and shook his hand. He looked nervous at first, but as they sat in Florence's living room, under an enormous portrait of her in a ballgown and jewels, done several years before, they all started to relax and have a good time.

Liz and Gabriel talked movies. He was starting a new one soon, and he said Florence had helped him immeasurably with the screenplay. She had just finished another book. And Jane was excited about the film they had just finished. It reminded Coco of the old days, when her father was alive, and they all talked about books, movies, new clients, and old ones, and movie stars came through their house constantly, and famous authors. It was the same atmosphere she had grown up in and was familiar to her. And she surprised everyone at lunch by saying she was thinking of going back to school.

"Law school?" her mother asked, looking stunned.

"No, Mom." Coco smiled at her. "Something useless, like a master's in art history. I think I might like to study restoration. I haven't figured it out yet." The idea had really taken hold in her head ever since she'd discussed it with Leslie two months before, and what she'd seen in Venice and Florence had spurred her on. "I can't spend the rest of my life walking dogs," she said softly, as her mother and sister smiled.

"You always wanted to do art history," her mother said kindly. Much to Coco's amazement, for once no one was criticizing her, and telling her what was wrong with her, and how stupid her plans were. It had started with Jane the night before. Coco wasn't sure if she had changed, or they had. They had certainly all chosen different paths. Liz and Jane were having a baby. Her mother was in love with a man nearly half her age. And Coco had just walked away from the love of her life. It struck her, as she looked at them, that they had lives and she didn't. She had chosen to stay off the track for nearly four years now. Maybe it was time to move forward again. It felt like she was ready to do that, even without Leslie in her life. She needed a fuller life of her own, with or without him. The black sheep was returning to the fold, and for once they had the grace not to say it.

Coco sat next to Gabriel at lunch, and enjoyed an interesting conversation with him about art, politics, and literature. He wasn't the sort of man who would have appealed to her. He was a little too Hollywood, in a way that Leslie wasn't. Gabriel was slicker, and part of the scene, but he was intelligent, and attentive to her mother. Florence was absolutely thriving on his attention, and she looked radiant and young. He was taking her to the Basel art show in Miami the following week. They were going skiing in Aspen after Christmas. They had seen all the recent art shows and plays. He took her to the symphony and the ballet. They'd been to New York twice in the last six months and seen every play on Broadway. It was obvious that their mother was having a good time, and even though his age shocked them, Jane and Coco agreed on the way home that he wasn't a bad guy.

"It's kind of like having a brother," Coco commented, and Jane laughed. He had talked about babies with her, since he had a two-year-old. He'd been divorced for a year and said the marriage had been a huge mistake, but he was glad to have his daughter, particularly now. Clearly, he and Florence weren't going to be having children. "Do you think she'll marry him?" Coco asked with a look of wonder.

"Stranger things have happened, particularly in this family," Jane commented, sounding more like her old self, but with more humor. She was definitely mellowing a little, or even a lot. "But to be honest, I hope not. She doesn't need to get married at her age. Why screw up what they've got? And if it doesn't work out, she doesn't need all the mess and headache of a divorce."

"Maybe she does need to get married," Coco said pensively. "But what is she going to do with a two-year-old?" Gabriel sounded like he was very attached to his daughter.

"The same thing she did with us," Jane chuckled. "Hire a nanny." All three of them laughed at that, and they chatted amiably through the evening, and Coco went back to San Francisco the next day. They invited her to stay for the weekend, but she wanted to get home. She was still feeling fragile.

Before she left, Jane took her aside and talked to her again about Leslie. "Don't give up on him yet," she said quietly, as Coco finished packing her bag. She was back in her old sweatshirt and jeans for the flight. It made her look like a kid again, but Jane was finally realizing that she wasn't. "He loves you and he's a good man. It wasn't his fault that that happened, and he must have hated it too. The last thing he would want is for you to get hurt. It sounds like a nightmare for both of you."

"It was. How can anyone live like that?"

"He'll figure it out so it doesn't happen again. It must have been a hell of a wake-up call to him. Everyone is a little nuts in L.A. I'm actually thrilled to be going back to San Francisco. It's more exciting down here, but I think it's a hard place to bring up kids. It's all about showing off. The values seem all wrong. It just wouldn't seem right to me to raise a child here."

"Yeah, and look how they turn out," Coco teased her. "I'm a hippie, and you're gay." Jane laughed at that and hugged her.

"You're not such a hippie anymore. Maybe you never were, I just thought so. And I'm glad you're thinking about going back to school. You could go to UCLA if you live down here with him," she said practically, and Coco looked panicked, so Jane backed off. She just hoped Coco didn't give up on him entirely. It made her sad for both of them. And she was actually sorry when Coco left. It had been a wonderful Thanksgiving, and Gabriel was even a pleasant addition. He had promised to come to Christmas in San Francisco with Florence. They were going to stay at the Ritz-Carlton and bring his daughter.

Coco was thinking about all of it as she flew back to San Francisco. She had left her van at the airport, and was relieved to drive back to Bolinas. It had been nice to see her family for two days, but she needed time to herself. She was still too sad about Leslie to want to be with people all the time. She needed time to mourn. She appreciated what Jane had said about him, but she knew better than anyone, after what had happened in Venice, that she couldn't lead that life. It was one thing to be the girlfriend of a movie star, it was another thing to be attacked by thirty men who could have killed them. She still remembered the feeling of terror as they surrounded them in the back alley, and later when she fell into the boat. If loving him meant living that way, she couldn't do it.

She let herself in to the cottage and looked around. It looked familiar and comfortable, like crawling back into the womb again. The weather was cold, and she wrapped herself in a blanket and went out to sit on the deck. She loved the beach in winter, and there were a million stars in the sky. She lay on the deck chair, looking at them, remembering when she'd been there with Leslie, and a tear crept slowly down her cheek.

Her cell phone rang then, and she dug it out of her pocket. It was from a blocked number, and Coco wondered who it was.

"Hello?"

"Hello." There was a small funny voice at the other end. "This is Chloe Baxter. Coco, is that you?"

"Yes, it's me," she said, smiling. "How are you?" She wondered if Leslie was with her, and had made it for Thanksgiving. Maybe it was a ploy to talk to her. But if so, she didn't care. She loved talking to Chloe. "How are the bears?"

"They're fine. And me too. How was your turkey?"

"Very nice. I had it with my mom and my sister, in L.A."

"Is that where you are now?" She sounded very interested, and as usual, very grown up.

"No, I'm at the beach. Looking up at the stars. It's late for you. If you were here, we could toast marshmallows and have s'mores."

"Yumm," she said, and then giggled.

"Did you have Thanksgiving with your daddy?" Coco couldn't resist asking, although she didn't want to pump her for information. She wondered if he was standing there or even knew that she was calling. Chloe had a way of doing what she wanted, without prompting from anyone else.

"Yes," Chloe said with a sigh. "He brought me a dress from Italy. It's very pretty. He just left for L.A. tonight."

"Oh." Coco didn't know what to say.

There was a pause, and then Chloe went on. "He says he misses you very much."

"I miss him too. Did he tell you to call me?"

"No. I lost your number. I got it off his computer but he doesn't know." Coco smiled at what she said. It was so like her to do that. "He says you're mad at him, because some very bad men attacked you both and you got hurt. He said you broke your wrist when they pushed you. That must have hurt a lot."

"It did," Coco admitted. "It was pretty scary."

"That's what he said too. He said he should have stopped them, but he couldn't. And now he's very sad, because you're so mad at him. I miss you too, Coco," she said sadly, and tears filled Coco's eyes again. This was hard. It reminded her of the wonderful time they had shared with her in August.

"I miss you too, Chloe. And I'm very sad too."

"Please don't stay mad at him," Chloe said sadly. "I want to see you when I come out. I'm spending Christmas with him in L.A. Will you be there?"

"I'm spending it with my mom and sister in San Francisco. My sister is having a baby pretty soon, so we have to stay here."

"Maybe we could come up," she said practically. "If you invite us. We could come to see you at the beach. I'd like that."

"So would I. But it's kind of complicated right now, because I haven't seen your dad in a while."

"Maybe he'll call you," she said hopefully. "He's going to be working on his movie. He's moving back into his house in L.A."

"That's nice," Coco said noncommittally, but she was touched that Chloe had called. She had missed her too.

"I hope I see you soon. My mom says I have to go to bed now," she said with a yawn, and Coco smiled.

"Thank you for calling me," Coco said, and meant it. It was almost as good as hearing from him.

"My dad says he can't call you because you're so mad at him. So I thought I'd call you myself."

"I'm glad you did. I love you, Chloe. Happy Thanksgiving."

She made a gobbling sound, and Coco laughed. She was truly the perfect combination of child and adult. She had just turned seven. "Happy Turkey to you too. Night-night," Chloe said. And then she hung up. Coco sat holding her cell phone, looking up at the sky, wondering if the call from Chloe was a sign or a message for her. Probably not, but it had been very sweet. She sat on the deck and thought about it for a long time.

Chapter 19

Leslie didn't call her when he got back to L.A. As Coco was, he was still feeling traumatized by what had happened in Venice. And he loved Coco too much to ask her to risk her life for him. He knew how much she had hated it when her father had been threatened years before, and the nightmares she'd had as a result. He couldn't ask her to live that way forever, for him. But his heart ached every minute of the day. All he could think of was her.

And Coco didn't call him, either. She berated herself every day for her cowardice. She had a broken heart, which ached every time she thought of spending the rest of her life without Leslie. But now, living with the risks it entailed seemed worse. She wanted a normal life with him, not a permanent diet of the insanity they'd lived through in Venice.

As a result, the silence between them was deafening, but there was nothing left to say. The fact that they loved each other wasn't enough anymore. It didn't protect them from the dangers of his world and fame. Their lives were incompatible, so there was no point torturing each other by staying in touch. And she knew she didn't need to explain it to him again. They had both said it all the last time they spoke, the day after she got home. And she knew he understood and respected her fears. Coco was trying to let it drift away, but the feelings were still there and probably would be for a long time. Maybe forever. And the pain of losing him.

She ran into Jeff at the trash cans one day, and he commented about what a nice guy Leslie was, how he acted like any other normal guy, and didn't put on airs because he was a big star. He said he liked him a lot, and had missed seeing him. Coco nodded agreement with him, and as she listened, she was trying not to cry. She had had a bad day. Every day was hard now. She was dreading Christmas this year. It was going to be so lonely without him. They had planned to spend it together. And now he'd be spending it with Chloe in L.A. And she was going to be with her mother and sister, and their significant others.

Even the house in Bolinas looked sad to her now. Everything looked faded and tired. And she finally put Ian's diving gear away. It depressed her seeing that too. And she had put the photographs she had of Leslie in a drawer. The only one she left out was a photograph she had taken of him and Chloe the day they built the first sand castle. Chloe looked adorable in it, and she didn't have the heart to put that one away too.

Chloe hadn't called her again. She had thought of buying her a Christmas present, but she thought it was mean to try and hang on to her. She had to let go of both of them now, no matter how cute she was, or how much she loved him.

By the time Christmas Eve came, Coco hadn't spoken to Leslie in seven weeks. She tried not to keep track of it, but she always knew. It had been exactly fifty days. She hated herself for remembering it. One day she would no longer remember how long it had been, just years.

She was planning to stay at Jane's on Christmas Eve. They had already turned the guest room into a nursery, and they were putting her in a smaller guest room downstairs. She knew that it was going to be hard to stay in the house again. Everything about it reminded her of Leslie now, and the months she had lived there with him.

Her mother and Gabriel and his daughter had arrived in San Francisco that afternoon. They went straight to the Ritz-Carlton to get organized. They hadn't brought a nanny with them, and Gabriel was going to take care of her himself. Florence was a little anxious about it, she had admitted to Jane. She hadn't been around a child that age in a long time.

"Well, that's what you get for having a young boyfriend, Mom," Jane teased her, and she laughed about it with Coco when she arrived.

They were spending Christmas Eve together, as they always did, and Christmas Day, and that night everyone would go home. Her mother and Gabriel were going back to L.A., since they were leaving for Aspen the day after Christmas. And Coco was going back to the beach. But for twenty-four hours, they would be a family, however unorthodox they were. And they seemed to be getting more so every year. Now Liz and Jane were going to have a baby, and her mother had a boyfriend young enough to be her son, and his two-year-old who could have been her grandchild. "We're not exactly your standard family anymore," Jane commented, as she walked Coco to her room downstairs. "Maybe we never were." And then she looked at Coco strangely, as though thinking back to the days when they were growing up and their father was alive. "I was so jealous of you then," she said in a quiet voice. "Dad was so nuts about you. I always felt like once you came along, I didn't have a chance. You were so little and so cute. Even Mom was excited about you for a while. She had so little time to give either of us, there just wasn't enough of her to share. I hope my kids never feel that way about me."

"I always thought you were the star, and there was no room for me," Coco confessed. She had said it to her therapist two years before, and it almost felt better saying it out loud to Jane.

"Maybe that's why I was so hard on you." Jane looked at her apologetically. "There was hardly room for me in that house, and then you came along. There was never enough love to go around."

"They were both such busy, important people," Coco said thoughtfully. "They never had time to be parents."

"And we never got a chance to be kids. We both had to be stars. I bought into it. You didn't. You just said to hell with it, and threw in the towel. I've been trying to impress them all my life. And in the end, who gives a damn? Who cares how many movies I produce? This baby is more important than that," she said, rubbing her belly, which got bigger every day. She almost looked like a cartoon of a pregnant woman now.

"It sounds like you're on the right track," Coco said gently, and gave her a hug. It was more than she could say for herself. They all had partners, she didn't. She had walked away from the man she loved. "Are you thinking of having more kids?" Coco asked her then. Jane had just referred to "kids," plural, instead of one.

"Maybe," Jane said with a smile. "Depends how this one goes, and how cute he is. If he's as big a brat as I was, I may have to send him back. You were pretty cute though. It just made me hate you more." Leslie had been right. Jane was jealous of her, and what she was saying now was finally letting the air out of that balloon. The air was pretty stale by now. They were no longer competing for their mother's attention, and their father was gone.

And these days, their mother was more interested in Gabriel than in them. She had already told Jane that she and Gabriel would be in the Bahamas when the baby was born. They would come to see it when they got back. It was who their mother had always been. The men in her life had changed, but she never had, and at her age, there was no chance she ever would. They had both made their peace with that.

"Liz and I have been talking about another baby," she admitted to Coco. "Next time we might do a donor egg from me, if mine are holding up, and donor sperm, and let Liz carry it. I'm glad I did it this time, but to be honest, I hate being fat. I'm turning forty in two months. Being fat on top of it is just too goddamn much. Maybe I am like Mom," she laughed. Their mother was the vainest woman in the world. Jane turned to Coco with a hesitant look then and sat down on the guest room bed. The weight of the baby was too great now to allow her to stand up for long. She could hardly walk. "Is there any chance that you'd like to be with me when the baby is born? I've been wanting to ask you, but I didn't know how you'd feel about it. Liz is going to be there, but I'd love to have you there too." There were tears in her eyes as she asked, and Coco sat down on the bed next to her and hugged her with tears in her eyes too.

"I'd love that," she said, and held her sister for a long moment. She felt honored that Jane would want her there. She wiped the tears from her cheeks then and laughed. "Hell, it may be the only chance I get to see a baby born, now that I'm committed to being an old maid."

"I don't think you have to worry about that yet," Jane said, smiling at her. "I guess you haven't heard from Leslie?" she asked cautiously, and Coco shook her head.

"I haven't called him either. Chloe, his little girl, called me on Thanksgiving. She says he misses me. I miss him too."

"So call him, for chrissake. Don't waste all this time."

"Maybe I will one of these days," Coco said with a sigh, but Jane knew she wouldn't. Coco was too scared and too stubborn. She almost wanted to call him herself, but Liz didn't think she should get involved. It was up to them. Jane was dying to give them a helping hand.

They went back upstairs then, and Coco laughed at her as she waddled up the stairs. She was excited about being at the birth. Jane told Liz as soon as they walked into the kitchen. She was putting the finishing touches on dinner for that night.

"Thank God, you'll be there," Liz said, looking relieved. "I have no idea what to do. We took Lamaze classes and I've already forgotten everything. This is such a huge deal." Liz smiled at Coco as she said it.

"Yes, it is," Coco agreed, in awe of the whole process, and impressed by the noticeable changes in her sister. The atmosphere between Coco and Jane had changed considerably in the past two months. After years of resenting each other, and each of them feeling wounded, they were finally friends. It was what Coco had hoped for all her life.

They sat at the kitchen table talking for a while, and Coco told them about the maple syrup incident the day she and Leslie met. Liz had hysterics as she listened, and Jane nearly fainted when she heard it.

"Thank God I wasn't here. I would have killed you!"

"I know. That's why I never told you. We were swimming in maple syrup until Leslie cleaned it up."

"Remind me not to ask you to house-sit again."

They finally went upstairs to get dressed, and Coco went downstairs to her room, relieved not to see the bedroom that she and Leslie had shared. They were going to show her the nursery later, but she was determined not to set foot in the master suite. It would just hurt too much. She was having a hard time getting over him, and Liz and Jane both knew it. Their mother still didn't know what had happened and never asked.

She and Gabriel arrived promptly at seven, with his adorable two-year-old daughter in tow. She was wearing a red velvet Christmas dress with matching bows in her hair, and black patent leather Mary Janes. Gabriel had dressed her himself. And they brought a collapsible playpen with them so they could put her to sleep when she got tired. She seemed like a very well-behaved little girl. Their mother talked to her like a small adult, which reminded Coco of Chloe.

Florence was wearing a very chic black cocktail dress, and Gabriel was wearing a dark blue suit. They looked smashing together, as Coco picked Alyson up and played with her, while Liz made her mother and Gabriel martinis. In a funny way, they were playing the role of the parents, and whenever she was around her mother, Coco felt like a child again. She used to feel that way around Jane too, but it had changed.

Jane whispered to her in the kitchen that Gabriel dressed like a fifty-year-old man.

"That's a good thing or they'd look ridiculous together," Coco whispered back, as Liz shook their martinis, "because Mom thinks she's twenty-five."

"Shit," Jane said out loud, "the whole goddamn world is confused."

"We certainly are," Coco said, laughing. "You're married to a woman, and Mom's in love with a child." The three of them stood around the kitchen table laughing, as Florence and Gabriel came to get their martinis, and Coco was happy to babysit for them. His daughter was adorable, and she was mesmerized by the Christmas tree Liz had put up in the living room. All Jane had been able to do this year was lie on the couch and watch.

"I can't believe I've got another five weeks to go. I feel like I'm going to have it tonight. Or I wish I would. One of these days, my stomach's just going to explode," Jane said as she walked into the living room with them and collapsed on the couch again.

"Don't forget to call me as soon as you go into labor," Coco reminded her, now that she was part of the team. She could hardly wait.

Liz had prepared a beautiful dinner for all of them. They started it off with caviar, followed by roast beef, Yorkshire pudding, mashed potatoes, minted peas, salad, and dinner rolls. It was an elegant meal, and to top it all off she had prepared traditional plum pudding with hard sauce for dessert. By the time they sat down to the meal, Alyson was sound asleep in her playpen. She was the perfect child. She was going to sleep in their room at the Ritz-Carlton that night. Florence said she had brought earplugs in case she cried, and Gabriel just laughed. He seemed to have endless tolerance for Florence's quirks, and looked at her with adoring eyes.

They went back to the hotel around ten o'clock with Alyson sound asleep in her father's arms. They had a limousine waiting outside, and they left with Florence in a swath of fur, and Gabriel in a good-looking black cashmere coat, as they thanked them for the meal and promised to be back at noon the next day. After that, the three younger women hung out in the kitchen and cleaned up. Liz was making turkey the next day. Jane had hardly been able to eat that night. The meal was delicious, but she said she had no more room. The baby was hogging it all. And she had heartburn all the time.

"This isn't as easy as it looks," Jane complained, rubbing her back. She was getting more and more uncomfortable now.

"I'll give you a backrub when we go to bed," Liz promised. She was truly the perfect partner, and Coco told her sister she was a lucky woman. It didn't strike her as odd that her sister was gay, and never had. Coco had always known her that way, and was very comfortable with it. She had always told her friends at school that Jane was a lesbian, and didn't see anything unusual about it.

"You were actually pretty funny then," Jane reminisced with a chuckle as the others cleaned up. "You told someone I was a leprechaun once, and when I corrected you, you said you thought it was the same thing."

It was midnight when they all went to their rooms, and Coco lay in bed downstairs, thinking of the months she had spent with Leslie in that house. She wished that he and Chloe were there. Christmas would have been perfect for her then. As usual, she was the odd man out. She wondered what they were doing that night. She knew that Chloe was with him, and wondered if they had put up a tree, if they were with friends, what kind of Christmas they were going to have, traditional or free-form. She would have loved to share it with them, but she couldn't. The paparazzi that were part of his life had changed everything. Her life was simpler now, she reminded herself. But also incredibly sad. The next day she would go back to her house at the beach, and Jane and Liz would have each other. And her mother and Gabriel would be flying to L.A. and then Aspen. She had made a decision that had seemed the right one at the time, and now she had to live by it. The alternative was too hard. Whether or not she loved him was not the question. Being able to share his life for better or worse was the key issue for her and the answer was that she couldn't.

Coco was up before the others the next day. She went to the kitchen to make herself a cup of tea, and saw that Liz had already started the turkey. She had gotten up at six to do it, and gone back to bed.

Coco wandered around the house while she waited for Jane and Liz to get up. It was an odd feeling being back here again. She saw Sallie and Jack lying side by side in the kitchen, and even that made her think of him. She didn't know what to do anymore to drive him from her mind. Probably only time would do it.

"You're up early," Liz said, when she came down to check the turkey again at nine. Coco had been up for hours. She'd been sitting by the tree, looking forlorn when Liz saw her. She didn't say anything about it to her, but she could see what she was thinking. Missing Leslie was written all over her, and Liz felt sorry for her.

They sat in the kitchen for a while and talked, but not about him. And at ten o'clock, Jane came downstairs and joined them. She said she already had heartburn.

"You're having the next one," she said, looking pointedly at Liz.

"I'd be delighted," Liz said, as Coco offered to make breakfast.

"You're a menace in the kitchen," Jane growled at her, and Coco laughed.

"You're right. I inherited it from Mom."

"You did not," Jane disagreed with her. "Dad was a lousy cook. Mom doesn't even know where the kitchen is."

"I think Gabriel likes to cook," Coco added. "At least we know she won't starve in her old age, if she ever lets the cook go."

"Do you really think they'll last?" Jane asked with a look of disbelief. It was hard for her to imagine. She was sure it was a passing thing, and he would eventually come to his senses, and find someone his own age. But she had to admit, he seemed happy with her mother, and not in the least bothered about the vast expanse of years between them.

"I think if she were a man, we wouldn't even ask that question," Coco answered. "Men Mom's age marry women younger than Gabriel all the time, and no one even questions it. Sixty-two and thirty-nine wouldn't surprise anyone, if their sexes were reversed."

"Maybe you're right," Jane said. "The weird thing is that they actually look right together. He's kind of stuffy for a young guy."

"I wouldn't go out with him," Coco said, and they all laughed. He seemed a lot older than Leslie, and in fact was only two years younger.

"Well, you know we wouldn't go out with him," Jane said, and they laughed harder. "But I know what you mean. He's kind of old-fashioned. Nobody wears suits all the time these days, but he does. Mom loves it. Actually, he looked like that the first time I met him, long before he got involved with Mom. I guess he has a thing for older women."

"Apparently," Coco said. "Or just Mom. He worships the ground she walks on. And the truth is that if he sticks around, it'll make life a lot easier for us in a few years. She'll be happy." Jane nodded as she thought about it. Coco had a point.

"What happens when she gets old? I mean really old?"

"The same thing that happens to all of us," Liz added. "You hope your partner doesn't die, or leave you. At some point, it happens," she said, looking tenderly at Jane.

"I'm never going to leave you," Jane whispered softly. "I promise."

"You'd better not." Liz leaned over and gave her a kiss.

"Well, I'm leaving you both," Coco said with a yawn as she got up from the table. "I have to get dressed. Mom will be here in less than an hour," she reminded them. They all went back to their rooms then and reappeared, nicely dressed, shortly before noon.

As always their mother arrived promptly, in a white Chanel suit, black alligator pumps, and the sable coat she'd worn the night before. She was wearing pearls, and her makeup was perfect. Gabriel was wearing gray slacks and a blazer and another Hermès tie with his pale blue shirt. They looked like a spread in *Town & Country*. Coco and Liz were more casual, and had worn nice slacks and sweaters, except for Jane who was wearing a bright red tent, and looked miserably uncomfortable all through lunch.

They exchanged presents before lunch, and everyone loved what they'd been given. Their mother had given them the same thing she did every year. She gave them each a check, and a slightly smaller one for Liz. She said she was always afraid of buying the wrong thing and preferred that they shopped for themselves. She had given Gabriel a Cartier watch that he was wearing, and she was wearing a very good-looking diamond pin on her suit, from him. And Florence gave Alyson an enormous doll in a pink dress that was almost as big as she was.

They sat down to lunch at two o'clock, and stayed at the table until four. After that, they sat in the living room, talking and drinking coffee. And then, their mother and Gabriel and Alyson left with all their presents. They were flying back to L.A. that night to drop Alyson off at her mother's, and leaving for Aspen in the morning.

Coco stayed till six to help them clean up, and then she said her goodbyes. They told her she could spend another night, but after two days of family, she thought they'd want to be alone, and she wanted to get home. So she took Sallie and drove back to Bolinas in the van. The house seemed empty and cold when she got in. She lit a fire, and sat down on the couch, staring at it, thinking about the past two days. She didn't allow herself to think of Leslie, or even Chloe. She had to be grateful for the life she had. And it had been a very nice Christmas. Her new rapprochement with Jane was a blessing in both their lives and was long overdue.

Coco went to bed early and was up at seven. She sat on the deck and watched the sun come up. It was a new day, a new life, and she was reminding herself again of how lucky she was, as she heard the bell clang on her gate. No one ever rang the bell. Most people just walked up to the house and knocked. She was still wearing her pajamas with the hearts on them, and she wrapped herself in the blanket she'd been wearing on the deck and walked around the house to see who it was.

Her long auburn hair was blowing in the wind and she hadn't combed it. It was cold out, but the sky was clear and blue. When she looked toward her gate, she saw them. Leslie was standing there, his hand on the latch, and his eyes locked on hers. He wasn't sure if he had done the right thing. Chloe was standing next to him in a bright blue coat, with her long braids and her big smile. And she was holding a present. The minute she saw Coco, she waved and bounded through the gate by herself.

"She wanted to see you," Leslie explained as Coco hugged her and walked through the sand on bare feet. She stood looking up at him as though she were seeing a vision.

"I wanted to see her too," Coco said, "and you. I miss you." And before she could say anything else, he took her in his arms and held her. He didn't want to hear another thing, he just wanted to hold her and smell her hair and feel her in his arms again.

"It's cold out here," Chloe complained, as she looked up at them. "Can we go in?"

"Of course we can," Coco said, as she took her hand, and turned around to smile at him. He had done the right thing.

The house looked the same to him, and he saw the photograph of him and Chloe. He smiled a long slow smile at her, and she mouthed "I love you" over Chloe's head.

"I love you too," he said clearly.

"What's for breakfast?" Chloe intervened, and then handed Coco her present. She sat down on the couch to unwrap it. It was a small brown teddy bear, and Coco smiled, gave her a big hug, and told her she loved it.

"How about waffles?" Coco answered her question. "And s'mores."

"Yes!" Chloe clapped her hands in glee as Coco went to the kitchen, and put the kettle on for tea. She kept glancing over at Leslie as though he might disappear. It had been a long two months without him, and she wasn't sure yet what this meant. She was just glad he was here.

They sat down to breakfast together, as Chloe told her all about their Christmas. They had decorated a tree, and gone to a hotel for dinner, and last night, they had decided to come and see her. They had taken a plane to San Francisco, and they were staying at a nice hotel because her father had said that it was too late to drive to the beach the night before. He said it would be rude, even though Chloe didn't think so. So they had come this morning instead. And now here they were. She beamed at both of them as she said it, and Coco smiled first at her, and then at Leslie.

"That was a very, very good idea," Coco said.

Chloe looked at her father immediately. "See, I told you she'd be happy to see us!" The two adults beamed at each other over the child's head.

Coco got dressed after breakfast, and they went out for a walk on the beach. It was the day after Christmas, and a number of people were walking.

"I missed you incredibly," Leslie told her, as Chloe ran ahead to pick up shells on the sand.

"Me too."

"I didn't know what you'd think if we just showed up. I didn't think you'd want to see me. Chloe said you did."

"She called me on Thanksgiving, it was the next best thing to talking to you." She looked up at him again, as though he were a dream.

"Coco, about Venice . . ."

She shook her head and put a finger to his lips as they stopped walking and looked at each other. "You don't have to say anything . . . I realize that I don't care about the paparazzi, or the fan magazines, or any of it, even if it does scare me to death . . . I just want to be with you. I love you too much to let that keep us apart." She knew it the minute she saw him. It was what he had come here to hear, but hadn't dared to hope for. She had been sure of it when he appeared at her gate. And what Jane had said on Thanksgiving had haunted her, about not giving up on him yet.

"I love you. I swear I'll never let anything like that happen to you again. I'll kill them first."

"I don't care . . . we'll get through it together . . . if they drive us crazy, we'll move. We'll go somewhere else. We can always hide out here." She smiled at him, and he held her.

"I was dying without you," he said in a deep husky voice.

"Me too."

"Where do you want to live?" He was willing to go anywhere for her.

"With you."

They walked slowly down the beach after Chloe. And when the wind picked up and it got too cold for them, they went back to the house and lit a fire.

Coco made lunch for them, and afterward Leslie took out the

trash for her. It was overflowing. He saw Jeff, the fireman, at the garbage cans, and he gave Leslie a broad grin and a slap on the shoulder.

"Nice to see you back," he said, shaking hands with him. "I hear you were making a movie in Venice. We missed you. My damn car's a mess again. I think it's the transmission."

"I'll take a look at it later," Leslie promised.

"We missed you around here," Jeff said with an intense look, meaning Coco. But he had missed him too.

"Thanks. I missed you all too." Leslie went back inside to Coco then, who was playing card games with Chloe. After that, they watched a movie on TV, he took a look at Jeff's car, and told him he might have to sell it. Coco made pizza for dinner. They tucked Chloe into Coco's bed, and they lay on the couch for hours, talking about their plans. He had to work in L.A. for the next three months, finishing the movie. His house was empty again, and he was living there.

"I can't leave for another month, but then I could come down and stay with you. We can see how it works, and if they drive us crazy. If they do, we can figure out something else. But we might as well try it down there first. That's where you live." She had made her peace with it the moment she saw him. It was about the person, not the place, and Jane had been right again. You didn't run away because the going got tough, if you loved someone. She knew that. She just got scared in Venice, and after that she got lost in her own fears.

"How's your wrist?" he asked, looking worried, and he wanted to cry when he saw the small scar on her hand. He kissed it, and then she kissed him.

"My wrist is fine. It's my heart that was broken. You just fixed it. I'm all better now." He smiled and pulled her into his arms.

"Chloe is a lot smarter than we are. She said I had to come here and fix things with you. I wanted to, but I was afraid to. Everything got so screwed up in Venice, I didn't think I had the right to do that to you again, or ask you to take that chance."

"You're worth it," Coco said quietly. "I'm sorry it took me so long to figure that out." He nodded and just held her. It didn't matter how long it had taken, he was back. And then he thought of something else.

"Why can't you come down for another month?"

"Jane's baby," she said, smiling at him. "I promised I'd be there. He's due in five weeks. And I need to wrap things up here anyway."

"What are you going to do with your business?"

"Give it to Erin, I think. I have to talk to her about it, but I'm pretty sure she'd like that. She hates her other job, and she can make a decent living at it. I did." She smiled broadly at him. "I want to go back to school. I can apply to UCLA."

"Art history?" She nodded.

"I want to figure something out so I can travel with you."

"I'd like that a lot." He looked relieved. "My next two pictures are in L.A." It meant he would be home for the next year. And they both hoped that the paparazzi wouldn't drive them insane. He had already hired a security service to stand guard in an unmarked car outside his house. He wasn't going to take a chance on another Venice happening again, to any of them. And once they lived together, hopefully they'd be old news.

He lay holding her for hours, and then finally went to sleep with Chloe in her bedroom. He hated to leave Coco alone on the couch, but she told him he should. She didn't want Chloe to wake up alone.

"She might think we were doing that disgusting thing she told us about once," she teased him, and he laughed.

"You'll have to remind me how to do that. I think I've forgotten."

"I'll remind you when I come to see you in L.A."

"When will that be?" he asked, looking worried. He didn't want to go for another month without seeing her.

"How does next weekend sound to you, unless you want to come here?" All the pieces of the puzzle were falling back into place again.

"Either way," he said, as he kissed her again before leaving her for the night. They had a lifetime to work out the details.

Chapter 20

For the next four weekends, she and Leslie took turns visiting each other, in L.A. and at the beach. Her visits to L.A. were uneventful. Paparazzi waited outside restaurants for them, and occasionally stood outside his front gate to take pictures of them as they drove away. A photographer followed them around a supermarket once, but it was so minor compared to what they'd experienced in Italy that neither of them cared.

They went to UCLA together to pick up an application. And he came to Bolinas twice after Chloe went back to New York. He was still on break from the movie for the holidays, and when he came to San Francisco, they had dinner with Jane and Liz. Leslie was startled when he saw how big she was. By then, she could hardly move.

"Don't laugh at me," Jane scolded him. "It's not funny. You should try feeling like this. If guys had to do this, no one would have kids. I'm not sure I could do this again myself."

"Next time, it's my turn," Liz said longingly. She had fallen in love with the idea of her carrying a baby born of Jane's eggs. They were talking about doing that within six months. Liz could hardly wait. But first, Jane had to deliver this one. She had admitted to Coco several times that she was scared, mostly because the baby was so big, and the whole process seemed terrifying to her.

They were both happy to see Leslie again, and to see Coco looking so happy. It had been agonizing watching her misery after Venice. She had mourned Leslie even more than Ian.

Leslie talked to Jane about the movie he was doing. He complained about Madison, and Jane laughed. She had worked with her too, and knew what he was dealing with. Madison was seven months pregnant by then, and they had to shoot around her a lot of the time, and use stunt doubles for anything requiring her body to be seen. The director was furious with her for not telling them she was pregnant when she started the picture. But they were making it work, at considerable expense to them.

And on his last weekend in Bolinas before going back to work, Leslie helped Coco pack some of her things. She was sending a vanload down to L.A. She was keeping her house at the beach. They still weren't sure where they'd wind up in the end, but it no longer mattered. They were together again, and their relationship was better than ever.

She had handed her business over to Erin, which gave her free time to spend with Jane. The baby was only days away. Jane was so bored that Coco and Liz took her out to dinner one night. They had spicy Mexican food, which someone had told Jane would bring on labor. She was willing to try anything. All she got out of it was heartburn. And Coco took her for long walks at Crissy Field. They had just come back late one afternoon, and were chatting in the kitchen, when Jane gave her a startled look.

"Are you okay?" Coco asked her. They were all beginning to feel like the baby would never come. Their mother was on vacation in the Bahamas by then. And they had promised to let her know when it was born.

"I think my water just broke," Jane said nervously as a pool of water spread around her, where a sea of maple syrup had once been.

"Well, that's good news," Coco said, smiling at her. "Here we go." She helped Jane into a chair on a towel, while she mopped up the floor.

"I don't know what you're so happy about," Jane said tersely. "I'm the one who has to go through this. You and Liz just get to watch."

"We'll be right there with you," Coco reassured her, and then helped her upstairs to her bathroom. Her clothes were soaked. "Should we call the doctor?"

"Not yet. The contractions haven't even started yet." She put on a terrycloth robe, wrapped herself in towels, and lay down. "I wonder how long this is going to take."

"Hopefully not long," Coco said, trying to sound convincing. "Why don't you try and get some sleep before it really starts?" Jane nodded and closed her eyes, as Coco turned off the light and pulled the shades. And then she went back to the kitchen and called Liz, who was doing errands downtown. She was excited to hear the news and said she'd be home in half an hour. Coco told her that since the contractions hadn't started, she didn't think there was any rush.

"Once her water's broken, that may not be the case." She had read all their books on pregnancy again and was well informed. "Keep an eye on her. The contractions could start right away."

Coco made herself a cup of tea and went upstairs quietly, and she was amazed to find her sister clutching the bed in agony, in the midst of a contraction that didn't seem to stop. Jane couldn't even talk until it was over.

"When did that start?" Coco asked with a look of concern. She didn't want Jane to have the baby at home, but they were a long way from that.

"About five minutes ago. That's the third one I've had. They're really hard, really long, and they're coming pretty fast." She had another one shortly after, and Coco timed it. It lasted a full minute, and they were three minutes apart.

"Why don't I call the doctor." Jane nodded and gave her the number. When the nurse answered, Coco told her what was happening. She wanted to know if the contractions were regular, which they weren't because it had been five minutes since the last one, so they were getting farther apart. The nurse told her that they might stop again for a while. But if they were consistently five minutes apart or less, to bring her in. She was going to let the doctor know to expect them anytime within the next few hours.

Nothing happened then for ten minutes. And Jane was having another contraction when Liz walked in. She rushed to the bed and held Jane's hand. She put her hand on her belly, and it was rock hard.

"They really hurt," Jane said to Liz.

"I know, baby," she said gently. "It'll be over soon, and then we'll have our little boy."

Coco left the room to call Leslie and tell him what was happening. He was quiet for a second and then said, "I wish it were ours."

Coco had thought of that too. "How's she doing?" he asked, sounding concerned.

"It looks like it hurts a lot."

"It does." He had been there for Chloe's birth, and it had looked awful to him. But Monica still insisted that Chloe was worth it. "Send her my love." Coco went back into the bedroom to tell Jane, and Liz was helping her sit up. She was going to the bathroom every few minutes and doubled over with pains on the way. She could hardly walk.

Liz turned to Coco with a look of worry mixed with excitement. They had waited a long time for this and now it was finally happening, but she hated to see Jane in so much pain. "They're still irregular," Liz told Coco, "but she's having a lot of them, and they're very strong. I think that's because her water broke. The books say it can go at a galloping pace after that. Maybe we should take her in." It was hard to decide.

"I'm not galloping anywhere," Jane said miserably through clenched teeth as she leaned on Liz. "I want something for the pain." She was planning to have an epidural at the hospital, but they couldn't give her anything at home.

They waited for another half hour, and by then the pains were four minutes apart. It was time to go. Liz helped her put a sweatsuit on, and slippers. It took both Liz and Coco to get her to the car. Coco was glad the hospital was nearby. And once they got her there, they could hardly get her out of the car. She was crying with the pains.

"This is much worse than I thought," she said to Liz in a hoarse voice.

"I know. Maybe they can give you an epidural right away."

"Just tell them to shoot me when I come through the door." She had another pain then and leaned on Liz while Coco ran inside to get a wheelchair. She told a nurse they were bringing her in. They got Jane into the wheelchair a minute later and wheeled her in, as the nurse smiled at her.

"How are we doing?" the nurse asked as she took over and wheeled Jane to the elevator as Coco and Liz followed, looking slightly frantic. This had gotten rough faster than they thought it would.

"We're not so great," Jane said in answer to the nurse's question. "I feel like shit."

"We'll get you all set in a few minutes," the nurse said in a soothing tone. They were at labor and delivery only minutes after they'd come in, and the nurse who had wheeled her in turned her over to the labor nurses on the floor.

"The pains are three minutes apart," Liz explained as Jane had another contraction and clutched her hand.

"Okay, let's take a look," the admitting nurse said cheerfully. "We'll give your doctor a call in a few minutes when we know where things stand." She didn't say it to her, but sometimes even with heavy contractions, there wasn't much progress. She asked who was coming into the exam room with her, and both Liz and Coco said they would. "Are we waiting for Dad to arrive?" the nurse asked brightly.

"No, we're not," Liz said quietly. "I'm Dad." The nurse didn't bat an eye, and escorted all three of them into the room. She had dealt with couples like them before, more and more in recent years. Parents were parents, whatever sex they were. She smiled at both

Coco and Liz, and helped Jane out of her clothes. They wrapped her in a hospital gown, and got her onto the bed where she would go through labor and deliver. And with apologies for any discomfort she might cause, the nurse put on latex gloves and did the exam. Jane had a pain right in the middle of it and clutched Liz's arm. And before it was over, she started to cry. It took a long time, and the nurse apologized again.

"I'm sorry, I know that was painful. But we have to know where you are. You're at five. I'll give your doctor a call and let her know, and I'll get the anesthesiologist down right away to start the epidural."

"Will it hurt?" Jane asked miserably, glancing from the nurse to Liz and Coco. She was still in agony from what the nurse had just done. Nobody had told her it would be like this. It was the worst pain she'd ever felt.

"It won't hurt after you have the epidural." She hooked up a belt with a fetal monitor then, so they could check the baby's heartbeat and her contractions. It was official now. Jane was in labor. Liz was smiling at her with love in her eyes. "Do we know what the baby is?" the nurse asked before she left the room.

"It's a boy," Liz said proudly as Jane closed her eyes. Coco hated to see her sister in so much pain, but she was happy for her too. It was a little scary watching it all happen. She had never seen a birth before, even in a movie. Just puppies being born, and that was a lot easier than this.

"Well, it looks like you're going to have your little boy in your arms tonight," the nurse assured them. "Things are moving along very nicely." And with that, she disappeared as Jane had another pain. It was a big one. The nurse came back with a clipboard for

Jane to sign and Liz to fill out. Jane had preregistered two weeks before so they had her in the computer. They just needed her signature for any emergency procedures. Technically, Liz couldn't sign for her, but she did, and had Jane sign too. They were in this together.

The nurse was back for the next contraction, and the anesthesiologist was with her. He explained the procedure for the epidural to them, while the nurse checked again, and Jane burst into tears.

"This is awful," she said to Liz breathlessly. "I can't do it!"

"Yes, you can," Liz said quietly, trying to keep her eyes locked onto Jane's.

"We're at six," the nurse told the doctor, and he looked concerned.

"If this goes too quickly, we may not be able to do the epidural," he said to Jane as she lay there and sobbed.

"You have to. I can't do this without one." He looked at the nurse, and he nodded.

"Let's see if we can get it in." He told her to roll over on her side and round her back for him. She was having another pain and she couldn't do it. She felt as though everything was out of control in her body, and people were doing terrible things to her and wanting her to do things she couldn't. It was the worst experience of her life.

The anesthesiologist managed to get a long catheter into her spine, and then began to feed in the medication. He had her roll on her back then, and the next pain hit her like a tidal wave. She had another one right after, and the medication had had no effect yet. He explained to them that she might be too dilated for it to

take effect, and then suddenly the pains stopped. Nothing happened for a full five minutes, which was a relief to Jane.

"The epidural could slow things down," he explained. And then
as quickly as they had stopped, the contractions started again.
Jane said they were worse than before. It went on for another ten
minutes, and then the nurse checked her again, and Jane cried out
in pain and shouted at the nurse.

"Stop doing that!" she screamed at her. "You're hurting me!"
And then she just lay in bed and sobbed. The epidural had done
nothing for the pain so far.

"I'm going to put in some more medication and see if that works
better for you," the anesthesiologist said calmly as the nurse reported to him.

"We're at ten. I'll get her doctor."

"Did you hear that?" Liz said to her. "You're at ten. That means
you can push. The baby will be out soon." Jane nodded, looking
dazed, and the monitor showed that she was having another contraction, but this time Jane didn't react to it. The medication was
working. Everything was happening very fast. They had only been
there for an hour, which felt like a lifetime to Jane.

Her obstetrician walked into the room five minutes later. She
smiled as she said hello to Jane and Liz, and they introduced her
to Coco.

"We're having quite a party here," she said cheerfully. "I've got
good news for you, Jane." She leaned down close to her so she'd
listen. "With the next contraction, you can start pushing. We're going to get that little boy into your arms as fast as we can."

"I can't feel the contractions now," Jane said, looking relieved.
Her eyes were glazed, as Coco and Liz exchanged a worried look.

"We may lighten up on the medication a little, so you can help us push," the doctor told her, which panicked Jane.

"No, don't," Jane said, starting to cry again. Coco was shaken watching her tough older sister disintegrating before her eyes.

"She's doing fine." The doctor smiled at Liz and Coco, and the nurse put an oxygen mask on Jane as the anesthesiologist left the room. He had another epidural to do for a C-section but said he'd be back. It was a busy night at the hospital. The nurse said there were a lot of deliveries that night.

The monitor said she was having another contraction. They set Jane's long legs up in stirrups and told her to start pushing. Another nurse came in to help. She had a nurse on either side of her, the doctor at the foot watching for the baby's head, and Liz up close to Jane's face. She felt surrounded by people, and they kept telling her to breathe and push. Nothing happened for a while.

Jane pushed for an hour and nothing changed as Coco watched. Everyone was intent on what was happening, and another nurse came into the overcrowded room with a plastic bassinet.

"I can't do it," Jane said, sounding exhausted. "I can't push anymore. Get him out."

"No," the doctor said cheerfully from the foot of the bed. "That's your job. You have to help us now." They told her to push harder and asked Liz to brace Jane's shoulders, while each of the nurses braced her feet. The anesthesiologist came in then, and the doctor told him to ease up the medication, and Jane begged him not to. It went on for another hour. She'd been pushing for two hours by then, and nothing was happening. The doctor said she could see the baby's hair, but that was all she could see so far.

They did an episiotomy then, and used forceps. It took another hour and Jane was screaming, as Coco stood on one side of her, and Liz on the other, and she had to keep pushing until she said she was dying. She let out a hideous scream that Coco thought she would remember forever, and slowly, slowly, the baby's head started to come out of her until there was a little face looking up at them with wide eyes. Liz and Coco were crying, and Jane was staring down at him, and her face turned purple as she pushed harder. They got his shoulders out and then the rest of him, and there was a long wail in the room and this time it wasn't Jane crying, it was their baby. They cut the cord, wrapped him in a blanket, and laid him on Jane as she sobbed and looked at Liz in agony and elation. She had never done anything so hard in her life and hoped she never would again.

"He's so beautiful," they all said as they looked at him. They took him to clean him off and weigh him, while they delivered the placenta and sewed Jane up.

"He weighs nine pounds, fifteen ounces," the nurse said proudly and then handed him to Liz. "You delivered a ten-pound baby," she told Jane. It had taken her three hours to push him out. It was easy to see why. He was huge, and Coco looked at him in amazement. They let her hold him, and then she gave him back to Jane. She put him to her breast, and he lay there sucking quietly with big blue eyes, staring at his mother. He had beautiful hands and long legs just like hers. Liz was standing close to her, kissing her and smiling and talking to their baby, who seemed to recognize their voices as he looked at Liz and Jane.

Coco stayed with them for another hour until they took Jane to a room. She was exhausted. Liz was spending the night, so Coco went back to the house, still in awe of what she'd seen. She kissed

Jane and Liz before she left and congratulated them, as Liz picked up the phone to call Jane's mother and tell her Bernard Buzz Barrington II had finally made his appearance, and all of them were thrilled.

When Coco got back to the house, she called Leslie and told him all about it, and how painful it had been for her sister. But how happy she looked when he was born.

"The next one will be ours," Leslie said gently. "Tell Jane and Liz congratulations for me." He promised to come up that weekend to see him, and then Coco was going back to L.A. with him. The baby had arrived two days before his due date. And now it was Coco's turn to begin a new life. It was exactly eight months since the day they met. It had taken almost as long as Jane's baby.

Chapter 21

As he had promised to, Leslie came up on Saturday. Jane was home from the hospital by then. She was weak, sore, and ecstatic. She and Liz fussed constantly over the baby. The baby nurse they'd hired was there and showing them everything they needed to know about caring for him. Jane was nursing. It was a perfect time for Coco to leave.

Leslie and Coco had dinner with Jane and Liz that night, and Leslie held the baby, and looked very comfortable with him. Coco said a tearful goodbye to her sister. She felt closer to her now after sharing the birth.

Coco and Leslie flew to Los Angeles the next day, and Leslie had filled the house with flowers for her before he left. Everything was immaculate and looked perfect. He had cleared two huge closets for her. And there had been no paparazzi outside when they got there. His security service was patrolling the house.

He even made dinner for her that night.

"How did I ever get so lucky?" she asked in wonder as she kissed him.

"I'm the lucky one," he said, looking at her with wonder. He still couldn't believe she was finally with him. They had both passed the test in Venice, and the two agonizing months after. There was no question in their minds now. They knew they belonged together.

They called Chloe that night and told her Coco was there and had moved in. They had told her she would, when Chloe went back to New York at New Year's, and she was thrilled. She could hardly wait to come out and see them.

"Are you going to have a baby now?" Chloe asked pointedly, and Coco wondered if she was worried, as Jane must have been when she was born. She didn't want that to happen to Chloe. There was enough love for all of them, and she wanted Chloe to know that.

"Not yet," her father answered solemnly, but he hoped they would.

"Are you getting married?" she asked with a smile in her voice.

"We haven't discussed it yet, but if we do, we won't do it without you. I promise," her father told her.

"I want to be a bridesmaid."

"You're hired. Now all we need are the bride and groom."

"That's you and Coco, Daddy," she said, laughing. "You're silly."

"So are you. That's why I love you," he teased her. And after they hung up, he turned to Coco, who had been listening on the other phone. "She has a point, you know, about our getting married. I'm a respectable man. You can't expect me to live in sin with you. That would be very brazen of you. And think what the tabloids would do with *that*! 'Major movie star lives with dog-walker.' Positively shocking," he said as he kissed her.

"I'm not a dog-walker anymore. You don't need to worry," she said, rolling over on their bed with a look of pleasure. She still felt like Cinderella. Even more so now. The glass slipper was hers and it fit her to perfection.

"Well, even though you're not a dog-walker, I do have a reputation to worry about. What do you think? Should we do it? Just to give Chloe a shot at being a bridesmaid? I think that's an excellent reason myself. The other reason of course is that I love you insanely, and before you run away from me again, I'd like to establish some ownership here. Will you marry me, Coco?" He had slid off the bed, and was kneeling next to it, looking into her eyes with a serious expression. He looked as though he were about to cry from the emotion. And Coco felt moved to tears as she listened.

"Yes, I will," she said quietly. Their life together was about to begin. She was going to be Cinderella forever. She had found her handsome prince. "Will you marry me?" she asked him just as tenderly.

"With pleasure." He smiled and climbed into bed with her. It was her first night in their new home, the one they would share for better or worse, or until the paparazzi did them in.

Chapter 22

Jane and Liz had spent the whole morning overseeing the flowers. The caterers had been in the kitchen since late the night before. The house looked spectacular with white roses everywhere and topiary trees covered with them. Jane had to stop giving instructions to the moving men, to nurse the baby, and then came back to change everything around again. They were expecting a hundred people by six o'clock, and she wanted everything to be perfect. She had the baby nurse sewing white ribbons on garlands the florist was putting on the staircase. The baby was four months old, and he was so big he looked a year old.

The activity in the house was overwhelming, and at four o'clock, Liz and Jane went upstairs to get dressed, and the baby nurse put the baby down for a nap. He was an easy baby, and she loved working for them. She said they were the nicest couple she'd ever met. Jane still hadn't gone back to work. And Liz was planning to do artificial insemination in July, using Jane's donor eggs. Jane had just turned forty, but her FSH tests showed that they were holding up. And Liz wanted to carry Jane's child. Buzz had been a wonderful addition to their life. They hoped the next one would be a girl.

"Maybe we should get married," Liz suggested as they shared the bathroom to get dressed.

"I'll do it if you want to, but I've felt married to you for years in my heart," Jane said with a smile.

"So have I," Liz said as she zipped up Jane's dress. She was wearing a pale blue cocktail dress, and Liz was wearing gray satin. They had seen to every possible detail, and were proud of the results. And it felt right to both of them that it should happen here, where it all began.

They were back downstairs at five-thirty just in time to greet Jane's mother and Gabriel. Not surprisingly their mother was wearing a champagne-colored satin suit that was almost white. Jane had made a bet with Liz that she would do something like that, and wear white or close to it to her daughter's wedding. It was so like her, and totally predictable.

"She wouldn't dare," Liz had said. "She wouldn't do that to Coco."

"Ten bucks says she would," Jane said firmly, and Liz had taken the bet. And as Florence came through the door, Jane turned to Liz with a broad grin. "You owe me ten bucks." They both laughed. And greeted Gabriel, who was wearing a very proper dark blue suit, and carrying Alyson, who had just turned three. He and Florence had just celebrated the second anniversary of their union. And they were going to Paris and the South of France in July. They were going to stay at the Hotel du Cap, and then Florence had chartered a yacht for them for two weeks to go to Sardinia and visit friends. Gabriel hadn't made a movie all year, he was too busy traveling with Florence. Liz commented that she looked happier every time she saw her. Liz didn't say it, but she had never seen her as happy when she was married to Jane's father. Gabriel was good for her. And he looked comfortable and relaxed. Their life together was one long vacation. He had just moved into her house.

Leslie's parents had come from England and were chatting with Jane and Liz. All of the guests had arrived by six-thirty. Coco was waiting downstairs so no one would see her, when Leslie arrived with Chloe. She was wearing a pink organdy dress that reached the floor, and she looked like a little princess. Liz told her that and she beamed. She wanted to play with the baby, but Jane was afraid he'd spit up and ruin her dress, so she told her she had to wait till later.

The music began at six-thirty as they heard a helicopter whirring overhead. There were police guarding the house outside, and motorcycle cops cruising the street. They looked up at the helicopter and identified it as press. There was a photographer hanging out a window with a long lens. The cops shrugged. They wouldn't get much. Everyone was inside.

And when the caterer told her to, Coco came upstairs. She entered from the dining room, looking stately and spectacular in a white satin dress that molded her figure, and trailed behind her. There was a long train, and all she could see as she walked through the crowd seated in Liz and Jane's living room was Leslie, with the bay behind him and Chloe at his side. It was all she needed to see and all she wanted now. There was a helicopter flying past the house and she didn't care. She knew what it was, and that there were probably a lot of them in their future. All that mattered was Leslie, and Chloe, and the life they would share.

They exchanged their vows as everyone watched them and her mother cried. She was holding Gabriel's hand and pressed it lightly when the groom said "I do." And then Leslie kissed Coco, and their life began.

It was a perfect wedding and exactly what Coco had wanted. Her family was there, and the people they loved and who loved them. Leslie's friends had come up from L.A. His family had come from England, and Jeff from the beach was there. He and his wife had been immensely flattered to be asked. They had had the wedding at Jane's house to avoid the press. It was safer here, behind closed doors, in her sister's home.

They were going on a honeymoon by chartered plane to an undisclosed location and taking Chloe with them. Coco had wanted her to come, and Leslie hoped she would have a little brother or sister soon.

There was a dance floor in the dining room, and people wandered through the garden on the warm night. And a disco had been set up with a Lucite floor over the swimming pool. It was the best party San Francisco had ever seen.

At midnight, after they served the wedding cake, Coco walked halfway up the stairs to throw her bouquet. She aimed it carefully and hit her in the chest. She didn't want her mother to miss it. Florence caught the bouquet and pressed it to her heart as Gabriel smiled at her. He knew what she had in mind, and it was fine with him. They shared a last dance after the bride and groom left, and he kissed her. By then, Jane and Liz were downstairs doing the samba in the disco with all of Leslie's friends from L.A.

Leslie, Coco, and Chloe drove off in a limousine. The police held the crowds back, and the helicopter whirred overhead. Two motorcycle cops were riding ahead of them, and they sped off to the airport with Chloe between them. Coco was smiling, and Leslie looked like the happiest man in the world. The three of them were holding hands.

"We did it," Coco whispered to him with a victorious look. The paparazzi hadn't grabbed them. No one had gotten hurt. No one had terrified them or Chloe. They were safe, and together, and they had gotten there just the way he said they would.

"So are you going to do it now?" Chloe asked her father as they drove away.

"What?" He was looking at Coco, and his mind was on other things.

"The disgusting thing." Chloe giggled.

"Chloe!" He scolded her and then grinned. "I have no idea what you mean."

"You remember. When Mom said that . . ."

He cut her off quickly. "Never mind."

"Okay," she said, smiling up at Coco. "I love you guys," she said happily. She loved her dad, and Coco was her best friend.

"We love you too," Leslie and Coco said in unison, and then leaned over to kiss over her head, and then bent down to kiss her. And as they sped toward the airport, Coco smiled at Leslie. He had been right after all. Things had worked out just the way they should. One day at a time.